"You are *not* going to traipse down to the wh  **eleven o'clock at night.'**

A little thrill ___ ouldn't help it. "He' ___ re.

"Who said he's going to see me?

She waved her hand over Ryan's imposing form. "Little hard for someone like you to blend in."

"I have my ways."

"As long as you stay out of sight. I don't want you spoiling my meeting."

"How about saving your life?" He pushed back from the table and stepped around it to pull her chair out for her. "Is that okay with you?"

She nodded as silly schoolgirl butterflies took flight in her belly.

She'd have to watch herself with this man, in more ways than one. Because she couldn't let a sexy grin and a pair of strong arms deter her from exacting her revenge.

THE WHARF

BY
CAROL ERICSON

MILLS & BOON

Published in Great Britain 2014
by Mills & Boon, an imprint of Harlequin (UK) Limited,
Eton House, 18-24 Paradise Road, Richmond, Surrey, TW9 1SR

© 2014 Carol Ericson

ISBN: 978-0-263-91370-5

46-0914

Carol Ericson lives with her husband and two sons in Southern California, home of state-of-the-art cosmetic surgery, wild freeway chases, palm trees bending in the Santa Ana winds and a million amazing stories. These stories, along with hordes of virile men and feisty women, clamor for release from Carol's head. It makes for some interesting headaches until she sets them free to fulfill their destinies and her readers' fantasies. To find out more about Carol, her books and her strange headaches, please visit her website, www.carolericson.com, "Where romance flirts with danger."

To my editor Allison, who gets it

Chapter One

The clanging of the halyards against the masts of the sail-boats docked at the pier echoed across the water, sounding like a death-knell chorus.

"He wants revenge against you for tricking him, and he's gonna get it if you don't watch yourself."

Kacie Manning's back tingled with the warning, as if someone had already placed a target there. She peered at the man three feet away from her. His face was obscured by a baseball cap pulled low on his forehead and a bandana hiding his mouth and chin.

"Would you be willing to go to the police and tell them what you just told me? He can't make threats like that from prison."

The figure hugging the shadows hunched his shoulders. "I'm not getting on his bad side. The man's a straight-up psychopath. If the warden pays him a visit, Dan's gonna know who talked."

Kacie hugged herself, dipping her hands into the sleeves of her baggy sweater to ward off the chill of the night... and his words. "How's Dan going to get the word out on the street? The prison monitors his communication."

The man whistled between his teeth, and the bandana puffed out from his face. "I thought you knew Daniel Walker. You wrote a book about him, didn't you?"

"You know that, or we wouldn't be here."

"Then you should know what he's capable of, Kacie. He ain't just a psycho. He's a crafty psycho."

Goose bumps raced across her flesh, and she rubbed her arms. This ex-con obviously knew Daniel Walker well. Not everyone did—his own family sure hadn't. "Did he actually confess to the murders?"

"No way." He scratched at his chin beneath the bandana. "He's too smart for that. He still wants to keep on pretending. He started talking to me about karma one day before my parole. I didn't know what the hell he was talking about, but then he explained it's like revenge, comeuppance. And he told me you were gonna get yours."

"Why are you telling me this? Why are you warning me?"

"I dunno." He shuffled a step closer, careful to keep his face in the darkness. "You're a pretty little gal, Kacie. I saw you once or twice when you came to the big house to interview Walker."

She tried to swallow, but her dry throat wouldn't allow it.

He'd seen her at Walla Walla? Maybe Walker had sent *him* to take care of his business. She shuffled back a few steps. "That still doesn't explain why you'd risk Walker's anger to warn me."

"You remind me of my sister a little bit." His eyes glittered in the dark. "Besides, I ain't risking nothing. It's not like you're going to go running to Walker telling him someone from the state pen warned you about him, right?"

"Of course not."

A squeaking noise to her right made her grit her teeth. She jerked her head to the side and spotted a shopping cart rumbling around the corner, with a ramshackle man in rags steering it.

The parolee across from her swore and spit from beneath his bandana.

The homeless man trundled toward them, one wheel of his cart squealing and wobbling over the cement walkway.

Kacie held her breath as he drew next to them.

"Can you spare some change?" His hand was already protruding from the dirt-encrusted sleeve of his jacket.

Her informant had ducked back into the shadows, but his voice lashed out at the transient from the anonymity of the darkness. "Move it along, buddy."

The homeless man must've heard something in the other man's voice because he thrust his cart in front of him and picked up his ambling pace without a word or backward glance.

The transient had enough street smarts to recognize a dangerous man when he heard one. What was her problem? Could she even trust an ex-con wearing a bandana across his lower face?

She scooped in a breath of salty air. "Like I was saying, I have no reason to tell Walker anything."

"You sure he didn't charm the pants off you? Make you wet?" The man chuckled low in his throat.

Kacie clenched her jaw where a muscle jumped wildly. He was just trying to make her uncomfortable, push her buttons.

She snorted. "Did you read my book?"

"I don't read no books, but I heard about it. You tried and convicted the guy all over again and kicked him for good measure."

"Then you should know his smooth talk didn't work on me."

"You're a good actress, Kacie."

She flinched. She wished he'd stop using her name. They weren't friends. They weren't even acquaintances.

"Why do you say that?"

"'Cuz Walker thought he had you eating out of the palm of his hand during all those interviews you two did together."

"Oh well." She tossed her hair over her shoulder.

"That's why he was so pissed off. It's not just that you wrote a book that made him look bad. It's that he thought he had you."

"He thought wrong." And she'd done nothing in the interviews that would've made him think otherwise. She'd come into the project suspecting an innocent man had been convicted of murdering his wife and children. Several interviews later, she knew she was dealing with a sociopath, a *guilty* sociopath.

"Yeah, he had you all wrong." He adjusted his cap with a hand sporting a tattoo of a cross on the back. "That's why he wants to kill you."

The wind whistled in from across the bay and blew right through her. She huddled into her sweater further. "Thanks for the heads-up." She dug into her pocket for a hundred-dollar bill, creased it and held it out to him.

Stepping back, he sucked in a breath. "I ain't no snitch. I didn't tell you for money."

"I'm sorry. I didn't mean to offend you." She crumpled the bill in her fist and shoved it back in her pocket. "I appreciate the warning, that's all."

"Sure, sure. I told you. You remind me of my sister."

He pivoted, melting into the shadow of the building.

Kacie took one step away and cranked her head over her shoulder. "What were you in for?"

The voice came from the darkness like disembodied evil. "Killing my sister."

Kacie's hand flew to her mouth and she stumbled toward the weak light spilling from the ticket booth for the submarine. Her heart hammered so hard she wouldn't have been able to hear footsteps even if they were coming straight toward her.

This time she didn't care if she gave him the satisfaction of knowing he'd shocked her.... He had. She broke into a jog, heading for the lights at the more popular end of the wharf—not that teeming crowds met her here, either. Late on a Sunday night, Fisherman's Wharf wasn't exactly crackling with tourists and street performers. The fishermen had hauled in their catches many hours before and would be ready to go out in a few more. The hipsters and club hoppers were ducking in and out of bars in other areas of the city—other areas where the air didn't reek of fish and resound with the clanging of masts.

Her footsteps carried her past the darkened and shuttered restaurants, past the homeless people huddled on benches or in doorways. She kept glancing over her shoulder, half expecting to see the masked face of the sister-killing parolee. He'd probably just been trying to yank her chain. Was there anyone in prison who didn't lie?

If San Francisco were the type of city where you could hail a taxi on the street, she'd do it. No point in standing on a dark corner placing a call and waiting for one to show up.

Her legs moved faster. A few die-hard T-shirt shops still hoped for the odd tourist on a late-night souvenir run. The lights spilling from their windows tempered her pulse rate.

When she hit the street that led to her hotel, her breathing almost returned to normal.

A hotel near Fisherman's Wharf wouldn't have been her first choice, but Ryan Brody was staying there, so it was good enough for her.

He had at least two brothers living in the city, so she couldn't figure out why he didn't stay with one of them. Maybe there was a rift in the family.

Her lips stretched into a humorless smile. If that was the case, it couldn't happen to a better bunch.

Brody. The name filled her with unspeakable rage.

Kacie let out a pent-up breath as she hiked up the sidewalk to her hotel. A few more people, other than the transients who owned the night, crisscrossed the street and wandered into the shops still selling their wares.

Kacie greeted the bellhop as she stepped through the doors of the hotel. "Is the hotel pool still open?"

"It's open twenty-four hours, ma'am."

"Thanks."

When she got to her room, she fired up her laptop. She planned to find out the identity of her talkative ex-con. As the computer booted up, she shed her clothes and wriggled into a bikini. Then she grabbed the hotel-issued terry-cloth robe and threw it over the back of a chair.

She leaned over the laptop, her hands hovering above the keyboard. What was the murder of a sister called? Fratricide? Or was it something different for a sister?

She tapped the keyboard. He'd been imprisoned at Walla Walla, but that didn't necessarily mean he'd committed his crime in Washington.

She twisted her stiff neck from side to side and then shoved the computer away. She could do this the next morning before she met with Ryan Brody. Right now, she needed a little relaxation.

She slipped her arms into the robe and knotted the sash around her waist. Twisting her hair around her hand, she headed for the bathroom. Her toiletry bag hung on a hook on the back of the door, and she dug inside one of the pockets until her fingers tripped across a hair clasp.

She secured her hair, dropped her key card in her pocket and pulled her door securely closed behind her.

The vacant indoor pool beckoned. She shrugged out of

the robe and draped it over a chair. She jerked her head toward some splashing coming from the hot tub. Three teenage boys rose from the bubbling water in unison, steam floating off their bodies.

They better not be heading toward the pool. She sat on the edge and lowered herself into the lukewarm water. She kicked off the wall, and the water enveloped her as she sliced through it, her arms windmilling and her flutter kick just breaking the surface.

In, out, in, out. Her regulated breathing calmed her and cleared her brain of all the ugliness she dealt with on a daily basis—all the ugliness yet to come.

She finished her laps and, placing her hands flat on the deck, hoisted herself out of the pool.

One glance at the hot tub and a trail of water leading to the door told her the boys had left. She made a beeline for the sauna. She pulled one of the heavy doors open and poked her head inside where the dry heat blasted her. It was blissfully empty inside. She spread her towel out on one of the wooden benches and stretched out on her back, crossing her arms beneath her head.

She'd play it cool with Brody. She'd play it nice and civil—just like she had with Daniel Walker. Not that Ryan Brody, youngest police chief in the state of California, was a serial killer.

But his dad was.

She stretched out her legs and wiggled her toes. It felt great, but she couldn't take much more than ten minutes in the sauna.

A sound at the doors had her doing a half sit-up. She stared at the heavy wooden doors but nobody entered the sauna.

Good. Maybe someone had heard her in there. She rolled to her stomach, burying her face in her arms.

Sweat trickled down her back and dripped from her elbow. Sitting up, she dabbed the corner of her towel between her breasts.

She swung her feet to the floor and ladled a small amount of eucalyptus oil over the hot rocks. They sizzled and the fresh scent of eucalyptus soaked the room.

She took a few deep, cleansing breaths and then stood up and pushed at the door. It wouldn't budge.

She wiped her hands on her towel and grabbed one of the door handles with two hands and gave it a shove. Wedging her shoulder against the wood, she drove into one door and then the other. The doors stayed firmly in place and now her shoulder hurt.

What the hell? The bellhop had told her the pool area was open all night and the sign on the door had verified that. There was no way they'd be locking up now. And why would they lock the sauna from the outside?

She pushed at the doors again and heard a rattle against the wood.

"Hello? Is anyone out there? Can you open the doors?"

Only the hissing and dripping of the rocks answered her.

She scanned the walls of the sauna for a phone, an emergency shutoff or a call button and saw nothing but smooth, dry wood.

"Hey!" She pounded her fists against the doors. "I'm in here."

Sweat poured off her face and she mopped it with her towel. Trickles of it ran down her chest to her belly and more droplets crept down her spine.

Her breathing shortened and she parted her lips to drag in a long breath. The dry air filled her lungs.

She dumped another ladle of oil on the rocks and gulped in the rising steam.

Someone had to come in there shortly. If the pool was

open twenty-four hours, maybe the cleaning crew came in the middle of the night.

She tried one of the doors again, driving her shoulder against it. Again, she heard a rattling on the outside. Was there something blocking the door? A sauna wouldn't have a lock on the outside.

She planted her feet on the wood floor and flattened her palms against the double doors. She dug in and pushed with her entire weight. One of the doors moved past the other about a half an inch.

She pressed her eye to the crack, but the doors were too thick and there was very little space between them.

She put her lips to the space between the doors and screamed. "Help! I'm locked in the sauna."

The yelling weakened her, and her knees wobbled. She put a hand out for the bench and sank to its hot surface, which scorched the backs of her thighs. Everything was hot now.

She ran her tongue around her parched mouth and tipped her head back to peer at the ceiling. She eyed a square vent with mesh across it. Could she fit through that? Where did it lead?

She stood on the bench and reached for the vent, her fingertips skimming the mesh. She rolled up her towel and stood on top of it. She slammed the heels of her hands against the vent and then noticed the screws.

With nothing gained except sore palms, she lowered herself to the bench.

Her robe. She'd left her robe hanging over one of the chairs. Maybe someone would notice it from the gym that looked out onto the pool and come out to pick it up.

She pressed her face against the double doors again and screamed. "Help! I'm in the sauna."

She was going to meet her death in a hotel sauna. A

laugh bubbled to her lips. Her parents were going to have a helluva lawsuit.

She pressed her hands to her hot, moist face and her eyelids fluttered. How long had she been in there? Maybe she'd just pass out, and they'd find her in the morning.

She dropped to the bench before her knees could buckle under her. She'd try screaming again in a minute or two—when she got her breath back.

A voice! Had she imagined it?

She hopped up, adrenaline surging through her body. "Is someone there? I'm in the sauna."

Scratching and scraping noises echoed from outside the sauna and the doors wobbled. Then they flew open and cool air rushed into her wooden prison.

She heard a male voice, strong and angry. "What the hell happened?"

Her legs couldn't support her and she fell forward.

Her rescuer caught her in a pair of solid arms, and for a moment she melted against him. "Thank you. Oh my God, I was trapped in there."

"You're burning up. You need water." The man took a step back and tilted up her chin.

Her gaze met a pair of murky green eyes, which widened and grew lighter.

Her mouth dropped open, and her body jerked. She'd just fallen into the arms of the enemy.

Chapter Two

Ryan swallowed and then choked. "I'll be damned."

Kacie Manning's eyelids drooped and her body went limp again. He swept her up in his arms and carried her to a chaise longue. "Hold on. I'll be right back."

He dashed into the gym next door and grabbed his bottle of water from the floor next to the fly machine. By the time he'd returned, Kacie had opened her eyes, but they still hadn't lost their glassy look.

He held the bottle to her dry lips. "Drink this."

She parted her lips and he tipped the water into her mouth. She sputtered and coughed, then chugged half the bottle.

He poured some of the water into his cupped hand and splashed her face. She blinked a pair of impossibly long lashes and sniffled.

"Sorry, but you need to cool down."

"I—I'm okay." She reached for the bottle and downed the rest of the water.

"How long were you in there?"

"I have no idea. Was it locked from the outside? Why didn't it open?"

He held up a finger. "Hold on."

He grabbed the empty bottle, filled it up from the water

dispenser in the gym and swung by the sauna to pluck the pool net from the tiled floor.

He sat in the chair next to Kacie's chaise and handed her the bottle. "More."

While she wrapped her lips around the bottle, he held up the pool net by its long handle. "This was shoved across the doors."

"What?" She dropped the bottle onto the tile, where it spun, its mouth ending up pointing his way.

"I was working out in the gym. I just sat down on the fly machine and noticed the handle of the net wedged between the door handles of the sauna. I didn't know if it was a joke or what, but it looked dangerous."

"Someone shoved that across the handles while I was in there." She dabbed wet fingers across her forehead. "But it was no joke. I was getting weak and dehydrated."

"Was there anyone out here when you went into the sauna?" Her flushed red cheeks and bright eyes made her look younger than her picture.

"There were some teenage boys horsing around in the hot tub when I first came down, but they'd left by the time I hit the sauna."

"They could've come back."

Her eyes darkened to rich chocolate and her nostrils flared. "Maybe. I'm reporting it to the hotel."

"Of course."

It seemed ridiculous to introduce himself now after he'd held her half-naked body in his arms, but protocol demanded it if they were going to work together. He cleared his throat and thrust out his hand. "I suppose we should start from the top with a more formal introduction. I'm Ryan Brody. It's nice to finally meet you in person, Ms. Manning, even though the circumstances could've been better."

"Kacie Manning." She gripped his hand in a firm shake and then her face reddened even more as she glanced down at her wet bikini, plastered to her body and covering just the bare essentials.

Dropping his hand as if he had the cooties, she jerked upright and swung her legs from the chaise.

He hunched forward in his chair, ready to catch her in case she toppled over. "Whoa. You shouldn't be making any sudden moves. Do you want more water?"

"I want," she said, her gaze darting across the pool, "my robe."

"I don't think that's a good idea yet." He swirled his finger in the air. "You want to give your skin plenty of ventilation."

It sounded good, anyway. Truth was, he didn't want her covering up that beautiful body just yet. The small triangles covering her breasts and nestled between her legs left the rest of her curves on stunning display. The photo on her book cover of her in a blouse and jacket hadn't done her justice. She'd probably sell even more books if she posed in this bikini.

Good thing she couldn't read his male-chauvinist thoughts. His earnest look must've won out over his lustful one because she collapsed against the chaise longue, crossing her legs primly at the ankles.

"You're right." She pressed the back of her hand to her cheek. "But I think my body temperature is returning to normal."

At least someone's was.

He scooted his chair closer to her and leaned forward, brushing her wet hair aside and skimming his fingers across her forehead. "You're hot."

Her gaze slid to his face and she folded her arms across

her chest. "I think maybe I should get back to my room, get some clothes on and report this to the hotel."

"I'll help you." He scooted his chair back and held out his arm for support as she rose from the chaise.

She ignored him, but not for long. As she straightened up, she swayed to the side and clutched at his proffered arm.

He curled the other one around her bare waist. "Take it easy. Just lean on me."

She took a few shuffling steps and then dragged in a long breath. "I think I'm good now."

"I can carry you up to your room. It'll make your complaint to the hotel even better."

Her dark eyes flashed and he felt their heat. He'd gone too far.

He raised his hands, palms facing forward. "Just a thought."

She swept her robe from the back of a chair and folded it around her body. The entire pool deck seemed to drop a few degrees.

By the time she reached the door to the hallway, her steps were steady. She turned toward him. "What are you doing at the hotel? I wasn't expecting you until tomorrow."

"I left work early and decided to make the drive down tonight instead of in the morning. Don't feel compelled to move up our meeting time from lunch tomorrow just because I'm already here."

"Lunch still works for me." She shook her head and smiled. "Crazy way to meet."

"I'm just glad I decided to hit the gym for a late workout."

"Me too."

She checked out his shoulders and arms, visible in his

49ers muscle T, making him glad he'd just been pumping iron.

He ushered her into the elevator before him. "Floor?"

"Fourth."

He got off on the fourth floor with her, and she raised
her eyebrows. "Are you on this floor, too?"

"One more up, but I'm not leaving you alone."

"I'm not going to faint, Brody."

"You never know. You were sweating buckets."

"That must've looked...attractive." She shoved her key
card into the door and a row of green lights flashed.

"That looked scary. You lost a lot of fluids in that
sauna."

She shoved her door open and then spun around, wedging her hands on either side of the doorjamb. "You can
wait out here while I change. If you hear a big thump, you
know I went down."

The door slammed in his face, and he jumped back. A
little hostile, but he could understand why she wouldn't
want a strange man lounging in her hotel room while she
got dressed.

And they *were* strangers, despite their intimate begin-
nings on the pool deck.

When she'd first called him a few months before, he had
recognized the name. Hell, he'd already read her book on
Daniel Walker. Fascinating stuff—former college-football
player, respected businessman, Pop Warner coach—went
berserk and murdered his entire family.

When she'd proposed writing a book on his own family
tragedy, it piqued his interest. Kacie Manning, like many
others, believed in his father's innocence, and she had the
resources, research skills and platform to prove it.

In the end, he'd had to run it by his brothers, especially
Sean and Eric, the two oldest. They'd known Dad the best

and had been affected by the dark cloud over the Brody name more than he and his younger brother, Judd, had been.

He'd braced himself for their opposition, but they surprised him by agreeing, or at least not objecting. They'd even uncovered a few pieces of evidence about the old case that Ryan planned to hand over to Kacie.

A loud thud resounded from Kacie's room, and he banged on her door. "You okay in there?"

The door eased open and she poked her head out. "I'm still upright, but my suitcase isn't—fell off the stand."

"Are you ready?" He nodded at the water bottle in her hand. "Keep hydrating."

"I'm so hydrated I'm ready to float away." She stepped out of her room, pulled her door shut and shoved her key card in her back pocket.

As he followed Kacie down the hallway, he scanned her fully clothed form. The addition of a faded pair of jeans and a baggy T-shirt did nothing to conceal her attractiveness. Damn. At the pool, he'd figured his male libido had just been reacting to the way she filled out that bikini.

But this new iteration of Kacie Manning heated his blood as much as the bikini-clad one. The soft denim of her jeans tightened in all the right places, accentuating her rounded derriere. She'd finger-combed her shoulder-length copper hair into tousled, damp waves that looked as if she'd just had a roll in the sheets.

He couldn't help it. Her appearance tweaked all his male parts. He had a hard time reconciling this lush body with the mind that had written that unflinching portrayal of a killer and sociopath.

Of course, if he ever admitted that thought to his brother's fiancée, Christina, she'd slap him upside the head.

Passing the elevator, she pointed down the hall. "Stairs."

He reached the door before her and held it open. "After you."

Walking closely behind her down the stairwell, he had a hard time concentrating on the steps and almost tripped on the last one.

"I thought I was the unsteady one." She pushed through the fire door and strode into the deserted lobby. Her flip-flops slapped against her feet as she marched to the front desk.

The hotel clerk put down his coffee and met her eyes across the counter. "Good evening. My name is Michael. Can I help you?"

Kacie flattened her palms on the shiny wood and hunched forward. "Well, Michael, someone locked me in the sauna over an hour ago."

The man's eyes bulged from their sockets. "The sauna doesn't lock from the outside."

Pushing the waves from her face, Kacie shook her head. "I don't mean locked. Someone used the handle of the pool net to wedge the doors closed."

"That's terrible! Are you okay? Do you need a doctor?"

"I'm fine…now." She jerked her thumb over her shoulder. "He was in the gym and noticed the net. He let me out."

"It's lucky you're both night owls. Did you see who did it?"

"No. There were some teenage boys in the hot tub earlier, but I don't have any proof that they did anything."

Ryan rested his arm on the counter. "Do you have a camera out there?"

"Sorry. We don't." He grabbed the receiver of his phone and barked into it. "Wesley, we have a situation in the lobby."

Kacie sighed and straightened up. "Then I don't know what you can do about it. The pool area and gym were empty when I went into the sauna. I heard a noise at the door about five minutes after I went in there. That must've been when the idiot decided to play his dangerous joke."

A security guard crossed the lobby, his rubber-soled shoes squeaking on the marble tiles. "What's the problem?"

"Miss...?" Michael raised his brows at Kacie.

"Manning, Kacie Manning."

His forehead furrowed. "Wesley, Ms. Manning was the victim of a rather dangerous practical joke. Someone wedged the sauna doors shut while she was in there."

Wesley tipped back his hat and scratched his forehead. "You don't say. That's a pretty stupid thing to do, especially at this time of night. Did you see anyone?"

"Just a few teens earlier, but they'd left by the time I went into the sauna."

"Yeah, I saw those boys. I had to kick them out of the business center tonight. They were dripping water all over the computers and accessing porn sites." Wesley cleared his throat. "Sorry, ma'am."

Kacie waved her hand. "Oh, I know all about pornographic sites and that teenage boys—and even grown men—are big fans of them."

Ryan slid her a sideways glance. Was that for his benefit? He'd better get his mind out of the bedroom and keep his eyes off her assets.

He stood tall and squared his shoulders. "If the boys were still wet, it sounds like they came straight from the pool. Where'd they go after you kicked them out of the business center?"

"I watched them get into the elevator, and I didn't see them again. I'm assuming they went back to their rooms, but they could've snuck back down to the pool."

Drawing her brows together, Kacie said, "I don't think

they had enough time if they were fooling around in the business center after they left the pool."

The security guard turned to Ryan. "Sir, did you see anyone in the gym?"

"Nope."

"The best I can do is talk to the boys if I see them again." He wagged his finger at Kacie. "You need to be more careful, young lady. Didn't your mama ever tell you to let someone know where you're going at all times?"

Kacie covered her twitching lips with her hand. "No, sir, but that's good advice."

Wesley tugged his pants over his significant belly and sauntered away.

"Sorry about that, Ms. Manning. Wesley's kind of old school."

"I didn't mind."

"We do want to make this up to you, however. I'll check with management, but I'm going to suggest we comp your stay with us, Ms. Manning." He bent his head over his keyboard and started tapping.

"Thanks, Michael." Kacie pointed at Ryan and mouthed the words *You too?*

He shook his head. He hadn't been the one sweating it out in the sauna.

Michael looked up from his task. "Oh, this is a coincidence."

"What is?" Kacie folded her hands on top of the counter.

"I left a message on your hotel phone earlier, probably when you were by the pool. I knew your name sounded familiar."

"Oh? What was the message? I didn't notice one on my phone."

"It's a package, actually. Some transient came in here with it, said a woman had dropped it out front. Your name was on it, and when I looked it up, I discovered you were a guest at the hotel."

"A package?" She shoved back from the counter and shrugged at Ryan. "I wasn't carrying anything except my purse when I walked back to the hotel tonight."

Michael rubbed his chin. "It had your name on it. I put it in the back. I'll get it."

"That's weird. I didn't bring any package with me."

"Maybe someone was supposed to deliver something to you and left it with a doorman or bellhop, and it got left outside. At least your name's on it, and the transient brought it in here."

"I hope it's not important. That's a pretty shabby way to treat something important."

Michael scurried from the back, balancing a lumpy, brown paper–wrapped package on his outstretched palms. He presented it to Kacie, her name scribbled in black felt pen across the outside. "Here you go, Ms. Manning. If there's anything we can do to make your stay more comfortable, please don't hesitate to ask."

"Thank you." She took the package from his hands and spun around. "I'm going to open this now."

She crossed the lobby and sank to the cushions of a love seat facing the door.

Ryan sat across from her and whipped out his knife. "Do you need something for the twine?"

"Yes, please." She held the package out to him, and he sliced the blade through the twine wrapped around the brown paper. It covered something soft and shapeless.

Placing the package in her lap, Kacie began unwrapping it. When she folded back the last piece of paper, she gasped and jerked back.

He lunged out of his chair, falling on his knees in front of her. "What is it? What's wrong?"

Holding the object with the paper, she turned it toward him. A rag doll with blond braids smiled at him with her stitched-on mouth.

His pulse slowed down. "A doll? Are you a collector?"

She shook the toy at him, and the braids flopped back and forth. "This isn't just some random doll."

His gaze tracked from the black button eyes of the doll to Kacie's own round eyes taking up half her face. "Obviously. What is it?"

"Daniel Walker's daughter was clutching this doll when he murdered her."

Chapter Three

The doll grinned at her with a mouth that resembled a slash of blood, calling up images of the original doll at the Walker murder scene. Kacie pressed two shaky fingers to the red yarn on the rag doll's face just to make sure it wasn't blood.

"Kacie, what does this mean?"

She raised her head, her eyes locking onto Ryan's as he put a steadying hand on her bouncing knee. The gesture had an immediate effect on her and she took a deep breath. She didn't have to face this alone right now. "Zoe Walker had a doll just like this one. When they found her body, she had one arm wrapped around her doll—this doll."

"I remember the doll from your book. This one's not yours, is it?" He flicked the paper with his fingers.

"No. This is the first time I've seen a doll like this since I saw the original. Someone sent this to me. That homeless guy didn't find a package outside the hotel. Someone probably paid him to deliver it to this hotel."

As a shiver rolled through her body, she pushed the doll from her lap, where it landed on the carpet still cradled in the brown paper.

"Wait." Ryan picked up two corners of the wrapping. "This might contain some evidence—fingerprints, hair, clothing fibers."

She shifted away from the doll as he placed the package next to her on the cushion and carefully folded the paper around the toy.

"Do you want to tell me why someone would want to send this particular doll to you?" He sat back on his heels as if he had all night to wait for an explanation.

She had no intention of making him wait that long. Despite her revulsion toward all things Brody, she couldn't deny the trust this man fostered in her bones.

He'd saved her from the sauna. His capable hands, square jaw and broad shoulders signaled stability and security. His green eyes reflected sincerity—when they weren't darkening to something more like lust, which happened anytime they wandered over her body.

The fears of the night, beginning with the fratricidal ex-con, flooded her senses, and her pulse rate galloped a mile a minute. She filled her lungs with a deep breath from her nose and expelled it through parted lips to ward off the rising panic and rushing adrenaline.

"Kacie, are you okay?" Ryan squeezed her knee.

"Fighting off an anxiety attack." She pointed to the ceiling. "I'll tell you all about this doll and who sent it from the comfort of my own room while holding a glass of wine in one hand."

"You got it." He sprang to his feet and held out his hand. "I'll help you up. One of my officers suffers from panic attacks, and she always gets a little dizzy."

She gripped his warm hand and struggled to her feet. "You have a cop working for you who has panic attacks?"

"Shh." He held his finger to his lips. "That's top secret."

"But you're her boss."

"That's right. She's a good cop. She told me about the attacks and it doesn't need to go any further—not that I think you'll go running to the Crestview City Council to report us."

Leaning against him, she tilted her head the other way to survey his face. "That's decent of you."

"I have totally selfish reasons. Like I said, she's a good cop and she makes the department and me look good."

She licked her lips. *Yeah, he probably likes the way that cop's backside looks in uniform.*

He kept his hand on her back and the package tucked under his other arm as he guided her toward the elevator. "I think we can skip the stairs this time."

As the doors closed, she stepped away from his warmth and wedged her shoulder against the cold mirror inside the car. "This has been quite a day—full of shocks and surprises."

She counted among those shocks and surprises her immediate attraction to Ryan Brody. The guy had it all in the looks department, including a killer bod, but she'd known that before their face-to-face meeting. She'd seen pictures of him and had even had her P.I. do a little surveillance on him in Crestview.

Brandy, the female P.I. she used, had gone a little overboard with some of the private pictures she'd gotten of Ryan with her long lens.

When Kacie had shuffled through the photos, including quite a few shirtless ones and even a grainy picture of Ryan coming out of his shower, she'd accused Brandy of forming an obsession over her subject.

Brandy, a lesbian in a committed relationship, had just winked.

Kacie's physical attraction to Ryan made up only part of the equation. The guy had rescued her from a scorching sauna. What girl wouldn't feel overwhelmed by that?

And then there was the way he had looked at her.

She glanced down at the body that for years had compelled her to sip diet sodas and munch raw veggies, while her two sisters and her mom could seemingly eat whatever they wanted and still maintain their svelte figures.

Ryan had eyed her as if he wanted to toss her over his shoulder and throw her down on the nearest bed or bend her over the nearest kitchen counter or take her against the wall—any wall.

She pressed her cheek against the cool glass of the mirrored elevator.

"Are you going to faint? Because I can carry you back to your room—piece of cake." He snapped his fingers.

The elevator doors whisked open and she stepped into the hallway, looking over her shoulder. "I'll save you the strain on your back."

His eyebrows jumped to his hairline and he cocked his head. "You're as light as a feather."

Great. How many weaknesses and insecurities could she reveal to him in the course of one night?

She invited him into her room and immediately abandoned the idea of the glass of wine. After the accusations against, and subsequent suicide of, his father, Ryan's mother had turned to drugs and alcohol. Kacie didn't want Ryan thinking she was a lush on top of all the other flaws she'd put on display that night.

Crouching in front of the little fridge, she asked, "Water? Something else?"

"If you're still having that wine, I'll have a beer—and I'll pay you back."

"I decided against the wine. Do you still want the beer? It's on the house."

"I still want the beer, and I'll still pay you for it."

She wrapped her fingers around a chilled bottle and held it up. "Is this okay?"

"That'll do." He reached over and took it from her and then twisted off the cap. "Now, tell me about that doll."

She snapped the lid on a diet soda and perched on the edge of the bed. "Like I told you before, the little Walker girl had the same doll. A strand of Walker's hair was found on the doll, and it was stuck on top of the blood smears. Walker's defense team and the prosecution went back and forth on this point. Walker's attorneys claimed that it wouldn't be unusual for a piece of their client's hair to be on his daughter's doll, and the prosecution argued that it got there *during* the murder."

"It was a significant piece of evidence."

"Yes."

"So, who sent you the doll and why?"

She pleated the bedspread with her fingers. "I think Walker sent it to me as a warning."

As Ryan sat next to her on the bed, she proceeded to tell him about her meeting with the ex-con and Walker's threats against her.

When she finished, he whistled between his teeth. "You're telling me earlier tonight you met with some ex-con who said he had info that Walker was after you?"

"Yep." She took a long pull from her can of soda, the bubbles tickling her nose.

"Damn, you live dangerously, woman."

"That's what I do. Do you think it was any picnic going to interview Walker at Walla Walla on visiting day?"

His gaze left her face and made a detour to her body before returning. "Umm, no. No picnic at all—for you."

It was a good thing her temperature was still slightly elevated because her cheeks warmed again at his taking inventory of her. She pursed her lips. Did he think she'd sashayed into the prison visiting room in a bikini?

"Did you catch this parolee's name?"

"No, but his initials are DB. That's how he signed his texts, anyway." She formed her fingers into a gun and pointed it at him. "That reminds me. He said he was in for murdering his sister. I was going to try to look him up."

"I can help you with that." He pushed off the bed and sauntered over to her laptop on the desk. "I can search for him on the law-enforcement database."

"That would be awesome. I was just going to try to search for fratricides in Washington that occurred about twenty years ago." She flipped up her laptop and turned it toward him.

"Why twenty years ago?"

"From what I could tell, the guy didn't look any older than fifty, so I figured maybe he served twenty or twenty-five years before his parole."

Ryan entered a website address and typed in a user-name and password at the log-in screen. "System's down. We'll check again tomorrow. I think you need to get to bed anyway."

Alone. Get to bed alone.

"I'm much better, thanks, but I'd appreciate it if you could stash that doll in your room." She drew up next to him, bumping his shoulder, and logged off the computer.

"No problem. I'll stuff her in my closet just so no one thinks I'm sleeping with dolls."

She jerked her head up and searched his face for a sign of the double entendre, but his clear green eyes, crinkling at the corners, showed only humor. All this talk of beds and sleeping had fired up her imagination again.

"Yeah, you wouldn't want that getting around your department." She backed away from him and swept his beer from the credenza. "Do you want to take this with you?"

"No, you can toss it." He grabbed the package with the doll wrapped inside and tucked it under his arm. "Do you want me to send this to the lab at the SFPD? Even though my brother's still on leave, I have connections there."

"I'll think about it, thanks."

He saluted and grasped the handle of the door, pulling it open. "Good night. We're still on for lunch tomorrow, right?"

"Yes, and now we have an advantage because we've already met. We can get right down to business."

"Yeah…business."

He stepped into the hallway and pulled the door closed, and Kacie let out a long breath.

That man had a way of making her feel like a siren or a femme fatale.

She fell across the bed, dangling her legs off the side. It didn't matter how Ryan Brody made her feel. She still had a job to do, and that meant proving his father's guilt beyond a reasonable doubt.

KACIE PICKED UP the receiver of the ringing phone once and dropped it back in its cradle, further burrowing into the pillows. She could sleep another few hours, but she'd been looking forward to this day for a few years. Never mind that Ryan had sort of spoiled the occasion by being even better looking in person than in his pictures and by saving her life and then saving her sanity by taking that doll away. Never mind all that.

It was game time.

An hour later she put the finishing touches on her makeup, dabbing the excess shine from her lips. She'd dressed in one of her prison outfits—a slim skirt that hit below the knee with a matching jacket—demure, plain, nothing to draw the unwelcome attention of the convicts at Walla Walla or Ryan Brody. He'd already seen her in next to nothing, but that was the night before. This was a whole new day.

She slipped her feet into a pair of low-heeled shoes and hitched her laptop case over one shoulder and her purse over the other. She even had the restaurant picked out for lunch, unless Ryan wanted to go somewhere else. She'd let him choose.

She always let them think they had the upper hand. It had worked with Daniel Walker up until the moment her book came out and he'd realized he'd been duped.

And apparently her trickery still burned a hole in his gut.

She made it to the hotel lobby fifteen minutes early and perched on the edge of the same love seat where she'd unwrapped that doll the night before.

She hunched her shoulders against the chill rippling up her back. What kind of man would send the same kind of doll his daughter had been hugging the moment he ended her life, as a warning? A sick one. But then, she'd only come to realize that about Walker later.

Like many others, she'd been swayed by Walker's good-looking, grief-stricken face…until she met the man.

She glanced up when the elevators across the lobby dinged open. Ryan strode through the doors and his head jerked in her direction like a heat-seeking missile.

She'd been waiting just five minutes, so he liked being early to meetings, too.

She still had the advantage of watching him approach. If everything that had happened the night before hadn't transpired, what would her first impressions of this man be?

Tall, good-looking, built, confident, maybe a little cocky. She sucked in her lower lip. This wasn't working. She couldn't forget the night before—his concern, his consideration, his blatant attraction to her.

"You're early." He offered a handshake. "I'm Ryan Brody, Ms. Manning. It's a pleasure to meet you."

She gripped his hand. "Are you trying to press the reset button? It won't work. I just tried it."

He squeezed her hand and wouldn't let go, as a smile spread across his face. "You're right. It doesn't work. I already know way too much about you."

At least he had the decency to keep his eyes on her face this time, but it didn't matter. Parts of her body tingled that didn't have any business tingling under her proper skirt and blouse.

He finally dropped her hand, and she smoothed her palms across the front of her linen skirt. "I don't know nearly enough about you, so I propose we get started. I made a reservation at Mezza Luna in North Beach, unless you have a preference for something else."

He spread his arms, and the cotton of his T-shirt tightened across his chest. "I'm a little underdressed. I thought since we were old friends, we'd be going more casual."

"You look fine." And *fine* had a whole other meaning for the way his jeans hugged his muscular thighs and tight backside.

"I can run up and throw on a sports coat, even though the summer weather is finally starting to peek through the fog."

"Mezza Luna isn't that formal, but it's a good place to conduct business. I like to feel like I'm dressing for work because this *is* my job."

"If you're sure they won't kick me out."

"I'm sure." She pointed to the front doors of the hotel. "I called ahead for a taxi. It should be here in about five minutes."

"I'm impressed you're so organized after the night you had."

She crossed her arms across her waist. "Speaking of which, where's the doll?"

"Stashed in the closet. Are you sure you don't want me to send it to the SFPD lab for analysis?"

"It's not against the law to send someone a doll, is it?"

"No, but if we can link it to Walker…"

"Oh, I know it's Walker. The ex-con told me Walker wanted to make my life a living hell, and the doll is his first shot."

"He's not going to have a second." He placed his hand on the small of her back and steered her toward the taxi, which had just pulled up.

Somehow she believed it when he said it.

He opened the door of the taxi for her and she slid across the seat, giving the restaurant's address to the driver.

It didn't take him long to get there, speeding through the streets, dodging cable cars and buses and maneuvering around pedestrians. The taxi squealed to a stop in front of the restaurant, and Kacie insisted on paying.

"Tax write-off for me."

Ryan took a detour to the men's room, leaving Kacie to confront the unfriendly hostess, who acted as if she were guarding the gates of Fort Knox.

Kacie dug in her heels. "Our reservation is for 12:45, and I requested a specific table. I don't think I should have to wait for that table."

The hostess pursed her lips and tapped her pencil on her reservation book. "We have a very important person coming later, and he always likes that table."

"Is there a problem with our reservation?" Ryan raised his brows at the hostess, his mouth turning up at one corner.

The hostess brightened up, flashing a set of white teeth

and pulling back her angular shoulders. "Not at all, sir. I'll seat you immediately."

Her slim hips swaying in front of them, she led them to their table.

If Ryan thought that woman had any intention of kicking him out of the restaurant for dressing too casually, he hadn't checked his reflection in the mirror.

Kacie pulled out her chair before Ryan could do it for her. He must have that effect on all women, not just her. She'd been silly to think his attention to her was anything more than his customary way of relating to women. Women loved him and he loved them back.

Good. She tugged on the lapels of her jacket. That made her job a lot easier.

Made lunch a lot easier, too. The hostess ensured that they had warm bread and cold water on their table in record time.

Kacie flicked open the menu, while munching on a piece of that bread drenched in olive oil.

"I've never been here before. Have you?" Ryan ran his finger down the sheet of daily specials.

"Once or twice. Everything's good."

"I think I'll go with the fettuccine with clam sauce."

"Excellent choice." She dabbed her fingers on the napkin in her lap. "Do you want to get down to business?"

"Sure, but can we finish last night's business first?"

Last night's business when she'd been ready to turn down her sheets for him at the crook of his little finger?

"We had unfinished business?"

"The security guard. Did he ever get back to you? Did he ever talk to those teenage boys?"

"I didn't hear from him, and there was a different clerk at the front desk this afternoon."

A waiter approached their table and took their order. When he left, Kacie pulled out her mini-recorder.

"I hope you don't mind if I tape our interview."

"Nope." He dug into the bread basket and dropped a piece on his plate. "You must have some fascinating recordings of Dan Walker."

"I do. A lot of times, it wasn't until I listened to the recording that I got to understand the man, as much as you can understand a sociopath. He's very distracting to talk to—he's such a good actor."

"And I'm not." He spread his arms. "What you see is what you get."

A total hunk with a protective streak a mile wide and a smile that could melt the insides of the snootiest, skinniest restaurant hostess in North Beach.

Kacie cleared her throat and set up her recording device. "That's good to know."

As she placed her finger on the record button, Ryan put his hand over hers like a caress. "Can I ask you a question before we get started?"

When he touched her like that, he could ask her anything. She flicked his hand off hers and pressed Record. "Go ahead."

He glanced down at the red light blinking on the recorder. "Why my father's story? Why are you interested in writing a book about a twenty-year-old cold case?"

"Because it *is* a cold case. Your father, an SFPD homicide detective, was suspected of being the Phone Book Killer, a serial killer he was investigating himself, but nobody ever proved it."

"A lot of people said he proved it when he jumped from the Golden Gate Bridge and the murders stopped."

"Damning evidence, but there are so many more who believe he was set up, and now all four of the sons he left behind are in some type of law enforcement. It's a great story." She shrugged her shoulders, stiff from her lies.

"You can count my two older brothers among those who believe in our father's innocence. They've recently stumbled across some new evidence and have agreed to give it to me to pass along to you."

Her water sloshed as she set down her glass. "Sean and Eric know I'm writing a book about the case?"

"Yeah. They're okay with it. I told them your angle is that someone set up Joseph Brody."

They wouldn't be okay with it if they knew her true purpose…and her true identity.

"Great." A smile stretched her lips. "And I'd love to see that new evidence. What do you remember about that time?"

"Not much. I was young and confused, and then I lost my dad, who was a larger-than-life figure for me." His green eyes darkened as he took a sip of water. "Do you still have both of your parents?"

"Y-yes."

He splayed his hands on the white tablecloth in front of him. "It's hard to explain the loss of a parent, especially at a young age. You can't begin to understand the hole it leaves."

Oh, but she could.

"You're right."

"And then I lost my mom." He studied his fingernails. "She turned to prescription drugs and alcohol, and Sean had to take over the parenting duties."

"Your mom passed away." She knew the whole painful Brody story.

"Not until I was an adult, but it was still tough. So many wasted years."

Their food arrived, and Kacie turned off the recorder.

Ryan's soulful eyes and sensitive mouth were going to make this a lot harder than she'd anticipated.

The smell of garlic and fresh clams wafted from Ryan's plate, putting her chopped salad to shame. She dug into her rabbit food as he twirled his fork into his creamy pasta.

They ate in silence for a few minutes before he pointed his fork at her salad. "Is that all you're having?"

"It's a big salad."

"It's a salad." He held his fork out to her, tightly wrapped in fettuccine, the savory steam curling beneath her nose. "Try some of this."

She tapped her plate. "Put it here."

"Then you'll have to twirl it up again. Here." He hunched forward, the fork centimeters from her lips.

She opened her mouth and he placed the fork against her tongue. She sealed her lips around the tines and sucked the pasta into her mouth as he drew the fork out with a flourish.

Tingles raced up her inner thighs and circled her belly. She grabbed her napkin and pressed it against the lower half of her face while she chewed. This craziness had to stop.

"Good, huh?" He grinned, but his heavily lidded eyes looked more seductive than smiley.

"Very good." She dropped the napkin from her still-warm face. "Now I will return to my regularly scheduled salad."

"Just let me know if you want another…taste."

She waved down the waiter. "More iced tea, please."

She had to find some way to stay cool. Did all this sex appeal come naturally to Ryan Brody, or was he cranking up the charm for some ulterior motive? She'd already told him she planned to focus the book on proving his father's innocence. He didn't have to butter her up.

Her gaze dropped to his strong hands as he ripped a roll in two and smeared a pat of butter across one half. Although she wouldn't mind if he buttered her up, down and sideways.

She'd *never* felt this way about a story resource before.

Holding up the roll, he asked, "Do you want the other half?"

"No, thanks." She pushed her plate away, dabbed water droplets from the tablecloth with her napkin and repositioned her recorder on the table.

"Whenever you're ready."

He polished off the rest of his meal, including the rest of her roll, and then perused the dessert menu. "Do you want to share a dessert?"

"I'm good."

He ordered a coffee instead and leaned back in his chair as he stirred in a swirl of cream. "Fire away. Ask me anything you want about my father's case. If I don't know the answer, I'll ask my older brothers."

Kacie flipped open her notebook, which contained sheets of printed-out questions. She dived in.

"The Phone Book Killer case was unusual from the get-go, wasn't it? After the first two victims, the killer started communicating with your father, one of the detectives on the case, claiming he was selecting his victims out of the phone book."

"That's right. Serial killers have been known to contact the police to brag and taunt, and the Phone Book Killer singled out my dad. Of course, that's one of the aspects of the case that caused some doubt about my father. Why him?"

"Good question." She drummed her fingers against the tablecloth. "Then he kidnapped your brother. Was that some kind of warning?"

"According to Sean, that's what my father thought. It

was the killer's message that he could get to any member of my family."

"But your brother wasn't harmed, which became another oddity of the case."

Ryan raised his shoulders and let them drop. "People say Joey Brody staged the kidnapping to divert suspicion from himself."

"Then the evidence from your father started to pile up— missing days from work, plaster found in the trunk of his car, the same type of plaster used in casts, which the Phone Book Killer was wearing to disarm his victims."

"Too pat. Too easy." He massaged the back of his neck. "In hindsight, it smells like a setup."

As she reeled off the elements of the case against Joey Brody, Ryan had an answer for every one of them. He had emphasized that his older brothers believed without a doubt in their father's innocence, and Ryan's hot defense of Joey Brody put him firmly in that camp.

Of course they were all in that camp. Admitting your father had blood on his hands had to be hard.

After another hour of question and answer, where they saw the restaurant clear out and received several visits from their waiter with more coffee and iced tea in hand, Kacie clicked off the recorder.

"I really appreciate your openness. It can't be easy. Y-your dad sounds like he was a great cop."

And Daniel Walker had been a great football player.

He shrugged. "Life is full of trials and tribulations. How about you? You look like you've had it pretty easy—smart, attractive, successful."

Straightening her shoulders, she folded her hands on top of the notebook. "I've been lucky. I have a wonderful family. Great parents, two older sisters."

"I hope you appreciate that."

Anxious to hide the emotion that had overcome her, she swiped her recorder from the table and ducked down to stuff it into her bag. "Oh, I do, but you're right." She popped back up with her phone and wallet in hand. "We all have our…disappointments in life."

A loud voice carried across the mostly empty restaurant. "Kacie Manning, right?"

She jerked her head up and zeroed in on a pudgy man with a black goatee making his way toward their table. "Do I know you?"

He stuck out his hand. "I'm Ray Lopez. I'm a reporter with a local TV show."

Great. That's all I need.

"Good to meet you, Ray." She gestured toward Ryan. "This is Ryan Brody. Chief Brody."

"Oh, hey. No introductions necessary. I know who Chief Brody is. I'm like this—" he held up two fingers pressed together "—with Sean and Eric. Eric's fiancée, Christina, and I go way back."

Ryan shook Lopez's hand, sizing him up with one glance. "Sure, I know who you are."

Kacie's gaze bounced from Lopez to Ryan. Sounded as if Ryan wished he didn't know Lopez.

"I'm a big fan of yours, Kacie. Is it true you're doing a book on Joey Brody?"

"You know, I'd rather not discuss that." She swirled the ice in her water glass and took a sip.

"Say no more." Lopez raised his hands. "It's just that I've been trying to get exclusives for years with the Brodys. Guess I'm the wrong sex or something."

Ryan tossed his napkin onto the table. "Excuse me?"

"Just a little joke, Brody. I'd rather work with Kacie Manning than with me, too." He winked and sauntered back to the hostess stand.

"What a jerk." Kacie rolled her eyes.

"He's been kind of a local fixture here the past few years."

"Does he really know your brothers?"

"Yeah, but Sean just tolerates him and Eric can't stand him." Ryan made a move for the check, which had been perched on the edge of their table for an hour. "Let me get this."

She beat him to it, snatching it up and pressing it to her chest. "Tax write-off, remember?"

As she snapped her plastic down on the tray, Ryan tapped her phone on the table. "You have a couple of messages."

"I heard them come through earlier." She picked up the phone. "Didn't want to disturb our flow."

"Yeah, we do have a flow, don't we?"

The hostess with the mostest had extricated herself from Lopez, who'd since left the restaurant. She parked herself next to Ryan's chair, batting her fake eyelashes. "Is there anything else we can do for you today?"

"No, thanks. Sorry we took up this table all afternoon."

"No problem." She waved her perfectly manicured nails. "I could see you were hard at work over here. If you like to play as hard as you work, a friend of mine is having a party tonight at a private club. I could get you in as my…guest."

Kacie clenched her teeth as she tapped her phone to view her messages. He could do whatever he wanted while he was here, including partying with pretty people, as long as he made himself available to her for their interviews and a few field trips.

But she didn't even hear his response as she read over her second message. The blood drained from her face and her head felt like a balloon ready to float away.

"Kacie?"

She glanced up from the display to meet Ryan's eyes, wide and questioning.

"Are you okay?"

The hostess backed up from the table. "I'll let you two finish your business."

Kacie dragged in a breath and released it through dry lips. "It's my contact from last night. He wants to meet again tonight."

"The ex-con?" He snapped his fingers for the phone. "No way."

She raised her brows. When had she appointed him her master scheduler? She handed him the phone anyway, realizing she'd have a hard time saying no to this man.

He peered at the display and read it aloud. "'Meet me same place as last night, same time. More info. DB.'"

He handed the phone back to her. "You recognize that number?"

"It's the same one he used before and the same initials." She pressed her damp palms against her napkin, still crumpled in her lap. "Maybe he knows about that doll. Maybe he saw who gave it to the homeless guy."

"Maybe you should ignore him."

"I can't. He's warning me about Walker."

"Or he's doing Walker's bidding. You ever think of that?"

"Yes. I'm not stupid."

"Oh, I know that, but you're not thinking clearly right now. You are *not* going to traipse down to the wharf alone at eleven o'clock at night."

"I have to go. He might have important information about Walker's next move against me, maybe something I can give to the police this time."

Ryan held up his hands. "You weren't listening. I said you weren't going there *alone*."

A little thrill raced down her back. She couldn't help it. "He'll never talk if he sees you there."

"Who said he's going to see me?"

She waved her hand to indicate his imposing form. "Little hard for someone like you to blend in."

"I have my ways."

She added a tip to the bill and scribbled her signature. As she tucked the receipt in the side pocket of her purse, she said, "As long as you stay out of sight. I don't want you spoiling my meeting."

"How about saving your life?" He pushed back from the table and stepped around it to pull her chair out for her. "Is that okay with you?"

She nodded as silly schoolgirl butterflies took flight in her belly.

This was exactly the effect Daniel Walker wanted to have on her—wrap her around his little finger, tell her sweet little lies.

What could Ryan Brody's motive possibly be? To make sure she wrote a favorable book about his father? She'd already told him she planned to do so. Did he doubt her?

She'd have to watch herself with this man, in more ways than one. Because she couldn't let a sexy grin and a pair of strong arms deter her from exacting her revenge on his father.

Her mom deserved justice.

Chapter Four

Ryan slung the towel over his shoulder, his gaze riveted on the pool area where three teenagers roughhoused in the water. They had to be the same ones from the night before.

He pushed through the glass door separating the weight room and the swimming area, and the humidity of the pool deck seeped into his flesh. The soles of his running shoes squished the wet tiles as he crossed to the edge of the pool. He squatted beside it and called out, "Hey."

Three faces turned toward him, a sullen look already forming around the mouth of one of them.

He was the one who answered. "Yeah?"

"Were you guys in here last night? In the hot tub?"

The three of them exchanged quick glances, and another teen spoke up, an earnest look on his face. "Yes, sir. We were in the hot tub late last night."

"Did you happen to see a woman out here?"

"Yeah, she went into the pool."

"She was smokin' hot for a cougar." The first boy to have spoken up stuck his tongue out of his mouth and flicked it up and down.

Ryan's hands, resting on his knees, curled into fists.

"Shut up, man." The Boy Scout punched his friend in the shoulder, then turned his attention back to Ryan. "Why are you asking? Did something happen?"

Flexing his fingers, Ryan dropped one knee to the deck. "Someone played a trick on her in the sauna."

The sullen one lost the attitude and the smirk and said, "She was still in the pool when we left."

The other two teens nodded in agreement. "She was swimming laps when we bolted."

"Did you see anyone else out here? In the gym?" Ryan pushed to his feet.

"No, sir."

"All right. Thanks." Ryan exited the pool area, mopping his face with the towel.

He believed them. According to the security guard, those boys were probably messing around in the business center at the time Kacie was in the sauna. Besides, would they play a trick like that on a smokin'-hot cougar?

They got half of that right. Kacie was smokin' hot, but she was no cougar—at least not for him.

He filled up his water bottle from the gym's dispenser and then tossed his towel in the bin. She'd shot him down when he asked her to join him for dinner that night, but they planned to get together before her meeting with DB to give him another crack at finding the guy in the law-enforcement database.

As far as he could tell, Kacie had spent the afternoon holed up in her hotel room—working, she said. He smacked the elevator button with the flat of his palm. That woman ran hot, very hot, and cold.

Women. He sure loved 'em, but he couldn't even pretend to understand 'em.

He'd spent his afternoon dropping that doll off at the local precinct, touching base with his brother's fellow officers and then tracking down his younger brother.

He knew Judd was going to be out of town again, but he'd managed to catch him for about an hour before he headed to the airport, this time to work for the Saudi royal family. His P.I. brother had been getting higher-end gigs lately, a step up from spying on errant spouses.

Ryan shook his head as he slipped his key card into his door. He'd barely recognized Judd with his suit sleeves covering his tattooed arms, his long hair slicked back.

Once again, Judd had offered up his apartment to Ryan, but Ryan had passed. Judd was careless with his business and his women. Ryan didn't want any surprises in the form of irate females dropping in—either ones Judd had spied on for their husbands or ones he'd loved and left.

That was the excuse he had given Judd, anyway. If he took his brother up on his offer, he'd have to check out of this hotel. And Kacie Manning was in this hotel, one floor below him. He wasn't going anywhere.

He showered, changed and ate a burger at the restaurant in the lobby. Then he showed up at Kacie's door, five minutes early.

She'd stacked the remnants of her own room-service meal on the credenza. Papers and notebooks littered the desk around her laptop. She'd swapped her business attire for a pair of black jeans and a dark green top that accented the copper highlights in her hair and an expanse of soft, creamy skin above the neckline.

Wedging her fist on one curvy hip, she tapped the toes of her bare foot. "You're early—again."

"Am I?" Had he betrayed his eagerness to see her?

"I was just going to clean up." She flicked her fingers toward the abandoned dishes.

"Let me." He hoisted the tray and carried it toward the door.

She scooted around him to pull the door open and then leaned against it while he pushed the tray against the wall in the hallway.

He rose, dusting his hands together. "I ran into those teenagers at the pool today."

"Really?" She let the door slam. "Did they fess up to anything?"

"Just that they thought you were smokin' hot." He would leave out the cougar part.

Color rushed into her cheeks, and she snorted. "Must've been all that steam from the hot tub obscuring their vision. So, they didn't see anyone else out there?"

"No." He tilted his head and hitched his thumbs in his pockets. Was she fishing for a compliment or did she really not understand the impact of that body on a red-blooded American male?

She ducked her head and fussed with the laptop, her hair creating a veil over her face.

Nope. She didn't get it. Self-confident about everything except her looks. He knew the type.

"I couldn't get back to that system you were using."

"I'll find it." He sidled next to her at the desk by the window and brushed her arm with his fingers as he reached for the keyboard.

Standing shoulder to shoulder with her, he felt her body quiver. Must be the excitement of discovering the identity of her contact. Couldn't have been because of their close proximity, since she'd been shoving him away from her with both hands ever since he'd carried her bikini-clad body from the sauna.

He pointed to her screen background, a middle-aged couple with a spaniel between them. "Your parents?"

"And their faithful dog. They've had him for fifteen years."

He studied the pair, a sleek blonde with straight chin-length hair and a balding man who looked fit for his age. Kacie must have taken after her dad because she didn't resemble her mom at all.

He entered a URL and typed in his username, password and number from his token. The system whirred to life and he let out a breath. "It's up."

Kacie stepped away from him and planted a chair between them. "Have a seat. I'll give you what I know."

He settled on the edge of the chair, his hands hovering above the computer as he waited for it to connect. When the search bar appeared, he turned his head to look at her. "Date of incarceration?"

"Can you enter a range of dates?" She leaned over him and her fragrant hair tickled his cheek.

He swallowed. "Yeah."

"Maybe twenty or twenty-five years ago."

He typed in the date range. "Location?"

"Let's go with Washington State." She jabbed her finger at the display, and the side of her breast skimmed his upper arm. She pulled back.

He got rock hard. He squeezed his eyes shut and gritted his teeth. "Washington. Crime?"

"Murder."

He entered the man's heinous crime, but even that couldn't tame the heat surging through his body. He'd need a cold shower for that.

"I can't exactly enter his initials, but I can enter *B* followed by an asterisk and that should give us everyone with a last name starting with that letter—unless he's lying to you."

"An ex-con lying? Say it ain't so." She knelt down beside his chair.

"Then this is it." He entered the initials in the name fields and clicked the search button.

A little hourglass blinked in the center of the display.

"Uh-oh. This could take a while."

"We have time." She rose from her seated position and

tapped at the clock in the lower right corner of the screen. Then she settled back on the floor. "Did you have a good afternoon?"

Leaning back in the chair, he stretched his legs out to the side. "I took that doll to the SFPD."

"You didn't have to do that. There's no crime."

"Doesn't matter. They know me there from my brother Sean, and besides, it's professional courtesy."

"Did you give them any details?"

"They didn't ask, and I didn't tell."

"Well, thank you." She folded her hands in her lap. "Did you get a chance to visit some old haunts in the city?"

"I dropped in on my brother."

"I thought he was on extended leave."

"My other brother—Judd."

"He's the youngest, right?"

"Youngest and wildest."

"He's a P.I."

That wasn't really a question. She seemed to know his family history as well as he did. "Yep."

"Why didn't you just stay with him?"

"He was on his way out of town, too. He's been doing some bodyguarding, and this time I think he's guarding a suitcase full of jewels instead of a person." Ryan's gaze dropped to the top of her head. Besides, all the excitement he needed was right here at this hotel in Fisherman's Wharf.

"Wow, I bet he has some stories to tell."

"If he does, he keeps them to himself." He jiggled the mouse to wake up the display. "Just last month he was working as a bodyguard for some pop princess on tour in Hawaii."

She snapped her fingers. "Oh, oh, I know who that

is, but her name escapes me now. Aren't you just a little bit envious?"

Right now, working with Kacie and enjoying the way her quick mind picked up on his next thought and their easy back-and-forth banter, he didn't envy anyone. "Naw. That's Judd's thing. He's kind of rootless. I like my small town."

"Of course, you did have an opportunity tonight to party with that attractive hostess." She threw up her hands. "Don't let me get in your way of a good time. If you want to check it out after we meet my informant tonight, go for it."

He drew in his eyebrows. Was she trying to push him into that hostess's arms? "Ah, not interested."

"Not a party kind of guy?"

He would prefer a party of two in that king-size bed across the room. Leveling a gaze at her, he said in almost an undertone, "I like certain kinds of parties."

She jumped to her feet and brushed off the seat of her snug jeans as she wandered to the window.

His voice must've betrayed his meaning, and it sure did fluster her. Either she wanted nothing to do with him, or he was growing on her.

"If you change your mind, I'm sure she'd welcome you with open arms."

The beep of the computer saved him from trying to analyze her obsession with sending him away with some other woman.

He hunched forward and scrolled through the entries. "There are quite a few here, but it won't be an impossible task to comb through them."

"Too bad we can't split them up."

"We can't." He rose from his chair and dragged the other one next to his and patted the seat. "So you might as well sit down next to me."

She moved the chair a few inches away from his and

sat on one corner, ready to take flight if necessary. "Okay, what do you do, just click on the entry?"

"That's it."

They spent the next fifteen minutes selecting the cons, and Kacie's shoulders began to get sore from holding them stiffly so she wouldn't accidentally brush against Ryan again.

When she'd accidentally mushed her breast against his biceps, she had nearly melted into a puddle. Of course, her chest had done a bunch of mushing against his when he'd carried her out of the sauna, and she'd been wearing a lot less then, but she'd been half out of it and hadn't yet formed this powerful attraction to him.

She rubbed the back of her neck as Ryan clicked on another possible suspect.

He swung his head toward her. "Are you tired?"

"My neck and shoulders are tight. I already put in a few hours of computer time this afternoon."

"Why don't you go stretch out on the bed? If anything looks promising, I'll call you over."

Her gaze darted to the bed and back to the computer. What would be worse, lying on a bed in the same room as Ryan or continuing to sit inches away from his hard body, inhaling his fresh, masculine scent?

She pushed back from the desk so fast her chair tipped back.

"Whoa." Ryan caught it and righted it.

She scurried to the bed, dragged the pillows from beneath the bedspread and punched them into position. Then she hopped onto the bed, her head sinking against the pile of pillows.

"Let me know if you find anything, and help yourself to the mini-bar."

He hunched over the laptop and continued tapping and clicking.

Good move. Her head began clearing once she was out of the Ryan realm. Without all his manliness parked next to her and invading her senses, her muscles relaxed and her breathing deepened. The sounds from the computer became hypnotic and she closed her eyes.

Rough fingertips dabbled against her cheek and she burrowed into the pillows, a smile curving her lips.

"Kacie?"

"Mmm." Warmth spread through her body and she felt safe, like the first time her foster parents brought her home.

She rolled to her side and flung out her arm. Her hand hit an immovable object, and she peeled open one eye.

Perching on the edge of the bed, Ryan smiled at her. "You dozed off."

She opened her other eye, noticed her hand resting against his thigh and snatched it back. She grabbed a pillow and hugged it to her body, bringing her knees to her chest.

"Was I out long?" Had she been snoring? Drooling? She wiped the back of her hand across her dry mouth.

"About an hour."

"Sorry." Why wouldn't he remove himself from the bed?

"No worries. You looked so peaceful over here I didn't want to disturb you."

She rubbed her eyes and scooched up to a sitting position, still clutching the pillow to her chest. "Did you find anything?"

"I did, just now." He jerked his thumb over his shoulder.

"You found DB?" Her fingertips buzzed and she dropped the pillow to her lap. She would've swung her legs off the bed, but Ryan's six-foot-something frame of solid muscle blocked her way.

He must've read the trapped-animal look in her eyes

because he eased off the bed and took a step back. "It looks like DB is Duke Bannister. He was convicted of first-degree murder and sent to the big house for twenty-five to life. Served twenty-two of those years and then got paroled last year."

Tossing the pillow to the side, she scrambled from the bed. "Who'd he kill?"

"His sister."

She tripped and he caught her around the waist. "Careful."

"Bannister told me I reminded him of his sister."

"Even more reason for me to come with you tonight." Ryan gave her hip a pat before releasing her.

Taking his vacated place in front of the computer, she dragged the chair forward and studied the screen. "Now that I know who he is, I can dig around his background and see if I can find out whether or not he's working for Walker."

"You may be able to find that out tonight."

"How?" She pushed her bedhead hair from her face. "He's not about to tell me if I ask him."

"You won't have to ask him. If he attacks you, you'll have your answer."

She hunched her shoulders. "That's not going to happen."

"Really? The dude killed his own sister."

"Okay, maybe you're right, but you're my muscle tonight." She bit her lip and busied herself printing out Bannister's page, second-guessing her plan to meet with Ryan in person. She'd have been better off conducting an interview with him over the phone or even over the computer. The man's presence was scrambling her thoughts and overloading her senses.

"We have about forty minutes. I'm going to get ready. Can we meet in the lobby in a half an hour?"

"Sure."

She strode to the door and opened it wide, watching him as he moved from the room into the hallway. "Thanks for doing all the work while I snoozed."

"No problem. It looked like you needed the rest."

She pulled the door closed and banged her forehead against it. She needed to wrap up this interview process and get down to the business of proving Joseph Brody's guilt beyond a shadow of a doubt.

She brushed her teeth, finger-combed her hair and stuffed her feet into a pair of canvas shoes. They'd do if she had to take off in a sprint.

Ryan had beaten her to the punch again, greeting her with a big smile in the lobby ten minutes early.

"Are you always early?" She threw her sweater over her shoulders, letting it hang.

"Are you?"

"Pretty much."

"Me too."

Drawing her small purse across her body, she asked, "How is this going to work?"

"Tell me where you met him last time. You start out first and I'll follow you, slinking along in the shadows. I won't be far behind you at any given time, but you won't see me and neither will Bannister."

"Should I use a code word or something if I get into trouble?"

"If you want to play spy games, go for it. Otherwise, a good old-fashioned scream will work."

"I mean—" she stepped through the front door of the hotel and nodded at the doorman "—if I start feeling nervous and I just want you to be primed and ready."

"I'm always primed and ready."

He winked at her and she rolled her eyes, but she could believe it with that body. "You know what I mean."

"I do. How about 'sauna'? It's where we first met, where I rescued you from danger the first time."

"The first time?" She raised her eyebrows. "Do you think there will be a second?"

"There could be tonight—that's the point."

"Okay, 'sauna' it is." She gave him the location of her first meeting with Bannister and set out ahead of him, her footsteps jaunty and her head held high.

The usual transients went about their usual business, but this time she eyed each one, wondering if he could have been the one who delivered the doll to the hotel.

The moist air off the bay caressed her face and worked through the waves of her hair. Even though she'd left the city as a child for Seattle with her new family, the smells and feel of San Francisco had never left her—and never would.

She cranked her head over her shoulder once, but couldn't see one trace of Ryan. He was probably taking a different route to stake out a good location, and with his dark clothing and 49ers cap pulled low on his face, he'd blend right into the scenery of the wharf.

Knots formed in her belly as she waited to cross the street before hitting the walkway along the wharf. Most of the restaurants were shutting down for the night or trying to, and all of the street performers had rolled up their props and gadgets from the sidewalk. Tourists still crisscrossed the streets, weaving in and out of the shops still open for business. The homeless population, the silent army of the night, shuffled from doorway to bench to bus stop, searching for a place to park their possessions.

She strode through the crosswalk and turned left toward

the less-populated area of the wharf, its tourist attractions long closed for the day. She spotted the low-slung building where she'd met Duke Bannister—assuming that was his actual name—the night before and dragged in a long breath.

Her gaze scanned the vacant side of the building. The last time he'd come from around the corner of that building. Easier for a surprise attack?

Tensing her muscles, she lightly clenched her hands at her sides. If Bannister got to her before Ryan got to him, she planned to do a little damage of her own first.

She slowed her steps and cleared her throat. "DB?"

If she used his real name, she might spook him. And she definitely wanted to hear what he had to say.

She froze. Had she heard a cough?

"DB?" She reached the building and trailed her hand along the damp metal, stopping at the corner.

"I-it's Kacie."

A soft sigh floated from around the corner of the building. Was he playing some kind of game with her?

"Are you there?" If Bannister was lurking around the corner in a suspicious manner, Ryan would notice that. Wouldn't he?

She held her breath and gripped the edge of the building. She leaned forward, turning her head to the side. A man sat on a bench facing the water, a hat perched on his head, one arm resting across the back of the bench.

"DB, it's Kacie." She crept forward, the soft soles of her shoes a whisper on the pavement.

Her jaw ached with tension, and her little sips of air had her lungs burning. She couldn't see his other hand, which could've been resting in his lap. Holding a weapon?

Her first swallow became a lump in her throat and she tried again. She approached DB from the back and laid a hand on his denim-clad shoulder.

Her fingertips met moisture. She snatched her hand back and peered at her fingers in the dim yellow light spilling from a bulb on the outside of the building.

The smell of blood invaded her nostrils—heavy, metallic. Rubbing her sticky fingers together, she circled the bench and dropped to her knees in front of DB.

Blood soaked the bandana around his neck as it gurgled from a gash across his throat.

As Kacie screamed "sauna," one thought pummeled her brain.

Duke Bannister's sister had finally gotten her justice.

Chapter Five

Ryan jumped from behind the barrels on the wharf and sprinted toward Kacie, her howl echoing in the night.

He pulled his gun from his pocket and charged toward the figure reposing on the bench, ready to do him physical harm if he had one finger on Kacie.

No need.

Kacie had fallen onto her backside, her hands spread before her.

Bannister's head lolled back, as if he were taking in the night sky, his denim shirtfront and blue bandana loosely tied around his neck soaked with blood. Someone had slit his throat from ear to ear, creating a grisly second smile.

Ryan dropped to the ground and pulled Kacie away from the dead man. Bannister's blood smudged her splayed hands, and without their support, she tilted to the side, in danger of falling over.

He wrapped an arm around her shoulders and pulled her close against his body. "Shh. Don't worry. I'm right here beside you."

She sobbed against his arm. "The blood, the blood."

Ryan placed his firearm back in his pocket and exchanged it for a cell phone. He called 911, then hooked his arms beneath Kacie's to bring her to her feet since she seemed incapable of movement.

"Hey, what happened, man? Is the lady okay?"

Ryan glanced over his shoulder to see a transient hunched over his shopping cart. "She's okay, but this guy is dead. Did you see anything? See anyone hanging around here?"

"Nope." The guy took off faster than he'd probably ever moved since he'd been on the streets.

Carrying Kacie toward a chain-link fence across from the bench, he whispered soothing words against her soft earlobe. "It's okay. I have you."

Her eyes grew wide and she clutched his T-shirt with both hands, forgetting they were stained with Bannister's blood. "What if he's still here? What if Walker is still here?"

He wrapped his arms around her trembling body and stroked her hair. "Walker's not here. He's locked up, remember? Nobody's going to hurt you."

She sniffled and burrowed against his chest.

His arms tightened around her trembling frame, and she molded against his body, melting into him. He could stand there all night holding her if it weren't for the dead guy they had to deal with.

Sirens swooped down to the wharf, bringing out the night owls, who began to form clusters around the bench. The SFPD soon had the situation in hand, taping off the area and keeping the looky-loos at a distance.

Sergeant Curtis approached them first. "You called this in, Brody?"

Curtis worked homicide with his brother. Ryan tucked Kacie against his side and extended his hand. "Good to see you, Sergeant. I missed you when I was at the department earlier today. This is Kacie Manning. She had a meeting with the guy, and I tagged along. We believe he's an ex-con named Duke Bannister."

"Kacie Manning." Curtis snapped his fingers. "You wrote that book on Daniel Walker—fascinating read."

Kacie peeled herself from Ryan's side and drew back her shoulders. "That's right. This man did time with Walker. He had some information for me, and that's why I was meeting him."

"Did either of you see anything out here?" Curtis swirled his finger in the air.

"No. I didn't realize Bannister was dead until I approached him from behind and touched his shoulder." She held out her hands. "I got his blood on my hands."

"We'll want to take a swab of that, Ms. Manning, and then you can clean up." He snapped his fingers for a tech.

"A transient came by soon after we discovered the body, but he claimed he hadn't seen anyone and then took off in a hurry. I, uh—" Ryan gestured toward Kacie "—had my hands full and couldn't detain him."

"No problem. A lot of these guys on the wharf are regulars. We'll have our guys put the word out. We'll offer an exchange of money for info. If someone saw something, the smell of cold hard cash usually brings them out of the woodwork. Do you think the information he had could've led to his murder, Ms. Manning?"

Kacie's eyes darted to Ryan's face and then back to Curtis's. "I'd met with Bannister before. He told me at that time Walker had it in for me."

Curtis whistled. "Do you think this is Walker's long hand from prison?"

"It could be."

Ryan joined in and told Curtis about the doll and how he'd dropped it off earlier today at the station. "Your lab guys have it now."

"We'll contact the warden at Walla Walla. He can have a little talk with Walker or more closely monitor his communications or do whatever he thinks necessary." Curtis leveled a finger at Ryan. "In the meantime, stay close to this guy. If you got a Brody on your side, you ain't doing half-bad."

After they answered a few more questions, a tech took a sample of blood from Kacie's hand, handed her a moist towelette and they were free to go.

Their shoulders bumped a few times on the walk back to the hotel. When the police showed up, Kacie seemed to have recovered, morphing back into the hard-nosed reporter.

And that was a good thing, but one part of him liked the way she clung to him, needed him. He wanted to be there for her.

She peppered him with questions and suggested likely scenarios all the way back to the hotel.

When the doors of the elevator slid open on the fourth floor, she held up her hand. "I'm okay, really."

"I know that, but what kind of cop would I be if I didn't see you safely to your room after the night you just had?"

She blinked. "I guess that sense of duty never goes away, does it? Even when you're off the clock."

"Funny thing about cops." He stepped out of the elevator and took her elbow. "We're never off the clock."

"I saw that with a lot of the men and women I interviewed for the book on Daniel Walker."

She'd allowed him to touch her, but that soft, yielding woman in his arms at the wharf had turned rigid and cold. If she wanted to keep this strictly business, he could comply.

When they reached her door, he dropped his hand. "Why do you think Walker had Bannister killed? Maybe he found out that Bannister already told you about his plan for revenge, so he killed him for punishment."

Folding her arms, she leaned against her door. "Or

maybe Bannister was about to give me more details about Walker's scheme, a scheme he didn't want revealed, something Walker may have told him in prison."

"It's in the warden's hands now."

She glanced down at her own palms, still stained with Bannister's blood despite the towelette. "My hands." Her gaze shifted to his shirt. "And your shirt. I'm so sorry. I ruined your shirt."

"This old thing?" He plucked the black T-shirt away from his chest. "I can toss it. It's seen better days."

And now it could die happy after having this woman pressed against it for five whole minutes.

"At least it's not soaked through. Is it?" She tapped a finger against the stiff cloth of his shirt.

"I don't think so." He pinched the hem of his shirt and yanked it up, exposing his stomach and chest. Dropping his chin to his chest, he said, "Nope. It didn't go through."

When he looked up, she dragged her gaze from his bare skin. A rosy color stained her cheeks and she expelled a quick breath through parted lips.

Good to see his charms held some fascination for her.

The shutters dropped over her eyes again and she made a turn for the door. "I'm going to scrub my hands with soap and water and get to bed. We have a busy day tomorrow."

He let his T-shirt fall. "Sweet dreams. I'll see you downstairs for breakfast at nine."

IT TOOK HER three tries to unlock her door with Ryan still breathing down her neck, his muscles covered only by that thin black T-shirt.

When the green lights finally signaled success, she gave him a halfhearted wave and scurried inside the room, letting the door shut heavily behind her.

Why had she fallen into his arms so easily? Did she

have a choice? She'd just discovered a dead man awash in his own blood, for heaven's sake! She would've fallen into the arms of that homeless guy if he'd been handy. Ryan had just been handy.

But did handy have to feel so good?

She cranked on the water in the shower and stepped in. She cupped the little bar of soap in her hands as she held them beneath the warm stream. She lathered up her hands again and again, watching pink water swirl down the drain. The red from the scrubbing soon replaced the red from the blood. She toweled dry and dropped the towel to the bathroom floor.

Tomorrow she'd face the day with a fresh outlook. The warden at Walla Walla would handle Daniel Walker and get him off her back. Then she'd be free to pursue the Brody story.

Back on solid footing, she wouldn't need to run to the all-too-welcoming arms of Ryan every two seconds. Then she could get started on what she had come here to do— prove Joseph Brody's guilt as the Phone Book Killer beyond a reasonable doubt.

THE FOLLOWING MORNING, she didn't even try to race Ryan downstairs. Let him have that petty victory. But as luck would have it, she beat him anyway. She took a table on the rim of the hotel restaurant and positioned her chair to face the lobby.

She generally liked to be waiting for her subject because she felt it gave her the upper hand, an opportunity to study her specimen before he knew he was being observed. In Ryan's case, it had the opposite effect.

As soon as he appeared in the lobby, her pulse quickened.

He exchanged a few words with the hotel clerk at the desk that had the clerk smiling from ear to ear. The hostess at the restaurant practically tripped over herself waving him to the table, and more than a few female heads turned as he threaded his way through the tables.

When he aimed that smile her way, Kacie experienced that newly familiar feeling of heat surging through her body and tingles spreading through her lady parts.

"Good morning. How'd you sleep?"

"Surprisingly well." To keep busy, she stirred way too much cream in her coffee. "Last night… Well, not that I'm happy someone is dead, but it's almost a relief to have Walker's threats out in the open. The warden can deal with him now."

He took his place across from her. "I wouldn't waste any tears on Bannister. The cops found two knives on him— one in his jacket pocket and one in his boot."

She choked on her sip of coffee. "He could've…"

"That's right. He could've been planning something for you. Maybe he didn't have any more information about Walker. Maybe he wanted to get close to you again."

"So, in a weird way, I owe Walker a debt of gratitude for getting rid of Duke Bannister."

"In a *really* weird way. I'm glad you're feeling better." He called the waiter over and ordered a cup of coffee.

"I'm ready to put all this behind me." She meant not only Walker and Bannister but also her insane attraction to Ryan Brody. She'd have to suppress that and get down to business.

"I hope you can. I hope the warden at Walla Walla deals with Walker." When his coffee arrived, he pointed to the cream next to her saucer. "Any of that left?"

She shoved it across to him. "We're going to take our first field trip to the Golden Gate Bridge. Are you okay with that?"

His spoon stopped short of his coffee and he sucked

in a quick breath. "I don't think we're going to find any evidence there."

"This first part—" she drew a circle on the table with her fingertip "—isn't about finding evidence. It's more about setting the mood. This has to be a story as well as just a report on the facts of the case. You know that, right?"

"I read your book." He rested his chin on top of his steepled fingers.

"I hope it's not going to be too hard on you." She laced her own fingers in her lap, resisting the ridiculous urge to caress his forearm.

"It won't be easy going through it all again, but if it proves my father's innocence, I'll walk through fire."

He may have to before this was all over because she planned to reveal his father as a killer. Then all this tension between them would blow up into smithereens.

They finished their breakfast and headed out to the parking structure where Ryan had left his car, a small SUV. He maneuvered through the streets of the city like a pro and pulled into the visitor parking for the bridge.

Kacie released her seat belt. "Where'd you learn to drive like that? I thought you lived in a little hick town up north?"

"I drove all around this city as a teenager. I wasn't always a hick." He winked at her.

"Hey, I'm not casting stones. The town I live in is no thriving metropolis."

He rested his hands on the steering wheel. "Did you grow up there?"

"My parents are in Seattle. I grew up there."

"And your sisters?"

"My sisters? How did you know I had sisters?" Her heart drummed a beat in her chest. Had he been checking up on her? How much could he have discovered through his police connections?

"Yesterday during our interview, you told me you had two older sisters."

"Oh yeah. One still lives in Seattle—married, children—and the other lives down in L.A., engaged." She'd have to watch her tongue around him.

She scrambled from the car and grabbed a light jacket from the backseat.

Shoving his hands into his pockets, he ambled to her side of the car and peered at the blue sky. "Not sure you're going to need that."

"It is a nice day, but it's always breezy on the bridge." She draped the jacket over her arm. "Ready?"

They crossed the parking lot and walked toward the pedestrian entrance. When they reached the walkway, tourists, cyclists and photographers joined them, while cars whizzed past on the road.

Ryan walked beside her, his head turned toward the bay. Did the view bring him pleasure, like it did most of the other pedestrians, or pain?

He stopped and grasped the low barrier, hunching his shoulders. "This is it."

She drew beside him, drinking in the view of Alcatraz and the city skyline floating between the blue of the bay and the blue of the sky. "This is a beautiful stop, but there are so many great views."

"No, I mean, this is it." The wind played with his hair, flattening it against his head as he looked down.

Then it hit her and her stomach dropped. "This is the exact spot where your father died?"

"This is where he jumped."

This time she did reach out, covering his hand with hers. "I'm sorry. We didn't have to... You didn't have to..."

He cranked his head around and his eyes blazed at her for a second. "You wanted to come here. You wanted to come and see where it all ended. Well, this is it. This is the spot."

A muscle twitched in her eye. Was he angry at her for foisting this on him? Ryan seemed like such an easygoing guy, but his hard mouth and harder eyes hinted at depths of rage she hadn't seen or expected.

Would this rage bubble over when he found out the truth?

By then she'd be far away, her lifelong goal reached. She brushed a wisp of hair from her face. "Do you want to leave?"

His shoulders dropped and he ran a hand through his thick, windblown hair. "No."

"His body was never found."

"Currents carried him out to sea."

"Were there any witnesses?"

"One." Turning sideways, he leaned on the barrier. "A woman was taking in the early-morning view. She'd noticed a man quite a distance from her. She watched as he climbed over the barrier and disappeared."

"She called the police?"

"She used one of the phones on the bridge to call the coast guard, but his body never turned up."

Kacie shivered despite the sun on her back. "Their station is so close I'm surprised they didn't find him."

"It happens. The current was swift that day. The police found my father's jacket and wallet on the ground and later they located his car in the parking lot—the same lot where we just parked."

"Have you or your brothers ever spoken to this witness?"

He cocked his head and pressed his back against the

barrier, spreading his arms along the top like a tourist posing for the camera. "I never have. If they did, they didn't tell me about it."

"I'd be curious to talk to her, if she's still alive. Do you know?"

"I know she was a young woman—early twenties."

"Do you remember her name?"

"I don't, but it would be in the case file for my father's suicide, and that's at the department."

"You can get your hands on that, right? You're the victim's son and you have connections."

"Uh-huh."

His gaze shifted away from her face and over her left shoulder. This visit had really affected him.

She cleared her throat. "I'd like to have a look at that file. Sometimes a fresh pair of eyes can yield some new insight."

"Uh-huh."

His eyes narrowed and his body tensed.

"Do you want to...?"

He swore and pushed past her.

As she stumbled, she twisted around just in time to see him lunge over the barrier—another Brody over the bridge.

Chapter Six

The barrier dug into his rib cage as he balanced on top of it, his hand grasping the straps of the woman's backpack.

"Don't do this."

She turned her head to look up at him with blank, red-rimmed eyes.

Kacie ran up beside him and dug her fingers into his arm. "What are you doing?"

"Call the cops from the phone. There's a woman on the ledge."

Kacie gasped and spun around.

The woman below him continued to stare at him, but she'd stopped struggling. She'd dropped to her knees on the steel ledge that ran almost the entire length of the bridge. There was nothing between her and a long drop into the choppy bay.

"Are you ready to come up now? Think about your family."

She sniffled and straightened up to her full height.

Ryan still held on to her backpack, but she could slip out of it at any second. He extended his other arm. "Grab on to me."

She glanced back at the endless sky in front of her, and Ryan's heart skipped a beat. Then she wrapped her hands around his arm.

He braced his feet against the barrier and hoisted her up and over it. She fell on top of him with a squeak, then rolled off him and curled into a fetal position on the ground.

Several pedestrians had watched the drama unfold. They formed a semicircle around him and the woman, who couldn't have been much older than twenty-five.

Kacie pushed through the onlookers. "The cops are on their way. I can see one coming on his bike."

The officer rode up with another officer right behind him. They dispersed the crowd and crouched beside the woman, who was still coiled into a ball.

Sirens followed, and the woman was lifted to her feet and bundled into the back of the squad car. The officer on the bike asked Ryan a few questions, got his name and number and pedaled off.

"Oh my God. I can't believe that happened right when we were here." She'd clapped a hand over her mouth and her eyes widened above it.

"It's a shame it happens at all. That woman was clearly in need of some help."

"Ryan Brody, you're such a hero. You put yourself in danger to save that stranger."

"Not at all. I was never in any danger of going over. She was small and light. Ask me if I'd have done it for some big bruiser."

Like Dad.

"I'm sure you would've tried. How often are people rescued from suicide attempts on the bridge?"

"I like to think more than are successful. The authorities try to keep a close eye on the activities up here."

"A closer watch than in your father's day."

"Definitely." He flexed his fingers, which had cramped up while holding on to the woman. "Now, let's get some lunch and visit the station for that case file. Unless you didn't get everything you needed here."

"Are you kidding? I got more than I bargained for." She touched his shoulder. "Thank you for coming here with me today. I see that it was difficult for you."

He stopped walking because he didn't want her to remove her hand from his arm, to scare her away. "Just because it's tough doesn't mean you flinch or turn away."

"Of course, if you hadn't been here, you wouldn't have saved that woman's life. She might not feel thankful now, but maybe she will later." She smoothed the material of his shirt before dropping her hand. "It all happened for a reason. Now, let's get that lunch."

Forty-five minutes later, Ryan took a big bite of his burger and mopped the grease from his chin as he watched Kacie stab an anemic piece of lettuce. "You sure do like your rabbit food."

"Some of us—" she waved her fork at him "—don't have time to spend hours in the gym or whatever you do to maintain that hard body."

She noticed? Did she take him for a gym rat, flexing in front of a mirror? "I have to stay physically fit for my job."

"Well, I don't." She added a tomato to the forkful of lettuce and popped it into her mouth.

"You don't need to be physically fit. You're physically fine." He didn't need a woman pumping iron alongside him. He preferred the contrast of a soft body next to his, and Kacie Manning had the kind of body a man could sink into.

Her cheeks reddened to match the tomatoes on her plate. "Are you going to follow up on that woman?"

"Yeah, I'll make a few calls, but they probably have her on a fifty-one-fifty hold. Maybe they can get her back on her meds and back on her feet, if that's what drove her to the bridge."

"It happens a lot, doesn't it? People jumping from the bridge?"

"About two or three times a month. And more attempts from people crying out for help."

"Like today. I don't think she was really going to jump. Do you?"

"I have no idea. I'd think if you're going to do it, you just do it, instead of hanging out on the ledge. I saw her slide over, and I thought she was gone, but she was crouched on the ledge."

"Exactly—it was a cry for help and you were there." She pushed back her chair and reached for her purse. "I'm going to use the ladies' room before we leave." She thumped her wallet on the table and slipped it open to a row of cards. She selected one and placed it on the table. "Use this for the check."

When she disappeared around the corner, he grabbed her card. He could at least pay for one of these meals.

He flipped open her wallet and it fell open to a plastic insert of pictures. A pretty young woman with coppery hair smiled at him from the plastic sheath.

He hunched over and studied the picture. The woman, with her voluptuous figure and full lips, resembled Kacie a lot more than the Nordic-looking family on her laptop.

A hand reached over his shoulder and smacked down on the wallet.

"What are you doing?"

He glanced up to meet Kacie's flashing brown eyes, their gold flecks throwing off sparks.

He held up his hands. "I'm not stealing your cash. Just the opposite. I was putting your card away. This lunch is on me for a change."

Her nostrils flared as she swept the wallet from the table and dropped it into her purse. "I told you. These meals are tax write-offs."

"Who's the woman in the picture? The one in the green dress?" He handed his credit card to the waiter.

"She's, uh, my grandmother when she was a young woman."

"I thought so."

Her eyebrows jumped. "You did?"

"I mean, not your grandmother, but I figured she was a relative. You look like her."

"She was my father's mother. She died young."

"Pretty lady."

"Thank you." She gulped the rest of her water and smiled brightly. "Ready to head to the station?"

Thirty minutes later, Ryan led the way into the hubbub of the big-city squad room. His brother had tried to lure him there a few times with job offers, but Ryan had preferred the peace and quiet of Crestview.

He stopped by Lieutenant Healy's office first. They shook hands and he introduced him to Kacie.

Healy's eyes lit up, but Ryan couldn't tell if it was from the way Kacie filled out her jeans or because he recognized the name.

"Kacie Manning—I enjoyed your book. Loved how you nailed that SOB Walker to the wall."

Okay, so maybe Ryan was the only one with impure thoughts about Kacie.

Kacie and the lieutenant shook hands. "I'm glad you appreciated that. Walker sure didn't."

"I got the lowdown from Curtis on that parolee's murder. We contacted the warden at Walla Walla. We'll let him handle Walker, but we still need to find out who did his dirty work."

"I hope you do because I think he's the same one who sent me a doll at Walker's bidding."

Healy puffed up his chest. "Don't worry. We'll nail him. You have other fish to fry right now, don't you?"

Ryan jabbed a finger at his own chest. "Are you calling me a fish?"

"Yeah, a shark." Healy wagged his finger at Kacie. "Don't let him fool you, Ms. Manning. He might come off as the carefree, easygoing brother, but all these Brody boys are harder than granite and just as uncompromising."

Ryan narrowed his eyes at Healy. The lieutenant and his brother didn't get along, and Ryan sensed that his animosity carried over to him.

"If you could keep me posted on Duke Bannister, I'd appreciate it—professional courtesy."

Healy shrugged. "Sure thing. How does your brother feel about this book?"

"All of my brothers are on board with it. We'd like to get to the bottom of what happened."

The lieutenant's lips spread into a mirthless smile. "Careful. You might not like what you find at the bottom of it all."

"We're willing to take that risk. As part of this—" he circled his finger in the air "—process, do I have permission to look up the case files?"

"*Mi casa es tu casa,* Chief. My house is yours."

He and Kacie moved toward the office door, and Ryan made a half turn in time to catch Healy checking out Kacie's derriere.

The lieutenant dragged his gaze up to Ryan's face. "Yes?"

"Any news on the attempted suicide this morning?"

"Oh yeah, I heard you were involved in that, too." He

sat down behind his desk and folded his hands. "She's on psych hold."

Ryan dropped his chin to his chest in a curt nod, then placed his hand on the small of Kacie's back to propel her out of the office.

As they walked to the elevator, Kacie leaned over to whisper in his ear. "Does he have something against you?"

"He doesn't like my brother Sean." He jabbed the elevator button. "Sean shows him up all the time. Makes him look bad. The lieutenant got written up a few months ago for not acting on a hunch of my brother's that turned out to be right. A woman got murdered because of it."

"Guess I should watch my back around him."

Yeah, because he's watching your backside.

Ryan sealed his lips and ushered Kacie into the elevator.

He didn't need to be her personal protector. She was a grown woman and had probably been handling unwanted male attention for years. She'd been handling his for the past few days.

He pushed the button for the basement.

"Next stop?" She folded her arms and wedged a shoulder against the elevator.

"Records."

The musty smell of the records lockup hit him as he opened the door, but the smell of a flowery perfume replaced it.

Marie Giardano peered at them through the mesh screen that guarded her counter, and her red lips broke into a wide smile. "If it isn't one of the Brody boys come to brighten up an old lady's day."

He strode across the room and curled his fingers around the edge of the screen. "You look as beautiful as ever."

She snorted but her eyes lit up. "You boys always say that, but you all come in here with other women in tow."

Ryan reached out and pulled Kacie toward the counter. "Marie Giardano, this is Kacie Manning. She's writing a book about Dad."

Marie pursed her lipsticked mouth into a straight line. "Really. You're the one who wrote that book on Daniel Walker, aren't you?"

"I am. Did you read it?"

"Nope." She jerked her thumb over her shoulder. "I get my fill of that stuff on the job. I stick to romance with a happily ever after."

Kacie blinked her eyes at Marie's hard tone.

"Kacie's going to find out the truth about Dad, Marie. She's going to set the record straight."

"Uh-huh." She turned back to Ryan. "What can I get for you? It's been a constant parade of Brody brothers this summer. When's that tough guy Judd going to pay his homage?"

"Judd's out of the country right now, but you can help me find the file on Dad's suicide."

"Really?" Her eyes slid from his face to Kacie's. "Why do you need to dig around in that?"

"I told you, Marie. Kacie's writing a book. We want to start with the end. We're going to try to find the woman who witnessed Dad jumping from the bridge that morning."

"Cookie Phelps."

"Cookie?"

"She was a hooker walking across the bridge that morning, probably after a night of seeing johns. Who knows? Maybe she was planning her own jump that morning."

"That's weird." His pulse ticked up a notch and he looked at Kacie to gauge her reaction.

Her eyes took up half her pale face and her breath quickened between parted lips.

She'd had a stronger reaction than he'd had to the identity of the witness.

Marie drummed her long nails on the counter. "What's weird about it? This city is full of hookers. Who else would be out and about at that time of the morning?"

"It's her presence on the bridge at precisely that time that's unusual. Chances are she was considering a jump. Why else would she be there? To sightsee? To take pictures in the dark?"

"So, maybe your father saved one more life before he died. Cookie saw him go over and changed her mind."

"She was interviewed?"

"Of course. She called it in."

"I want that file, Marie."

"If you can find it, you can check it out. Lieutenant Healy already phoned down with his blanket approval for any file you want."

She tapped on her keyboard and jotted down a few numbers on a slip of paper. "Here's the row and shelf."

"Thanks, Marie. Can I check it out or do I have to look at it here?"

"You can check that one out. It's just paper—no evidence." She buzzed the cage open, and Ryan held the door open for Kacie.

Kacie smiled her thanks at Marie, who had already turned back to her computer.

When they got to the row in the back of the room, Kacie trailed her hand along the boxes, reading out the numbers. She turned abruptly, almost running into his chest. "She doesn't like me much, does she?"

"Didn't seem like it. Maybe it's just the claws coming out from one femme fatale to another." He winked.

Rolling her eyes, she said, "She knew your father?"

"She was good friends with my father and mother. After

Dad died, Marie would drink with my mom, just to see her home safely." He located the box and pulled it from the shelf. "She probably just doesn't like the idea of a book coming out and dredging up painful old memories."

He balanced the box on a rolling stool and flipped off the lid. "There's not too much in here. I'm just going to take the whole box if Marie lets me."

"That woman would let you get away with murder."

"She's loyal, but not that loyal."

"Figure of speech, Brody." She replaced the lid and smacked her fist against it.

Ryan hoisted the box in his arms, and Kacie led the way out of the maze of metal shelves stuffed with cold cases. The files for the Phone Book Killer were there somewhere, and he was sure they'd get to those in due time.

Marie looked up from her keyboard. "Got what you need?"

"Right here." Ryan patted the side of the box. "We'll return it tomorrow."

"Take your time, and send Judd over when he returns to U.S. soil."

"Will do."

"Thanks. Nice to meet you, Marie." Kacie waved as she held the door open for Ryan and the box.

Marie flicked her long fingernails in their general direction.

"Oh boy." Kacie pulled the door closed with a click.

Twenty minutes later, when they reached the elevator of their hotel, Ryan's finger hovered between two buttons. "Your room or mine?"

"Let's stick to my room. It's closer."

Clutching the box to his chest, he waited while Kacie opened her door. She stepped inside the room and wedged her foot against the door to hold it open for him.

He squeezed past her into the room, and she sucked in a breath. He dropped the box to the floor by the window and pulled out the two bulging file folders. Then he walked to the table and placed them side by side. "Lotta stuff here for one suicide."

Kacie joined him at the table and spun one of the folders around to face her. "No wonder. This is for a different case—domestic violence."

"Someone misfiled something." He dropped the extra folder back into the box and thumbed open his father's case.

Kacie placed a hand on his forearm. "Are you sure you're up to this? I can go through it myself."

He covered her hand with his. "Do you think I lost it on the bridge?"

"It upset you, being in that spot, and I don't blame you."

"It was eerie, but don't you think I've been there before? As soon as I was old enough to take the Muni to the bridge, I checked it out."

"I can certainly understand that, but if you'd prefer not to look at this file…"

"It's just words on paper. It's not like the coast guard ever found his body and took pictures."

She disengaged her hand from his and pulled her chair to his side of the table. "Okay, then. Let's take this from the top."

Facing her laptop, she pushed it back on the table. The movement woke up the display, and Kacie jerked her head up and gasped.

His gaze darted from the blue screen to Kacie's tight face. "What's wrong?"

"Someone's been in my room."

Chapter Seven

Ryan's body tensed and he looked ready to tackle someone. That was what she liked about him—he was always ready.

"How do you know? Is something missing?"

"It's my laptop." She jabbed a finger at the blue display with the log-in prompt glowing white against it. "When my computer goes to sleep, it displays my screen saver, that picture of my parents. The log-in prompt stays there only after several incorrect log-in attempts."

He pushed back from the table. "You're sure?"

"That's how I configured it, or at least that's how the self-described computer geek in my apartment building configured it."

"Look around. Is anything else different? Missing?"

She hopped up from the chair and took a turn around the room. Everything seemed as it was. She yanked open the dresser drawers and poked her head in the closet. She flipped on the lights in the bathroom and ran her hand along the vanity. She called over her shoulder. "I don't see anything different."

"Are you sure about the laptop?"

"Yes."

"You know how computers are. They act up, have glitches."

"Are you trying to convince me someone *wasn't* in my room?"

"There's no other evidence."

"This isn't a case you have to bring to the D.A., Chief Brody. I just have a feeling."

"But you didn't have this feeling until you saw something unexpected on your computer. Do you also have a feeling it's Walker?"

"Maybe the warden had a talk with him, but Walker hasn't gotten the word to his minion yet to lay off."

"You said failed log-in attempts. So let's say Walker's minion was in here. Did he fail to log in to your computer?"

"Yes." She entered her password and her folders popped up on her desktop display.

"Why would Walker want to get in to your computer?"

"Just to mess with me, Ryan. Put me on edge."

"Do you want to call hotel security?"

"I wouldn't know what to report. I don't even know what this guy looks like. Walker wouldn't send someone who stands out into a hotel. He wouldn't get past the front desk."

"Why don't you check your files to make sure everything's okay?"

She did a cursory check through her folders, which she backed up every day anyway, and again nothing was amiss.

"Okay, maybe it was a computer glitch, but next time I leave the room I'm going to put some trigger in place, a thread across the door or something."

"Maybe you need a full-time bodyguard. Too bad my brother's out of town."

She looked at him through her lashes. She already had one Brody looking out for her.

Finding nothing else, they returned to the file on the suicide, reading aloud snippets of paragraphs.

Kacie tapped a pencil against the page. "It was foggy that night. I'm wondering if Cookie was closer than she claimed to be."

"Why would you think that?"

"You know how it can get on the bridge with the fog rolling in. Sometimes you can't see your hand in front of your face, and yet Cookie saw a man throw himself over the barrier from twenty feet away."

"What's your point? Why would she lie about her location?"

"I don't know. Maybe she was close enough to stop him and didn't do anything. Then felt guilty about it later."

"Maybe." He folded the corner of that page and flipped to the next. "She used one of the emergency phones on the bridge to call—no cell phones back then."

"The coast guard responded within two minutes of the call and didn't find a thing. The police questioned Cookie and then let her slide back into oblivion. She certainly didn't seek the limelight or her fifteen minutes of fame."

"I wonder if she went back to hooking." He dragged her laptop toward them. "I'm going to search for Cookie and see if she's still in the city."

Kacie continued to thumb through the file as Ryan worked his magic on her computer. She'd have to remember how easy it was working with a cop. They had inroads that she and her P.I. could only dream of.

"This is interesting."

She hunched forward. "What?"

"Looks like Cookie got out of the life after my father's death."

"Maybe it scared her straight."

"Really straight. She's working as a Realtor now."

"Good for Cookie. Is her name still Cookie?"

"She's using her real name now, Cynthia Phelps."

"I'm sure she sells a lot more homes with that name." She drew her brows together and clicked her fingernail against the table.

"Why so thoughtful? Are you thinking of investing in real estate now?"

"Phelps. That name sounds familiar."

"Maybe you saw one of her signs. They'll make it easier to locate her."

She snapped her fingers and lunged for the box. "Phelps—the domestic-violence case."

She yanked the folder out of the box and smacked it against the table. Swirls of dust danced along the beams of sunlight coming through the windowpane.

She ran her finger down the first page. "Yep. Cynthia Phelps called the cops on her boyfriend, Frankie Lawson."

"At least that explains how the file got dropped in with this one—witness in one case, complainant in the other." Ryan stretched and then laced his fingers behind his head.

Kacie continued to skim the file. Her finger ran across the name of the arresting officer and then moved back. Her mouth fell open. "Ryan."

"What?"

"You're not going to believe this."

"Let me guess. Frankie was her pimp."

"That may be, but there's something else—Joseph Brody was the arresting officer."

"What?" Ryan dropped his hands and snatched the file from her. He held the paper close to his face and swore. "What are the chances of that?"

"It's such a coincidence. This arrest happened years before the suicide, before your father was a homicide detective."

"Now we really have to track her down and talk to her." He smacked the file onto the table. "I wonder if she even recognized my father as the cop who came out to her place."

"Where did you say she works now?"

He spun the laptop around to face him. "Bay Realtors. I think we need to look at an open house today."

KACIE LEANED FORWARD in the passenger seat of Ryan's car, her nose almost touching the windshield. "Looks like that couple is heading out."

"I hope they made Cookie an offer to put her in a good mood." He slipped the key from the ignition. "She probably doesn't want to be reminded of her past now that she has a squeaky-clean life."

"That's why it's best we do this here, away from a possible husband and her squeaky-clean home."

They approached the house, located in the Sunset District, and tapped on the open door as they crossed the threshold.

Kacie called out. "Hello?"

An attractive blonde with a neat pencil skirt and a tucked-in blouse showcasing her slim figure emerged from the kitchen, carrying a plate of chocolate-chip cookies.

She smiled. "Hello. Just in time for a fresh batch. Would you like one?"

"No, thank you." Kacie stepped away from the table so Cynthia could put the plate down.

"I'll have one." Ryan selected a cookie from the plate and bit off half, the warm, gooey chocolate melting in his mouth.

He saw Kacie trying to catch his eye, probably to see if he recognized the significance in Cookie offering cookies, but he avoided her smirk.

"Do you prefer to look around on your own or would you like me to show you the place?"

"Actually, Cynthia—" Ryan plucked a napkin from the white tablecloth and dusted his fingertips "—we're here to talk to you about something else."

Cynthia's eye twitched and she smoothed her skirt with nervous hands. The life clearly still haunted her.

"Who are you?"

He reached into his pocket and pulled out his badge. "I'm Chief Ryan Brody. Yeah, *that* Brody. And this is Kacie Manning. She's a writer doing a book on my dad. You knew my dad, didn't you, Cynthia?"

She folded her hands in front of her, her white knuckles almost matching her cream-colored skirt. "Of course I knew Joseph Brody. He was a good man."

"A good man who you saw jump off the Golden Gate Bridge."

"That's right." She lifted her chin. "I didn't know it was Joey Brody at the time. If I had known, maybe I could've done something to stop him."

"So you're saying you didn't find out it was Joseph Brody who'd jumped off the bridge until later?"

"That's right." Her gaze darted toward the front door as if she were planning an escape from her own open house. "The cops never even told me. I read about it along with everyone else."

"When you found out it was Detective Brody, it must've been a…shock." Kacie touched Cynthia's arm in a sympathetic gesture.

"I was even more upset when I found out who it was." Cynthia grabbed the edge of the tablecloth and twisted it between her fingers. "Joey Brody saved my life once. If I had known that was him on the bridge, I would've done anything to save his life. Anything."

"Did the cops at the time make the connection between you and my father? Did they realize he'd arrested your pimp several years before?"

Glancing over her shoulder, she said, "No. They didn't know, or at least they didn't ask me about it. When I read the story in the newspaper, I didn't bother telling them. I was still in the life. I didn't need to remind the cops about that."

Kacie picked up a cookie from the plate and broke it in two, showering crumbs on the tablecloth. "What were you doing on the bridge at that time of the morning, Cynthia?"

She dropped the tablecloth and began picking at the cuticles of her manicured nails. "It wasn't closed to pedestrians. I was just walking, like anyone else."

"At the break of dawn? In the fog?"

"It's not against the law." She pulled back her shoulders and brushed the crumbs from the table into a napkin, which she then crumpled in her fist. "What do you want from me, Chief Brody? I never saw your father's face that morning. I didn't talk to him. He didn't say a word. One minute there was a man on the bridge through the fog. The next, that man had hoisted himself over the ledge, like so many before him and so many since. I told you. I would've given my own life to save your father's."

Ryan took her cold hand in his and she jerked back. He rested the pad of his thumb against her racing pulse. "I don't want anything from you, Cynthia. I just wanted to look at the woman who was the last person to see my father alive. I think my dad would've been pleased that it was you—someone he had helped in another life."

Tears flooded her blue eyes, eyes that had seen too much. "Just so you know, I never believed any of that stuff about your father. He was no killer. I guess it all just got to be too much for him. Sometimes it just gets to be too much."

"I appreciate that." Ryan squeezed her hand. "My brothers and I don't believe it, either, and neither does Ms. Manning. That's what this book is all about. We're going to clear his name."

A commotion at the front door signaled another set of potential buyers. Cynthia whispered, "Be careful," and she yanked her hand away from his as she greeted the newcomers.

Ryan pocketed one of Cynthia's cards and grabbed Kacie's elbow to steer her out the door. "Thanks, Cynthia. We're interested and we'll talk to our Realtor about an offer."

When they hit the sidewalk, Kacie spun around. "What was that about?"

"Just trying to help her out. If those people think there are other interested buyers, it might light a fire under them."

As she shook her head, the sun glinted off the copper strands in her hair. "Not that. She told us to be careful. What did she mean?"

"You heard that, too?" Ryan rubbed his knuckles across his chin. "I thought I'd imagined it."

"Why would she say that?" Kacie paced away from him, tossed her cookie halves in the gutter and made her way back, poking her finger against his chest. "And why was she so nervous?"

"She's a former hooker running from her past. Why wouldn't she be nervous around a cop? Or two people showing up while she's trying to do her job and questioning her about her old life?"

"It was more than that, Ryan, and you know it. She's

hiding something about that night—or rather, that morning."

He took her hand and pulled her toward the car parked at the curb. "Maybe it's like we were speculating before. She was there to jump, saw someone else jumping and had a change of heart."

"Then later found out the person who had jumped was the cop who'd intervened in her conflict with her pimp, probably saving her life. It sounds so unlikely. Maybe he arranged to meet her there that morning."

"What are you implying, Kacie? My father had Cookie join him at the bridge to make sure he had a witness? I don't think he'd do that to her."

Leaning against the car, she placed her hands on his shoulders. "Is that why you're denying the coincidences in her story? You're afraid it'll make your dad look cold and unfeeling?"

"I don't know." He ducked his head, pinching the bridge of his nose. "You're right. Cynthia was agitated. Why did she keep saying she'd have done anything to save my father?"

"Maybe he did have her meet him there to witness the jump. She agreed to help him out and then felt guilty about it. Maybe she knew why he'd called her there." She smoothed the cotton of his T-shirt against his shoulders, and then she folded her arms over her chest. "There's something not quite right about the whole scenario."

He cranked his head over his shoulder to take in the for-sale sign. "We should question her again."

"I agree, but that's not going to happen right now while she's showing a house. If she sees us out here waiting for her, she'll never let that couple go."

"Right again." He walked around to the passenger side of the car and opened the door. "Let's give her some breathing room."

Ryan didn't have much to say on the ride back to the hotel. Throughout the conversation with Cynthia, he'd felt as if there was another subtext to her words. What had she been trying to tell him? He slid a glance at Kacie in the passenger seat. And would she be more willing to tell him if he questioned her alone?

He parked the car, and they entered the hotel elevator. When they stopped at Kacie's floor, Ryan held the door open and said, "Do you want me to come with you to your room in case your trigger has shifted?"

Before Kacie had walked away from her room, she'd placed a toothpick against her door. He'd kept trying to tell her that anyone on a hotel hallway could knock it over without necessarily opening the door of her room, but she seemed to think the trick would work well enough.

"I can always use a little backup."

She crooked her finger at him. He would've followed her anywhere. When they reached her door, she crouched down. "The toothpick is still leaning against the door."

"Same spot? Someone could've noticed it and replaced it."

"It's in the same spot. I counted the threads of carpet from the doorjamb."

"Where do you learn this stuff?" He held out his hand and she dropped the toothpick into his palm.

"Where anyone learns anything these days—the internet."

"Dinner later, or are you going to stick to your room again?" He tossed the toothpick from hand to hand, practicing his nonchalant look.

"I'm up for a working dinner—say, seven o'clock?"

A working dinner beat a pathetic table for one and a pay-per-view movie. "Lobby at seven o'clock."

She shut the door on Ryan and the toothpick and did a

quick survey of the room. Nothing was out of place, but she still felt on edge.

Maybe it was that whole interview with Cynthia Phelps. The fact that she'd already had an association with Joseph Brody and then happened to be on the bridge to witness his jump was weird enough, but add to that her jittery manner at the open house and one plus one was definitely adding up to something more than two.

She sat on the edge of the bed and kicked off her shoes. She'd meant what she'd said to Ryan about a working dinner. If she kept her mind on work, it would leave less room for her emotional response to him and his hot body.

And that was all it was. He was a good-looking guy with juicy slabs of muscle. Any woman could appreciate that, but it didn't require any action on her part. She sucked in her bottom lip and then bit it.

Stop thinking about him in that way.

She had a job to do—prove Joseph Brody's guilt—and no sexy son or loyal friends would deter her. Both Marie Giardano and Cynthia Phelps had Joey Brody's back, and neither one of them seemed all too pleased with her or the prospect of her book.

They knew him, or thought they knew him, and wanted to protect him. Even Daniel Walker had his defenders, and every serial killer in lockup had enjoyed marriage proposals from the outside.

Kacie stepped out of her clothes and tossed them on the closet floor. She showered and changed into a skirt to keep the dinner professional. Of course, the skirt was a flowery number that hit about midthigh.

Biting the inside of her cheek, she turned in front of the mirror to check the back view. She reached for the waistband when a knock on her door made her jump.

She peered through the peephole to see Ryan waving. He was taking this punctuality thing way too far.

Glancing down at her bare chest, she swept a T-shirt from the bed and pulled it over her head. She opened the door a crack. "You're early."

"I dropped by to pick up the file on my dad's suicide. There was something I wanted to check before dinner."

She widened the door and made a sweeping gesture with her arm. "Enter. It's on the table where we left it. I'm still getting ready."

He squeezed past her into the room, checking her out from head to bare toes. "I'm glad you're not done getting dressed. I'm no fashion expert, but that shirt doesn't go with the skirt."

"Thank you for your advice, Mr. Givenchy." She plucked at the hem of her skirt and curtsied.

Ryan cocked his head. He sauntered to the desk and scooped up the folder. "You're getting a call."

She held up her hands and he tossed the buzzing cell phone at her. Cupping the phone in her hand, she read Unknown Number on the display. The unknown was nothing unusual in her line of work.

She answered. "Hello?"

"Why, hello, Kacie. This is Daniel Walker."

Chapter Eight

The low voice as smooth as a sharp blade sent a cascade of shivers down her back and she dropped to the edge of the bed. She'd never shown one ounce of weakness to Walker, and she wasn't about to start now. "How are you calling me?"

Ryan jerked his head up from the file and mouthed the words *What's wrong?*

Had the fear seeped into her tone? She cleared her throat and put her cell on Speaker.

Walker chuckled. "It's called a phone."

Ryan's brows collided over the bridge of his nose as he crossed the room in two steps and crouched beside the bed.

"You know what I mean, Walker." She met Ryan's eyes and dipped her chin as his mouth formed an O. "How is it you have access to a phone to call me?"

"All things are possible in prison, Kacie, my dear."

"The cops will be onto you if you decide to send your thug after me again."

He clicked his tongue and even that sound caused her to clench her jaw. "Kacie, Kacie, that's why I'm calling. The warden had a little chat with me and I assured him, like I'm assuring you now, I never sent anyone after you. I'm an innocent man, biding my time and preparing for my appeal."

"B.S." She bounded up from the bed, nearly knocking Ryan over, and paced to the window. "Duke Bannister warned me that you were coming for me, and then you had him killed."

"Who's Duke Bannister? Sounds like a boxer."

"He was a fellow inmate of yours at Walla Walla." She licked her lips. "Just stop it. You know who Bannister is."

"I'm afraid I've never had the...pleasure of meeting Mr. Bannister. Or does he prefer Duke?"

"He doesn't prefer anything now. He's dead."

"So, an ex-con comes out of nowhere claiming to know me and proceeds to warn you that I'm after you? Sounds perfectly logical to me." Walker coughed.

"Yeah, he warned me, and then I got locked in the hotel sauna, and I got that doll."

As the silence on the other line dragged on, she shrugged at Ryan. Maybe Walker had been busted for the phone use.

"Hello?"

"What doll?"

"Someone sent me a doll just like the one your daughter had. I got the message."

She heard Walker begin to sob and the sound had her bobbling the phone. She closed her eyes, fighting the sympathy that surged through her body. He didn't deserve it.

She heard shouts over the phone and then a harsh whisper from Walker. "It wasn't me. I didn't do it. I wouldn't do it."

Then the line went dead.

Planting her hands on the table on either side of her laptop, Kacie hunched over, the phone still clutched in one fist.

She felt the warmth of Ryan's presence behind her and then his strong fingers squeezing her shoulder.

"Are you okay?"

She took a deep breath and turned to face him, close enough for her breasts beneath the baggy T-shirt to brush against his chest. Close enough to see his green eyes changing color at the contact. "I'm fine. He's so good, so convincing, isn't he?"

"What do you think he meant at the end? He didn't kill his family, or he didn't have someone stalk you?"

"I don't know—probably both. To deny the one is to deny the other. If he never killed his family, he wouldn't be the type to go after me for proving he did. Threatening me would almost be like admitting his guilt—and he'll never do that, not as long as he has breath in his lungs."

"He seemed really broken up about his daughter."

"He's a good actor."

"Why would he go through the trouble of contacting you to tell you he wasn't threatening you?"

She shuffled away from him and peered out the window at the darkening street below. "I don't pretend to know what goes through the man's mind."

"Really? Because in the book you sort of did pretend to know what was going through his mind. Think about it. If he did discuss his plans with Bannister and then send someone to carry them out, why would he direct attention to himself by calling you, especially after the warden already talked to him about Bannister's murder?"

She yanked on the rod of the drapes. "He enjoys the attention, Ryan. He saw it as another opportunity to maintain his innocence to me."

"If you say so." He shrugged.

"Besides, I don't have any other enemies. Who else would be locking me in saunas and sending me dolls? Bannister was offed for warning me about Walker."

"Was he?"

"Of course. What are you talking about?" She folded her

arms over her stomach, grabbing handfuls of the T-shirt on both sides.

"You were going to meet him that night because he'd called you at lunch and said he had something to tell you."

"Yeah?"

"He'd already warned you about Walker. What more did he have to say?"

"Maybe he was going to tell me something about the doll." She bit her bottom lip, not enjoying the direction of the conversation.

"Why would he do that? If he even knew about the doll, he'd know that you'd figure out he was telling you the truth about his warning. What more would he have to say?"

"So what's your theory?"

"He was going to tell you the truth—that someone besides Walker had sent him."

She threw up her hands. "You're basing all this on Walker's insistence that he didn't do it. They all say that, don't they?"

"I'm just playing devil's advocate here." He tucked the file under his arm. "I still want to look this over. You can finish getting dressed, and I'll meet you downstairs in fifteen minutes."

He jogged up the stairwell to work off some tension. Kacie hadn't been wearing a bra beneath that T-shirt. She may have thought it was loose-fitting, but every time she moved, the soft material conformed to her breasts, making it hard to concentrate on the conversation...or just making it hard.

When he got to his room, he splashed some cold water on his face and brushed his teeth. Then he stretched out on the bed and skimmed through the file on his father's suicide again, flipping to the back pages.

At the time of his father's suicide, Cookie Phelps had

been a streetwalker, plying her trade in the Tenderloin and turning over most of her earnings to a pimp. How had she broken out of that cycle? Where had she gotten the money to attend real-estate classes and take the test for her license?

That had all happened in quick succession, shortly after his father's death. According to her website, Cynthia Phelps had been a Realtor for almost twenty years.

Had one event influenced the other? The thought that his father may have made some arrangement with Cynthia left a bad taste in his mouth.

He checked the time and stashed the file in the nightstand drawer. He'd bring all this up with Kacie at dinner. Maybe she could arrange to wear a potato sack, because that was the only way he was going to be able to focus on anything other than not peeling off her clothes.

No such luck.

The sway of her hips as she approached him in the lobby made the flounces of her skirt twitch back and forth. She'd replaced the baggy T-shirt with a V-neck sweater, and although she had her breasts properly ensconced in a bra, there was nothing proper about the way the soft material of the sweater hugged her assets.

He closed his mouth and hoped the drool hadn't made it to his chin.

Standing up at her approach, he smiled. "That sweater is a much better match."

"I'm glad you approve. I feel so much better about my selection now."

He pointed to her feet in a pair of low-heeled sandals. "Can you walk in those? I'm thinking seafood at the Wharf."

"No problem. I don't feel like battling traffic and searching for a decent place to park. Let's skip the big touristy places."

"Agreed."

They stepped into the cool night and Kacie threw a light jacket over her shoulders.

"Let's beat the light." Ryan grabbed her hand and pulled her into the crosswalk as the red hand blinked at them.

"You like living dangerously, don't you?" She freed her hand from his on the pretext of clutching the collar of her jacket. "Drivers in this city are an impatient bunch."

"You seem to know San Francisco well. Do you spend a lot of time here?"

"I…" She fussed with her jacket, finally shoving her arms through the sleeves. "I come here a few times a year—meetings, book signings. I like it."

"Do you like it better than Seattle?"

"Both cities have their charms." She stopped at the curb and smacked her palm against the light for the signal. "How about you? Do you miss it?"

"Crestview isn't that far away, and two of my brothers are here, so I come in at least once a month." He touched her elbow and pointed to the right. "This way."

Hunching her shoulders, she said, "I'm glad you said that. Bannister was killed in the other direction. Do the police have any leads in the case?"

"If they do, they're not telling me." He guided her around a crowd of people watching a man dressed up like a robot, his face caked with silver makeup. "But I'm calling the lieutenant tomorrow to let him know about Walker's call."

"Oh." She rubbed her nose. "Do you think that's necessary?"

"He's not supposed to be calling you, Kacie. He'd been warned. How does he have your number, anyway?"

"We were in very close contact at one time. I guess he kept my number."

He shook his head. "You never changed your number after giving it to a psychopath like Walker? Come to think of it, how did Bannister get your number?"

"I gave it to him after he emailed me from my website. With the type of writing I do, I need to keep the lines of communication open. It's a risk I'm willing to take to get and keep my contacts."

"Talk about living dangerously." He opened the door of the restaurant for her but felt like wrapping her in his arms instead. She might see herself as a tough cookie dealing with these criminals, but they saw her as an easy mark.

After the waiter brought their drinks and food, Ryan settled back in the booth and wrapped his hands around the chilly mug of beer. When Kacie pulled her mini-recorder from her purse, he groaned. "You're kidding."

She cocked her head. "I told you it was a working dinner."

"I didn't believe you."

"Why wouldn't you believe me? Did you think I'd need time to recover just because Walker called?"

"It's okay if you do." He flicked her wineglass with his finger, and the golden liquid inside shimmered in the candlelight. "I don't mind a little business with my pleasure, but can we do this without the recorder?"

She swept it back into her purse. "Done. Did you discover anything else from that file after you left my room?" she asked as she picked up her fork and dug into her salad.

"Just that Cookie turned her life around shortly after my father's suicide. She went from streetwalker to house seller in record time."

"Maybe the tragedy inspired her to do something more with her life."

"Possibly, but it takes some quick money to turn your life around like that."

"Are you suggesting she got it from your father?"

Ryan took a bite of his food and a long swallow of his beer, then placed the mug on the table. "I hate to even think it, but it sure seems like a coincidence that she winds up with the means to change her life after witnessing Dad's suicide."

"That's one proposition I would've liked to have heard."

"Maybe Cookie didn't know why he'd asked her to join him on the bridge."

"Why would he even want a witness? Wouldn't leaving his personal effects on the bridge be proof enough that he had jumped?"

"I don't know, Kacie. Maybe we're just reading way too much into Cookie's presence on the bridge. She was there, and she saw him, a cop who had arrested her pimp. Maybe it was what it was—a coincidence.

"I'm not sure questioning her again will do any good, but I might give it a try anyway." He dropped his napkin on the table. "The discovery of Cookie does indicate there's a lot of untapped information on my father's case. Who knows what more we'll find out when we start going through the case files—witnesses, suspects, victims."

Kacie slammed the glass she'd been drinking from on the table, and the water sloshed over the rim. "Sorry. You know, Ryan, I'm not sure we need to delve into all of that. This is more of a personal story from your perspective."

"Really?" He tapped his unused spoon against the table. "I thought the point of this book was to prove my father's innocence. That's why I signed on."

"And I think we can do that by telling your story."

"It's not my story, Kacie." He cocked his head. "It's

my father's story, and to get it right we need to burrow into the past."

She threaded her fingers together. "We'll have to dig into the case file after we pick it up from Records when we drop off the suicide file. Maybe we can split it up. I'll take the victims, and you can have...whatever."

"Yeah, and the best part is we don't even have to go back to Records to muddle through the stuff. My brother's fiancée made copies of everything in the case file and organized it."

"Even the pictures?"

"Everything."

"That's great." Kacie glanced at her phone. "Can we get going?"

"Dessert?"

"No, thanks." She pressed her fingers to her temples. "I'm not feeling that great."

She didn't even make a move for her wallet to pay for the dinner. He placed his own card on the table and covered her fidgeting fingers with his hand. "We'll take a taxi back to the hotel."

"That's okay. I could use the fresh air." She waved her fingers in the air to get the waiter's attention. "Where are these cataloged and organized notes?"

"In my hotel room. My brother Eric gave them to me before he went back to D.C."

"That's convenient." She took a sip of water and closed her eyes. Then she pulled in a long breath and straightened her shoulders. "Not sure if I'm up for any more work tonight. Maybe my body's trying to tell me to take it easy."

"Then let's get out of here so you can...take it easy."

By the time he'd paid the bill and they stepped out into the cool night, Kacie had gotten her color back.

"You're feeling better?" He adjusted her jacket around

her shoulders, and his fingertips brushed the smooth skin stretched across her collarbone.

Her eyes met his, and her lips parted. "I feel...fine."

She wriggled deeper into her jacket, and he had to stuff his hands into his pockets to keep from pulling her lush body into his arms.

"Great. If you start feeling lousy again, let me know."

She hooked her arm through his, pressing her shoulder against his shoulder. "What'll you do? Sweep me up in your arms again and carry me back to my room?"

The scent of her perfume and her soft hair tickling his chin overwhelmed his senses. Was she coming on to him? She'd been holding him at arm's length up to that point, despite his broad hints that she pushed his buttons in all the right ways. Maybe it was just because she'd been feeling faint. Once she came to her senses, she'd probably push him away again and insist on professionalism. So, should he take advantage of her momentary lapse of professionalism?

He left his hands in his pockets. "If you collapse on the sidewalk, I'll definitely call an ambulance."

"Oh, that's comforting." She rubbed her cheek against his shoulder like a satisfied cat.

This time the strands of her hair caught on his beard. He pulled one hand out of his pocket and curled his arm around Kacie's waist. He waited for her to pull away or engage with some distraction, like her phone.

She snuggled against him, her curves fitting against the hard lines of his body.

He tightened his hold, his fingertips sinking into the swell of her hip.

They strolled down the sidewalk, side by side, fitting in with all the couples on their date nights.

They stopped to watch the robotic man. Kacie pulled a dollar bill from her purse and dropped it into his bucket.

"Is that tax-deductible, too?"

She laughed, a warm, sultry sound that made him feel as if they shared some deep secret that set them apart from everyone else around them.

"No, it is not." Then she smacked his backside, allowing her fingers to linger and brush against the denim.

She'd better not have been teasing, because she'd just made him hard past the point of no return.

As their hotel rose before them, Ryan grabbed Kacie's hand and quickened his steps. When they hit the elevator, he punched the buttons for both floors. His room, her room—he didn't care where this happened.

But she apparently had a preference. When the doors opened on her floor, she punched the button to close the doors. When the car hit his floor, he took one step off the elevator, straddling the door, and she brushed past him into the hallway.

She glanced over her shoulder. "Are you coming?"

When she looked at him like that, he had every intention of coming. He followed her provocatively swaying hips toward his room and shoved his key card in the slot while she wedged a shoulder against the door.

He pushed open the door, and she fell into the room. He caught her shoulders and pulled her close, gazing into her liquid brown eyes.

Her lashes fluttered and she ran her tongue along her lips.

His tongue followed suit before he plunged it into her warm mouth. She closed around him and took a step closer, pressing her breasts against his chest, hooking one arm around his waist.

He let the door slam behind them and then deepened his kiss as he placed both hands on her derriere, pulling her close and fitting her against his pelvis.

She gasped into his mouth, her body going limp.

He backed her up against the wall and yanked the jacket from her shoulders. As it fell to the floor, he slid down the zipper of her skirt.

He didn't even have to pull it off. It joined the sweater on the floor. He ran one hand up her smooth thigh and traced the line of her panties with his fingertip.

She squirmed against him, but he had other plans. He grabbed the edge of her sweater and tugged it up. She raised her arms and he pulled it over her head and tossed it over his shoulder.

Her breasts, encased in a lacy black bra, heaved with her panting breath. With each expansion of her lungs, the flimsy lace could barely contain the smooth, milky flesh. The bra hooked in the front, making his life a whole lot easier. With one little twist, he unhooked the bra and Kacie's breasts spilled into his greedy hands.

He cupped them in his palms and ran the pads of his thumbs across her rosy, peaked nipples.

She hissed and threw her head back, banging it against the wall.

As he rolled one nipple between his thumb and forefinger, he dipped his head to suck on the other. At the contact, her hips lunged against his, and he grabbed a handful of her luscious backside to steady her.

He teased her nipple with his tongue and lips, blowing on it gently while he pinched her other nipple.

The sensations drove Kacie wild with desire.

Moaning, she thrashed her head from side to side and curled one leg around his denim-clad calf.

Her hands clawed at his T-shirt. He'd stripped her down to her panties and he still had every bit of clothing on. How had that happened? She'd planned to seduce him in a controlled manner, keeping him on a tight leash, and she'd wound up quivering, almost naked, against the wall.

He grabbed her hands with one of his, cinching her wrists together over her head as he continued focusing his attention on her breasts.

The tender suckling of the one contrasted with the almost painful tweaking of the other until she couldn't distinguish the pleasure from the pain and they merged into one overwhelming sensation of need.

She tried loosening her hands from his grip, but once she got them free, he flattened his solid body against hers. One hand came up behind her and yanked her panties down around her thighs.

He cupped her bottom and extended his fingers between her legs, thrusting them into her wet folds.

She whimpered. It was all she could manage.

His suckling of her breast became more insistent, alternating with and matching the thrusting of his fingers.

The dual attack made it hard for her to breathe, hard for her to think, hard for her to remember why she'd initiated this seduction in the first place.

The rough denim of his jeans and the soft cotton of his T-shirt pressed against her naked flesh. How was he fully clothed? He had her at his mercy, when she'd planned to have him at hers.

Her legs began to shake and tremble. His thrusting fingers had begun to probe and stroke. Heat filled her belly as coils of tension tightened her muscles.

Clenching her jaw, she dug her fingernails into Ryan's shoulders. Her leg crept up farther and farther until she had it wrapped around his thigh.

Then he raised his head from her breast and pressed his warm lips against her mouth. As his tongue invaded her, she exploded.

Her other foot came off the floor, and only Ryan's body kept her upright as she thrust her hips against him over and over as the waves of her orgasm claimed her.

He kissed the sighs from her lips as she descended from paradise. When she once again had her feet firmly planted on the carpet, Ryan pinned her with his gaze and reached down to unbutton his fly.

His erection had been straining against his jeans, and once free, his hard, tight flesh brushed her belly.

He placed a hand on her shoulder, nudging her down.

She dropped to her knees in front of him. He was still fully clothed except for his jeans and the underwear twisted around his muscular thighs, exposing his throbbing erection.

She trailed her fingernails up the insides of his thighs, and his big body shivered. She took him gently into her mouth and he groaned, plowing his fingers through her hair.

He said through clenched teeth, "I don't think this is going to last very long."

She answered by wrapping her arms around his hips and digging her nails into his muscular buttocks. The musky taste of him filled her mouth, and at this moment she wanted nothing more.

How did she think she could hold herself aloof from this man? Disengage herself from the hot passion that coursed between them? Maybe she'd been fooling herself. Maybe she always knew how it would end between them.

And this had to be the end. Once he learned her true identity and her true purpose, he'd end it himself.

Oh, but right now it felt like a beginning.

He growled, a deep, animalistic sound from the back of his throat, and tugged on her hair, urging her to stand.

He kissed the pulse throbbing in her lower lip while he nudged his knee between her legs. Her heart galloped, skipping several beats along the way when she realized he planned to take her right here against the wall.

"There's a bed in this room, you know."

"We don't need a bed." He nipped her earlobe, and she sighed.

He forced her legs apart and slid one hand between her thighs. She hitched a leg around his waist, and he drove into her, pinning her against the wall.

She didn't know how or when she'd managed to hook the other leg around his waist, but nothing was holding her up except him.

Wrapped around his body, she glanced over his shoulder into the mirrored closet door across from them and gasped. She resembled some wild creature, naked limbs wrapped around Ryan's body, appearing to be a part of him, belonging to him.

Then she squeezed her eyes closed as her core tightened. His thrusts grew deeper and faster until the pressure finally broke and she cried out with her release.

She melted around him as the sweet pleasure continued to soak into her skin. He had to support her thighs with his splayed hands as she continued to straddle him.

Then his body stiffened, and his muscles tightened beneath her hands. The force of his passion exploded within her, and he moaned her name over and over as he spent himself inside her.

She'd never heard a sweeter sound.

At last he buried his face in the curve of her neck as they both panted. "That was even better than I imagined it would be."

Her legs slid down his thighs, and she grabbed on to his shoulders. "And when exactly did you start imagining this?"

A slow grin spread across his face, and he pinched her chin. "From the moment I carried you from that sauna."

Her pulse quickened. "You didn't know anything about me."

He snorted. "That's never stopped a man from fantasizing."

"You're still dressed." Her hands slid down to the front of his sweat-soaked T-shirt and she plucked it from his chest. "How is that even fair?"

"It's more than fair." Taking a step back, he hitched up his jeans, and his gaze tracked down her nude body, leaving prickles of heat in its wake. Then he swept her up in his arms as if she weighed no more than a kitten and carried her to the primly made bed.

He dropped her. "Now, let me get a good look at you."

"Isn't that what you were doing before?" Warmth swept across her body and she crossed her legs. "And when do I get my turn?"

He pulled off his heavy motorcycle boots and dropped them one at a time on the floor. Straddling her, he pulled his T-shirt over his head, revealing an expanse of rippling muscles.

"That's more like it." She reached out her hands toward the ridges on his chest and traced one hard line with her fingertip.

He twitched beneath her gentle touch. "I'm not done with you yet."

She couldn't help herself. When he talked like that and his bottle-green eyes roamed over her body, she turned to clay, only too happy to allow him to mold and shape her to his pleasure…and hers.

She moaned, and he chuckled. "You'd better hang on because I'm just getting started."

She'd worry about the plan later.

KACIE WOKE WITH a start and squinted at the green numbers floating in the pitch dark. Ryan's slow, steady breathing stirred the ends of her hair, and his leg hitched over her hip pinned her to his body.

And what a body. She'd finally gotten her chance to do her own exploration, and the memory would be seared into her brain forever.

She squirmed away from him, and he didn't move a muscle. Before they'd drifted off to sleep, she'd scoped out the location of the box containing the case files organized by his brother's fiancée—a box she hadn't known existed until dinner. Now she swept her cell phone from the nightstand and aimed the little beam of light across the room and under the desk by the window. It didn't quite reach her target, but she knew the general location.

When she rolled off the bed, she shivered, but the room wasn't even cold. She shuffled her feet on the carpet as she quietly made her way to the box.

Holding the cell-phone light before her, she crouched next to the box and flicked off the lid. She dug into the first set of files and read the neat headings on the labels until she came to a thick folder bound by two rubber bands.

This had to be it. She peered at the label and nodded to herself. She snapped off the first band and then rolled off the other one.

She flipped open the file and began to thumb through the contents, inspecting each photo.

A light came to life across the room and she gasped, dropping the folder on the floor.

"What the hell are you doing?"

Chapter Nine

A pulse pounded against her temple, and she swallowed. "I—I had an idea and wanted to look up something."

Ryan's sleep-roughened voice rumbled across the room. "Are you kidding me? You're working?"

"Not exactly."

"Not at all. Get back to bed."

With trembling hands she gathered the scattered contents of the folder and hugged it to her chest. "Just a few more minutes. Go back to sleep. I'm sorry I woke you."

"I am, too, but now I am awake and I'll be damned if I'm gonna lie here while a naked woman is in my room working on the floor. Come on over here before I toss you over my shoulder and carry you back to bed. And don't think that wouldn't give me great pleasure...before I give you great pleasure."

The bed squeaked, and Kacie dumped the folder back into the box and tamped the lid back on it.

"No need to go caveman on me. I'm coming."

She extinguished her cell-phone light and stumbled back to the bed, where Ryan had flipped back the covers.

"Crawl in here, woman, and keep me warm." He patted the mattress.

She slid beneath the sheet, and Ryan pulled her back toward his chest, folding his warm body around hers.

He wrapped one arm around her, cupping her breast. "Brr. Seems like I need to warm *you* up. What possessed you to start working, stark naked, in the middle of the night?"

She yawned noisily and threaded her fingers through his. "I'll tell you in the morning."

BUT SHE DIDN'T tell him in the morning, and he didn't ask. Either he'd forgotten she ever left the warmth of their bed or he no longer deemed it important.

Fine with her.

She bit off the corner of her toast and waved it at his laptop on the breakfast table between them. "Anything important?"

"My assistant chief has everything under control. Most exciting thing I've missed is the town drunk falling off the wagon again and running his car into a ditch."

She dropped her toast and brushed the crumbs from her fingers. "Aah, small-town life. Is it enough for you?"

"Is it enough for *you*?" He clicked the keys of his keyboard without looking up. "You're outside of Seattle, right? Small town?"

"It suits me, but when I'm not spending my time writing and researching, I'm on the road. So, my small town is an oasis for me."

"Crestview is an oasis for me, too."

"An oasis from what?"

He tapped his head. "From the stuff going on up here."

"You seem well-adjusted to me." She tilted her head and tossed her hair over her shoulder. "All red-blooded American male."

"You got that right." He reached around his laptop and brushed a knuckle across her cheek. "But I've worked hard to reach this level of calm and serenity, and living in

Crestview helps. I work, I surf and I run the trails, and I have a tight-knit group of friends in town."

"And you have your brothers."

He choked on the sip of coffee he'd just taken. "I wouldn't exactly say hanging out with my brothers keeps me sane, but I think we've all worked through our issues in our different ways. This book and proving Dad's innocence once and for all will go a long way toward sealing the deal for all of us."

He took her hand and traced the pad of his thumb along the grooves of her knuckles. "Thanks to you."

"Save your thanks." She slid her hand from beneath his warm touch. He wouldn't be thanking her if he knew about her deception. Last night had changed so much between them, had changed her, but it couldn't alter her mission. She owed this to her mother. She had to see it through, regardless of her feelings for Ryan. Mom deserved justice even if her daughter had to make sacrifices. "I haven't done anything yet."

"You will. Any woman who gets up in the middle of the night to work after a couple of hours of passionate sex is going to get the job done."

She dropped her lashes and crumpled her napkin into a tight ball.

"What *were* you doing last night?" His gaze had returned to his laptop monitor, but his words seemed to hover over the table like an accusation.

"I was just wondering if Christina had anything in her notes about Cookie's previous encounter with your father."

His eyes flicked to her face and dropped again as she eased out a long, slow breath. "Did you find what you were looking for?"

"You rudely interrupted me and threatened to forcibly remove me from the floor. Remember?"

"Oh yeah. I would've had a lot of fun doing it, too." He wiggled his eyebrows up and down. "Cookie's having another open house this afternoon. I think we should pay her a surprise visit."

"Do you think it will do any good?"

"She's had some time to think about the past. Maybe she'll remember how my father helped her and decide to tell me the truth."

"If she hasn't already." She hunched over the table, clasping her hands in front of her, happy to change the subject. "Her nervousness might've just been coming from the fact that you brought up unpleasant memories from her past."

"Could be—" he tapped the screen "—but I have a sudden desire to see another house in the Sunset District, and maybe she'll put out more chocolate-chip cookies."

"What time?"

"Two to five. I figure we'll drop by closer to five to catch her alone."

"That'll work for me."

"Do you have plans?"

"I'm going to edit what I have so far as an introduction, so I'll be holed up in my room all afternoon."

"That'll give me time to do some work, too." He snapped his computer shut. "We can meet up again around four?"

"What kind of work?" She gripped the edge of the table. Maybe she should suggest they work side by side just so she could make sure he wasn't going through that box on his own.

His wide shoulders rose and fell. "Seems my assistant chief isn't that good after all. He wants me to look at a couple of reports and respond to a proposal from a new caterer trying to get a contract for our jail food."

"You have to deal with caterers as the chief of police?

Who knew?" She lifted one eyebrow and retrieved her purse from the back of her chair. As long as he didn't plan to go rummaging through that box—at least not until she got a crack at it first.

When the check came, Ryan let her pick it up this time to make her happy. She'd been on edge all morning. Did she regret the antics of the previous night?

He didn't.

Maybe it wasn't the smartest idea to bed the woman who was writing a book about your family, but she'd started it. He hadn't planned on taking her against the wall like that— or any other way—but she'd come on to him the previous night, no doubt about it.

He had no intention of turning down a lady like Kacie Manning. Was she regretting it now because he hadn't measured up in some way?

He pulled out her chair and she smiled her thanks as her gaze roamed hungrily over his body.

Hell no. He'd measured up in every way that mattered. But maybe she preferred her lovemaking slow and easy— nice and proper.

His eyes followed the sway of her hips as she wove through the tables of the restaurant.

Hell no. There was nothing proper about the way that woman liked to make love.

They were made for each other. They fit together like tongue and groove. Literally.

She made a sudden stop as she exited the restaurant and he stumbled against her.

"Sorry." He put a hand on her waist.

She shifted away from him and grabbed a newspaper from a rack. "My fault. I wanted one of these."

Definitely skittish.

She waved the paper at him. "Spencer Breck died."

"The billionaire who owns half the city?"

"Is there another Spencer Breck?" She studied the news-print and whistled. "He's leaving one big estate."

"I know his wife died a few years ago, but he has kids. I'm sure he'll leave a lot to charity, too. Nobody can spend that much money."

"He has one child—London Breck—beautiful, skinny and now wealthy beyond belief." She tucked the newspa-per into her bag.

"Poor girl." He punched the elevator button.

"You're kidding, right? She has everything."

Shrugging, he said, "All that money is nothing but trou-ble, and now there's going to be a lot of publicity because her father just died. Publicity is never good."

"Don't cry for London. That girl loves publicity—skinny-dipping in fountains, driving race cars, following rock bands."

"I guess some of us don't follow the gossip rags as much as others, so maybe it's not 'poor girl.' She sounds like a pain in the ass."

This time when the elevator reached her floor, she left him with a wave of her hand.

When he reached his room, he blew out a breath and shouldered open his door, letting it slam behind him. He pressed the palm of his hand against the wall where he'd pinned Kacie the night before and closed his eyes. He could almost detect her scent—sweet, musky and all woman.

He brushed his teeth and set up his laptop on the table by the window, kicking the cardboard box out of his way. The files within shifted and his gaze darted toward the box.

Maybe Kacie had been onto something last night. Had Christina made note of the fact that the only witness to his father's jump off the bridge knew him?

He lifted the lid from the box with the toe of his shoe

and pulled out the disheveled folder on top. The word on the label jumped at him: *Victims.*

In the dark, Kacie had grabbed the wrong file anyway. Any mention of Cookie wouldn't be in the file about the Phone Book Killer's victims.

He dropped that file to the floor and shuffled through the box. Christina hadn't created a separate file for the suicide. So maybe she hadn't made the same discovery about Cookie as he and Kacie had. Even more reason to talk to Cookie that afternoon.

He secured the lid back on the box and delved into Crestview police work.

Ryan worked through lunch since he and Kacie had gotten a late start that morning. He took a trip down the hallway and got a can of soda and a bag of chips from the vending machine.

As he popped the tab on the can, his gaze strayed to the box again. Christina had been so thorough about researching his dad's case, so thorough it had almost cost her the relationship with Eric. How had she missed that detail?

He swept his phone from the table and tapped on Christina's name in his address book.

She picked up after the first ring. "Hi, Ryan."

"Hey, Christina. Where are you?"

"I'm in D.C. with your brother. Is that why you called?"

That was Christina—all business. "No, I have a question about your research into Dad's case."

"How's the book coming? Have you met Kacie Manning yet?"

"I've met her and I have no idea how the book is coming. That's her business."

"Except you're calling me." She covered the phone and shouted an order to someone.

"Are you busy?"

"Not too busy to talk to one of my future brothers-in-law. What do you need to know?"

"Did you look into the woman who witnessed Dad's jump from the bridge?"

"Cookie Phelps, a hooker."

"Did you talk to her? Look her up?"

She cleared her throat. "No. I just got her name and statement from the case file on the murders."

"You never looked at the file on the suicide?"

"There was no file on the suicide."

"Sure there was…is. I picked it up from Records."

"That's weird. I never saw that file and nobody ever offered it to me."

"Well, I got it, and you wanna hear weird? My dad had arrested Cookie's pimp several years before Cookie witnessed his suicide."

Christina whistled. "That's a coincidence."

"Yeah, I guess so."

"You think there's some significance to it?"

"I met Cookie yesterday, and she was really nervous."

"Is she still in the life?"

"She's a Realtor."

"Makes sense she'd be jumpy about reminders from the past."

"Yeah, that's what Kacie figured."

"How is that intrepid true-crime writer, Ms. Manning? She must have some cojones to go toe-to-toe with that psychopath Daniel Walker."

"Umm, yeah." He took a sip of his drink, scrambling for a new subject or a way to end the call.

"Well, does she?"

Too late. He never should've taken a sip of soda. Christina was like a pit bull when she got hold of something. "Does she what?"

She sighed noisily. "Have cojones?"

"Not that I noticed."

Christina swore. "You're sleeping with her."

No wonder she was such a good FBI agent. His brother was in big trouble. "Because I didn't notice her cojones?"

She snorted. "Whatever. Keep us posted on what you dig up. And, Ryan?"

"Yeah?" He held his breath.

"Keep it in your pants."

He ended the call and shoved his phone across the table. Eric had told him that Christina was from a family of powerful *brujos,* and now he didn't doubt that at all.

He tapped his toe against the box. But not powerful enough to have gotten the suicide file.

He glanced at the clock on his computer and shoved it away from him. He had just enough time to go for a quick workout in the hotel gym, shower and change.

Maybe Kacie would agree to have dinner with him after they saw Cookie. The evening might not end up the same way it did the night before, but if Kacie wanted to dial back the passion and put him firmly in the friend zone, he'd comply like a gentleman.

That didn't mean he'd ever forget the previous night— the way she tasted, the way her smooth skin felt beneath his fingertips, the way she clung to him and took all he had to offer.

Better make that a cold shower.

KACIE STEPPED FROM the shower and pulled on a lacy thong and a matching bra—not that she planned on any high jinks with Ryan that night, but a girl never knew when she'd be in an accident and need to have her clothes sliced from her body. Best to be prepared.

Of course, if she did seduce Ryan again, she could place

herself back in his room in the dead of night and take another crack at the file in the box. All she needed was one picture.

And really, there wasn't much involved in the seduction of Ryan Brody. He wanted her—and she wanted him. That fact soothed her conscience. There was no trickery involved, at least during the seduction phase.

She studied her body in the mirror, naked except for the bit of froth between her legs. She cupped her breasts and ran her thumb across the reddish flesh where Ryan's beard had scuffed her. Closing her eyes, she sank against the vanity. She could make the sacrifice one more night to get her hands on that picture.

The knock on the door made her jump and her eyes flew open. She stuffed herself into the bra and tiptoed to the door. Pressing her eye to the peephole, she called out. "One minute, Brody."

She wriggled into a pair of skinny jeans and snagged a black camisole from the dresser drawer.

Panting slightly, she pulled open the door to her hotel room. "Are you early again?"

"Right on time." He tapped his watch. "Were you working or daydreaming?"

A little of both.

"All work and no play. I think I got a good start on the intro to the book."

She'd flung open the door and Ryan had stood with his shoulder wedged against the wall as she grabbed a blouse from the closet and shoved her feet into a pair of flats.

"Can I read it?"

She scurried to her laptop and made a few quick clicks with the mouse. "Not yet."

Not until I have another opportunity to savor every inch of your delicious body before you discover my true intent.

He threw up his hands. "Okay. Am I going to have to read it along with everyone else?"

"I think that's a good idea." She leaned close to the mirror and spread some lip gloss across her lips with the tip of her little finger.

"Just like Walker."

She dropped the tube of gloss. "What?"

"He didn't read the book until it was published, either, did he?"

"Nope. Do you want to get some dinner after we see Cookie?"

"Sure." His green eyes lit up, almost as though they were shooting sparks.

Oh yeah. Getting Brody back into bed tonight would be easy.

Ryan drove to the open house in his car, since parking on the residential streets of the Sunset District was easier and faster than taking public transportation. They pulled up to the curb across the street from the house, and Ryan pointed to the blue sedan parked in front. "That's her car, but I don't see any others. You think she's alone?"

"If she's not, we can pretend to be interested buyers until the real interested buyers leave."

They slid from the car, both of them snapping their doors shut as if fearing Cookie would hear them out there and take flight.

Kacie approached the slightly ajar door first and placed the palm of her hand against the green-painted wood. She eased it open and stepped into the house.

The smell of freshly baked cookies had her mouth

watering, and she winked at Ryan. "You're in luck. You can probably have all the leftover cookies."

He didn't return her smile. Instead, his gaze darted around the room as his jaw tensed.

His concern radiated out toward her. She scanned the empty living room and kitchen, her brow furrowing. "Do you think she saw us coming?"

Putting his finger to his lips, he shook his head.

Did that mean he didn't think she saw them coming or that he wanted her to keep quiet? And why?

Ryan poked his head into the kitchen. "Look at the cookies."

Mounds of dough crowded a cookie sheet, while the oven clicked and heated up the room.

"Looks like she left in a hurry." Kacie turned off the oven and backpedaled out of the kitchen. "Or maybe she's in the backyard with some potential buyers."

A side door led from the kitchen to a small patio. Ryan jiggled the handle and then opened the door. He shuffled onto the brick patio, and Kacie crossed the room to peer down the short hallway.

Maybe Cookie was in the bathroom.

"Cynthia?" Kacie took two steps down the carpeted hallway and froze. She tilted her head. Was that a noise? Was Cookie hiding from them back there?

"Cynthia, we just want to talk to you." Trailing her hand along the wall, Kacie took several more steps down the hall.

The door of the first room stood open, and she glanced inside. A lone wicker wastebasket gaped at her from its side in the center of the room.

She continued to the next open door and ducked her head inside. She stumbled backward, clutching her throat.

The room was empty…except for Cookie's bloodied and crumpled body in the corner.

Chapter Ten

She must've screamed.

"What is it?" Ryan bumped her shoulder as he crowded past her into the room. He swore and strode across the carpet, dropping to the floor next to Cookie's body.

"What happened to her?" Kacie felt like such a chicken, but she stayed back, clinging to the doorjamb.

"Call 911. She's still breathing."

Kacie twirled around to retrieve the purse she'd left on the kitchen counter. Now she really felt like a coward. The woman was alive and suffering, and all she could do was scream like a ninny.

She dumped the contents of her purse onto the counter and grabbed her cell phone. She babbled over the phone until the operator asked her for the address.

She knew the street name and stumbled outside to read the number from the front of the house.

Clutching her phone between clammy hands, she returned to the bedroom. Ryan had found a towel and was wrapping it around Cookie's head, stanching the flow of her blood.

"An ambulance is on the way. What happened to her? Is she going to be okay?"

"Someone beat her to a pulp." Ryan tucked in the ends of the towel to secure it and picked up Cookie's wrist to feel for a pulse. "As to whether or not she's going to be okay, I have no idea. She's in bad shape."

Kacie's stomach churned and she sealed one hand over her mouth.

Sirens wailed, and Ryan glanced up. "Go out front and meet them."

Grateful to have something useful to do, Kacie rushed from the room and tripped onto the porch. The ambulance came to a screeching halt behind Cookie's car, with two cop cars hot on its heels.

As she led the EMTs to Cookie's inert form, she told them as much as she knew. They got to work immediately as Ryan backed up, giving them space.

He held out his hands, stained with Cookie's blood.

"Did she say anything, Ryan? Was she conscious?"

"No."

The presence of the police officers halted any conversation between her and Ryan. She'd wondered how much of the truth Ryan was prepared to give to the cops, but she should've known better. He told them everything. Of course, they'd have probably figured out sooner or later that Ryan Brody, the police chief of Crestview, wasn't house shopping in the city.

Before their conversation with the police ended, the EMTs wheeled Cookie from the house.

"Wait—her purse." Kacie grabbed Cookie's purse from the counter, and her phone slid out. Her eyes shifted to the side, where Ryan was still talking to the cops, and then she snatched the phone and slid it into her back pocket.

Not everyone was as honest as Ryan Brody.

She dangled the purse from its handle. "Should this go with her to the hospital?"

"We'll take that, ma'am." One of the cops held out his hand and she hung the purse over his arm.

The police kept them for another fifteen minutes before releasing them, although the work of law enforcement had just begun. She and Ryan crossed paths with a horde of crime-scene investigators and additional cops and detectives.

When they got to the car, Ryan rested his hands on the steering wheel and blew out a breath. "Wow."

"What are you thinking, Brody?"

He turned his head and his jaw relaxed for the first time since they had entered the open house. "Are you all right? You were as pale as a ghost in there."

"I'm fine. You'd think I'd be used to it by now—two violent-crime victims in the space of a few days."

"That's right." He drummed his thumbs against the steering wheel.

"What do you think happened?"

"Someone came to the open house and beat her."

"I know that, but why?"

"Why do you think?"

She swallowed and ran her tongue across her dry teeth. "Because of us? Because she talked to us?"

He drove the heels of his hands against the steering wheel. "It seems that way, doesn't it?"

"Why?"

"Someone doesn't want her talking to us."

"Do you think," she said, licking her lips, "that whoever beat her up wanted her dead?"

"I don't think he cared one way or the other. Even if she doesn't die, she's not going to talk now. She got the message—loud and clear."

She gripped his forearm, her nails digging into his corded muscle. "What's going on, Ryan? Why would someone want to keep Cookie quiet? She witnessed your father's suicide. That's public record."

"She must know more." He smacked his thigh. "She knows something, or someone thinks she does. We had our opportunity to find out yesterday. We had the element of surprise, and we blew it."

"*She* blew it. She should've told us everything she knew yesterday. If she was scared or worried, maybe you could've given her some protection, or the SFPD could've helped."

"She was obviously scared. I should've pressed her."

"Shoulda, coulda, woulda. We didn't and she didn't, and now we just have to figure out who attacked her and why."

He jerked his thumb over his shoulder. "I'm hoping the cops can come up with some evidence—if we didn't destroy it all by traipsing through the house."

"I believe in being proactive." She patted her purse, where she'd slipped Cookie's phone. "If I had to count only on law enforcement in writing my book about Walker, I never would've had a book."

"What do you mean?" He raised an eyebrow at her.

She dug into her handbag and pulled out Cookie's phone. "I have this."

"Congratulations. You have a phone."

"Not just any phone." She tilted it back and forth. "Cookie's phone."

This time his eyebrows jumped to his hairline. "You stole a piece of evidence from a crime scene?"

"I don't see it that way. Cookie's murder is directly related to us, and we deserve to take a few matters into our own hands instead of relying on the SFPD to feed us info when and if they want to."

He shook his head. "You have a loose concept of ethics."

Heat flashed in her cheeks and she turned to her open window to gulp in a few breaths of fresh air. He didn't know the half of it. "Do you want to see Cookie's incoming and outgoing calls or don't you?"

His gaze strayed past her and took in the law-enforcement personnel scurrying in and out of the open house. "Not here."

He put the car in gear and pulled away from the curb. He cruised around the neighborhood and then stopped in front of a park. Punching on the dome light, he said, "Let's do this."

Kacie tapped Cookie's smartphone to wake it up. "Let's see. First, I guess we can see any recent calls."

She brought the phone beneath the light, and Ryan leaned in, his head touching hers. She ran her finger down five calls. "She doesn't get many calls for a Realtor, or else she deletes them."

"These three have names attached, so I'm assuming they're family or friends, but these two are listed as being blocked—one last night, one this morning."

She tapped on one blocked call but nothing happened. "I guess you can't call back a blocked number."

"What about any texts?"

She accessed Cookie's messages. "Ah, more prolific here, but it looks like they're mostly work-related—back and forths about properties, financing, open houses."

"Any messages about today's open house? Her assailant could've been posing as a house hunter. In fact, that's the most likely scenario."

"Here's a thread about it." She read the messages aloud to Ryan. "So, someone just double-checking the time and square footage of the lot."

"Is there a name associated with those texts?"

"No, but there's a phone number."

"How about—" he took the phone from her "—we send this person a text, posing as Cookie?"

"Go ahead."

He read his message as he entered it. "'Still interested in the house on Gladys? CP.'"

Kacie held her breath as Ryan cupped the phone in the palm of his hand. They both focused on the hypnotic blinking cursor for a good two minutes before Kacie released her breath.

"I guess he's not going to respond right away."

"Or ever. If this is our guy, he's gotta figure the police have his phone and are doing a little research."

She sat back and tilted her head against the headrest. "He's also gotta figure the police can trace that number, right? You *can* trace that number, can't you?"

"I can pull some strings and get a line on that number, sure."

"That's a start. What about those two blocked numbers?"

"I'll work on it."

Kacie covered her face with her hands and massaged her temples. "I don't get it. Why would someone want to harm Cookie?"

"Why would someone want to harm Dr. Franklin, my father's police therapist?"

"What are you talking about?" She peered at him through her fingers.

"When my brother Sean decided to question Dr. Franklin, he wound up having a heart attack. I approach Cookie Phelps, and she winds up in a coma. Someone doesn't want my father's case reopened."

"And the only reason for that is that someone doesn't want the truth to come out."

"The truth is he didn't do it."

She held up her hands. "Whoa. That was a big leap."

"Was it?" He cocked his head, his eyes narrowing. "The current story is that my father was the Phone Book Killer and then offed himself to avoid detection and prosecution. If that were the truth, why bother harming all these people twenty years later if all they were going to do was confirm that truth?"

"It could be the other way around." She folded her hands in her lap and stared at her white knuckles. "What if Dr. Franklin and Cookie had some irrefutable proof that your father *was* the Phone Book Killer, and someone wants to suppress that? After all, nobody ever proved that he was."

The silence from the other side of the car seemed to drag on forever. Kacie turned her head to take in Ryan's profile, which seemed carved from granite.

He spoke, barely moving his lips. "That makes no sense."

"I guess not. I'm just trying to look at all angles here." She nibbled on her lower lip and stared out the window. His supposition made more sense than hers, but what did that mean for her? What did it mean for the book? And more important, had she just revealed her hand to Ryan?

The chill from his side of the car almost had her reaching for her jacket.

He cranked on the engine. "I'm going to look into this phone number."

"After dinner?"

"Dinner?" He turned a pair of icy green eyes on her. "You really have an appetite after discovering Cookie?"

She swallowed past the lump in her throat as tears stung the backs of her eyes. *Idiot.* She'd leaked her personal agenda, and now that Ryan had gotten a glimpse of it, he no longer trusted her.

To be fair, she no longer trusted herself. Not where Ryan was concerned.

She knew the Brody brothers believed fervently in their father's innocence. They'd shut out anyone who challenged that belief.

And the irony of the situation was that she didn't even

know if she had an agenda anymore. She didn't know what to believe about Joseph Brody.

All she knew now was that she'd just lost the trust of a man she'd been falling for—a man she was having a hard time figuring out how to live without.

But she wasn't about to give up. Hadn't she always fought for what she wanted? With two beautiful older sisters, the biological daughters of her adoptive parents, she'd always felt as if she had to assert herself. She knew now that the struggle had been all in her head. Her parents hadn't really loved her any less than they had Fiona and Calista, but she'd always tried to get them to love her more because she had always felt less worthy.

She wasn't going to stand by and allow this amazing man to slip through her fingers. It was time to switch gears.

She put her hand over his. "I'm sorry. I'm sorry I doubted your father. Of course your theory makes much more sense than mine."

His arm tensed and then he turned off the car. "You don't have to apologize for doing your job. If we're going to get at the truth, we should discuss every angle, however sordid, however painful. Judd and I used to roll our eyes at Sean and Eric and how fierce they were in defense of Dad. Now I've gotten the same way. I've allowed myself to get sucked into this blood-is-thicker-than-water mentality where family can do no wrong."

"It's understandable, Ryan. If someone were making horrible claims about a member of my family, I'd probably defend that family member to the death."

He slipped his hand from beneath hers and squeezed her thigh. "But you're not just someone, and you're not making horrible claims. You're playing devil's advocate. I get it. You're doing your job, and I acted like an ass."

She put two fingers to his lips. "I totally get it, but I

didn't want to let your anger fester. I don't want any mis-understandings between us."

He puckered his lips and kissed her fingers. "Usually I'm the same way, but I admit it. This case has gotten under my skin, and now I feel responsible for Cookie's predicament."

"How were we supposed to know she'd pay for talk-ing to us?"

"Dr. Franklin paid, too."

"We don't even know that." Her stomach growled and she pressed a hand to it. "Would you really consider me a horrible person if I wanted to get something to eat? It doesn't have to be five-star or anything."

He chuckled and squeezed her thigh a little higher, which caused a slow flush to fan out across her skin. "I channeled Sean there for a minute. He's great at guilting people, too. I'm sorry about Cookie, but I'm also starving."

She slumped in her seat. "I'm so glad to hear you say that. Literally, I could eat anything."

"Tacos from a hole-in-the-wall stand?"

"Lead the way."

He revved up the car again and peeled away from the curb.

Twenty minutes later, they pulled into the crowded park-ing lot of a taco stand in South San Francisco. The lines at the windows curled around the parking lot.

"Looks like we're not the only ones who need a quick fix." She reached into the backseat for her jacket as Ryan pulled his car around the back of the building and parked it on some dirt.

They shuffled to the back of the line, and Kacie plucked Cookie's phone from her purse. "Are we going to try call-ing the number from the open-house texts?"

"Yeah, just not from our phones or the hotel."

"I guess we can try to find a pay phone."

"There are still a few of those left." He nudged her to keep up with the line. "Let's eat first and call later."

They each ordered a couple of tacos and Ryan added a burrito to his order. He paid in cash, and then they stood to the side of the window, waiting for their number to be called.

He tugged on the ends of her hair. "Grab that table over there, and I'll wait for our order."

She threaded her way through the lines at the windows and scooted onto a picnic bench next to a family of four.

Ryan had accepted her apology and had even called her forthright. She rubbed her twitching eye. She had to tell him the truth. He'd be angry at first, but then he'd appreciate her honesty. Wouldn't he?

There was no reason to keep the truth from him anymore. The book she'd planned to write had taken a detour. The same thing had happened with the Walker book. When would she learn about preconceived notions?

Of course, if she never revealed the truth to Ryan, he'd never know that she'd come into this project with an agenda. But if they ever ended up together, she'd have to tell him. She couldn't keep such a big secret from him.

She glanced up and spotted him carrying a box of food overflowing with chips. Could they really end up together? Did they have a chance?

He placed the box on the table. "I asked for extra chips and salsa, but I think they went overboard."

She dipped a chip into the salsa and held it up. "You can never have too much chips and salsa."

"Watch it. That stuff's hot." He straddled the bench across from her.

She bit into the chip with a crunch and the salsa dribbled down her chin. Before she had a chance to grab a napkin from the dispenser, he dabbed her chin with his thumb. "You're supposed to eat it, not wear it."

She chewed and swallowed, the salsa burning the roof of her mouth. "Thanks for that bit of advice."

They both dug into their food, and cheap tacos on the street had never tasted so good. For the duration of the meal, she forgot about Cookie and Daniel Walker and even Joseph Brody. For the duration of the meal, they were two people with an undeniable attraction for each other out on a simple date.

But the meal ended.

"I think I saw a pay phone across the street at the gas station." He crumpled the wrapper from his last taco and tossed it into the box. "You game?"

"Absolutely." She patted her face with a napkin. "No more salsa on my face?"

He wedged a finger beneath her chin and tilted her head back. "Your face looks perfect."

Oh no, she wasn't ready to give up any part of that.

They relinquished their coveted seats to another couple hovering nearby and shoved their trash into the garbage can.

The light changed and they dashed across the street to the service station. Ryan grabbed her hand and tugged. "I think it's on the side of the mini-mart. I saw it when we were driving up the street."

They turned the corner of the squat building that housed a small convenience store. A light glowed over the pay phone.

Ryan picked up the receiver.

"Does it work?"

"We'll soon see." He dropped a coin in the slot and snapped his fingers for the number on Cookie's phone.

Kacie brought up the text and read the number aloud to him.

He punched it in and listened, while she pinched his shirtsleeve. "Well?"

He slammed the phone back in the cradle. "No answer and no voice mail."

"That in itself tells me something." She shoved Cookie's phone back in her purse. "Who doesn't have some kind of message on their phone, especially if you're using that phone to look for a house?"

"I don't know. Maybe he only responds to texts."

"Well, he didn't respond to our text, either."

"I didn't expect much, Kacie. I'm still going to try to trace the blocked phone calls. I can call the station tonight and get one of my guys on it." He rubbed a circle on her back and it almost soothed away her disappointment.

She combed her fingers through her hair and clasped it into a ponytail. "I suppose if someone had answered the phone and confirmed he or she was a valid house hunter, it would've been a dead end. This at least leaves us an opening."

They jogged back across the street and squeezed between the cars in the parking lot to get to Ryan's SUV in the dirt.

"At least we didn't get towed."

"No ticket?" She peeked at the windshield. "Looks like you got away with your illegal parking job, Brody. Did you put some kind of cop vibe around the car?"

"Yeah, it's a secret shield."

He opened the door for her and she slid onto the seat, closing her eyes.

The car jostled as Ryan climbed into the driver's side. "Are you okay?"

"It's been a long day. Not what I expected. Can we call the hospital and check on Cookie?"

"Sure." He pulled out his own phone and called information for San Francisco General. The operator must've automatically connected him because he began speaking.

"I'm calling to find out about a patient who was brought in earlier by ambulance, Cynthia Phelps." He tapped her knee and shook his head. "This is Chief Ryan Brody from Crestview. I'm the one who found her. You can check with the SFPD."

He recited his phone number and dropped the phone in his cup holder. "They wouldn't give me any info, but she's going to check with the P.D. and call me back if they give the go-ahead."

"Sheesh, you can't even check on anyone's welfare anymore without a full-scale investigation?"

"Don't worry. I'll get the news one way or another."

He pulled out of the parking lot, his tires stirring up dirt and rocks on the way out. He merged onto the freeway back to the city and their hotel.

The hypnotic headlights and her full tummy had Kacie's eyelids drooping. If she hoped for a repeat of the night before, she'd better get a boost of adrenaline from somewhere.

Maybe just getting a glimpse of Ryan's hard body would be enough to jump-start her libido.

The car bounced as Ryan left the freeway and turned onto the Embarcadero. He made another turn and the tires squealed as Kacie's head bumped the window.

"Hey!" Her eyelids flew open. "What do you think this is, the Indy 500?"

Ryan clutched the steering wheel. "This car isn't behaving too well."

"Maybe if you'd spring for a newer model, Brody."

The traffic light ahead glowed yellow and the car

lurched and then flew through the intersection as the light turned to red.

She gripped the edge of her seat. "Wow, Brody, just because you're a cop doesn't mean you can get away with murder in this city."

She clapped a hand over her mouth. Bad choice of words. But before she had time to apologize, the car sailed through another intersection, narrowly missing two pedestrians.

"Brody! What the hell are you doing?"

"It's the brakes." He hunched forward over the steering wheel. "We don't have any."

Chapter Eleven

He stomped on the brake pedal again, but the car surged forward. Aiming for the side of the road, he reached for the emergency brake. He yanked it up and the car lurched and growled.

It didn't stop, but it did slow down.

Kacie gasped beside him. "Is it going to stop?"

"Not without a fight." He pumped the brake, and his foot hit the floor.

He rushed up on a car stopped at a crosswalk. He careened around it, blowing by the shocked faces of the pedestrians startled to a halt in the street.

He couldn't keep this up. The closer they got to the busy end of the wharf, the less space he'd have to maneuver in. He needed something to slow him down, some obstacle in his path.

"Make sure your seat belt's snug."

Kacie tugged on her belt. "What are you going to do?"

"Hang on."

The curb, a couple of benches…and barriers. His tires bumped the curb, and he aimed the car between two groups of people. His vehicle jumped when he hit the curb and plowed toward the first bench.

Kacie yelled something unintelligible.

They ripped through the bench to the sound of screaming metal. The car limped forward.

His body tensed as he made a beeline for the orange barriers stationed along the walkway. The car smacked the barrier, and the air bags exploded.

He grunted as the bag hit his chest. Kacie gave a muffled cry.

The car lurched back, finally at rest.

Ryan struggled out of the smashed car and ran to the passenger side. He didn't like the look of the black smoke curling up from the collapsed hood. He yanked open Kacie's door and helped her from her position pinned between the air bag and the seat of the car.

They both staggered away from the wreckage as alternating sirens filled the air.

"Are you hurt?" He turned Kacie to face him and touched the abrasion on her cheek.

She held her hands in front of her. "I think I'm okay. You?"

"Tossed around, but nothing broken."

"You have some glass in your hair. Close your eyes." She flicked his hair with her fingers.

"Don't cut yourself."

She grabbed his T-shirt. "What just happened, Ryan?"

"Someone tampered with my brakes."

Her eyes widened, and then the EMTs and the cops descended.

The men in white checked his vitals and bandaged a small cut on his hand. The police weren't as solicitous. They'd gotten a few calls about his reckless driving before the crash and weren't altogether convinced he wasn't drunk or crazy.

"It was the brakes. They failed."

He still had to blow into the cop's face, but since he

showed no outward signs of drinking and the cop couldn't smell any alcohol on his breath, he didn't have to take a Breathalyzer.

Once he showed the officers his own badge and they realized he was Sean Brody's brother, he got the kid-glove treatment.

Kacie didn't have any severe injuries, but that red spot on her face from the air bag was going to turn into a nasty bruise.

"Were you having problems with your brakes before, Chief Brody?"

"You call me Ryan, and no. I drove down here from Crestview and didn't have any issues with the brakes. Brakes were fine when we went to eat, and then it was sudden, like the lines were cut."

The officer raised his brows, but he wrote Ryan's suspicions in his notebook. "We'll have the car towed and our mechanic will check that. Anyone we need to question?"

Yeah, the same guy who'd beat up Cookie Phelps.

"I can't give you any names, but I'm almost positive this was no accident."

The cop took more information from Ryan and then offered to give them a lift to their hotel.

They made it back to the hotel and he didn't even have to ask Kacie to join him in his room. She collapsed on the bed, clutching the ice pack the EMTs had given her.

He pointed to the blue pack. "That's supposed to go on your face."

"When did he do it?"

He reached into his travel bag and pulled out a bottle, then popped a couple of ibuprofen in his mouth and chugged some water. "Must've done it while we were at the taco stand."

"That means…"

"Someone's been following us." He shook the bottle of gel caps at her. "I think you need a couple of these."

"No kidding." She held out her hands and he tossed her the bottle. "Maybe that's how he found out we met Cookie yesterday."

"Somebody knows we're working on Dad's case, and they want us to stop. Do you still think it's someone who wants us to preserve the commonly held belief that Dad was a serial killer?"

"I never said I believed that. I was just throwing out the possibility."

"Okay, I get it."

"Here's another possibility." She pressed the ice pack to her face and wrinkled her nose. "What if the brakes tonight don't have anything to do with Cookie or your father?"

He stopped pacing. "Really?"

"Think about it. Duke Bannister warned me about Walker. Someone locked me in the sauna, sent that doll and then killed Bannister. Maybe that's the person who tampered with your brakes. Maybe this is Walker's work."

"I think you've got it backward, Kacie." He rested his forehead against the cool glass of the window and watched a homeless man navigate his cart around a bus stop.

"What do you mean?"

"Maybe all of those previous incidents are connected to my father and this book. Maybe Walker was telling the truth for once in his life—he had nothing to do with the sauna or the doll or Bannister. After that interview you did on TV, plenty of people knew this was your next project."

She sat up and the ice pack fell to the floor. "You just rocked my reality. I never thought of that possibility before."

"I'm surprised. You're a good, insightful reporter. If you're in the business of looking at all possibilities, I'm shocked this one never occurred to you."

Hunching forward, she gathered the bedspread in her fists. "So, right from the beginning, before the two of us even met, someone was on my tail, harassing me, wanting me to believe Walker was after me. And all the time it was this book."

"That's what it's beginning to look like to me. This was never about Walker."

"Then Bannister was working for someone else." She bounced on the mattress, clapping her hands.

"That's what he wanted to tell you at the end. He was going to come clean about who sent him."

"He was murdered before he could do it."

"Just like Cookie was beaten before she could give us any more information."

"This is big, Brody, if it's true." This time she couldn't contain her excitement and she bounded from the bed. "We're onto something and maybe it starts with your father's suicide. Maybe he said something to Cookie before he jumped. Maybe he implicated someone else."

"And that someone else is alive and well in the city of San Francisco."

"Alive and well and targeting people who dare tell the truth or try to."

"There's just one problem." He crossed his arms and leaned against the window. "This is just a theory. We have no hard evidence to back it up, and we have no line on any suspects. We might as well be at square one."

"No, no." She shook her head and winced. "This is so much better than square one, Ryan. This is clarity. This is truth."

"This is supposition." Her reaction puzzled him. The pithy facts they had before them didn't warrant Kacie's level of excitement. Maybe she had a concussion. "Are you feeling okay?"

"A little sore. But more than ever I'm ready to tackle this project."

"I'm glad the car crash energized you, but you need to get some rest. We're both going to be feeling it tomorrow."

She folded her hands in front of her and dropped her lashes. "Can I stay with you tonight, Ryan? After everything that happened today, I'm feeling jittery. This person, whoever he is, must know we're staying in this hotel."

He crossed to the bed in two strides and gently enfolded her in his arms. He kissed the top of her head and the scrape on her face, which was already turning into a yellow bruise.

"Of course you're staying here tonight."

She held up one finger. "Give me a few minutes. I'm going to run to my room and brush my teeth and all that stuff."

"Do you want me to come with you?"

"I'll be okay. I promise not to get into the elevator with any strangers."

"I'll see you downstairs and wait outside your room just in case."

She kissed his mouth. "I knew you would."

Several minutes later back in her own room, Kacie changed into her pajamas. In the bathroom, she leaned toward the mirror and smoothed some night cream over the abrasion on her face.

She'd been so focused on her vendetta against the Brody family, she hadn't even considered there may be more to the story. Someone knew she was writing this book about Joey Brody and was trying to stop her from uncovering the truth—that Brody had been innocent.

That truth would smooth over everything between her and Ryan, giving them a clear path to some kind of relationship.

She just had one small detail to take care of first.

She wrapped the hotel robe around her body, grabbed

her purse and swung open the door to find Ryan propped up against the wall outside her room. "You didn't have to wait out here."

"No problem. Made me feel better to get a clear view of the hallway."

"All quiet?"

"Except for a couple too drunk to walk straight? Yeah."

She joined him in the hall and he escorted her back to his room. She hung her purse over the back of a chair and then stood in the center of the room, twisting her fingers in front of her.

Ryan turned on the radio and whipped the covers back from the bed. "My bed is yours."

She liked the sound of that. She shed her robe, crawled under the covers and fluffed up a pillow against the headboard.

He pulled off his T-shirt, and wearing a pair of boxers low on his hips, he slid into bed next to her.

Was she expected to keep her hands to herself with this prime male specimen sprawled out next to her?

He rolled to his side and slid his hands beneath her pajama top. As he cupped her breasts, he nuzzled her ear and whispered, "Do you always overdress for bed?"

Her nipples peaked beneath the rough pads of his fingertips and her insides melted.

"Do you?" She slid her hand along the waistband of his boxers and rolled them down to expose his readiness. He was already hard, his erection filling her hand.

He sucked in a breath and nipped her earlobe. "You've been manhandled enough today. I promise to take it nice and easy."

She sighed and yanked off her top. "You can take me any way you like."

His grin widened as he rolled on top of her and slid both

hands beneath her bottom, then moved down her body, taking her pajamas off along the way. "Let's start by releasing some of this tension."

He dipped his head between her legs, and she couldn't remember her own name, let alone the events of the day.

True to his word, they made love nice and easy, but every time he took her over the precipice she felt as if she'd died a thousand deaths.

Spent, they lay in each other's arms, their limbs tangled, their bodies joined with no beginning and no ending. The picture from the TV cast a flickering blue light across Ryan's strong face. How had she fallen so hard and so fast for this man?

She'd started this project placing Ryan Brody, all the Brody boys, in the role of the enemy. She couldn't help it. Even though the sons weren't guilty for the sins of the father, she'd put a black mark next to every Brody. But Ryan had torpedoed that role the very first night they'd met when he'd carried her from the sauna.

They'd do this together. They'd prove his father's innocence, perhaps find a measure of justice for her mother and write a kick-ass book in the process.

But first things first.

She picked up his heavy arm, which lay across her midsection, kissed the inside of his forearm and placed it across his chest.

He murmured and kicked one leg. She should wait until he was sound asleep, but then she'd be sound asleep, too.

She watched the reality show on TV for a few more minutes, listening to Ryan's steady breathing. She rolled away from him, and he tossed his head to the side.

She reached out and stroked the ridges of muscle that formed his chest. What a beautiful man—and he wanted her, thought she was beautiful and desirable. Made her feel beautiful and desirable for the first time in her life.

Her adoptive mom had always told her most men liked a woman with healthy curves, but it took Ryan Brody's unabashed lust for her body to finally make her believe it.

She kissed one of the brown nipples on his chest, her tongue flicking over the saltiness. He didn't move.

Releasing a breath, she rolled to the edge of the bed and swung her legs over the side. The bruised spot on her hip thudded with pain.

The glow from the TV cast enough light in the room that she could make it to the box by the window without tripping over anything. She knelt beside the box and tipped off the lid.

Her pulse quickened. The victim file was no longer on top, where she'd left it. Had Ryan been going through the files?

She dug in the box and found the file halfway down the stack. Glancing over her shoulder at Ryan's sleeping form, she pulled out the file and sat cross-legged on the floor with the folder in her lap.

She shuffled through the papers to get to each photo until she found the one she was looking for. She pulled the picture out of the stack and stuffed the file back into the box beneath the other folders.

With trembling fingers, she gripped the edges of the picture, her gaze sweeping the room. She couldn't very well go back to her room right now. If Ryan woke up while she was gone, she'd have way too much explaining to do. She'd have to hide it in this room and take it with her when she returned to her own room in the morning.

She considered and then rejected several options before deciding on her purse. She'd have to fold the picture, but she planned to shred it anyway.

She tiptoed to her handbag, still hanging on the back of the chair, and creased the photo in half before stuffing it into the depths of her purse.

She brushed her hands together. Ryan didn't ever have to know about that.

She crawled back into bed and snuggled against his warm body, running her hand up his muscular thigh before draping her leg over his.

This was going to work out. She'd make sure of it.

THE FOLLOWING MORNING, Kacie opened one eye and groaned.

Ryan looked up from the table by the window, fully dressed. "I think it's best if you hit the ibuprofen as soon as possible. I'm just beginning to be able to move my limbs without hissing in pain."

She smacked her lips and croaked. "Good idea."

"I put a couple of gel tabs and a glass of water on the nightstand for you."

"Thanks." She popped the pills and gulped down the water. "What are you working on so early?"

"I'm contacting my department to see if they can request a trace on that blocked phone number on Cookie's phone. It might lead to nothing, but then, that's why they're called leads."

"Glad someone's thinking clearly this morning."

He tapped some keys on the keyboard. "I need Cookie's number and the times of the calls. You still have her phone, right?"

"Uh-huh." She yawned.

"You put it in your purse before the accident last night."

Her heart slammed against her rib cage. "Yeah, it's still in my purse. I'll get it." She yelped as she scrambled to a sitting position.

"That's how I felt this morning. Let the meds take effect before you start moving around. I'll get the phone."

With her muscles screaming at her almost as loudly as the voice screaming in her head, Kacie clenched her teeth and sat up, flinging the covers from her body. "That's okay. I'll get it."

Too late. Ryan had her purse in his hands, spreading it open. "I'll find it."

"My purse is a mess. Toss it over here. I'll dump it out on the bed."

"I can do that here." Before she could say another word, he dumped the contents of her purse onto the table.

With wide eyes, she watched the folded photo drift to the floor. Maybe he'd leave it there.

He plucked Cookie's phone from the table. "Got it. That wasn't so bad."

He began to gather the rest of her items and shove them back into her purse.

"That's okay, Ryan. I'll do that."

"Sorry. Something fell on the floor." He crouched down and pinched the corner of the photo between two fingers.

Kacie held her breath, her heart pounding.

He couldn't have picked up the picture in a worse way. It flipped on its side as he dropped it onto the table, the stamp from the SFPD clearly visible.

He tapped Cookie's phone and Kacie's breath came back in short spurts. She eased from the bed. No sense in tempting fate. She had to get that photo back into her purse.

She made it halfway to the table when Ryan's gaze shifted from the phone's display to the photo on the table.

"What is this? It looks like a piece of evidence, a photo." He squinted at the stamp on the white background. "It's a photo of a victim."

Kacie reached out one hand. "I-it's…it's…"

Ryan unfolded the picture and smoothed it out on the table, his eyebrows colliding over his nose. "I know this picture."

Kacie crossed her arms over her belly, her nails digging into the flesh of her upper arms.

Ryan's head jerked up as he stabbed the photo with his index finger. "This is the same picture you have in your wallet. What the hell are you doing with a picture of one of the Phone Book Killer's victims in your wallet? Who is she?"

She dragged in a shaky breath and closed her eyes. "She's my mother."

Chapter Twelve

Ryan blinked. Her mother. Her mother was that cool blonde on her laptop. She'd told him this woman was her grandmother. He grabbed the picture and held it close to his face.

Grandmother? How could he be so stupid? Judging by the woman's hair and clothing, this photo belonged to the eighties. This woman was too young to be Kacie's grandmother—but not too young to be her mother.

He reread the label in the corner of the picture, the label that tagged this woman as a homicide victim.

The Phone Book Killer had murdered Kacie's mother twenty years before. The reality of it slammed against his chest, knocking the breath from his lungs.

He hunched over the table, flattening his hands against the surface on either side of the picture. The aches and pains of the car accident flooded his body until he became a single ball of hurt.

"Ryan."

He turned his head, and his eyes flicked over the naked woman standing before him, her arms crossed over her perfect body. Her delectable breasts heaving with every harsh breath. Her lush, lying lips parted and moist.

His hands bunched into fists on the table and a muscle in his jaw ticked wildly. He swallowed the rage at how she could keep something like this from him that threatened to overtake all his senses.

He cleared his throat to make sure he could speak. "Why did you want to write this book about my father?"

She brushed a hand across her face and trailed unsteady fingers through the tangles of her hair. "It's a good story, Ryan."

"Don't—" he held up his hand "—lie. And for God's sake, put some clothes on."

She pivoted and scooped up the pajama bottoms he'd removed from her body, inch by seductive inch, a million years before. She stepped into them and dug through the covers to pull out her pajama top. She pulled it over her head and sank to the edge of the bed.

"I wanted to write this book to get to the truth, to exact justice for my mother."

"I said, stop lying." He smacked his open hand against the desk, and the photo of the beautiful dead woman floated to the floor once again. "You thought you already had the truth, and you came here to crucify my father. Why else would you be lying to me all this time about your mother? You came here to put the nail in the coffin of his reputation. You came here to trick me, to use me."

She pinned her hands between her bouncing knees. "You're right. I thought your father was guilty of murdering my mother, but it wasn't my plan to trick you."

"But you did." He smacked his forehead with the heel of his hand, welcoming the pain. "The night before last and last night, too, you came on to me. You did it to get access to my room and this box."

He gave the box a vicious kick, and it flew in the air a foot before landing on its side, spilling its guts.

He laughed and the sound grated against his throat. "You were sloppy. When you filched the photo from the box, you should've run into the hallway and buried it in the trash can by the elevator. Flushed it down the toilet. Ripped it into small pieces and swallowed it. Instead, you put it in your purse."

"I wanted to tell you about my mother, Ryan, because I'd changed my mind. I realized that your father wasn't the Phone Book Killer."

"You wanted to tell me, so you stole the picture from the file and hid it in your purse? Uh-huh."

"I was going to tell you later."

He snorted. "You mean after you got me in bed a few more times and had me so crazy in lo…lust I wouldn't care that you lied to me from the start?"

She covered her face with both hands and her shoulders shook. He ground his back teeth as his natural instinct to comfort her flooded his chest.

Her muffled words came out on a sob. "I wanted to tell you, but I didn't know how. It seemed the damage had already been done."

"You're right. You should've been straight with me from the beginning. You could've come to me with the truth. I would've understood."

She hopped up from the bed. "You never would've agreed to work with me, and I didn't know you, didn't know anything about you. You were the enemy. Do you know how many years the name Brody filled me with rage? I thought your father had killed my mother. Everything I read about the case pointed to him. I wanted to be the one to prove it once and for all and bring some peace to my mother and the other victims of the Phone Book Killer."

She folded her hands behind her back and leaned against the wall, looking small and defenseless in her pajamas and bedhead hair.

She'd lost her mother as a child in the vilest way. The

Phone Book Killer had turned her world upside down and decimated the only family she had. She must've been adopted soon after that and taken away from her home and everything she knew. No wonder she hated the name Brody.

She must've read his softened expression because she stretched her hand out to him. "I'm so sorry, Ryan. I know now I never should've kept my identity a secret from you. And last night, the night before…there was no pretense. I could've found a million different ways to get into that box."

His jaw tensed. She'd crept around his room not once, but twice while he'd lain sleeping, naked, totally at her mercy in every way.

He pinched the bridge of his nose. "I need to be alone right now. This association, this project—it's over."

She sagged against the wall.

He turned his back on her. "If you need some kind of protection, I can call hotel security to check on you."

"I'm sure I'll be fine in the hotel."

She moved stiffly toward the desk and grabbed her purse. She left the photo of her mother on the floor.

When the door closed behind her, Ryan reached for the phone. He punched in the extension for the front desk and requested some security for Kacie's room. He explained how she'd been the guest locked in the sauna earlier in the week. Still fearing some kind of legal action, the manager agreed readily.

He swooped down and snatched up the photo. He fell across the bed on his back, holding the picture of Kacie's mother in front of his face. She smiled at him with Kacie's lips and reproached him with Kacie's eyes.

He tossed the picture onto the floor and rolled onto his stomach, scrunching a pillow into his face.

His hand skimmed a bit of lacy material and he pulled it from under the pillow. Kacie's silky thong tangled around his fingers, tying him up, binding her to him. He pressed it to his face and inhaled her scent.

He might be mad as hell about her deception, but it didn't make him want her any less.

THE TEARS BURNED hot trails down her face, stinging the abrasion on her cheek. On the floor of her hotel room, Kacie leaned her forehead on her knees, which were pulled to her chest, and her tears dripped off the end of her nose.

As soon as she'd gained a measure of Ryan Brody, the man, she should've told him the truth. Even when she still believed Joseph Brody was the Phone Book Killer and her mother's murderer, she should've come clean to Ryan. He might've ended the project then, but anything would've been better than the look on his face when he realized the truth. He actually believed she'd used him sexually to get to the folder in his room. She'd been speaking the truth, for once, when she'd told him that there were a million different ways she could've gotten her hands on her mother's picture.

She didn't need to land him in bed to do that. She'd *wanted* to land him in bed. If he really thought she'd been faking it with him, he must think she deserved an Academy Award.

She rubbed her hand beneath her runny nose and fell to her side. What did it matter now? She'd blown it. She'd blown the book. She'd blown any chance of discovering her mother's real killer. She'd blown a budding relationship with a decent man.

All because she hadn't trusted that man with the truth. Mom, her adoptive mom, had told her she'd regret not learning to open up more. When her parents had first adopted her, they'd sent her to a child therapist. She'd attended almost a year's worth of sessions before she began to feel comfortable with her new family. Then when she'd hit adolescence, her parents had sent her for another round of head shrinking when it became apparent she was playing fast and loose with the truth when she thought the truth would expose her to someone's displeasure.

Her therapist had diagnosed her with abandonment issues, and she'd been able to work through most of those feelings, but she'd never completely resolved them.

Now it had cost her—big-time.

She curled tighter into her fetal position and allowed the tears to flow unabated.

Someone tapped on the door and she rolled to her back, her pulse jumping in her throat. Had Ryan forgiven her? Was he going to give her a second chance?

She sprang to her feet and peered through the peephole. The disappointment at seeing a room-service waiter punched her in the gut.

"I didn't order any room service."

"I know, ma'am. Mr. Ryan Brody in room 582 ordered it for you."

"He did?" Her voice squeaked like a schoolgirl's. He did care. Maybe he was coming up to join her now.

She pulled open the door, smiling through her tears at the uniformed hotel employee in the hallway. A dark shape lunged from the side, and with a sickening thud, the waiter dropped to the ground.

Kacie choked out a scream and took a backward step into the room. Then she felt a prick on the inside of her wrist and she descended into blackness.

RYAN PACED THE FLOOR, tapping his phone against his palm. Why wouldn't Kacie be answering her hotel phone or her cell phone?

When she'd left his room, she'd been shaken up—not even dressed.

Once she was out of his sight, his worries began to build up. When the hospital called to tell him Cynthia Phelps was still in a coma, he couldn't shake off his concerns, no matter how infuriated he was at Kacie. He'd decided to at least check in by phone.

But she wouldn't answer her phone. It would be one thing if she was just ignoring his number on her cell, but he'd called her from his room phone, too, just in case. And it was highly unlikely she'd ignore a call from a number she didn't recognize. Not with her many true-crime contacts out there.

He shoved his key card in his back pocket and headed for the door. He jogged down the steps of the stairwell to the next floor and pushed through the fire door.

Adrenaline crashed through his body when he saw the crumpled body of a waiter in front of Kacie's hotel door.

He ran to the young man's inert form while digging his cell phone from his pocket. The kid had a lump the size of a melon on the side of his head and copious amounts of blood soaked the carpet beneath him.

He shouted into the phone for the front desk to call 911 and be on the lookout for a woman in duress, possibly in the company of a man.

He jumped to his feet and ran back to the stairwell. He wouldn't have taken her down the elevator since it opened right onto the busy lobby. If he had a gun to Kacie's back, he'd be taking a big risk going through the public place.

He knew this stairwell led to a side door and an alley to the street. His legs pumped like pistons as he ran down the stairs, taking about three at a time.

He heard a door slam below him and vaulted over the handrail, landing on the floor below. He started yelling, his shouts echoing in the stairwell. He needed to cause as much commotion as possible. It was still broad daylight.

He kicked through the final door, which led to a short hallway and a glass security door to the street. He yanked that open and stumbled onto the sidewalk, blinking in the sunlight.

The sight in front of him caused his heart to skip a bit. A man with a black stocking cap on his head was staggering down the alley, carrying Kacie's limp form in his arms.

Ryan shouted and sprinted toward him.

The man hit the sidewalk and dropped Kacie. He ran into the street, dodging cars. Ryan reached Kacie, her body unconscious on the sidewalk. He hovered over her as he watched her abductor hop over a fence and dart between two buildings.

He took a step into the street and Kacie moaned.

He couldn't leave her. He dropped to his knees and gathered her to his chest. "Kacie, Kacie."

He could hear the sirens arriving around the corner at the front of the hotel for the room-service waiter. He scooped up Kacie in his arms and carried her back through the side door of the hotel, past the stairwell and into the lobby.

A woman gasped. "Is she okay?"

"Not at all." He yelled for the front-desk clerk, and a few minutes later one of the EMTs who'd arrived earlier returned to the lobby.

"Was she hit on the head, too?" The EMT snapped on his gloves and lifted Kacie's eyelid.

"I don't think so. I didn't see any injuries on her body. Is the kid okay?"

"He'll be fine." He touched the bruise on Kacie's cheek. "What's this?"

"Air bag. We were in a car accident yesterday. She's going to be all right, isn't she?"

"I think she was drugged. I called for another ambulance. We're taking both of them in. Do you know what happened?"

"From the looks of it, someone used the kid to get her to open her door and then snatched her. I caught the culprit on the sidewalk outside, but he dropped her and took off. I would've gone after him, but I couldn't leave her unconscious on the sidewalk."

The man patted his shoulder. "Of course not."

An hour later, Ryan shifted in the plastic chair, stretching his legs in front of him. He jumped to his feet when the SFPD officer entered the room.

"She's okay?"

"She's gonna be fine." Officer Schrader scratched his chin. "What is it with you, Brody? Small-town chief of police comes to the big city, and violence and mayhem follow."

"It's this book, Schrader. It's my father's case. Someone doesn't want it reopened."

"That's what Sean thought, too. I don't know what's going on."

"Was Kacie able to give you a description of the man who abducted her?"

"Nope. But the waiter said the man corralled the waiter from another floor, forced him at gunpoint to go to Ms. Manning's room and stand at her door with his cart. When she saw he was hotel staff, she opened the door. The assailant, who was wearing a ski mask, hit the kid on the side of the head with the butt of his gun and injected Ms. Manning with a sedative. He then carried her down the stairwell."

"Did you check out the cars on that block? I'm sure he didn't intend to carry an unconscious woman in pajamas through the streets of the city. He must've had a car waiting for him."

"We're running them now. Did you get a look at him?"

"He never turned around. He heard me yelling and dropped her. I could see the black cap on his head. He must've still had the ski mask over his face. He seemed to be moving slowly, having difficulty carrying Kacie."

The officer nodded. "Deadweight's a bitch."

"Can I see her?"

"Ask the doc, but I'm done questioning her for now."

He had no intention of checking with anyone. He had let Kacie down. He never should've allowed her to return to her room by herself, hotel security or no hotel security.

He slipped through the automatically opening doors as two orderlies pushed a patient on a gurney through. He threaded his way through the emergency-treatment area, which was crammed with stretchers and harried doctors in white coats dashing from one curtained area to another.

Ryan peeked behind each curtain, backing away from patients in varying degrees of discomfort.

"Hey, you're not supposed to be back here." A nurse waved a pen at him.

Flashing his badge, he said, "I'm looking for Kacie Manning."

She shrugged and squeezed past him.

Behind the very next curtain, he found Kacie, her coppery hair gleaming against the white pillow and framing her white face.

She turned a pair of saucer-round eyes on him.

He grabbed a plastic chair by the side of her bed and straddled it. He took her limp, cold hand in his. "How are you feeling?"

Her tongue darted out of her mouth. "How did you know something was wrong? How did you know he had me?"

"I didn't know until I saw the waiter knocked out in front of your door."

"What made you come?"

"I felt uneasy." He lifted his shoulders. "I'd called hotel security to do a few extra rounds past your room, but the hospital had just called me to report that Cookie was still unconscious, and it reminded me of the danger you still faced."

She curled her fingers around his hand. "Ryan, I'm so sorry I didn't tell you about my mother."

"Let's leave that for now." He squeezed her hand. "The cop told me you didn't get a look at the man who abducted you. Ski mask?"

"Yes." With her free hand, she smoothed out the wrinkles on the sheet covering her stomach. "All I remember is his cold hand as he grabbed my arm and shoved a needle into it."

"You went out immediately?"

"Yeah. I don't remember a thing after that pinprick."

"He carried you down the stairwell and out the side door to the street. He was heading down the alley with you. I'm sure he had a car parked on the street. He couldn't very well have carried you down the sidewalk."

"Are the police checking on that?"

"They are now."

"He got away."

He released her hand and plowed his fingers through his hair. "I had a choice between leaving you unconscious on the sidewalk and going after him. I chose you."

"After what I did to you? If you had caught up with him, he could've given us answers."

"I wasn't going to leave you lying on the sidewalk, unprotected. For all we know, he could've been working with an accomplice, and someone else could've snatched you."

She folded her arms across her chest and hunched her shoulders. "Why did he want to kidnap me? Why didn't he just kill me in the hotel if he wants me to stop writing this book?"

"I don't know, Kacie. Maybe it was a warning. Maybe he was going to try to find out how much you knew first." He scooted his chair closer. "Did you notice anything about his hands or body before he injected you?"

She bit her lower lip. "He was covered from head to toe in black. I didn't see his hands. I just felt them on my skin."

"Was he tall? When I saw him, he was carrying you and running. He seemed to be struggling."

"I didn't notice his height, but the struggling makes sense if he's running with a woman in his arms."

"A young, fit man wouldn't have been having the same issues."

"Are you trying to say he was old and unfit?"

He sighed and slumped back in the chair. "Just grasping. It still doesn't make any sense to me."

A nurse whipped back the curtain and smacked a clipboard against her hand. "Good news, Kacie. You're out of here."

"Are you sure?" Ryan stood up and faced the nurse. "She was drugged and almost abducted."

"She didn't have much of the drug in her system and we were able to flush out most of it. She might be a little groggy and she shouldn't drive for a few hours, but she's good to go."

Ryan rolled his eyes. "I'll take her back to her hotel."

"I don't have any clothes." Kacie plucked at the paper gown covering her body.

"You have what you came in wearing, right?" The nurse pointed to a plastic bag on a cart in the corner. "Your stuff's in there, and we can give you some slippers."

"I was wearing pajamas."

"Hey, your pj's cover more than what most people wear on the street these days. Nobody's going to notice a thing." She plucked up the plastic bag and dropped it on Kacie's bed.

"Do I need to sign any kind of release form?"

"Right here." The nurse tapped the clipboard and then handed it to Kacie. "We already got your insurance info, so you're free to leave."

When she left, Ryan whistled. "This is another reason why I like Crestview. This place is an assembly line. I'll turn around while you get dressed."

"Nothing you haven't already seen, Brody."

And touched and tasted. He liked hearing that feisty tone back in her voice.

"Along with no shoes, I don't even have any underwear."

"I'm sorry. I should've thought to bring you some clothes when I grabbed your purse from your room."

"I'm glad you had the foresight to get my purse. I swear, I don't think these people would've treated me without a copy of my insurance card."

She ripped open the plastic bag and dumped her pajamas onto the bed. She snatched up the bottoms and wriggled into them beneath the sheet. Then she shrugged out of the paper gown and pulled her top over her head.

He averted his gaze from all that creamy white skin, but she'd had it right. Nothing he hadn't seen before. And felt. And tasted. And enjoyed.

Tossing off the sheet, she said, "I guess I'm ready."

He stood next to the bed and offered his arm, which she took. She rose to her feet, leaning heavily against him.

"Can you walk?"

"Sure." She took a few shuffling steps to prove her point.

"Hang on to me, and I'll get you out of here. I parked my rental car right in front, if they haven't towed me." He curled his arm around her waist and tucked her against his side as he maneuvered through the chaos of the emergency room.

His new rental welcomed them from exactly where he'd left it. He helped Kacie into the passenger seat and then dropped onto the driver's seat.

"You need some food."

"I need a shower first. I haven't had a shower since..." She trailed off, her cheeks sporting two red spots.

He got it. She hadn't had a shower since the day before, when they'd made love. Since before he found out her mother was one of the Phone Book Killer's victims.

"Shower first, then."

In less than an hour they were safely ensconced in her room. This time he didn't leave her alone and wouldn't—no matter how many lies she'd told him.

She stacked a pile of clean clothes in her arms and headed for the bathroom. "Make yourself at home. There's no telling how long I'm going to take in the shower."

"Take as much time as you need, and let me know if you feel dizzy or weak. I'm going to order some room service. Any preferences?"

"Food."

Kacie snapped the bathroom door closed and leaned against it. Where would she be right now if Ryan hadn't saved her? Getting tortured? Beaten like Cookie? Dead? What did that man want with her? He could've killed her in the hallway. Why hadn't he?

It couldn't just be another warning. She and Ryan had gotten that warning the night before in the car—stay away from this case or else.

She dragged the dirty pajamas from her body and tossed

them into the corner of the bathroom, then cranked on the water and stepped into the tub, grabbing the shower curtain as she swayed. Maybe she did need Ryan's help, but he'd probably see it as another ploy to seduce him.

Despite her lie, he had to believe everything she felt, that everything she did with him the previous two nights had come from the heart. He had to believe it, even though she'd given him every reason not to.

She turned her face to the warm spray and let it soothe her skin. He must have felt it, too, that connection between them. Maybe in some weird way, their connection had come from both of them having their lives upended by a serial killer.

She washed her hair and massaged some conditioner into it. Then she soaped up a washcloth and circled it on her skin.

"Are you okay in there?" The knock on the door made her drop the washcloth.

"Yes." She bent over at the waist to retrieve the washcloth from the tub and lurched to the side. "Oh!" She made a grab for the shower curtain, popping a few rings from the rod.

The bathroom door flew open, and Ryan emerged through the steam like some avenging god. "Did you fall?"

He flung back the damaged shower curtain and dropped beside the tub.

Kacie glanced at him from her embarrassing position of all fours in the tub, her hair still goopy with conditioner.

"I—I just dropped the washcloth and had a little trouble picking it up."

"You shouldn't be making any quick moves. And on top of it, you're probably still sore from the wreck yesterday." He placed both hands around her waist. "Sit down."

She rolled back to her bottom, folding her legs beneath her.

Taking the washcloth from her hand, he tapped her knee. "Stretch your legs out so you're flat in the tub. I don't want you toppling over again."

She obeyed and uncurled her legs, stretching them in front of her and scooting back in the tub.

He rose to his knees with the washcloth in his hands and finished the job she had started. She closed her eyes as he rubbed the washcloth across her flesh and down her back. He swirled it in circles down to where her backside met the porcelain. Then he swished it to her front, skimming it across her chest and beneath her breasts.

Now she really felt dizzy and it had nothing to do with that drug.

He dabbed her belly and flicked the washcloth between her legs and then swept it down the insides of her thighs.

He finished with her feet, massaging each toe as if she were some great work of art that needed precise cleaning.

"Can you stand up now to rinse off?"

After that sensuous washing, the only thing she wanted to do now was lie down—with him, on a bed, naked.

"Yes. Really, Ryan, you don't have to do this."

"Yeah, I do. Hang on to me."

She grasped his arm and he helped her stand.

He flicked up the lever for the shower and kept one arm firmly around her waist.

"You're going to get all wet."

"Too late. Rinse out your hair and I'll keep hold of you so you don't lose your balance again."

She let the water run across her body to rinse off the soap and then ducked her head in the spray.

Ryan turned off the water for her and with one arm reached for her towel on the rack.

Was he going to dry her off, too?

He tousled her hair first and then rubbed and blotted the towel across the rest of her body.

He could have taken her again, right against the wall. She wouldn't have fainted or fallen or lost her balance, but she might have screamed.

He flipped down the lid of the toilet and helped her from the tub. "Sit here and finish drying off—and leave this door open."

"You're soaking wet."

He glanced down at the T-shirt clinging to his chest and peeled it off in a single motion.

"There. Feel better?"

Moisture glistened on his smooth skin, enhancing the hard planes of muscle that shifted across his chest.

She swallowed. "Much."

"Holler if you need me. Room service should be here any minute." He stepped out of the bathroom, his wet T-shirt flung over one shoulder.

She finished drying herself and wrapped her hair in the damp towel. As she finished dressing, she heard a knock at the door. Ryan wouldn't open it and had the waiter leave the tray outside.

Did he think her abductor would try the same trick twice? After what had been going on, she'd been a fool to open the door to the waiter in the first place. She hadn't been thinking straight. She'd been excited at the thought of Ryan sending room service to her.

Heck, that shower scene had been a hundred times better than room service.

He called out, "Food's here. Are you doing okay?"

She checked her reflection in the mirror and shoved her damp hair from her face. She'd dry it after she ate.

She stepped into the room and spread her arms. "Presentable at last."

He grunted. "I thought you were damned presentable in the tub."

She ignored the comment. If they allowed this sexual tension to build between them again, there was only one outcome—bed. And she couldn't go there with him, not now. Not until they squared things between them.

"Smells good. What did you order?" She lifted the silver lid from a plate.

"Hamburgers, French fries and some salad, because you're always eating salad."

"The point is to eat salad instead of hamburgers and French fries, not in addition to." She snagged a French fry from the plate and bit into its salty, greasy goodness.

"After what you've been through, you deserve hamburgers, French fries *and* salad."

He dug into his own food, and she layered her burger with tomato, onion and pickles and took a big bite.

It tasted like heaven—calories be damned.

"Did you get any ibuprofen in the emergency room?"

"No. Don't they charge about twenty-five dollars for one pill?"

He shook a small bottle. "I have them for free. Aren't you still sore from the accident last night?"

She was sore from a lot of things. "I'll take one with my burger."

Ryan tapped one onto her plate and continued destroying his cheeseburger.

She finished her food and patted her mouth with a napkin. "I feel halfway human now."

"Good." He stacked his plate and hers onto the tray and poured himself another glass of iced tea from the pitcher. "Now tell me about your mother."

Her eye twitched above her bruised cheek, and she rubbed it. Guess he hadn't forgotten about her little lie.

"What do you want to know?"

"Her name, for starters."

"It's all in the file on the victims."

He shoved the tray out of the way. "I want to hear it from you—all of it."

"Her name was Layla French."

"Where's your biological father?"

The knife twisted in her gut. "I don't know. His name was Russ Langford, and he wasn't around. She'd always told me it was just the two of us. I always got the impression she'd never told him about me. Anyway, after my mother's murder, he never stepped up and I never gave him another thought."

"And the Mannings adopted you."

"I had no other family after the Phone Book Killer took my mom away from me." She sniffed but refused to let the tears fall. He'd see them as a ploy for sympathy. "The Mannings lived here, heard about my plight and petitioned to adopt me. Since there was nobody else beating down my door, Child Protective Services allowed the adoption. Then we moved to Seattle."

"Do you remember anything about your mother's murder?"

"She was here one day and gone the next. When my adoptive mom explained to me years later that Layla had been murdered, she told me that she'd been killed trying to help someone."

He nodded. "That's right. The Phone Book Killer used plaster to put his arm in a cast and then pretend he needed help."

"I just always like to picture it that way—she went out thinking she was lending someone a hand."

"And you always believed that someone was Detective Joseph Brody."

"Everything I ever read pointed to his guilt. Why would he jump from the Golden Gate Bridge at the height of the investigation if he wasn't guilty?"

"I've wondered that a million times." He rubbed his jaw and clasped his chin. "But why would someone threaten us for researching and writing this book if he were guilty?"

"That's what got me, Ryan. That's what changed my mind."

"Then why didn't you tell me about your mother?"

They were back to that. "Honestly?"

"Let's try that first—for a change."

She winced. "Because I wanted to protect myself. I knew how bad it would look if you found out."

"You figured I'd put the brakes on this project."

"I figured you'd put the brakes on us."

"And if there ever was going to be an us, exactly when did you figure you could safely tell me you'd believed at one point my father murdered your mother and you were out to prove it?"

She twisted her wet hair around one hand and studied the ends. "Maybe when we were bouncing grandkids on our knees."

His phone began to ring beside the glass and she nodded toward it.

"You'd better get that." It would save her from explaining herself any further. She'd spent two nights with the man and saw grandkids in their future. The embarrassing part of all that was she meant every word.

He looked at the lit display of his phone. "It's my department. Hey, Paul, whaddya got for me?"

His eyes narrowed to green slits and Kacie caught her breath. More bad news? Her aching body couldn't take any more.

"I see. Yeah, nothing we can do about that."

He ended the call and tapped his phone against his chin.

"Well?" She sat on the edge of her chair, gripping the sides.

"They did a trace on that blocked number on Cookie's phone."

"Who is it? Who called Cookie twice before she was attacked?"

"We don't know."

She slumped. "That's not helpful at all."

"We don't know who called because the trace goes back to a protected phone number."

"A protected phone number? What does that mean?"

"It's like classified information. Whoever called Cookie that day is someone in a position of authority. Seems Cookie had friends—or enemies—in high places."

Chapter Thirteen

"That doesn't mean this person in authority is the one who beat her."

"No, but it's another puzzle piece. Why would someone like that be using a protected number to call a Realtor? You'd think anyone house hunting would want to make communication as easy as possible."

"What kinds of people have these numbers?"

"Politicians, diplomats, police officers."

Kacie brushed some crumbs from the table and tipped them onto the tray. "I think we need to get to work on Christina's research."

"Did I say I wanted back on this project?"

"We can't stop now, Ryan. Don't give up on clearing your father's name because I betrayed you. It looks like we both finally have an opportunity to bring justice to our parents. We can't let that go, regardless of what is or isn't between us."

He stood, hoisted up the tray and walked toward the door. Kacie darted ahead of him and opened it for him.

As much as he wished there was nothing between them at this point, he couldn't deny his attraction to her. Hell, the smallest sound from the bathroom had him bursting into her shower. He knew what he'd find in there and he hadn't been able to stop himself. He'd wanted her smooth skin beneath his hands again. He'd wanted to climb into the tub with her and hold her, keep her safe.

He stood in the center of the room, hands on his hips. "Okay, let's go through Christina's research—together this time. I'll run up and get the box and you stay here, behind a locked door. Do not open it for anyone. I don't care if there are twenty room-service waiters outside bearing gifts."

"If I'm not opening the door, you'd better take this." She handed him her key card and he slipped it in his back pocket.

Five minutes later, he returned with the box in his arms and balanced it on his hip as he unlocked Kacie's door. He held his breath as he walked into the room, but she was sitting cross-legged on the bed, looking at her phone.

"Are you feeling up to this?"

She dropped her phone and snapped her fingers. "Bring it on. I'll be shuffling through some papers. It's not like we're doing hard manual labor."

"It's hard psychological labor." He tapped his head.

He joined her on the bed but put the box firmly between them.

"We can work at the desk if you like. I'm not so weak that I can't sit up in a chair."

"You may not be, but I am." He pinched his neck where it met his shoulder. "I'm still plenty sore from the car crash."

She reached behind him and plumped up an extra pillow. "Lean back."

Before he did, he grabbed a stack of files from the box and dropped them in his lap. "Let's start with the first victim."

"That would be my mother."

"I know, and I'm sorry, Kacie." He reached across the box and brushed the back of his hand along her cheek. "I never even told you that. I was so outraged that you'd kept your identity a secret from me, I never expressed my sympathy for your loss."

"We both lost, Ryan." She blinked her wide eyes. "I didn't expect your sympathy under the circumstances."

"Well, you have it. I'll take her case and you can look at the second murder victim, which is about the time the killer started contacting my father. Maybe a little distance and different perspective will do us both good."

He read through the file silently. Kacie's mother had been a waitress in the Lower Haight, at a seedy joint called the Hippy Shake, where the waitresses went topless more often than not. He slid a gaze at Kacie, who was engrossed in her own reading.

Layla French, if that was even her real name, had taken her baby daughter and left an abusive relationship with Russ Langford back home in Ohio. The cops contacted the ex-boyfriend, Kacie's father, in Ohio. Once the second murder occurred, the police had dropped the abusive-boyfriend angle.

This first case had seemed like a routine homicide investigation, with his father and his partner, Brett Stillwell, zeroing in on the fine clientele of the Hippy Shake. What had happened to the two Joes?

"Kacie, who was my father's partner on the second case?"

She lifted up the corner of a piece of paper. "Detective Stillwell. Why?"

He scratched his chin with the edge of the paper he was holding. "I always thought my father's partner was named Joe, like him. They called my father Joey and his partner Joe to avoid confusion."

"Could be Joe Stillwell. His first name isn't listed, or I haven't gotten to that part yet."

"I have. It's Brett Stillwell." He slid his phone from the nightstand and punched in Sean's number. His brother answered after two rings.

"What's up, Ry?"

Sean had given his department strict orders not to disturb him, so he knew nothing about the trouble—including the fact that Kacie Manning was the daughter of a murder victim—and Ryan intended to keep it that way.

He cleared his throat. "We're going through Christina's files and I have a question for you."

"Shoot."

"Who was Dad's partner in homicide?"

"For most of his career or during the Phone Book Killer investigation?"

"For most of his career."

"Joe Rigoletto. Joey and Joe."

"Why didn't he work this case with Dad? He was working with a Brett Stillwell instead."

"Joe Rigoletto was dead by the time of the first Phone Book murder."

"Dead?"

Kacie was peering at him over the top of the box, and he tapped Speaker for her.

Sean continued. "He died on the job, beside Dad. They were investigating a couple of murders related to a suspected drug dealer. They got a tip on the guy's whereabouts, and they were ambushed. Dad escaped injury but Joe wasn't so lucky. Happened about six months before the first Phone Book murder."

Kacie sucked in a breath.

"Who was that?"

"That was Kacie Manning." He glanced at the papers spread out on the bed. "We're working."

Sean shouted across the line. "Hey, Kacie, we're all looking forward to meeting you someday."

"Likewise."

"Is that it, Ry? Because I've got a lady waiting for me poolside."

"Yeah, and I can't wait to meet the woman who loosened Sean Brody up enough to get him to take an extended vacation."

"You'll meet Elise soon enough. You're gonna love her. She's sweet, straightforward, uncomplicated, honest—not at all like… Well, you'll meet her."

"Looking forward to it."

They ended the call and Ryan cupped the phone between his hands, his brow furrowing.

"She sounds like a paragon of virtue," Kacie offered.

"Huh? Who?"

"Elise." Kacie flipped back her hair along with another page of the file. "Sounds like a regular Mother Teresa."

"Umm, yeah. I heard from Eric that she's really nice, a kindergarten teacher from Montana or someplace like that. Not Sean's usual type, but then, his usual type never worked out for him."

"And who is this sweet, uncomplicated, *honest* woman not at all like?"

Ryan finally dragged his gaze away from the page in front of him and met Kacie's eyes. "What are you talking about?"

"Your brother, he mentioned on the phone that Elise was not at all like someone. Who's that someone?"

"Our mother. I told you, after Dad's death, she turned to booze and pills and never looked back. Her days were filled with hiding the stuff from us and obtaining it with phony prescriptions. Lies upon lies upon lies."

She looked down at her fidgeting fingers. "So, I guess

it's really important for you Brody boys to be with an honest woman, someone who will never lie to you like your mother did."

He snorted. "You'd think so, wouldn't you? But there's my brother Eric, who took back his fiancée after she kept his daughter from him. Can you imagine?"

"She had a baby with your brother and didn't tell him about it? And he took her back?"

"Extenuating circumstances. She had her reasons, and those two are made for each other—true love and all that."

"Must be nice."

Ryan tapped the tip of his pencil against the side of the box. "Don't you think that's weird?"

"That Eric took her back?"

"What? No. Don't you think it's weird that my dad's longtime partner in homicide died in an incident on the job six months before the case that would bring my dad down?"

"I guess Joey and Joe turned out to be the bad-luck duo."

"You could say that. But why is it that every time I look at this case, I find out something new and disturbing? You know my brother Eric was kidnapped during this case, right?"

"Yes."

"He just found out recently that some coven of witches was involved in his kidnapping."

Kacie hugged a file to her chest. "Do you think they also had something to do with the Phone Book Killer? Maybe he was a member of the coven? I don't remember the occult being associated with any of the slayings."

"It wasn't. I don't know where that leaves us, but I'd like to find out more about Joe Rigoletto's death."

"Marie Giardano?"

"Most likely."

Kacie uncurled her legs and stretched them in front of her, pointing her toes. "By the way, the killer started contacting your dad by leaving packages at the station for him. They contained notes with letters cut and pasted from magazines and bits of info about the crimes that only the killer could've known."

His gaze skimmed her calf where her pant leg had risen and settled on her delicate feet with her blue-painted toenails. What were they just discussing?

Notes.

He lined up his spine along the headboard, bumping his head against the wall. "The people who suspected him of being the Phone Book Killer always claimed he'd left those notes himself, maybe to garner publicity."

"Part of what led to their suspicions about him is that nobody ever saw anyone leave those notes." She crossed her legs at the ankle and began tapping her toes together.

Was she trying to torture him?

"Then they found some plaster in his car, suggesting he might have been making his own arm brace, just like the Phone Book Killer did." Ryan crossed his arms behind him, cradling his head against his laced fingers. "There had been one or two witnesses who reported that a man in a cast had been in the area where the victims were abducted."

"But nobody ever ID'd Joseph Brody. I'm not sure there was much of a case against him, just suspicion and innuendo."

He swung his legs off the bed and hunched forward on his knees. "A lot of that came from his own department, the brass."

"Usually a P.D. circles the wagons for one of its own. I thought your dad was a good cop, an excellent detective."

"Maybe they were worried about the stain on the department. From what I remember when Sean used to talk about this stuff all the time, there had been some bribery or something uncovered at the department not too long before these murders. They didn't want to go down that road again, so they jumped on the pithy evidence tying my father to the murders."

Kacie spread her hands. "There's so much here, I can't believe I ever thought your father was the Phone Book Killer."

"There's still a lot that doesn't add up. The biggest mystery of all is why he killed himself if he wasn't guilty."

"Maybe it had nothing to do with the case. Did you ever consider that possibility? Maybe he was ill or in some kind of other trouble. Gambling debts? Some kind of graft? You just said there'd been some trouble with the department prior to the murders."

"I suppose gambling and graft are better than murder."

She shoved a sheaf of papers from her lap and hopped from the bed. "I'm not trying to imply that your father was a criminal. Just looking at other possibilities. I spent too long with tunnel vision, believing what I wanted to believe."

"No offense taken. Just be honest with me, Kacie. That's all I ask."

"I swear, no more secrets." She drew a cross over her heart. "Back to the station tomorrow to conduct a follow-up? I want to know if they have any leads on Duke Bannister's murder."

"Then there's the attack on Cookie."

"There are so many loose ends, it's making me dizzy."

Closing her eyes, she massaged her temples and Ryan was at her side in a nanosecond. "Sit down. Let me get you some water."

She opened one eye and skewered him with it. "It was a figure of speech. I'm not really dizzy."

He squeezed her shoulders and laughed…and it felt good.

She felt good. "That's what you said when you headed into the bathroom, and look what happened in there."

"I toppled over reaching for the washcloth. It could've happened to anyone. I didn't need a shower assistant."

"I didn't hear you complaining." He raised one eyebrow at her, his blood stirring again.

"Who in their right mind would complain about…that?"

He traced her jaw with his thumb and then dropped his hands and stepped back. Could he trust this woman? Eric may have forgiven Christina for a much more egregious lie, but those two had history. He'd just met Kacie a week before, and she'd been lying to him from the get-go. What other secrets did she have up her sleeves?

She crossed her arms, tucking her fists against her body. "So, we'll meet tomorrow morning and head to the station?"

"You're not getting rid of me. I made a mistake leaving you on your own this morning."

Golden sparks flew from her eyes and her lush lips parted as her breath quickened.

"I'll bunk on the floor."

Her mouth snapped closed, and she compressed her lips into a thin smile. "Afraid I'll seduce you with my wicked, wicked ways?"

"Nope." He reached past her, grabbed two pillows and threw them on the floor. "I'm afraid of what I'll do to you."

WHAT HAD HE meant by being afraid of what he'd do to her? Kacie rolled onto her left side again to peer at the large, slumbering form on her hotel-room floor.

What did she know about Chief Ryan Brody anyway? One week before, she'd believed he was the third son of a serial killer, a killer who'd murdered her mother.

And now? Now she couldn't imagine her life without

him. She punched her pillow before scrunching it beneath her head. She'd come into this thing planning to remain cool, calm and collected. She'd pump Brody for information and tell her story, her way.

She'd been able to do that with a sociopath like Daniel Walker, but all her reason had flown out the window the minute Ryan had gathered her in his strong arms.

With thoughts of the murders spinning in her head and her sexy protector on the floor next to her, sleep was long in coming.

The next morning, Kacie woke up to the sound of the shower. She bolted upright. Ryan had packed up his make-shift bed, stacking the two pillows on the chair and folding the blanket on top of them.

Maybe if she heard a bump in the shower, she could come to his rescue. She'd be the best damned shower assistant he ever had. She'd soap up every inch of his body, not once but twice. She'd even climb in there with him. She'd kneel before him with the warm spray pounding her back, and she'd...

"Earth to Kacie."

She glanced up to find the object of her desire leaning out of the bathroom door, fully clothed. "I'll be done in a few minutes. Are you feeling okay?"

"I'm fine." Considering he'd just ruined a perfectly good daydream.

"Still sore?"

"Nothing a little pain reliever can't cure." And a warm shower with a special helper.

"I'll leave the bottle by the sink in here. I had to pop a few more myself. I think those air bags can do more damage than a steering wheel to the chest." He raised his inner forearms, which were still bruised by the air bag.

"Ouch."

"Do you mind if we stop off at my room so I can change into some clean clothes?"

"No problem." She stepped past him into the bathroom and started to swing the door closed.

He stopped it with his hand. "Are you steady on your feet now?"

Should she tell him another lie and say that she was about ready to collapse?

"I've had a good night's sleep and I'm fine. I'll leave the door unlocked if it makes you feel better."

"It would."

He removed his hand and she closed the door with a snap. She'd actually just told him another lie anyway. She did *not* have a good night's sleep.

She stepped into the tub and turned her back to the water. How could she have possibly slept with Ryan sprawled on her floor?

They could've shared the bed and kept their hands to themselves. She soaped up her hands and rubbed her body, her eyelashes fluttering. Who was she kidding? She wouldn't have been able to keep her hands to herself. Maybe if they laid a brick wall down the middle of the bed.

Ryan tapped on the door. "Doing okay in there?"

"Yeah, yeah."

"Is that what you call a short shower?"

It would've been short if she hadn't started daydreaming again and pretending her hands were Ryan's. They were a poor substitute anyway.

She turned off the water and toweled off before climbing out of the tub. She dressed in the bathroom and wiped the steam from the mirror with the towel, then pushed open the bathroom door and called into the other room. "We need to make a list of what to ask at the station. We've got the doll, Bannister's murder, Cookie's attack…"

He finished for her. "My car, your abduction and some questions for Marie about Joe Rigoletto."

She poked her head out of the bathroom. "Do you think the cops will run us out of town on a rail after all that?"

"I just know this all would've been easier if my brother were here."

"He'd come back if you called him, wouldn't he?"

"Sure, he would, but it's been so long since the guy's had a real vacation and even longer since he's had a real woman. My brothers and I have been telling him for years to relax, and now that he's finally taken our advice, I'm not going to reel him back in."

"Then you're doing the right thing. And he does have allies in the department."

"John Curtis. We can count on him."

"Then let's get going, after stops for clean clothes and breakfast."

When they hit the station, they made the rounds. The lab had gotten nothing from the doll that Daniel Walker denied ever sending to her, and the detectives had no leads on Bannister's murder or the attack on Cookie Phelps, who was still in a coma.

"Give me something, John." Ryan crossed his arms as he perched on the end of Detective Curtis's desk. "What about my car?"

"Aha!" Curtis held up one finger as he shuffled through some papers on his messy desk. "Your brake lines were cut."

"I figured that. Any idea who did it?"

"Someone who followed you to that taco stand in South San Francisco."

"That's brilliant. No wonder my brother insists on working with you."

"Ouch," John said with mock pain. "You small-town cops have no idea the pressures we face in the big city."

"I'll give you one more chance. Anything on the guy who tried to abduct Kacie?"

Curtis shook his finger at Ryan and smiled at Kacie. "You see? I was saving the best for last."

Kacie's pulse jumped. "You found him?"

"Not quite. Follow me to Lieutenant Healy's office. We got something from the hotel video camera."

Kacie squealed and grabbed Ryan's arm. "Finally."

"Don't get your hopes up. It's pretty grainy, but maybe you'll recognize the guy."

They approached Lieutenant Healy's office and Curtis knocked. "Brody and Ms. Manning are here to look at the video."

Healy looked up from his desk. "What the hell is going on here, Brody?"

"I guess someone doesn't want Ms. Manning to write this book."

"Drugging and kidnapping her is an odd way to stop her." He steepled his fingers and peered at Kacie over the pinnacle. "Are you sure this isn't related to your other book, Ms. Manning? The panic over the doll. Bannister's warning from Daniel Walker. Isn't this just more of the same?"

"I don't think so. Walker doesn't know or have any interest in Cynthia Phelps."

"Ah, but Cookie's predicament could be due to her past as a hooker. Some pimps never forget."

"If we can get to the bottom of all these attacks, maybe that's exactly what we'll discover, but we need to get to the bottom of them first."

He spun his laptop around to face them. "Then start here. Do you recognize that man? We're pretty sure he's the one who forced the hotel employee to deliver that room service to your door and then jabbed you with a needle."

She bent forward at the waist and squinted at the grainy footage. A middle-aged man with graying hair and what looked like a scarf around his neck loped through a side door of the hotel.

"Is that the best you got?"

"That's it, but if you look at his neck, that could be his ski mask pulled down."

"Yes, I see that."

"The hotel is sure he's no guest, and the timing of his entrance into the hotel matched the timing of your abduction."

"Wait—play it again and stop it when he turns his face to the side."

She stared at the profile of the man who'd drugged her and forcibly removed her from the hotel and felt—nothing. He was a stranger. Grayish hair curled at the nape of his neck, and his prominent nose might make him stand out from a crowd, but she didn't recognize him.

She turned to Ryan. "Have you ever seen him before?"

"Nope."

"Oh well, at least it's something. I'd probably recognize him if I saw him again, so he's lost the element of surprise."

Healy held up a pencil and tested its point. "Why do you suppose he tried to kidnap you?"

"I have no clue, but your tone of voice indicates you might."

Ryan had stepped closer to her, brushing her arm with his. "Let's hear it, Lieutenant."

"Just seems convenient that Brody here was able to rescue you in time, and the perp just drops you and is able to get away, even though he looks about half Brody's size and strength."

Ryan tensed beside her. "Go on."

"Would be a nice little companion story to the release of the book—author gets abducted while writing the true-crime story of the Phone Book Killer."

Ryan clenched a fist, and she covered it with her hand. "Yeah, okay, I want another bestseller so badly I'm willing to hire someone to bash a poor kid on the side of the head and inject me with a horse tranquilizer. Save your theories for the movie script, Lieutenant, and just do your job."

Curtis glared while Healy snatched his laptop. "We'll let you know if we discover anything else."

"I'm sure you will." Ryan applied pressure to the small of her back and she turned and walked out of the office.

After they had shut the lieutenant's office door and had walked halfway down the hallway, Kacie sputtered, "What a jackass."

Curtis patted her arm. "That's the lieutenant for you. Don't take it personally."

"Keep us posted, John. You know where to find me."

"You keep us posted, Brody. This whole thing is getting crazy."

Ryan jabbed the button for the elevator. "At least we know what the guy looks like—sort of. I think that hotel needs to upgrade its security cameras."

"They need to upgrade their entire security system. At the rate I'm going there, they'll have to comp me a full year's stay."

He held a finger to his lips. "Shh. Don't give Healy any ideas. He'll probably accuse you of trying to score freebies all over the city next."

"Wouldn't put it past him."

The elevator doors opened on the smiling face of Ray Lopez. He held up his hand in greeting. "How's the book coming along, Kacie?"

"Just fine, thanks."

"Call me if you want a coauthor."

When they got in the elevator, Ryan mumbled, "Talk about jackasses."

When they reached their floor, they opened the door to the records area.

A young blonde with a bright smile greeted them. "Hello. What can I do for you?"

Ryan's eyebrows met over his nose. "Where's Marie?"

"Oh, you haven't heard?" The woman looked both ways as if the boxes surrounding her had ears. "Marie's gone."

Chapter Fourteen

Blood thrumming against his eardrums, Ryan clawed at the mesh screen dividing him from this woman who wasn't Marie.

"What are you talking about? Where is she?"

The woman took a step back. "We don't know. Who are you again?"

Ryan fumbled in his pocket and whipped out his badge and ID. "I'm Ryan Brody, chief of police in Crestview. Detective Sean Brody's my brother."

"Okay, I know you. Anyway, Marie took off. Nobody knows where she went."

"What does that mean?"

"Wait a minute." Kacie tapped her fingertips against his forearm. "You mean she went on vacation?"

Ryan blinked. Maybe it was as simple as that. Just because Marie had been paranoid didn't mean she'd disappeared.

He took a deep breath. "Is that it? She took some time off?"

"I guess so, but she didn't put it on the calendar and she didn't tell anyone."

"What do you mean?" Ryan rattled the cage. "Why are you talking in riddles?"

The woman's skin flushed red. "I don't mean to, sir, but you're not letting me get a word in edgewise."

"She's right." Kacie squeezed his arm. "Let her start from the beginning. What's your name?"

The woman flicked her eyes toward Kacie and licked her lips. "My name's Sheila Moriarty. I'm filling in for Marie. Yesterday she just didn't show up for work."

Ryan opened his mouth, but Kacie pinched his side and he shut it.

"She's usually prompt, so when she still wasn't here by nine o'clock, someone called her at home and on her cell. She didn't answer. One of the officers dropped by her place and it looked like she'd taken off in a hurry. Her closet doors and dresser drawers were standing open. No purse, no phone, no car."

"No signs of violence?" Ryan finally uncurled his fingers from the mesh, but his heart was still pounding against his rib cage.

"Officer Reynolds didn't see any signs of violence. It looks like she left in a hurry."

"Did any neighbors see her leave?"

"You know what?" She grabbed a card and scribbled on it. "I'm going to give you Officer Reynolds's info, and you can ask him all the questions you want. In the meantime, did you come down here for something specific, Chief Brody?"

"Yeah, I came down here to talk to Marie, but since that's not possible, I want to look at anything you have about the on-the-job shooting of a Detective Joe Rigoletto."

Sheila wrinkled her nose as she typed on her keyboard. "That doesn't sound familiar to me. When did that happen?"

"About twenty years ago."

Sheila stopped typing and dropped her jaw. "I don't think I'm going to find that."

"It hasn't been filed electronically yet, but you probably still have the paper files."

"I have no idea how I'd find that." She spread her hands.

"I know Marie's system. Do you want to let us in and we'll give it a shot ourselves?"

She glanced over her shoulder. "I don't know."

"Look, nobody has to know, and I won't even sign your log."

Sheila chewed her bottom lip and then hit the buzzer that unlocked the cage. "I guess so. Just don't tell anyone I let you back here to roam around."

"Believe me, we're not telling anyone."

He placed a hand on Kacie's back and propelled her through the door, just in case Sheila changed her mind.

When they reached the dusty boxes in the back of the room, Kacie whispered, "What do you think happened to Marie?"

"I hope her paranoia got the best of her and she took off for parts unknown for a while. I just wish she would've gone through proper channels. She would've attracted less attention that way."

"Maybe something spooked her."

"There's a lot of that going around." He knocked on one of the boxes on the shelf. "Let's see what we can find."

They took down the files for the year they were looking for and began reading the labels aloud to each other. Then they started spilling into the next year.

Kacie stood on her tiptoes to peer at a box on the top shelf. "Maybe they don't keep the officer-involved shootings or deaths down here."

"Maybe."

"Why don't you ask John? He seems like someone you can trust."

He tugged on his earlobe and narrowed his eyes. "We're

in a police station. Are you implying we can't trust anyone here?"

"Marie didn't."

He ran his eye across the shelf where the file on Rigoletto's shooting should've been. Had someone beat them to it? And if so, why?

Why did nothing seem to add up anymore?

"Another dead end. Seems like we're running into a lot of those."

Kacie took his hand. "Maybe someone up there is trying to tell us something—maybe it's our parents trying to tell us something."

"Are you saying you want to give up on the story?"

She glanced down at their entwined hands. "When I wrote that book on Walker and began to realize he had killed his family, I was scared of facing such evil day after day when I interviewed him. I was afraid of tricking him, and I was afraid of what he'd do when he discovered I'd tricked him. But Walker was a known threat, and he was locked up. I don't know what, or who, I'm facing here."

He pointed to the ceiling. "You have a picture of the man who tried to abduct you."

"And it means nothing. I really don't know if I'd even recognize that face in a crowd. There are other forces at work here." She waved her arm around the records room. "Forces we can't see."

He pulled her close. "I'll be here to protect you, Kacie. You know that, right?"

"I knew it once, before you discovered my true colors."

Did she blame him for her kidnapping? He tightened his hold on her. "I should've never sent you back to your room alone that morning."

Her spine stiffened, and she drew back from his embrace. "That wasn't your fault, Ryan. You know how I got in trouble that morning? I put myself there with my lies. I'm surprised you even came back to check on me. I didn't deserve it. I came into this project with the intent of turning the tables on the sons of Joseph Brody."

"But it didn't work out that way. You were open enough to see the truth."

"It didn't work out that way because I wasn't counting on falling for one of the sons of Joseph Brody."

Did she think she had to tell him that so he wouldn't believe the two nights they'd spent together were a sham?

He brushed the hair from the nape of her neck. "It was all too fast between us."

"And because of that you think it wasn't real?"

He knew it was real on his end, but he wasn't going to open himself up to getting used. "One thing at a time, Kacie. We mixed adrenaline and lust into a high-octane cocktail that exploded in our faces."

Sheila called from the front. "Are you two done back there? I'm ready to lock up for lunch."

Ryan shrugged and said, close to Kacie's ear, "I guess we're done."

She pivoted out of his arms and strode toward the front of the cage. She smiled brightly at Sheila. "That's it for us."

"Didn't find anything?" Sheila's head swiveled from left to right, looking at their empty hands.

"We saw the area where the case files should've been, but they weren't there."

"Well, that's some old stuff." She jingled her keys in her palm as if to remind them she wanted them out.

"Thanks anyway, Sheila—and sorry for coming on so strong before. Marie Giardano's a friend of mine, and I'm a little worried about her sudden departure."

"I understand. We're all a little worried, but it looks like she left of her own free will."

As they walked out of the room, Ryan leaned toward Kacie. "I'm not so sure about that."

When the elevator doors closed, Kacie asked, "Are you going to talk to John Curtis about any of this? Rigoletto? Marie?"

"I was just thinking we should invite John to lunch."

"Sounds like a good idea."

They located John in the squad room and extended their invitation.

"Let me wrap up a few things," he said, "and I'll meet you at the sandwich place down the street. As for Marie, I think she's okay."

Later at the sandwich shop, they found a table. They picked up lunch and a couple of fountain drinks while they waited for John.

Ryan stretched his legs in front of him. "Is your book a complete shambles now?"

"It's not moving in a linear progression, if that's what you mean."

"Did the other one?"

"It was different." She chewed on her straw. "The case had already been solved. Walker had been tried and convicted by the time I wrote the book."

"But didn't you start that book believing he was innocent?"

"I was certainly willing to give him a chance. His defense seemed so compelling."

"How soon after you met him did you begin to doubt him?"

"It wasn't meeting him so much, because he's charming and convincing. It was reviewing the evidence. While the media were busy buying into Walker's B.S., they neglected to reveal some of the true facts of the case. I looked at those facts, and it became pretty clear to me. Then the book became more of a psychological study of Walker."

"The so-called facts of this case are a lot less compelling, aren't they?"

"That's just it—there are very few facts. Plaster in your father's car to make an arm cast? So what? He maintained it was planted, didn't he?"

"Yep."

"And there was no proof it wasn't—no receipts indicating your father purchased the materials, no witnesses putting your father near these victims. Nothing was there really, except the fact that the killer was communicating with your father and then the kicker, that your father jumped from the bridge."

"Yep, that was the kicker."

"Can anyone join this party?" Curtis hovered over the table, balancing a tray with a sandwich and a bag of chips on it.

Ryan kicked out the chair across from him. "Have a seat, John. We were just talking about my father's case."

"What else?" He sat down, unloaded his food from the tray and then twisted around to put the tray on another table.

"First off, what do you know about Marie's disappearance?"

"Not much, but she was dropping some pretty broad hints the day before she left. I think she was trying to tell me not to worry."

"Is this going to hurt her retirement?" Ryan shook the ice in his cup.

"Not if I can help it."

"Do you think she left because of us? Because of this book?"

"I wouldn't say you in particular, but it's been building.

Started with Sean's case. You know, our own fingerprint guy was the Alphabet Killer."

"Yeah, I knew that."

"Then your other brother Eric was out here looking into another set of murders. Nothing to do with your father's case, but he was snooping around in Records, too."

"Speaking of snooping around in Records, Kacie and I just went down there to look up the files on Dad's partner."

"Stillwell?"

"No, the one before that. Rigoletto."

"Killed in the line of duty."

"That's the one."

"Why are you looking into that, Brody?"

"That incident occurred about six months before everything started going downhill for my father."

"And you think they're related?"

"You can't deny it's a coincidence. Two partners dead within six months of each other."

"It happens, Brody. Maybe not in the small town of Crestview, but in the big city it's not uncommon. Lotta stress here."

"That's bull. Stress maybe, but death? Even for a big department like San Francisco's, deaths on the job aren't that common. I know that was before your time, but did you ever hear anything about it?"

"Detective Joseph Rigoletto's picture is hanging on the wall at the station, but I don't know much more about it. I think his widow's still alive and living in the city. Marie knew her."

"Who didn't Marie know?" Kacie balled up the paper from her sandwich and tossed it onto her tray.

"That's the point." Curtis made a gun with his fingers. "She knows too much and maybe that's why she took off."

"Will you help me look her up?"

"Do you mean, will I use the department's resources to locate her for you? Sure. You're my partner's brother. When's he coming back to work, anyway?"

"When he's good and ready."

Back at the station, it didn't take Curtis long to locate Joe Rigoletto's widow. He jotted down her address on a pink message slip and slid it across the desk to Ryan. "You didn't get this from me."

They drove south out of the city to Mrs. Rigoletto's home in the suburbs.

When they pulled to the curb across the street from the neat house, Kacie put a hand on his arm. "Do you think we should burst in on her unannounced? She's elderly, isn't she? Wasn't Rigoletto older than your father?"

"Yeah, but I don't want to give Mrs. Rigoletto a chance to suddenly head out of town on a much-needed vacation."

"Okay, I'll follow your lead."

Ryan knocked on the door. He could tell they were being looked over from the vantage point of the peephole.

He flipped out his badge and held it up. "Mrs. Rigoletto? I'm Chief Ryan Brody. I'd just like to ask you a few questions."

The dead bolt clicked and he blew out a breath.

When the door swung open, he raised his eyebrows. Either Mrs. Rigoletto had aged incredibly well, or Rigoletto had married a much younger woman.

"Mrs. Rigoletto?"

The woman narrowed her eyes. "No, I'm her daughter, Rebecca Leeds."

"I'm Ryan Brody. This is Kacie Manning. We'd like to ask your mother a few questions about your father's incident."

"Brody…?" Rebecca grasped the doorjamb. "I know

who you are. Do you really think delving into my father's death is going to help your father?"

"I don't know. Didn't you ever wonder how it came about that the two partners were both dead within six months of each other?"

"I was in my late twenties when it happened. Dad's death destroyed Mom, and then when your father committed suicide, she fell apart even more."

"Happened to a lot of people."

"I'd met your dad once or twice. He was a great guy. My father always sang his praises. Said he could retire with ease, knowing detectives like Joey Brody were taking his place."

"Does your mother remember much about your father's murder? I tried to find the case file, but I couldn't locate it."

"Does she remember much about my father's murder?" Rebecca widened the door and ushered them into the house. "Follow me."

They trailed after her into an airy, open kitchen where a woman with bright red hair sat at a table with a pair of scissors and magazines spread before her.

"Ma, this is Ryan Brody, Joey Brody's son. Do you remember Joey Brody?"

Mrs. Rigoletto turned a pair of faded blue eyes on him and arched one eyebrow. "Is he the plumber? Because that faucet is still leaking. Or is it a bunker?"

"Is what a bunker?" Rebecca shrugged at Ryan.

"The thing that's leaking."

"It's called a faucet, Ma. You were right the first time. Faucet."

"Are you the plumber?"

Rebecca rubbed her mother's back. "No, I'm Rebecca, your daughter."

"Tell the plumber to fix the bunker."

Rebecca turned the page of one of the magazines. "These are pretty dresses. Cut these out, Ma."

The scissors began to slice through the glossy pages, and Ryan shook his head at Kacie, whose wide eyes glimmered with tears.

Rebecca stepped away from her mother and pulled out a couple of stools at the kitchen island. "My mom can't remember what a faucet is. She's not going to remember what happened twenty years ago."

"I'm sorry, Rebecca."

"Yeah, life's a bitch and then you get Alzheimer's or… worse. Why are you looking into this now?"

Ryan straddled a stool. "Kacie's writing a book about my father. When I discovered his partner, your father, had been killed in a shoot-out six months before everything came down on my dad, I figured we needed to look into it more."

"You're brave, digging into all that old stuff. I like to pack it up and put it away." She glanced at her mother. "In some ways, the memory loss is a blessing."

Kacie asked, "What do you remember about that time, Rebecca?"

"It was an ambush. They were anxious to interview a drug dealer about a couple of murders on his turf. A snitch dimed him off, and your father and mine went out to an abandoned warehouse in the Tenderloin to track him down. They didn't even make it to the door. My father was gunned down in the street and yours took cover behind their car and returned fire, calling it in."

"Did the police ever make an arrest in the case?"

"Oh yeah." She folded her hands on the counter. "Turns out it was the snitch."

Kacie tilted her head. "Why'd he do it?"

"I don't know. Making points on the street? Maybe someone blew his cover and he had to prove himself. He didn't share his motives with us." Rebecca's knuckles turned white. "I only saw him once. He pled out and we went to the courthouse for his sentencing. He had dead eyes. No emotion whatsoever."

Ryan clasped the back of his neck. It was a rare snitch who turned on his benefactors. "Is he still in the joint?"

"He died in there several years ago—shanked. What goes around comes around."

Another death in a long line of them. Another dead end.

Tapping the counter, Ryan said, "Sorry to bother you, Rebecca. Thanks for the info."

She came around the counter and swept scraps of paper from the kitchen table into her hand. "Maybe you should just let it go, Ryan. Nobody who knew Joey Brody believed for one minute he was the Phone Book Killer."

"He did jump off the Golden Gate Bridge."

"That he did."

Mrs. Rigoletto dropped her scissors. "Joey Brody didn't jump off the bridge."

Rebecca crouched beside her mother. "Do you remember Joey Brody, Ma?"

"Is he the plumber?" Her restless, blue-veined hands hovered above her paper-doll cutouts.

Rebecca heaved a sigh, plucked up the scissors and shrugged at Ryan. "I'll call the plumber."

Ryan knelt before Mrs. Rigoletto, who was happily brandishing her scissors again, and placed a hand on her knee. "You take care, Mrs. Rigoletto."

Her face crumpled for a moment, and the blue eyes seemed to focus on his face. "Joey Brody never jumped from that bridge."

Ryan squeezed her knee. "Goodbye."

When they got to the front door, Rebecca waved a hand in the direction of her mother. "Sorry about all that."

"Is she ever lucid?" Kacie stepped onto the porch ahead of him.

"Occasionally. She goes in and out. More out these days."

Kacie took her hand. "Well, bless you for taking care of her."

"Oh, I'm no saint." Rebecca laughed. "There's a passel of Rigolettos, and we all take turns. We have a caregiver, too."

"Then you're all saints. Thanks for your time."

Ryan waved and turned toward the street. "That's gotta be tough. At least my mom recognized us even when she was in a drug-induced haze."

When they got to the car, Kacie pulled out a pad of paper and started jotting down notes.

"Are you putting down what she told us?"

"Every little bit helps. Detective Joe Rigoletto will have a place in this story, even if it doesn't lead us to the truth."

"It doesn't seem as if anything is leading us to the truth."

They drove back into the city, and as always, Ryan caught glimpses of the Golden Gate Bridge as he maneuvered the car through the city streets, cresting the hills. If those barriers on the bridge could talk...

He parked his rental car in the lot below the hotel, and they took the elevator up to the lobby.

As they ambled across the carpet, the hotel clerk, Michael, called to Kacie. "Ms. Manning?"

She pivoted on the carpet and mumbled to Ryan, "Are they going to compensate me for my near-abduction by giving me the hotel?"

"They should."

When they reached the counter, Ryan asked, "How's your employee? The one who got cracked over the head?"

"He's doing fine, but he's spooked."

"I heard he couldn't identify his assailant."

"The guy was wearing a ski mask when he approached him, but he looked at the video and ID'd the guy from his clothing. Hopefully, they can get him from that."

"I'm glad he's okay." Kacie tapped the counter. "Is that why you called me over?"

"No. Actually, someone left you a note at the front desk."

Ryan's pulse picked up. "Who? Did you see him?"

"I wasn't working at the time. We left a message on the phone in your room, but I saw your name on the note and when I noticed you come in I thought I'd save you a trip up to your room and back down here."

"I appreciate it. Do you have the note?"

He stepped back from the counter. "I have the envelope right here." He slapped the white envelope on the counter.

"Thanks." Kacie swept the envelope from the polished wood. She carried it to the collection of love seats where they'd opened the package containing the doll not more than a week before.

She sank to the edge of one of the seats and ripped the envelope open with one finger. She shook out the single piece of paper and gasped.

"What is it?" His fingers itched to snatch it from her hand.

"This may be the lead we're looking for."

"Kacie, what is it?"

She waved the paper at him. "Someone's finally willing to talk, someone who may know the truth."

He couldn't take it anymore. He plucked the note from her fingertips and the words danced before his eyes. *I know the truth and I'm ready to tell all.*

Ryan crumpled the paper in his fist and slammed it against his knee—not at all the reaction she was expecting from him.

"Did you read the rest of it? He wants to meet with me. He left a number."

"Who is this, another Duke Bannister? You're not meeting with this person."

"I'm going to call him, Ryan. This is how I get a lot of my leads."

"A lot of your leads end up putting you in harm's way."

She worked the crumpled paper from his fist and smoothed it out on her knee. "It's a phone number. It can't hurt to call."

"Let's take this upstairs."

Ryan kept a firm hand on her back as they went up to her room, as if he could protect her that way from the person who'd written her the note.

Who *had* written the note? Could it have been Rebecca Leeds, having had a change of heart? No, they'd just left her place. Marie Giardano?

As soon as her room door closed, she reached for her cell phone.

"Wait." Ryan put out a hand. "Call on Speaker. And there's no way you're meeting this person alone, if that's what he's asking. And we're calling the police this time."

"Okay, okay." She would have agreed to any of his terms at that point. They needed some fresh information, a fresh point of view.

With shaky fingers, she tapped in the number from the note.

A gruff voice answered after the first ring. "Kacie?"

Her heart skipped a beat. Did he have her phone number, too? "Yes. How'd you know that?"

"You're the only one who has this number, Kacie. Do you want the truth? You and Brody?"

Her gaze shifted to Ryan's narrowed eyes. "Yes, of course. You mean the truth about Joey Brody and the real Phone Book Killer, right?"

"That's right, sweetheart."

She hunched her shoulders. "What is it? What is the truth? Tell me now."

He laughed and coughed at the same time. "It ain't that simple. I want to meet you."

Ryan shook his head back and forth so vigorously a lock of dark hair fell over his eye.

"I'll meet you, but you have to satisfy some conditions."

"I'm the one with the 411. Why are you calling the shots? You remind me of someone."

"Let me guess—your sister?"

"I ain't got no sister."

"Good. I'm not meeting you alone."

"Bring Brody with you. Is that what you want? He deserves the truth, too."

Ryan's jaw tensed and a muscle jumped in his throat.

"I will bring him. When and where?"

"No time like the present. Meet me down at the wharf at eleven tonight."

"I met someone else at the wharf earlier this week. It didn't end so well."

"Duke? He was an amateur."

"You knew him?"

"I know his kind. In over his head."

"And you're not?"

"I never spent a day in prison, sweetheart."

"Congratulations. Where are we meeting on the wharf? At the busy end. Someplace public."

"No. What I have to say to you and Brody is private. I'm lettin' you bring your big, strong man with you. That should be good enough. And do I have to tell you no cops? Calling the cops will only hurt you."

Her eyes met Ryan's and she shrugged. "I don't know."

"Are you telling me Brody's too scared to meet with me?"

"I'm not too scared to meet with you, but if you so much as touch Kacie, you're a dead man."

"I believe you, Brody." He hacked out a cough again. "Eleven o'clock by the submarine. There's a nice view of the bridge from there."

He hung up before Ryan could respond.

Kacie cupped the phone in her hand. "It sounds promising, doesn't it?"

"Why? Just because some guy calls out of the blue, seems to know what you're working on and tells you he has information? This could be anyone, Kacie. I don't like it."

"Of course you don't like it, but it's the way I work."

"And this is the way *I* work." He punched a number into his own phone and said, "I need to speak to Detective John Curtis or Lieutenant Healy."

As he paused, she grabbed his arm. "He said no cops."

He held his hand over the receiver. "The cops are not going to stake out a meeting between an author and a source. I just want them to be aware of what's going down."

He got Curtis on the phone and told him about the anonymous phone call. "Yeah, I have my weapon, and I'll keep you posted."

"What are they going to do?"

"Nothing for now, but they might send a patrol car over if one's in the area. Maybe they'll just sit there as reinforcement in case he tries something."

"I have a good feeling about this, Ryan. I heard something in his voice."

"Yeah, cigarettes and hard living. Sounded a lot like Duke Bannister."

"With one major difference."

"He doesn't have a sister?"

"He's never been to prison."

The rest of the evening dragged by, and although Ryan managed to scarf down a big meal from room service, she barely touched her pasta.

She had instincts and she had a feeling about this one.

When the digital clock ticked over to 10:30, she put on a pair of running shoes and yanked a hooded sweatshirt from the hook by the door. "I'm ready."

"We're about a ten-minute walk from the sub. Relax."

"Impossible." She bounced on the edge of the bed.

Ryan knelt in front of her, placing his hands on her knees. "I need to get back to Crestview in a few days. When I go, I want you to leave this alone."

Her breath caught in her throat. She'd almost forgotten he had a job to get back to. She'd almost forgotten he had another life beyond this city, beyond this hotel, beyond this case.

"I can't leave it alone, Ryan." She curled her hands around his biceps. "I'm writing this book."

"When you started writing the book, you had no idea it would lead to dead bodies, disappearances and your own kidnapping. It's a good thing I was here through all of that, but I can't be here forever."

"You mean you can't be with me forever."

"I didn't mean that." He put his hands around her waist. "I can't say what's going to happen between us, but if anything does, it's going to have to be away from all this. It's the only way to tell if it's for real."

"I know what's real, Ryan Brody. My feelings for you are real." She rested her cheek on top of his hair. "Are you telling me there can be no us as long as I'm working on this book?"

"I don't know, Kacie." He kissed her and whispered in her ear. "It's time to go."

They walked to the wharf hand in hand. Was he right? Did the feelings they had for each other now exist in some alternate reality where fear and danger fueled their attraction? Would they have to step away from the fire to see the truth?

They crossed the street to the wharf and turned left, toward the submarine. A cop car crawled down the street and Kacie poked Ryan in the ribs. "Do you think that's our backup?"

"Possibly." He patted his jacket pocket. "I've got our first line of defense right here."

"I'm hoping it won't come to that. He'll give us the info we've been waiting for and slither back under his rock."

"Don't count on it." He squeezed her hand, but it didn't soften his words.

Their steps slowed as they approached the closed ticket counter for the submarine. Ryan turned his back to the counter, his posture erect and alert.

A man climbed the steps to the walkway. "You made it."

"We're here. Now, what do you have for us?" Kacie took a step forward at the same time the man stepped under the circle of light from the lamp hanging above his head.

"Stop." Ryan grabbed her arm and yanked her back. "Don't you recognize him, Kacie? He's the man who tried to abduct you."

Kacie stumbled back against Ryan's chest as she squinted across the darkness—same height, same prominent nose, same gray hair.

Her heart pounded. "It's you, isn't it?"

"Guilty as charged." The man spread his arms wide. "But I can explain."

Ryan drew his gun from his pocket and released the safety with a click. "You'd better start explaining right now."

"I just wanted to talk to you, Kacie."

"And *that's* the method you chose? Drugging me? Carrying me off in my pajamas?"

"It seemed like a good plan at the time. I had a car waiting by the side of the hotel. I was just going to whisk you away for a private meeting, a little one-on-one time."

"Why? Why all this scheming?"

"I figured if I told you the truth, you'd never agree to meet me."

"That you had information for me? Why wouldn't I agree to meet you?"

"It's more than that, sweetheart."

"Stop calling me that."

"What's the truth? Let's hear it." Ryan had taken a step forward, shielding her body with his.

"The truth? I'm your father, Kacie. I'm Russ Langford. Layla French was my girl. She had my daughter on February fourteenth—Kacie Louise. 'Louise' after my mother."

Her body stiffened as the truth of his words hit her. "Why now? Why are you contacting me now and what do you have to do with the Brody case?"

"The Brody case is *my* case."

Ryan waved his gun. "What the hell are you talking about?"

"Kacie, I'm your father and I'm the Phone Book Killer."

Chapter Fifteen

His words roared in her ears and seemed to echo up and down the wharf. Then she laughed, a high-pitched giggle that frightened her as much as his proclamation had.

Ryan wound his arm around her waist as if to hold her up.

He growled at the man. "What are you talking about? Your ex was one of the Phone Book Killer's victims."

"The first and the only one who mattered."

"Wh-what are you saying? You killed my mother?"

"She'd left me and had taken you with her."

"You abused her."

Ryan's arm tightened around Kacie's waist.

"That's what they called it, but what we had was explosive." He shrugged. "We lost control sometimes."

"*You* lost control."

"Wait a minute." Ryan squared his shoulders. "Are you saying you killed Layla French, and then someone else killed the others, and because the M.O. was the same, Layla's murder was tied to the others?"

"No, Brody. I'm saying I was the Phone Book Killer. I killed Layla, and then I killed the others to cover the motive. After Layla's murder, the cops were trying to find me in Ohio. I killed the others to get them off my trail."

"You killed other people just to cover one crime?" Her stomach flipped and she felt like vomiting.

"It's not like I hadn't done it before. There were a few people in Ohio I had to get rid of."

Kacie gagged and covered her mouth.

"That's one of the reasons Layla left me. She had her suspicions."

Ryan snorted. "So all that bull about true love is just that. You came after Layla because you were afraid she'd rat you out."

"There was that."

"And the notes to my father? The kidnapping of my brother? Why did you go through all that?"

He pushed his hands forward. "I didn't."

"Liar. The Phone Book Killer contacted my father when he started investigating the second murder."

"It wasn't me. I told you. I've never been to prison, and that's why. I always kept a low profile. I'd never contact a cop like that."

"You're saying some random person started sending those notes? And what about the kidnapping?"

"I never touched your brother. Why would I do that?"

"Oh, I don't know. You're a cold-blooded killer."

Kacie was leaning so heavily against him he was afraid she was going to fall over. Her body had started trembling and shaking.

"Believe me or not, Brody. I had nothing to do with your brother's kidnapping or those notes to your father."

"I don't believe you, Langford. Why are you coming forward now after all these years?"

He shifted from one foot to the other. "Because my daughter's writing a book, and I want to give her a story. I owe her that."

"You owe me that? You owe me my mother."

"You know, sweetheart, you ended up better off. That

nice family adopted you and moved you up to Seattle. Your mother was a whore."

Kacie's trembling stopped and her muscles tensed.

"Shut the hell up, Langford. You murdered your daughter's mother and you think she needs a story? What are you really after?"

"Okay, you got me. I also happen to be dying—lung cancer. What do I have to lose now?"

"Then you can end your miserable life by telling the whole truth. What happened to my father?"

"He killed himself, as far as I know. Once that happened, I figured it was a good time to leave the city."

"And Bannister? You killed him because he was going to tell Kacie the truth?"

"I never touched Bannister."

"You beat up Cookie for the same reason?"

"I don't know any Cookie."

"Just stop lying." Kacie took a step toward her father, but Ryan held on to her arm. "You're dying. Just stop with the lies, unless that's a lie, too."

He coughed as if to prove the veracity of his claim. "Why would I lie now? Everything I told you tonight is the truth. I killed your mother because she left me. She wasn't my first kill, and she wasn't my last. I tried to disguise my motive by killing others in the same way, and I did pick them out of the phone book, within reason. I did not send any notes to Detective Brody, I did not kidnap his son, and the only thing I've done since I've been back in this city is try to get close to you, sweetheart."

"Don't. Call. Me. Sweetheart."

Langford chuckled. "Feisty, just like your mother. But that feistiness got her in trouble. So watch yourself, sweetheart."

Kacie wrenched away from Ryan and flew at her father.

"Kacie, stop!"

Before Ryan could reach them, Langford had his arm around Kacie's neck and a gun to her head.

He raised his own weapon. "Let her go. This isn't what you came here for."

"It's not, but I won't put up with this stuff from any woman. And you wonder why I drugged you in the first place? I wanted to have control when I made my confession to guard against something like this."

"Now you've made your confession. Let her go and be on your way."

Langford tightened his hold on Kacie. "You're not going to write any of this until I'm gone, right?"

She coughed and gagged.

"She can't breathe. Let her go. Even if she does write your story, she can't prove any of it."

"I don't need the cops investigating me before I kick the bucket."

Kacie gasped. "I'm not writing this story. Let me go and disappear. I never want to see you again."

"I don't know. Maybe this wasn't such a good idea. I thought you'd be grateful. Instead you're just like your mother, just like Layla."

He wrapped his arm tighter around Kacie's neck and she kicked his shin. He staggered back and the hand with the weapon dropped.

Kacie twisted away from him, and Ryan charged. He knocked the older man backward.

Langford still had his weapon, and he swung it toward Kacie. Ryan rolled between them and tensed his body, ready for the bullet meant for Kacie.

The shot rang out and Langford grunted. Had he missed?

"Kacie?"

"I'm okay."

Another shot echoed along the wharf and Ryan twisted his body to get a look at Langford.

He had flung his arms out to the side, his gun inches from his hand, a pool of blood spreading along the pavement beneath his head.

"Is everyone all right?" A bright light flooded the area, and two uniformed cops rushed forward, brandishing their service revolvers.

Ryan squinted at them as he pulled Kacie into his arms. "Did you shoot him?"

"No, sir. We had a sniper set up. When he grabbed Ms. Manning and put a gun to her head, the sniper got to work."

A million questions assaulted his brain, but Kacie needed him. Deep sobs racked her body and he sat up against the chain-link fence, pulling her into his lap.

"It's okay now. It's okay. It's all over."

She raised her tear-streaked face. "It's not over. It's just beginning."

"No, no, Kacie. You're fine. It's going to be okay."

"It's not okay, Ryan."

"It's hard. I know it's hard, but we'll get through it together."

"All this time, I thought your father was the killer and he wasn't. It was mine. My father was the killer."

Epilogue

Kacie zipped up her suitcase and scanned the hotel room once more. "Do you think I should even leave a tip after everything I went through here?"

"Hey, it wasn't the maids' fault." Ryan pulled back the drapes, and sunlight filtered into the room.

She reached into her wallet and pulled out a twenty. "It's tax-deductible anyway."

"Are you going to be doing any writing in Crestview?"

She sat next to one of her bags on the bed and pinned her hands between her knees. "I don't know, Ryan. I need time to process all this. How do you deal with it? How do you come to terms with the fact that your father is responsible for taking human lives and causing such destruction and despair?"

"Why don't you talk to someone, Kacie? I know a great therapist in town. We work with her all the time."

"It's ironic, isn't it? All those years I blamed Joseph Brody for my mother's death, and it turned out to have been my own father."

"We'll see about that. When that DNA test comes back, it may turn out Langford was lying anyway. I don't know how much to believe about what he said."

Ryan insisted on giving her hope by suggesting that

Russ Langford wasn't really her father, but she'd rather not harbor that wish.

She tucked her hair behind one ear. "Why would he lie about being the Phone Book Killer? He never wanted the publicity for the crimes."

"That part makes sense, but what about all that other stuff? What about Bannister, the doll, Cookie, the initial attack on you in the steam room and someone trying to get to your computer? Even the brakes on my car. He denied all involvement." Ryan crossed his arms and wedged his shoulder against the window.

"I was thinking about that. Maybe the steam room, the doll and Bannister were all Walker's doing, his way of punishing me."

"What about Cookie? Walker had nothing to do with her beating, and we can't ask her because she's still in a coma."

"Did you ever think that what happened to Cookie was unrelated to everything else? Someone attacked her at an open house. Maybe someone from her past."

"And Marie's disappearance?"

"You said it yourself. She was paranoid." She clapped her hands together. "Maybe now that Russ Langford's confession is out there, she'll feel safe enough to come home. I already told Ray Lopez he's welcome to the Langford story."

"Is he picking it up?"

"I don't know. Without the Brody connection, he didn't seem quite as interested. He believes Langford was the Phone Book Killer, but he's still intrigued by the unanswered questions surrounding the case."

"For once, Lopez is right." Ryan scratched his chin and sat beside her on the bed. It dipped and she shifted against his solid shoulder.

"There's so much that doesn't make sense," he said,

"and we're still left with the greatest mystery of all. Why did my father jump from the Golden Gate Bridge?"

"A lot of people wonder that about their friends and relatives. None of us knows what drives other people. Your father could've suffered from depression. The case might have been the last straw."

"I don't know if I can ever accept that, Kacie."

"I know. There's a lot I can't accept." She took his hand. "But I can't deal with it right now, Ryan. I'm putting the book aside. I feel like I granted my mom a measure of justice."

"I think you did." He slipped an arm around her shoulders. "I'm sorry to keep harping on it. You need a break. Hell, I need a break."

"*She* needs a break." She pointed at the TV, where a horde of reporters was following London Breck out of the courthouse, yelling questions at her. The blonde in the large sunglasses didn't answer one of them, instead ducking into a waiting limo.

"I told you. Sometimes money is a curse." He squeezed her shoulder. "Let's get out of this city."

"You love this city. We both do."

"Yeah, but what did Cookie say? Sometimes it just gets to be too much."

Kacie turned and put her arms around his neck. "We have a chance, don't we, Ryan? I just want to start over with you, away from the drama and the danger and the lies. My lies."

He kissed her and she knew everything was going to be okay.

After he took her breath away, he traced her lips with his finger. "I'm going to take care of you in Crestview, and you can write whatever you want to write. There's a big mystery going on right now about who's stealing Mr.

Pritchard's tomatoes. The book could be explosive. Another bestseller."

Smiling, she rested her head against his chest. They could start over. She had found love—with one of the sons of Joseph Brody.

* * * * *

Don't miss the heart-stopping conclusion of
BRODY LAW *when Carol Ericson's THE HILL
goes on sale next month.*

"I'm scared."

Cooper nodded, and he reached out. Took her by the arm and pulled her to him.

Almost immediately, she felt him stiffen, and he no doubt would have stepped away from her if Jessa hadn't caught on to him. Why, she didn't know.

Okay, she did.

It was because that brief moment in his arms had felt darn good. Reassuring. And safe. She hadn't felt safe in days, but it was a mistake to look for that safety in Cooper's arms. And the sound that rumbled in his throat let her know that he agreed.

But he didn't move.

Neither did she.

Jessa just stood there with one of his arms hooked around her. Their gazes met. Held. And she felt that tug again. The one deep in her belly that she didn't want to feel.

"This is not going to happen between us," she reminded him, and herself. "It can't."

MAVERICK
SHERIFF

BY
DELORES FOSSEN

MILLS
BOON

Published in Great Britain 2014
by Mills & Boon, an imprint of Harlequin (UK) Limited,
Eton House, 18-24 Paradise Road, Richmond, Surrey, TW9 1SR

© 2014 Delores Fossen

ISBN: 978-0-263-91370-5

46-0914

Harlequin (UK) Limited's policy is to use papers that are natural, renewable and recyclable products and made from wood grown in sustainable forests. The logging and manufacturing processes conform to the legal environmental regulations of the country of origin.

Printed and bound in Spain
by Blackprint CPI, Barcelona

Imagine a family tree that includes Texas cowboys, Choctaw and Cherokee Indians, a Louisiana pirate and a Scottish rebel who battled side by side with William Wallace. With ancestors like that, it's easy to understand why *USA TODAY* bestselling author and former air force captain **Delores Fossen** feels as if she were genetically predisposed to writing romances. Along the way to fulfilling her DNA destiny, Delores married an air force top gun who just happens to be of Viking descent. With all those romantic bases covered, she doesn't have to look too far for inspiration.

Imagine a family tree that includes Texas cowboys, Chinese, and Cherokee Indians, a Louisiana pirate and a British rebel who battled side by side with William Wallace... which makes for the thrill they'd to meet the likes of CJ's VIDAL? Dashing miners and farmers and labour captain. Delores Fossen looks as if she were good any predisposed to written romances. Along the way to publishing her CJ's deadly exploits carried an earlier tag-mark and improved looks of violence doesn't. With all these romantic laurels, one senses she doesn't have to look out the monster end of

Chapter One

The moment Sheriff Cooper McKinnon stepped through the hospital's emergency room doors, he spotted the woman running toward him. Not hurrying.

Flat-out running.

He'd only known the running woman, Jessa Wells, for a few months now. Since she'd moved to Sweetwater Springs to take the job as the town's assistant district attorney. A move that continued to be a thorn in Cooper's professional and personal sides.

Like the woman herself.

But that wasn't a thorny look she was giving Cooper now. She was a mess.

Her light brown hair was tangled on her shoulders, and there were small nicks and cuts on her face. White powder from a car's deployed air bag was clinging like dust to her already pale gray skirt and top. Everything about her expression was an emotion he knew all too well.

Fear.

Remembering that fear, and the panic, it felt as if someone had just punched him in the gut. *Mercy.* Despite his feelings about Jessa, Cooper prayed her situation turned out better than his.

One lost child was enough.

"Hurry," Jessa insisted, catching his arm and practically dragging him out of the E.R. waiting room and into a side corridor. "Dr. Howland's ready to draw your blood."

She was ashy pale—the only spots of color were those wide blue eyes. Desperate eyes.

Yet something else Cooper understood.

"It's my son," she said, though he didn't know how she managed to speak with her breath gusting like that. She was dragging in air through her mouth at a much too fast rate.

"Yeah. When the doctor called me, he said your boy, Liam, was two years old and that he'd been hurt."

Jessa managed a shaky nod. "We were in a car accident. Someone sideswiped me." She gave a hoarse groan. "And his spleen ruptured. I didn't even know that could happen to a toddler."

Lots of bad things could happen to babies and toddlers, and Cooper wished he didn't know that firsthand.

She threw open the door to an examining room. Not an empty one, but there was no sign of her son inside. Just Dr. Howland, his nurse Tammy Karnes and a table set up for Cooper to give blood.

Other than the panicked mother and the feeling of urgency, this was familiar ground for Cooper, since Dr. Howland often called him to donate blood. This was a first, however—a child who might literally die without it.

"Thanks for coming so fast," Dr. Howland greeted.

The doc looked every day of his sixty-plus years this morning. Heaven knew how many life-and-death situations like this he'd faced over his long career as a small-town doctor. How many babies he'd delivered.

And saved.

Heck, he'd delivered Cooper and his two brothers and had saved them a time or two over their years as law enforcement officers. He hoped the doc could do the same for Jessa's little boy.

Cooper took off his Stetson and got on the table, his belt holster and gun clattering against the metal side. The nurse didn't waste any time swabbing his finger. All routine. She jabbed it to get the drops of blood that she needed for a quick test to make sure he wasn't too anemic to donate. While she scurried away to do that, the doctor rubbed his arm with antiseptic and inserted the needle.

The wait began.

It wouldn't be long, but it would no doubt seem like a lifetime to Jessa. She stood at the end of the table, her gaze firing all around, mumbling a prayer under her breath.

The door flew open and the nurse hurried back in. "We're good to go."

That was the only green light the doctor needed, because he turned on the machine and got Cooper's blood flowing into the collection bag. It seemed the doctor was collecting a lot for a toddler, but maybe it was necessary if Jessa's son had lost a lot of blood.

"I was so thankful when Dr. Howland told me you were a match for Liam," Jessa said.

Or rather that was what she tried to say. Her voice cracked, and that too-fast breath caught up with her. Obviously it'd made her light-headed, and she wobbled enough for the doctor to reach out and take hold of her. Dr. Howland tried to move her to the chair in the corner of the room, but Jessa frantically shook her head and stayed put.

"We're lucky," the doctor added. "AB negative is the rarest blood type."

What the doctor didn't say was what he'd told Cooper when he called him. That if Cooper hadn't been nearby, just up the street at the sheriff's office, then Jessa's son would have had a much slimmer chance of pulling through this injury.

"I know you hate me," Jessa mumbled. She blinked, but there were no tears. They would no doubt come once the shock wore off. "But thank you for doing this. *Thank you.*"

Cooper didn't disagree with the hate part, though he probably should have tried to play nice. But he couldn't. Jessa was in shock and panicky now, but the bottom line was that she was trying to destroy his family. And him specifically.

Too bad she was doing it legally.

"I heard your mother's coming back to town," Dr. Howland tossed out there, casting an uneasy glance first at Jessa. Then at Cooper. The nurse, Tammy Karnes, made some uneasy glances of her own.

Because this was a powder keg of a subject. One that Cooper couldn't dodge since he was confined to the table with a captive audience. However, he didn't have to blab his head off about the details, either.

"Yeah, she's coming back," Cooper confirmed. Jewell McKinnon was indeed returning to Sweetwater Springs after being gone for twenty-three years.

It would *not* be a happy homecoming, and that was a massive understatement.

"Well, I'll try to get you out of here as fast as I can," the doctor assured him. "So you can be home when she arrives."

"No need for fast." Cooper didn't have a firm time for his mother's arrival, and nobody in his immediate family was pushing for one. Not even Jewell herself, since she was trying to make travel arrangements not just for Cooper's twin sisters but also for her stepson.

For support, no doubt.

Good thing, too, since Jewell wasn't likely to get any support from the now ex-husband and the three sons she'd abandoned.

Including Cooper.

"Besides," Cooper went on, "Jessa here has plans to have Jewell hauled off to jail as soon as her feet land on Sweetwater Springs's soil. She'd have me hauled off, too, if she could ever find proof that I stonewalled this investigation and tampered with evidence. Since I didn't do those things, there's no proof for her to find."

"Someone tampered with that crime scene and the box of evidence," she mumbled.

Yeah. Someone had. Cooper had seen the photos, and someone had tried to do a cleanup. But it sure as heck hadn't been him. He'd been just a kid at the time of that crime scene.

As for the evidence, well, there was something missing, all right, including the collection log. So they didn't even know what'd been taken.

Again, not his doing.

"I figure Jewell will go straight to the county sheriff's office and just turn herself in to the deputy there," Cooper clarified. At least that was what he was hoping she'd do, so it would prevent Cooper and his family from having to deal with her.

For the time being, anyway.

Jessa nodded, and despite the terror that she was no doubt feeling, he could see her slip into her assistant district attorney mode. "Your mother murdered a man, and even though the body wasn't found, there's enough evidence left to confirm it was murder. She has to pay for that."

Yes, there was enough evidence. *Blood.* Fitting, since

that was what had brought him to Jessa today. It could save a life, but with the large quantities found at the crime scene, it meant the loss of life.

In this case, it did indeed mean murder.

That wouldn't have concerned him so much if the murder charges hadn't brought Jewell back into their lives. Where the old wounds and memories would rip at his whole family. Especially his father, who could end up being implicated in this old crime, as well. He could thank Jessa for that and her vendetta-like investigation that had brought them to this.

Well, not to the hospital.

No way had she counted on something like this interfering with her plans to arrest a woman for a twenty-three-year-old murder.

"Ironic, huh?" Cooper said, looking at Jessa. "Of all the blood in Texas, your son's had to match mine?"

"Yes," Jessa quietly agreed. No more professional facade. "I wish I'd matched, but I didn't. And there wasn't time to try to track down his birth parents. Liam needs a transfusion now." She paused, shook her head. "I'm sorry if this brings back any bad memories for you."

They weren't talking about Jewell now but his late son, Cameron. Something Cooper damn sure didn't want to discuss with Jessa. But he'd never had any luck fighting back those bad memories.

He didn't have luck with it now, either.

As his blood flowed into the bag, the memories flowed, too. First of the storm nearly two years ago. Such a small, ordinary thing that'd had life-changing consequences. His wife, Molly, had driven Cameron into town for his six-week checkup and his shots. Molly had been dreading those. Cooper, too. He'd planned to meet them at the clinic so they could hold each other's hands and get through yet something else that was supposed to be routine.

Then the storm got worse.

The floodwaters came.

And in the exact moment that Molly's car had reached the Stone Creek bridge, it'd washed out.

Taking Cameron and Molly with it.

Cooper squeezed his eyes shut, trying to push away the images. Finally, he gave up and let them bash at him like angry waves, punching into him until he wasn't sure if it was blood or ice being drawn from him.

He hadn't been able to say goodbye to his son. Hadn't been able to bury him. Because his body had never been found.

Unlike Molly's.

Her lifeless body had been found in the creek. Now she had a grave with an empty space next to it, and there were days, like now, when Cooper had to fight hard not to wish he was in that ground beside her.

"Done," the nurse said, and Dr. Howland took the blood bags and hurried out. Jessa was right behind him.

The nurse eased the needle from his arm and positioned a bandage over the puncture before she attempted to help Cooper to his feet. But he waved her off. He'd never gotten dizzy after a donation, and the only thing he wanted to do was get the heck out of there.

Of course, that meant making plans to face Jewell, her stepson and Cooper's fraternal twin sisters, whom Jewell had taken with her when she left the ranch. Funny that seeing his estranged mother now seemed a better option than staying here with these memories eating away at him.

Cooper pulled down his shirtsleeve and went out the

door, only to find Jessa there, pacing and looking ready to explode.

"Dr. Howland said I had to wait here," she blurted out.

Man, her voice was trembling all over, and for a moment he considered offering her a shoulder, but then he thought better of it. With their bad feelings for each other, even a genuine shoulder offer would seem hollow.

"Once your boy gets the blood, he should be all right," Cooper told her. It wasn't much of a reassurance. Heck, it might not even be true, but it was something he would have wanted her to say to him if their situations had been reversed.

"I can't do this." She was past the frantic stage now, and the tears came.

Oh, mercy.

He really didn't want to deal with this, and looked around for someone to take over comfort duty. Of course, there was no one else. Any other day, there would have been all sorts of people milling around. But apparently the fates had it in for Jessa and him today.

"Where's your son?" Cooper asked, hoping that by talking she wouldn't shatter into a million little pieces. It'd worked in the collection room when she had slipped into her district attorney mode for a couple of seconds.

She pointed to the room behind her. Surgery. Well, that explained why Jessa hadn't been allowed in.

"How strong's your stomach?" he asked.

Jessa blinked, clearly not expecting him to ask that. "At the moment not very strong, but if you're asking if I want to see my son in surgery, I do."

He was afraid she'd say that, but since he had already walked out on this limb, Cooper kept right on walking. He led her farther down the hall and into a room with a set of stairs.

"There's an observation deck," he explained. "They bring in medical students sometimes."

And sometimes he'd used it to check on the status of a perp or a victim who'd been injured. Cooper had stood right in that very spot to watch Doc Howland dig a bullet from his brother's chest. That had turned out all right.

Maybe the same would happen today.

Maybe.

Jessa hurried to the glass, her breath instantly fogging it. Her son was indeed on the table, though Cooper couldn't see much of him because of the green sea of scrubs surrounding him. Cooper's blood was there, already flowing into the boy.

Man, he looked so little.

Hardly more than a baby.

"The surgeon seems to be finishing up," Cooper told her. "Everything looks good."

Well, the machines were all beeping and doing the right thing. That had to be good. Ditto for the fact that no one appeared to be in panic mode. Except for Jessa, that was. Even Dr. Howland was standing near the surgeon, just calmly watching.

"I can never thank you enough," she repeated.

And just like that, she came at him, and despite how he felt about the woman, it was the terrified mother whom he put his arms around.

"You don't have to thank me." Cooper tried to ease her away, but she stayed put. Pressed against him.

This wasn't a man-woman thing, but maybe because he was so raw from the memories, he got another punch of feelings that he didn't want to have. Jessa was attractive, and his stupid body didn't let him overlook that. When Cooper felt that too-familiar curl of heat go through him, he untangled himself from her and stepped back.

Way back.

Getting involved with a convicted felon would cause him less trouble than getting involved with this woman.

Jessa didn't seem shocked that he'd pushed her away. Only a little embarrassed that she'd sought out comfort from him in the first place. She snapped back to the window, her gaze fastened to her son.

"What are the odds that you'd be here right when Liam needed you?" he heard her say.

A different kind of uneasy feeling went through him.

Yeah, what were the odds?

Cooper tried to stop any crazy thoughts from flying through his head, but he failed at that, too. He was failing at a lot of things today.

"How old did you say your son is?" he asked.

"Two."

"And his birthday?"

The sharp look Jessa gave him made him wish he'd used a little more tact in asking that question. A stupid question. Because her son had nothing to do with Cameron.

"March 3," she finally said.

Cameron had been born on February 27 of that same year. So it was close, but not the same.

Not that it would have mattered if it had been.

His son had washed away in the flood. His son, with the same rare type of blood as Cooper had.

And Jessa's adopted son.

Less than six percent of world's population had that blood type, and no one else in the county that he knew about. Even his brothers had dodged the rare-blood-type bullet that Cooper had managed to get from a bad combination of Jewell's B-negative and his father's A-positive blood.

Cameron, however, had inherited it.

That uneasy feeling got worse.

Cooper couldn't stop himself. He moved to the glass, stepping all the way to the side until he could get a look at the little boy.

There was an oxygen mask on his face, but it didn't conceal his forehead. Or his hair.

Oh, mercy.

The uneasy feeling slammed into him like a Mack truck.

That was the shape of Cooper's forehead. The color of his hair.

And even though it didn't make sense, Cooper had to wonder if he might be looking at the son he'd thought he had lost.

God, was that Cameron?

Chapter Two

Jessa didn't know what had caused that bleached-out look to appear on Cooper's face, and she wasn't sure she wanted the answer. Something about this just wasn't right.

But then, how could it be?

Cooper had saved her son, and yet she and the sheriff were basically enemies. On opposite sides of the law, and it didn't help that he was the top lawman who ran this town. Heck, one of his brothers was the deputy and another was a Texas Ranger, making this a situation of her against an entire family of testosterone-heavy, badge-wearing cowboys.

Even now, with her mind a tornado of emotions, that bothered her.

Cooper and his brothers could be manipulating evidence, and no telling what else to shelter their father from the fallout of a crime their mother had committed. Jessa was actually thankful for that aggravating reminder.

Because it was better than thinking about what was going on below them in surgery.

It broke her heart for her baby to be here on that operating table. Maybe in pain. And with no certain outcome. Yes, the doctor had said he'd be okay. Cooper had said it, too. But Jessa wouldn't believe it until she could hold Liam in her arms again.

The tears came again, though she tried her best to blink them back. They tumbled down her cheeks, and this time Cooper didn't move to pull her into his arms.

Good thing, too.

Everything inside her was tangled into one giant, raw nerve, and she didn't need to be leaning on this man.

"Will you call his birth parents and let them know what happened?" Cooper asked.

"No." It took her a moment to pull herself out of her thoughts and fears to answer him. "It was a private adoption. The records are sealed." She paused, noted his weird expression again. "Why do you ask?"

He lifted his shoulder in what was probably meant to be a casual shrug, but that wasn't a casual look in his eyes. "I just wondered what would happen if he needed more blood. They won't let me donate any more for a while."

Sweet heaven. She hadn't considered that. Cooper and she were at odds, but his blood had saved her baby's life. And she might have to ask him to do it again.

But what if he couldn't?

Since she suddenly felt as if her legs might give way, Jessa groped behind her to locate one of the metal chairs and dropped down into it. "Liam has to be all right. He's all I have."

"Yeah." And with just that one word, she heard the old scars that had created this dark and brooding lawman. "There are other donors out there with my blood type. None in this area, but Dr. Howland's probably already put out the call to make sure he has enough blood on hand."

That helped. Well, as much as a basic reassurance

could help. The only thing that would truly get her through this was having her baby well.

"Keep talking," Cooper insisted. "They're doing all they can do for your boy, and for his sake, you can't fall apart."

He was right, but Jessa thought she would explode if the surgery didn't end now. God, how did other mothers handle this? It seemed impossible.

Cooper buttoned the cuff on his dark blue shirt and eased down next to her.

Not directly next to her, though.

He put his cocoa-brown Stetson in the seat between them. Only then did she realize she'd never seen him without the hat that was nearly the same color as his hair. The Stetson had seemed like part of his cowboy-cop uniform—like his boots, badge and jeans.

Yet another thing that was off.

He had on the other *uniform* items, but without that Stetson on his head, he no longer looked like the formidable lawman she'd been battling for weeks.

As if to anchor his hands in place, he hooked his thumbs over the belt holster that held both his gun and his badge. What he didn't do was take his attention off her son.

"Why'd you go the adoption route?" he asked.

Jessa kept her attention plastered to Liam, too, and tried to tamp down her breathing. "You mean there's something you don't know about me? I figured you had run a thorough background check by now."

"Oh, I have. I know you're thirty-three. Divorced. And you were an assistant D.A. one county over before you moved here. Nothing in that background check said why you adopted."

No. It wouldn't. Résumés and records didn't reveal a

need so deep that she'd ached for it. "Because I wanted a child, and I figured there were plenty of children out there who needed a parent."

Besides, she'd given up on finding Mr. Right to help her make a baby and a family. There'd been too many Mr. Wrongs in her life for her to keep believing that particular fantasy, and she hadn't wanted an unfulfilled fantasy to get in the way of what she wanted most—motherhood.

"It's funny," she added. "But just this week I requested information about Liam's birth parents. You know, family history stuff in case something like this happened. If I'd gotten the info sooner, I would have known about his rare blood type. I could have told the doctor straight off and it wouldn't have wasted precious minutes."

"They still would have had to test him," Cooper assured her. "They can't go pumping blood into somebody without confirming the type."

True. But Jessa couldn't help but think that she could have done more. Every second had been critical, and she prayed those lost seconds hadn't hurt her son's chances of making a full recovery.

"How'd this car accident happen?" Cooper asked. "You said someone sideswiped you?"

Jessa certainly hadn't forgotten about the accident that had brought them here. In fact, she would press Cooper for a thorough investigation later, but it was hard to remember the details with all these emotions cutting through her. Still, she tried. Best to tell him before she forgot anything.

"I was on Silver Mine Road, less than a mile from my house, and this truck came out of nowhere. The driver must have been on one of those old ranch trails because he pulled out right behind me. He was going so fast and tried to pass. That's when he hit my car, and I went into the ditch. He stopped for just a second or two, but then this other car came, and the driver of the truck sped off."

Thankfully, the other driver, Herman Hendricks, a rancher who owned the property not far from hers, had called the ambulance right away.

Cooper made a sound to indicate he was thinking about what she'd said. "And you didn't get the truck's license plate number?"

She shook her head. "I barely had time to think. The air bags deployed, even the one in the back where I had Liam strapped into his car seat." The guilt tore through her, and she had to choke back a sob.

"This is my fault," she managed to say. "Liam's favorite toy is this hard plastic horse, and I let him hold it while he was in the car seat. The air bag must have hit the horse, and that's what ruptured his spleen."

Cooper huffed. "Even if that's what happened, you had no way of knowing that some fool would force you off the road." He paused. "Did you recognize the truck?"

Another head shake. "And I wasn't really looking for side traffic. I mean, there's usually no one else on that part of the road at that time of morning. It was a miracle Mr. Hendricks was there."

She'd allowed herself to be lulled into a false sense of safety. And she'd desperately wanted safe. That was why she'd moved her son to the small rural house three miles outside of town.

Cooper looked ready to launch into more questions, but his phone buzzed. He stretched out his jeans-clad leg so he could take it from his pocket. They were close, practically shoulder to shoulder despite the seat with his Stetson between them, so she could see the name on the screen.

Colt McKinnon.

His brother, the deputy.

Cooper didn't put the call on speaker, but it was impossible for her to miss what Colt said in the otherwise soundless room. "Jewell and the others are coming in the day after tomorrow. They're not going straight to the county sheriff's office, though. They're coming out to the ranch."

His mouth tightened. "Why the hell are they going there?"

Colt didn't answer right away. "Dad asked her that, and Jewell reminded him that she owns the ranch. Not him. Not us."

Jessa hadn't thought it possible, but Cooper's mouth tightened even more.

The ranch's ownership wasn't a surprise. She knew that Jewell owned it outright, an inheritance from her own grandfather before she'd married Roy McKinnon. But Jessa was surprised the woman would play the ownership card when she had to know she wouldn't be welcome there.

"Jewell wants the guesthouse fixed up for her stepson and the twins," Colt added. "She says they'll be staying there while she's awaiting trial."

Jessa silently groaned. Oh, mercy. Cooper's mother was really pushing it hard. Even though her daughters were Cooper's full-blooded siblings, Jessa had heard that he hadn't seen them since they were kids. Thankfully, Jewell wouldn't be bringing her second husband, since he'd passed away years ago. Still, it'd be a mess since it would no doubt be months before the trial even started.

"What about the arresting officer?" Cooper asked. "Will he come out to the ranch for her?"

Cooper said *arresting officer* as if it were some kind of bug to be squashed. She hadn't expected a different reaction. Nor had Jessa had a choice in requesting someone from outside of Sweetwater Springs. She couldn't expect Jewell's own sons to make the arrest. The FBI was out, too, since Jewell's stepson was an agent. Ditto for the Rangers, because Cooper's brother was one.

That left the county sheriff, but that was a conflict of interest, too, since the county sheriff's father was the very man Jewell was accused of murdering. That was why Jessa had gotten permission from the state attorney general for a county deputy to do the deed. Hardly in the county deputy's job description to make an arrest for a murder in a town that had an entire law enforcement team, but it seemed the best alternative considering the circumstances.

"Are you out at the accident scene where the A.D.A. was run off the road?" Cooper asked.

"Yeah. No skid marks, but I can see the point of impact on her car where she was sideswiped."

"Look for tracks on the ranch trail several yards before the impact. Jessa says that's where the truck came out."

Cooper had used her given name, but he hadn't said it with any kind of affection. In fact, it'd seemed to stick in his throat, but it would have seemed petty to call her Ms. Wells after she'd launched herself into his arms earlier.

Something Jessa already regretted.

No sense breaking down the kinds of barriers that needed to stay in place.

"How's her boy?" she heard Colt ask.

Since Cooper's gaze was still on her son, he had a quick answer. "Surgery's finishing up now."

"You okay?" Colt said after pausing.

"Fine." Cooper jabbed the end-call button so hard she was surprised his phone didn't shatter.

Like her.

The panic was boiling through her again, and since it did indeed seem as if the surgery was wrapping up, she headed for the stairs. Cooper followed. Well, he ambled along behind her anyway, and caught up with her when she stopped outside the operating room doors.

She wanted to burst into the room, to beg for any information anyone could give her, but being closer to Liam didn't lessen the panic. It only made it worse.

Jessa started pacing.

"You should go," she said to Cooper. Though she didn't want him to leave. Yes, it was crazy, but he might be the only person nearby who actually knew what she was going through.

"I got a few minutes." Though he did check the time on his phone. "I need to do some paperwork, but it can wait."

There wasn't as much venom in his voice as she'd expected. Especially considering the massive amount of venom that'd been between them since she'd requested the county sheriff reopen this investigation.

"You think I'm on a witch hunt to have your mother arrested," she said. She didn't want to have this discussion with him, but after what he'd done for her and Liam, Jessa wanted to give him an explanation.

Well, as much as she could give, anyway.

Cooper already knew about the forensics. He'd no doubt studied every last detail. Twenty-three years ago, there'd been enough of Whitt Braddock's blood found in a hunting cabin on the grounds of his massive ranch for him to be declared dead, despite the fact his body was missing.

Dragged from the cabin, from the looks of it.

Rumors were rampant that Whitt and Jewell had been

having an affair, and that she'd killed him in the heat of passion when he'd tried to break things off with her and go back to his wife. The rumors had stayed just that.

Rumors.

Until Jessa had arrived in town as the new A.D.A., and she'd requested items taken from the old crime scene be tested. Jewell's DNA had been discovered on both the bed sheets and the knife that'd been found near the scene.

"I'm just sorry your mother's the target of my investigation," she added.

Cooper spared her a hard glance. "It's not my mother I'm worried about. She can take care of herself."

There it was. The venom. It wasn't aimed at her but rather his mother. Of course, Jewell had abandoned her husband and sons when she'd fled town under a cloud of suspicion. Cooper, his brothers and his father had to resent that, and it showed in his voice.

The door behind her finally opened, and Jessa turned so fast that her neck popped. It was Dr. Howland, and even though she'd never been happier to see someone, she couldn't read his expression.

He tugged the surgical mask off his mouth and nodded. "Liam's going to be okay."

The relief was instant, flooding through her and turning her legs to mush. If Cooper hadn't taken hold of her arm, she probably would have just crumpled to the floor.

Maybe sensing that Cooper wasn't exactly comfortable with rescue detail, the doctor took over. "Come on. They're moving him to the recovery room soon, and you can see him."

Despite everything feeling wobbly, Jessa got herself walking. She could see her little boy and make sure for herself that he was indeed okay. Thankfully, she didn't have to go far. Just two doors down, and Dr. Howland opened it for her and ushered her inside. Liam wasn't there yet, and she prayed she didn't have to wait much longer.

"I'll be back in a minute," the doctor told her, and stepped into the hall where Cooper was still waiting.

"All right, what's wrong?" she heard the doctor ask him.

Puzzled, Jessa stayed in the doorway, peering around the side, and she tried to hear Cooper's response. But he just shook his head and mumbled something she didn't catch.

Maybe this was about his late wife and child. Maybe the ordeal had brought back bad memories. Of course, the sheriff was about to face a whole boatload of new bad memories thanks to his mother and Jessa's investigation.

Since this was likely a very private conversation, Jessa started to move away so she wouldn't be able to hear. Then Cooper pulled in a hard breath and turned to the side so that she couldn't see his expression. But she could tell from his body language that whatever was bothering him wasn't good.

"I need you to run a DNA test," Cooper said to the doctor. She missed whatever he added to the request.

DNA? So maybe this wasn't personal. Maybe it had something to do with a case. Except she knew all of his investigations, and there wasn't one that required any kind of DNA test.

"I can get a court order," Cooper went on. "Or we can do this quietly. For now. If anything turns up, then I'd have to make it official, of course."

The doctor didn't say anything for several moments and shook his head. "I'm afraid you'll need that court order for this."

If Cooper had a reaction to that, she couldn't see it.

He simply nodded. "You'll have it within the hour. Then I want the test done ASAP."

"Sure. Once I have the order." Dr. Howland paused again. "Whose DNA are we comparing to his?"

Cooper turned and delivered his answer from over his shoulder. "Mine."

Chapter Three

Cooper's mind wasn't where it darn well should be. Even two days after donating blood, his thoughts were still on the little boy, Liam, at the hospital. The boy who now had Cooper's blood in his veins.

He'd already made at least a dozen calls to find out his condition. The boy was recovering, something Dr. Howland kept saying every time Cooper asked. That was good. But it wasn't the same as seeing Liam.

Or knowing the truth about his paternity.

It was such a long shot that this boy could be his son. But after living with no shot at all for nearly two years, Cooper had grabbed on to the sliver of hope as if it were a lifeline.

But it was a lifeline that he had to push aside.

Because all hell was about to break loose.

He'd had to make a lot of waves to get that court order for the DNA test, and by now half the county had probably heard about his request, or rumors of it, anyway.

Including Jessa.

She hadn't contacted him about it yet, which meant by some miracle she hadn't heard or either she was still too worried about Liam to do anything about it.

Cooper was worried, too. For the boy. For this blasted

hope that he couldn't tamp down. For the test result that he should have in the next twenty-four hours or sooner.

And worried for what the coming days would bring with Jewell's arrival.

Unfortunately, he couldn't push the latter aside because it was driving up the ranch road directly for the house he called home.

"Figured she'd be driving something flashier than that," his kid brother, Colt, mumbled. He had his attention fixed to the white car that was kicking up a trail of dust as it made its way to the house.

Cooper hadn't given a thought to the kind of vehicle. Only the occupants inside. Judging from the way his brother Tucker grunted, he'd done the same.

The three of them stood, shoulder to shoulder, with Cooper in the middle, Tucker on his right, Colt on his left. They'd all worn their badges, holsters and guns. But then, they were rarely without them. Same with the Stetsons, though Colt's and his were dark brown. Since Tucker was a Texas Ranger, his was white.

Cooper hoped they looked intimidating as hell.

Because the last thing he wanted was Jewell and the kids she'd raised on the very land that he, his brothers and dad had worked while Jewell had been off enjoying her life with her second husband.

"Not sure I'll even recognize her," Colt added.

Yeah, because he'd been only nine when she'd walked out twenty-three years ago. Just a kid. Heck, Tucker had only been eleven and Cooper thirteen, but he hadn't been able to get the image of her out of his head.

The image of her leaving.

Her exit and the affair she'd had with Whitt Braddock had crushed his dad, and because of all the pain she had caused, Cooper had made sure any good memories of her were gone, too.

Now here they were.

Right smack-dab in their faces.

"That's her, huh?" Cooper heard the woman say.

It was Arlene Litton, the weathered-faced horse trainer who'd been with them as long as Cooper could remember. Wearing dusty jeans and a plaid shirt that'd seen much better days, she clomped up the side steps of the porch that stretched across the entire bottom floor of the two-story house and joined them.

"You boys okay?" she asked, sounding more like a mother than their horse trainer.

None of them attempted to lie. They weren't okay, and they wouldn't be until Jewell was behind bars. Not until all their names were cleared. And not until Jewell's *kin* was off the ranch.

"When's the county deputy gonna be here to arrest Jewell?" Arlene asked.

"Hopefully any minute," Tucker answered.

Cooper echoed that but hoped the only arrest warrant the sheriff would have would be for Jewell.

Before the car accident, Jessa had been gunning to add another warrant—for Cooper—for obstruction of justice because she thought he'd tried to stonewall her investigation. He hadn't exactly cooperated, especially with anything that would have brought his father into it, but he darn sure hadn't obstructed anything, either.

As if he could have with the hardheaded Jessa hon-choing the investigation.

The car pulled to a stop in the driveway. The windows were heavily tinted, so dark that Cooper couldn't see inside. No one hurried out, but the door to the house opened, and his father stepped onto the porch with them.

Cooper had hoped he'd stay inside, but then that wasn't something his father would do. Roy McKinnon wasn't the sort to avoid trouble.

And *trouble* opened both backseat car doors.

A woman stepped out, the spitting image of Jewell. Or at least the Jewell whom Cooper remembered from over two decades ago. Shoulder-length blond hair, slender, almost frail build. In fact, she actually looked frail, something Jewell never had.

"Hello," she said, looking up at them. And she had to look up, all right, because there were twelve steps leading up to the porch. Something Cooper and his brothers had joked about often. But jokes aside, it gave them the catbird seat of sorts, and it put some much needed distance between Jewell and them that Cooper had no intention of narrowing.

"I'm Rosalie," the woman added, her voice as frail as the rest of her.

Rosalie, one of Jewell's twin girls, and his sister. Biologically, anyway. He hadn't seen her since she was barely six years old, but Cooper felt an instant connection with this woman that he darn sure didn't want to feel. He knew from background checks that Rosalie had given birth to a little girl about six months earlier, and the child had been kidnapped from the hospital nursery.

Never to be seen again.

Yeah, there was a connection, all right, and Jessa's hurt little boy had only made that wound fresher for Cooper.

Rosalie stayed by the car and looked over the top to the other side of the vehicle when her fraternal twin got out.

Rayanne.

Nowhere near frail looking.

She had a sturdy build, and her mop of brown hair

was gathered into a ponytail. For the most part. Strands of it flew in the steamy August breeze.

Rayanne was wearing jeans, not the designer kind, either, and she had a silver star badge clipped to her leather shoulder holster. She'd been a deputy in a small town two counties over for going on five years now. Her experience showed on her face.

And in that snarl.

That was a McKinnon snarl, one that Cooper recognized because he'd seen it too often in the mirror.

Why the heck did she have to look so much like, well, family?

"Pleased to meet you, too," Rayanne said with a hefty dose of sarcasm in her voice. She turned her eyes on Roy. "Daddy," she said with even more sarcasm and a chip on her shoulder that was bigger than the Smith & Wesson she was toting. Maybe because she blamed Roy for all of this.

Well, the blame was in the car, not with his dad.

"Oh, she'll be fun," Arlene mumbled, mimicking Rayanne's sarcasm.

The driver's-side door opened. Still no Jewell. But it was trouble of a different kind.

FBI agent Seth Calder.

Black hair, black suit and slick black mirrored shades covering his eyes, he stepped out, his phone anchored between his shoulder and his ear. He had that arrogance of a fed written all over him.

Cooper hated him on sight.

The breeze caught the side of his jacket, whipping it back, and the sun hit his holster and badge just right so it glinted in Cooper's eyes. Cooper had to blink and look away for a second.

If his stepbrother even spared them a glance, Cooper

couldn't tell. Of course, it was hard to tell much of anything with those sunglasses hiding his eyes.

"Oh, my," Arlene said under her breath. "He looks like something that just stepped out of my dreams."

Cooper and Tucker shot her a glare. "What kind of dreams?" Cooper snarled.

Arlene lifted a graying eyebrow that'd looked as if it'd never been near tweezers. "The sort you don't want to know I have."

Normally, Cooper would have appreciated the woman's attempt to lighten things up, but there was nothing normal about this.

Still not acknowledging them, Special Agent Calder went to the passenger-side door and opened it. How gentlemanly of him.

Jewell finally made an appearance.

Unlike her stepson, her attention did go straight to them, and a weak smile bent her mouth before it faded in a flash.

She'd changed more than Cooper had thought she would. She still had the blond hair, no grays, and there weren't a lot of wrinkles. She'd been well kept over these years, but her eyes looked old. Maybe because she'd lived with killing a man and abandoning her family all this time. He wanted to think she'd suffered for that, anyway.

"Cooper," she said, her voice small. Her gaze slid to his brothers, and she whispered their names before she settled on Roy. "I know you don't want us here, but the ranch is theirs, too."

"Not his," Tucker said tipping his head to Mr. FBI.

"Seth, too. I adopted him."

"She's my mother," Seth verified, none too friendly like, and he finally put his phone away. He looped his arm around Jewell's waist. "And just so we get this straight, we're here to clear her name."

"Even if it means sullying yours," Rayanne added, and her gaze went right to Roy. Her father. But clearly she didn't think of him that way. Probably because she'd been raised by Jewell's second husband.

"We'll see about that," Cooper fired back at them, and that probably would have started a big family ruckus if Roy hadn't stepped in front of them and if Rosalie hadn't stepped in front of her lot.

It was obvious who the peacemakers were.

And weren't.

Cooper gladly put himself in the second category. He didn't want peace with Jewell or the kids she'd chosen to raise.

"Why don't you show them to the guesthouse, Arlene," Roy suggested.

"Not me." Rayanne grabbed a beat-up gym bag from the car. "I'm not a guest." She marched up the steps as if she had a right to do just that, her gaze locking with Cooper's. The glare she gave him was really a dare, challenging him to stop her from going inside.

"Rayanne, there's plenty of room in the guesthouse," her sister reminded her.

Rayanne didn't take her eyes off Cooper. "I'm a McKinnon, just like you. And besides, there are only two bedrooms in the guesthouse, and I prefer not to have to share a room with my sister. I don't *lay* well with others."

Cooper didn't doubt that one bit and was about to point to the guesthouse anyway, but his father stepped to the side. "There are plenty of rooms upstairs, including yours and Rosalie's." Roy looked at Rosalie then. "You're welcome to join her."

"No, thank you." Rosalie scowled at her sister. "I'm

sure everyone would be more comfortable if Seth, Ray-anne and I were in the guesthouse."

"Didn't come here to make people comfortable, did I?" Rayanne mumbled, and she pushed past Cooper and went inside.

"I'll show the others to the guesthouse now," Arlene insisted.

It wasn't far, just about twenty yards from the main house, and Jewell no doubt knew the way since her own daddy had built it. However, Arlene's offer was a good one because this family gathering needed to end now.

And not just because Cooper was ready for it to end.

He saw the other car approaching, and even though he didn't recognize the vehicle at first, he recognized the driver when she braked to a noisy stop and threw open the car door.

Jessa.

And she didn't look happy.

Great, she'd found out about the DNA test and would want answers.

"Are you here to take me in?" Jewell immediately asked her.

"No." In fact, Jessa did a sort of double take as if surprised to see Jewell and her entourage there. And maybe she was truly surprised. Because her focus zoomed straight to Cooper.

"We have to talk," Jessa said, and it didn't sound like an invitation, more like an order.

Arlene went down the steps to show the others to the guesthouse just as Jessa stormed up them. His father and brothers gave him a questioning look, but Cooper couldn't explain things yet.

Because he didn't know what to explain.

"This way," Cooper said.

He didn't take Jessa through the main entry but to the side porch so they could go into his home office. It wouldn't exactly be private if Jessa raised her voice.

Something she might very well do.

But his father and brothers were no doubt wrapped up in dealing with Jewell's arrival. Once he'd dealt with this fire, Cooper had to make sure his dad was as okay as he could be under the circumstances.

"Why?" Jessa demanded the moment she stepped inside his office.

Since that *why* could cover a lot of territory, he just waited for her to finish. Cooper reached behind her and shut the door, and his arm accidentally brushed against hers. She jumped as if he'd scalded her.

"You had my son's DNA tested," she went on. But that was as far as she got. Her chest started pumping as if starved for air, and she dropped back and let the now closed door support her.

Jessa wasn't quite as frantic as she had been two days ago at the hospital, but it was darn close. The tiny nicks were still there on her face from her encounter with the air bag, but no business suit today. She was in pants and a sleeveless white top, and she had her hair pulled back in a ponytail. The dark circles under her eyes let him know she hadn't been sleeping.

Neither had he.

It'd taken every ounce of willpower for him not to rush back to the hospital to get a better look at the little boy.

"How's Liam?" he asked. Not avoiding her question. Nothing could do that. He was just delaying it because he truly wanted to know how the toddler was doing.

She glared at him for so long that Cooper wasn't sure she'd answer. "He's better, but you already know that.

You've called at least a dozen times checking on his condition."

He had. Cooper also knew Liam was doing so well that he'd probably be released from the hospital tomorrow. Jessa's mom had flown in from Dallas so she could stay with him during his recovery and help Jessa out. Her mom was no doubt with Liam now, since to the best of his knowledge, this was the first time in two days that Jessa had left the hospital.

"He'll make a full recovery?" Cooper asked.

Again, she glared. "Yes. In fact, he already wants to get up and run around. Now, why?" she added without pausing.

Cooper pulled in a long breath that he would need and sank down on the edge of his desk. "Because of the blood-type match. And because we never found my son's body."

Even though she'd no doubt already come up with that answer, Jessa huffed and threw her hands in the air. "And what? You think I found him on the riverbank and pretended to adopt him? Well, I didn't, and Liam's not your son. I want you to put a stop to that DNA test."

Cooper shook his head. "If you're sure he's not my son, then the test will come back as no match."

Her glare got worse. "You're doing this to get back at me." Her breath broke, and the tears came.

Oh, man.

He didn't want this. Not with both of them already emotional wrecks. They were both powder kegs right now, and the flames were shooting all around them. Still, he went closer, and because all those emotions had apparently made him dumber than dirt, Cooper slipped his arm around her.

She fought him. Of course. Jessa clearly didn't want

his comfort, sympathy or anything else other than an assurance to put a stop to that test. Still, he held on despite her fists pushing against his chest. One more ragged sob, however, and she sagged against him.

There it was again. That tug deep down in his body. Yeah, dumber than dirt, all right. His body just didn't seem to understand that an attractive woman in his arms could mean nothing.

Even when Jessa looked up at him.

That tug tugged a little harder. Because, yeah, she was attractive, and if the investigation and accusations hadn't cropped up, he might have considered asking her out.

So much for that plan.

"I hate being like this," she said in a breathy whisper. "Hate that all of this is happening." Jessa eased back, looked up at him. "Please tell me you're not doing this because you hate me."

"I'm not doing this because I hate you." And since they were both wearing their hearts on their sleeves, Cooper went a step further. "I don't even hate you. I just don't like what you're trying to do to me and my family."

"It's my job. It's not personal. But this situation with Liam feels personal."

"It *is* personal. I lost my son, and there's a small chance that he's still alive."

Just saying that was too much, and it was Cooper who moved away from her. He wouldn't let her or anyone else see how close this was to breaking him, but it'd brought back all the old memories and gouged into wounds, making them bleed and fester all over again.

"How old was Liam when you adopted him?" Cooper asked.

"Three months old, but that doesn't matter," she

quickly added. "I checked, and Liam was born four days after your son."

"Birth records can be altered."

That did it. Jessa the A.D.A. was back. Her chin came up, and even though there were still tears in her eyes, she managed to look tough as nails.

She wasn't.

Cooper was betting she was on the verge of falling apart. Especially if what he was about to show her made the connection that he hoped it'd make.

He took the silver framed photo from his desk. A photo he looked at every single day, wishing that his life hadn't turned on a dime. Cooper didn't need to look at it now. He'd memorized every detail. It was a picture of Molly sitting in one of the rocking chairs on the front porch. She was holding a tiny Cameron in her arms. The sunlight on their faces.

Keeping his attention pinned to Jessa, he handed her the photo, and after giving him a glance, she studied it.

There.

He saw it in her eyes. That flash of surprise. Maybe even recognition. Because the baby in the picture was only two months younger than Liam was when Jessa adopted him. If Liam was his son, then there'd be a resemblance.

"All babies look the same," she said. But the color had drained from her face.

Cooper figured his color was gone, too, and for a moment he thought he might disgrace himself by dropping to his knees.

His baby was alive.

Well, maybe.

He couldn't jump off that ledge just yet, even though he'd felt more hope than he had in nearly two years.

What he needed now were the results of that test, and he reached for his phone to call the doctor again.

However, Jessa's phone buzzed first.

Without taking her gaze off the photo, she blindly groped in her pocket and pulled out her cell. One glance at the screen, however, and she practically tossed the photo back at him so she could hit the answer button.

"Mom, is everything okay?" Jessa quickly asked.

"No," he heard the woman say.

Cooper's heartbeat doubled, and he reached over and moved Jessa back a bit so he could hit the speaker button on her screen.

"What's wrong?" Jessa's voice was trembling now, and she was already opening the door.

"Jessa, you need to get here right away," her mother insisted. "And bring Sheriff McKinnon with you. Someone's trying to kidnap Liam."

Chapter Four

"Why isn't my mother answering her phone?" Jessa snapped, and she tried again. But like the other dozen times, the call went straight to voice mail.

"There are plenty of dead zones in the hospital," Cooper told her. "And maybe your mother turned off the ringer because she's hiding."

It sickened her to think of her mother running through the hospital, trying to protect Liam while kidnappers chased after them.

"Hurry," Jessa said, but she knew Cooper couldn't drive any faster without risking an accident. Still, she wouldn't care if they wrecked as long as she could just see her son.

And prevent him from being kidnapped.

Everything inside her was racing. Her heart. Her breath. The horrible thoughts firing through her head.

The loud wail of the siren didn't help her nerves, but she was thankful for them. Because of the siren and the flashing blue lights, other drivers were moving out of Cooper's way, shaving off precious seconds. Maybe that would be enough.

It *had* to be enough.

She couldn't muffle the sob that tore through her

throat. Why was this happening? Why had everything in her life turned upside down?

Another sound shot through the truck, and because her nerves were so frayed, it took her a moment to realize it was Cooper's phone. She didn't see the screen before he sandwiched the phone between his shoulder and his ear.

"It's Reed," he told her.

Reed Caldwell, one of his deputies, and it wasn't Reed's first call but rather his third since this nightmare had begun. Cooper's brothers had called him, also. Tucker and Colt were headed to the hospital in another vehicle.

"No. Stay back," Cooper said to the deputy. "If possible, get me a photo. I'll be there in about five minutes."

That might be five minutes too late.

"Reed's on the scene," Cooper relayed to her the moment he ended the call. "And he just got an update from the security guard. There are two masked men in the hall of the pediatric ward. They're armed, and they've taken a hostage."

Jessa pressed her fists to the sides of her head. "Please, not Liam or my mother."

"No. Not them," Cooper quickly assured her. "They grabbed a nurse when she tried to stop them from entering Liam's room. She screamed, alerted the security guard, and that's when the men put a gun to her head. The security guard wisely backed off and called Reed."

"But what about Liam and my mother?"

"Reed talked to your mother right after she called us. She phoned the 9-1-1 dispatcher, too, and he got her number from them. Reed told her to take Liam into the bathroom of his room and lock the door."

That was a start, but it wasn't nearly enough. Not for her son, her mother or the poor nurse who'd tried to protect Liam.

"There's probably no reception in the bathroom," Cooper went on. "The walls are concrete block."

Jessa prayed that was the only reason her mother wasn't answering the calls. Her mother was a strong, levelheaded person, but an ordeal like this could cause anyone to panic.

"What do these men want?" she asked. "Why did they try to take Liam?"

Cooper shook his head, and for a split second his gaze met hers. She saw the same fear mirrored in his iron-gray eyes that was no doubt in hers. "They've yelled out that they want to talk to you."

Her heart slammed against her chest. So they knew who she was.

Jessa had held out hope that this was some kind of misunderstanding—maybe a situation of mistaken identity or some kind of custody dispute. But if these men had tried to kidnap Liam and then demanded to talk to her, then the chances of a misunderstanding were slim.

"This could be connected to one of your cases," Cooper added. He jammed even harder on the accelerator to pass a car. "Once Liam's safe and these idiots are behind bars, I'll find out."

His jaw muscles were tight again, as were most of the muscles in his body. He seemed absolutely determined to help her son. And she prayed it wasn't because he believed Liam was his. He wasn't Cooper's. He couldn't be.

That was another thing she'd get straight as soon as this was over.

"You told your deputy to stay back," she reminded him. "Why?"

He took the final turn to the hospital. "I don't want to give them a reason to start shooting. Once all the deputies are in place, I'll try to negotiate with them."

Cooper didn't seem like the negotiating type, but she was. She'd give the men whatever they wanted as long as they left Liam alone.

Without taking his attention off the road, Cooper made another call. "Colt, as soon as Tucker and you arrive, head to the back entrance of the hospital. If it's not clear, clear it. Then get upstairs. Go in low and quiet. Stay out of sight." He paused, glanced at her. And blew out a long breath. "If you need to shoot, just don't miss," Cooper added.

That sent a new round of fear and panic through her. God, she had to get to her baby.

Cooper's phone dinged just as he pulled into the parking lot, and he glanced down at the screen before he handed his phone to her. "Reed just sent me this photo."

It was a grainy shot, obviously taken from a distance, but Jessa could see the two men wearing dark masks. Both were bulky, both armed, and one was indeed holding a terrified-looking woman in front of him like a human shield. The other one was behind his partner. Out of the direct line of fire.

These were the men who wanted her son, and Jessa wished she could reach through the phone lines and stop them.

"I know they're wearing masks, but look at the body language and the hair," Cooper instructed. "Could one of those men be the person who sideswiped your car?"

Jessa's shoulders snapped back. "You think these things are connected?" But she immediately realized they could very well be.

Mercy, why hadn't she thought of it earlier? If that accident hadn't been an accident, then she should have figured out she and Liam were in danger.

Jessa had to shake her head. "I don't recognize anything about them, but then I barely got a glimpse of the driver."

Cooper gave a weary sigh and braked to a stop directly in front of the emergency room doors, where there were people and staff hurrying out. Jessa reached for the door handle, but he stopped her.

"Look, I know I stand zero chance of asking you to stay in the truck, so here are the rules," he said. "No matter what happens, you stay behind me. No going nuts and trying to get to Liam. No doing or saying anything unless you've cleared it with me first. I sure as hell don't need to babysit you while I'm trying to save Liam."

That stung. Because she didn't need him babysitting her. But Jessa agreed with Cooper only because she wanted him to hurry so they could get inside.

Cooper drew his gun, and she threw open her door at the same moment that he did and ran toward the emergency room. It wasn't easy because there were about a dozen panicked people still trying to get out. Cooper and she made it through the crowd and bolted up the stairs to the pediatric unit.

They didn't get far.

Deputy Reed Caldwell was there, stooped behind a wall while he peered into the hall. The moment Reed spotted his boss, he shifted over so that Cooper could take the lead. He did. Cooper took aim at the gunmen.

"My brothers just arrived," Cooper said.

Jessa glanced out into the hall, but she didn't get a good enough look before Cooper gave her a warning glare to get back.

"Tucker and Colt are at the other end of the hall, behind the gunmen," Cooper whispered to her. "I'm Sheriff Cooper McKinnon," he called out. "Let the hostage go, put down your gun and let's talk."

Jessa held her breath, praying they would but figuring it was unlikely they'd comply. The men had taken a huge risk in coming here like this, and that meant they wouldn't want to go away empty-handed.

"You wanna protect the little boy inside that room?" one of the men shouted. "There's only one way to do that. Tell Jessa Wells to step out now, or I start shooting. You've got thirty seconds to decide if it's the kid or her."

COOPER HAD TO catch Jessa again to stop her from bolting toward the gunmen. But she didn't exactly cooperate with his attempt to restrain her. She fought, trying to push him away.

"You heard what they said," she snapped, hysteria in her voice.

"Yeah, and I don't believe them. You shouldn't, either. They're criminals, Jessa, and if you go out there, at best they'll gun you down. If you're not so lucky, they'll start shooting up the place, kidnap Liam and take you both to a secondary crime scene. I'll let you guess what they plan to do with you, but I'm thinking it won't be fun for you or Liam."

That froze her, thank goodness, and the tears spilled down her cheeks before she dropped back. Cooper hadn't thought the tears would bother him that much. After all, he'd seen Jessa crying just two days earlier while Liam was in surgery and again when she challenged him about Liam's paternity. But this was different.

Okay, *he* was different.

Because as long as there was a chance that Liam was his, then it upped the stakes a thousand times over. And Jessa was one of the few people who was as aware of that as Cooper.

"You can't let them take him," she whispered. Her

mouth was trembling. The rest of her, too. And her eyes begged Cooper to make this situation right.

"I won't let them," Cooper promised, though he had some doubts about the plan he'd come up with.

"Well?" the man shouted. "What'll it be? Because time's up."

Cooper ignored him. "Call Colt," he whispered to Reed. "Tell them to fire on my count of two. The nurse is a head shorter than the gunmen. That gives them six good inches, and I want both men taken out together. I don't want one of these idiots to get off a shot and hurt their hostage."

Reed nodded, did as he said and then moved just to the side of Cooper so he'd be able to fire if necessary. And it just might be necessary if this plan went south.

Cooper glanced down the hall, past the waiting gunmen. The thirty-second time limit was long since up, and it was showing in their body language. They were getting antsy, and the last thing he needed were itchy trigger fingers in an already volatile situation.

"If you think I'm just going to let you walk out of here with the A.D.A. and her son," Cooper told them, "then you're a special kind of stupid. Put down your guns now!"

That stirred them up. They cursed. Fired nervy glances all around them. Trying to figure out what to do.

Had they really thought he wouldn't challenge them or try to stop them? Maybe they'd heard of the discord between him and Jessa and thought he'd turn a blind eye so they could kidnap her.

He wouldn't do that. Not ever.

Cooper took a deep breath. Readied his gun. And nodded for Reed to do the same.

"On the count of three, put down your guns," Cooper called out to the men. He added a quick silent prayer and shouted, "One."

Cooper checked to see if the men had come to their senses. They hadn't. They were cursing now and dragging their captive toward Liam's door. A door they were no doubt ready to bash open so they could take the little boy.

That wasn't going to happen, either.

"Two!" Cooper shouted.

Everything seemed to happen at once. The gunman darted away from his comrade and reached for the door. In the same motion, he fired a shot at Cooper.

Cooper ducked back, dodging the bullet, but two thick blasts followed. Not from the gunmen. These had come from the other end of the hall, where his brothers were. He looked out, spotted both of them on each side of the corridor. Cooper spotted the gunmen, too.

Both on the floor.

They weren't dead, but they'd been injured and were writhing and groaning. They were loud, but not nearly as loud as the nurse. Screaming, she bolted away from the men and ran right toward him.

"You're okay," Cooper assured her and handed the woman off to Reed. He had to move fast because Jessa started sprinting, headed directly for Liam's room.

She'd have to go past the men to get there.

Cooper caught up with her, pulling her behind him, and he kicked the men's guns away from their hands. The moment he did that, a medic came forward. So did his brothers, and Cooper knew the situation was under control. Jessa, however, wasn't.

"I have to see Liam," she insisted.

"Yeah, I know." Cooper felt the same, and he didn't

have the same ties to Liam as Jessa did. She'd raised him. Still, the urgency pressed down on him like a lead weight.

Cooper eased open Liam's door, and with his gun still at the ready, he peered inside. No other gunmen. Thank God. So he continued to the bathroom.

"Mrs. Wells?" Cooper tapped on the jamb. "It's Sheriff McKinnon."

He heard movement, and it wasn't long before Jessa's mom opened the door. She was holding a sleeping Liam in her arms.

"Is he okay?" Jessa didn't wait for her mother to answer. She gently took Liam and pressed a flurry of kisses on his face and head.

"He's fine," her mother answered.

But Cooper couldn't say the same for the woman. She was shaking so hard that she collapsed into Cooper's arms. "It's okay," he assured her. "You're safe now."

But for how long?

Cooper didn't have an answer for that—yet.

"Wait here," he said to the women, and he went back into the hall to see if he could get some quick answers. Apparently luck wasn't on his side today, because both gunmen were unconscious. And they were both bleeding a lot. It meant no answers now. Maybe not ever if they didn't make it through this. Still, it was better than the alternative of having a dead nurse and Jessa and Liam kidnapped.

"Can you handle this?" Cooper asked, his gaze going first to Colt before swinging to Reed.

Both his deputies nodded.

That was the only assurance Cooper needed.

There was a crowd of people now. Medics and doctors who'd responded to treat the wounded men. Some gawkers, too. Cooper picked through the group until his attention landed on Dr. Howland.

"I have to get Liam out of here," Cooper said. "He'll need a car seat and his meds."

The doctor didn't argue. "We can use my assistant's car. It has an infant seat already in it. I'll get her keys and my bag so I can go with you."

Cooper didn't argue, either. Despite Jessa's earlier assurances that Liam was making a speedy recovery, Cooper figured he'd need medical care for a while.

It didn't take long for the doc to return, and Cooper went back into the room. He pulled the blanket from Liam's crib and draped it over the toddler.

"Come with me," Cooper told the women. He positioned himself in front of them as they made their way into the hall.

The wounded gunmen were gone, no doubt on their way to surgery, but there were large pools of blood on the floor.

"Follow us out," Cooper said to his brother Tucker. It wouldn't hurt to have some extra firepower if things turned bad again.

With Tucker behind them, Cooper led Jessa and her mother around the blood as best he could, and they followed Dr. Howland down the corridor.

"Where are we going?" Jessa asked. She was holding Liam as if he were a thin piece of glass ready to shatter.

Cooper glanced around to make sure no one was in hearing range. There wasn't anyone. They had the hall to themselves.

"We're going somewhere you aren't going to like," he mumbled.

Cooper was taking Liam, Jessa and her mother home with him.

Chapter Five

Nothing about this felt right.

Jessa stared down at her sleeping son, thankful that none of this seemed to be affecting him.

But it was certainly affecting her.

The spent adrenaline had left her bone tired, but despite that she hadn't slept more than a few minutes in the guest room at the McKinnon ranch. Her mind was still wired, and the thoughts of how wrong this was kept going through her head.

Along with the sound of those shots.

She would always hear those. Would always remember how close they'd come to her baby.

And she would never forget that Cooper and his brothers had been the ones to keep Liam safe. Of course, Cooper might have had an ulterior motive for what he'd done.

Because he might believe Liam was his son.

Just the thought of that revved up her heartbeat and caused her breath to go thin. Jessa tried to tamp down her emotions. No need to worry about what might be, and she refused to believe that Liam was Cooper's lost child. Her life and luck couldn't take another bad turn like that, and she had to be due for the peaceful life that she'd planned with her son.

Of course, Cooper might be making the same plans.

Jessa glanced at the laptop still open on the guest bed where she had tried to sleep. She'd closed the email containing the background check on Cooper that she'd asked a P.I. friend to do, but she didn't need to see the report to remember what it'd said.

From all accounts, Cooper had been crazy in love with his wife, Molly, but they'd gotten off to a rocky start. Molly had literally broken her engagement to another man to start seeing Cooper, and the other man—Donovan Bradley—had then in turn tried to have embezzlement charges filed against Molly for the cattle-broker business they'd run together. The charges hadn't stuck.

But the gossip had.

There were plenty of rumors that Cooper had slept with Donovan's fiancée just to get back at the man for an old feud between the former friends turned enemies. Jessa had seen photos of Cooper and Donovan together on the high school football team and again on the rodeo circuit—definitely friends in those days—but something had caused a rift. Rumor had it that Donovan had gotten too friendly with Cooper's aunt, who was close to their age. Another side believed that Cooper was at fault with his sexual pursuit of Molly.

Jessa wanted to believe the rumors. She wanted to believe anything that would help her discredit Cooper, but she hadn't found a shred of proof that he was anything but a badge-wearing cowboy who actually knew the meaning of justice.

And keeping his jeans zipped.

Unlike Donovan, he hadn't left a string of broken hearts throughout the county.

Jessa's phone vibrated, and she silently groaned at the name she saw on the screen. It was yet another badge-wearing cowboy.

County Sheriff Aiden Braddock.

Aiden's father, Whitt, was the man Jewell was charged with murdering.

Jessa had worked closely with Aiden to bring the charges against Cooper's mother. For months the investigation had consumed them. Now she had something else more important to consume her—keeping her son safe and making other arrangements that didn't involve staying on the McKinnon ranch.

Jessa stepped out in the hall to take the call so that she wouldn't wake Liam, and she nearly ran right into Cooper. He'd obviously just showered. His hair was still damp, and he smelled, well, better than he should have. Something musky and manly that seemed to alert every nerve in her body. Ditto for his cowboy-cop "uniform" of worn jeans, a pale blue button-up shirt and scuffed cowboy boots. His badge was clipped to his belt.

Next to the silver rodeo buckle.

If she'd had any doubts that he was a cowboy, that would have rid her of them.

"That'll be Sheriff Braddock," he said, tipping his head to her still-vibrating phone. Mercy. The sight of Cooper had made her forget all about it. "He just called to tell me that Jewell turned herself in to the county deputy and she's now under arrest."

Since it wasn't a conversation she wanted to have in front of Cooper, she let the call go to voice mail. Better to get any details later after she'd worked out some details and rules of her own.

"I didn't tell Sheriff Braddock or anyone else that you were here," Cooper added.

Good. For now, the fewer people who knew where she was, the better. "Any updates on the would-be kidnappers?"

"One didn't make it. The other came through surgery

all right but is still too weak to talk. Colt's posted outside the guy's door in case someone tries to help him escape. Colt will call to let me know when I can question him."

Jessa hated those men, but she wished both were alive and ready to spill why they'd tried to take her baby.

Cooper glanced down at her clothes as if he'd never before seen jeans on a woman. And he hadn't on her. She always tried to dress the part of the D.A. when she went out, even just to get groceries. Yes, it might seem silly, but she wanted to be set apart, wanted the locals to respect her for the job.

But the jeans clearly didn't get much respect from Cooper.

However, they did garner a long look. One that made her feel as if he was trying to undress her.

Cooper glanced over her shoulder, his attention landing on the crib. "Is Liam okay?"

But he didn't just ask the question. Cooper slid past her, his arm brushing against hers, and went into the room. He stayed back from the crib, but he could no doubt see her baby's face. Yes, it was petty, but she stepped between them. However, since he was taller than she was, he'd have no trouble getting a second look.

"He's fine," she snapped, her voice still a whisper. "The doctor examined him before he left last night, and your sister came by a half hour ago to check his bandage. She said he was fine, and then she and my mother went to the kitchen to get something to eat."

His sister Rosalie, who was a pediatric nurse. For Liam's sake, it was convenient that she was at the ranch with them, but her mere presence was another sticking point. Because the only reason Rosalie was there was to help clear her mother's name. That put Jessa and her at odds.

In theory, anyway.

But Rosalie hadn't shown any resentment whatsoever. She'd examined Liam as if he were her own child and had promised to check on him as long as needed.

Hopefully, that wouldn't be long.

Jessa motioned for them to go back out in the hall. She didn't want Cooper standing there staring at Liam. Especially staring at him with that hopeful, pained look in his eyes.

Cooper followed her. Finally.

"I'll need to make arrangements to leave," she started. But that was as far as she got.

"Not yet. I want you, your mom and Liam here until I have a handle on who's after Liam and why."

Jessa groaned. "That could take days or more."

"Or less," he quickly argued. "We'll start with the gunmen, and once we know who they are, then we can work backward to find out who hired them." He paused a second. "Any idea who that would have been and why?"

She shook her head. "Maybe it's someone connected to your mother."

A muscle flickered in his jaw.

"I'm not accusing you," Jessa explained. "But there are others involved in the murder investigation."

"My brothers. My dad. And my mother's three other kids. Yeah, I know what you think of us. I can personally vouch for my brothers and Dad. Rosalie, too," he added almost hesitantly. "The other two, Rayanne and Seth, are law enforcement officers."

It wasn't exactly an endorsement of the last two's innocence, but there was another player in this.

Jewell.

"Do you think your mother murdered Whitt Braddock?" Jessa came out and asked.

"I don't care if she did."

Yes, he did. The wounds were still there. After all, his mother had abandoned him and his brothers. Jessa couldn't imagine doing that to Liam, but then she also couldn't imagine being a married woman, having an affair and then killing her lover.

But that was exactly what Jewell had done.

Well, it was what the evidence pointed to her doing, anyway.

"When I was at the hospital giving blood," Cooper continued, "you said you'd made some inquiries about Liam's birth parents, so that you'd know the family's medical history. Who exactly did you contact?"

She blinked and had to think hard to remember that conversation. "My adoption attorney, Hector Dixon. Why, you don't think he had anything to do with this, do you?"

Cooper lifted his shoulder. "I need to look at all possible angles. Maybe Hector contacted someone who got spooked."

Even though he hadn't come out and said it, Jessa knew where this was going. "You think the adoption was illegal—"

"Again, I'm looking at all angles. How'd Hector react when you asked him about the birth parents?"

Jessa opened her mouth to assure him that Hector had reacted as expected. But he hadn't. "He seemed nervous. Maybe distracted," she corrected. "He's a busy man, and I called him out of the blue. He might have thought I was questioning the way he handled the adoption."

At least she hoped that was all there was to it.

"I'll get him to the sheriff's office and question him," Cooper insisted.

Again, she nearly jumped to assure him that it wouldn't be necessary, that she'd talk to her lawyer herself. But this was an official investigation now. Besides, Hector might have some idea why this had happened, and if he did, he might know something that would somehow keep Liam safe.

"What about your personal relationships?" Cooper asked. "Maybe your ex wanted to make trouble for you?"

Jessa felt the heat rise in her cheeks. Cooper knew. Of course he did. He had access to police records from all over the state. He would have seen the report that she'd filed when her ex-husband, Rick Bolton, had beaten her. Maybe Cooper had even seen the bloody and bruised photos taken of her so he could be arrested for assault and battery.

"My ex hasn't been in touch with me for nearly three years," she settled for saying. "I'm not even sure where he is."

She braced herself for Cooper's argument. That Rick could have decided to get even with her for the eight months he'd spent in jail. But no argument—Cooper's eyes met hers for just a moment before they darted away. In that second of time, she thought maybe she'd seen some sympathy.

But she had to be wrong about that.

He was still too enraged about her bringing Jewell back to Sweetwater Springs and therefore back into his life.

"Where'd your lawyer get Liam?" Cooper asked.

They were back to the illegal adoption theory, and while it was a definite sore point, it was something she, too, wanted to know. It wouldn't help if she just buried her head in the sand.

"It was a private adoption, but let me call Hector now and find out."

She stepped away from Cooper before she could hear

any reason he might have for her not doing that. But he didn't object. Instead, when she took her phone from her pocket and pressed Hector's number, Cooper just stayed in the doorway, looking at Liam.

"He's not yours," Jessa insisted. "If he were, I'd know it. I'd feel it in my heart."

It was a stupid argument. One that clearly didn't convince Cooper. He just made one of those annoying sounds that could have meant anything. Jessa didn't get a chance to continue the one-sided disagreement, because Hector answered.

"Jessa," he greeted. "I heard about your car accident. Are Liam and you all right?"

It seemed the right thing to ask, but Jessa's nerves were too close to the surface for her to take anything at face value. "We're fine, but that's not why I'm calling. I need to know what you learned about Liam's birth parents."

"Nothing," Hector readily admitted. "Look, I've been trying, but the birth mother was adamant about this being a closed adoption. She left no contact information whatsoever."

That wasn't unusual. Often a teen mother would close that door of contact as her way of moving on and detaching herself from the child.

"What adoption agency did you use?" Jessa pressed.

Hector hesitated. It wasn't a pause. Jessa could feel the difference, but she prayed she was wrong. She didn't want any hesitations when he came to this.

"No agency," Hector finally said. "The woman I used is more or less a broker, and she's got a good reputation for her placements."

Jessa was listening to every word, but she lost her focus when Cooper went into the room with Liam. She went after him.

"Birth mothers who want to do private adoptions contact this broker," Hector continued, "and she in turn contacts the attorneys of prospective birth parents who are willing to pay medical bills and maybe even give compensation. Like you did."

She had. A total payment of nearly fifty thousand dollars, which was almost every bit of the inheritance she'd gotten when her father died six years earlier. Jessa would have paid a heck of a lot more than that. But again, that wasn't what had her attention now. Cooper had it. And she found him right by the crib, staring down at Liam.

Then she saw something else.

Cooper smiled.

The corner of his mouth lifted, the simple gesture flickering the muscle in his jaw. It was short-lived when his gaze landed on the bandage across Liam's stomach. The incision beneath it was already healing, but the bandage was a reminder that she'd come close to losing him.

"Jessa?" Hector said. "Did you hear me?"

No. She hadn't. "I'm sorry, this is a bad connection," Jessa lied.

"I said in our case, the broker contacted me because she'd heard through mutual friends that you wanted to adopt a newborn."

It all sounded reasonable. So reasonable that it might even appease Cooper.

"What's the broker's name?" Jessa asked. Best to finish this conversation fast so she could maneuver Cooper out of the room and away from Liam.

But Hector didn't do much to finish things. His hesitation lasted a lot longer than the first one. "Her name is Peggy Dawes, but please don't contact her. She prefers not to deal directly with the adoptive parents."

Tough. This broker would deal with her. "I need her

phone number. Before you say no, it's important. Yesterday someone tried to kidnap my baby, and I want to know why."

"Good God. And you think Peggy has answers about that?" He didn't wait for her to respond. "She won't. Heavens, Jessa. How could you think that? Peggy did you a great service by locating a baby for you, and you can't go around questioning—"

"I'll thank her," Jessa interrupted. "Now give me her phone number."

The seconds crawled by before she heard some rustling on the other end of the line and then Hector rattled off the number. Jessa made a note of it on her phone's notepad.

"Thanks," Jessa mumbled.

"Don't thank me. I'll keep looking for info on Liam's birth parents, but I'm not doing you any favors by giving you Peggy's number."

Jessa froze. "What do you mean?" But she was talking to the air because Hector had already hung up.

"Anything wrong?" Cooper asked.

He'd no doubt seen the concern on her face, but Jessa shook her head and showed him the number she'd taken down. "It's for Peggy Dawes, the baby broker my attorney used. Hector is still looking for information about Liam's birth parents."

Cooper nodded and pressed in Peggy's numbers on his phone's keypad.

"No!" Jessa insisted. "I don't want you to call her. I'll do it. I don't want her to think she's under investigation or something."

"She *is* under investigation," Cooper fired back, and he would have pressed the call button if Jessa hadn't caught his hand to stop him.

Jessa was about to launch into another argument, but the sound stopped both of them. Not a gunshot or some other nightmarish noise.

Liam stirred. "Mama." And he reached for her.

That got her hand off Cooper, and she shoved her phone into her pocket so she could gently lift Liam into her arms. He showed no signs whatsoever of being in pain, though he did point to his bandage. "Got boo-boo."

And then his attention went to Cooper.

Liam eyed him as if sizing him up, but then his attention landed on the shiny badge and rodeo buckle. "Up." Liam reached out for Cooper to take him.

It felt as if someone had punched her. Jessa didn't want her baby in the arms of the man who might try to take him away from her.

But that was exactly what Cooper did.

He eased his hands around Liam and lifted him into his arms. Liam didn't try to inspect the shiny things that had caused him to reach for Cooper. Her son just studied him.

Then Liam smiled.

Cooper closed his eyes a moment, and she could almost see the painful memories tightening the muscles in his face. Heaven knew how much he'd grieved when he'd lost his son in that flood. Jessa suddenly knew how painful that would have been, because she was feeling a little of it now.

God, she couldn't lose him. *Wouldn't*. Because she refused to believe Cooper had any kind of claim on the child she loved more than life itself.

Cooper's phone buzzed, and he hesitated as if deciding whether to answer it. He had no choice, of course, because it could be about the investigation, but it meant handing Liam back to her so he could answer it.

"It's Colt," he relayed to her, and he stepped away from the crib to take the call. He didn't put it on speaker, and Jessa couldn't hear what Colt was saying, but she prayed it wasn't more bad news.

She watched, waited and kept Liam close.

"Yeah, I heard you," Cooper said to his brother. "No, I'll handle it. I'll talk to her."

Mercy, that didn't sound good.

"We have IDs on the gunmen," Cooper explained the moment he ended the call.

Jessa was afraid to feel any real relief, but that was a start. Cooper had already said if he had names, he could begin to look for connections.

"The surviving one is Vernon Graham," Cooper went on. "He's awake and says he wants you to offer him a plea deal for a lighter sentence."

"What will he give us in return?" Jessa asked, and she was almost afraid to hear the answer. So far, nothing about this situation was good.

Cooper paused a heartbeat, his gaze fastening to hers. "Graham says he'll tell us the name of the person who hired him to kidnap Liam."

Chapter Six

"You don't have to do this," Cooper reminded Jessa one more time. "In fact, I'd rather you didn't."

She shot him a glare, kept her arms folded over her chest and continued to stare out his truck window at the passing countryside. "I want to hear what this woman has to say," Jessa mumbled.

This woman was Peggy Dawes.

Vernon Graham had given them Peggy's name as part of a plea deal. Judging from Jessa's scowl and body language, she wasn't pleased about the gunman's revelation that Peggy was the one who'd hired him to kidnap Liam. And there was a good reason for Jessa's anger.

It meant the kidnapping attempt was linked to the adoption. And it also could mean the whole adoption deal had been illegal.

But now Cooper was the one to snarl.

If Liam was indeed his son, then how the heck had Peggy gotten her hands on him?

Unfortunately, he could think of a few scenarios that tightened the knot in his gut. Maybe Peggy or one of her baby-brokering henchmen had caused his wife to be swept away in the flood. Or it could have gone in a different direction and Peggy merely could have found Liam.

Of course, that led him to the next question of why she hadn't just called the cops and reported it.

There was also another possible conclusion.

Maybe the gunman had out-and-out lied.

That also didn't help with the knot, because it still meant this was somehow connected to the adoption. After all, how else would the gunman have known the woman's name?

He would soon know the answer to that, since he was headed out to Peggy's San Antonio house to have a little chat with her. Cooper had considered just hauling her into the sheriff's office for questioning, but the woman didn't have even a parking ticket, much less a criminal record. Also, other than the accusations of would-be kidnappers, there were no flags to indicate she was doing anything illegal. Heck, he couldn't even find a connection between her and the gunman, Graham, who'd accused her of wrongdoing.

Well, he couldn't find the connection yet, anyway.

But if either Graham or Peggy confessed to anything, Cooper would be making an arrest today. That was why he'd wanted his brother along.

Jessa's phone buzzed, and she snatched it up and put it to her ear, but not before Cooper saw that the call was from her mother. "Is something wrong?" Jessa immediately asked the caller.

"No, everything's fine," he heard Linda say.

Thankfully, Jessa and he were close enough that he had no trouble hearing the conversation. He'd taken precautions when Jessa had said she'd be going with him to see Peggy. Cooper had put all the ranch hands on alert, and Tucker was standing guard. Rayanne was also in the house, but he hadn't even bothered to ask her to help. Unlike Rosalie, Rayanne didn't seem to be the helping sort.

Still, there were plenty of things that could go wrong that didn't involve security, so Cooper listened carefully to what Linda had to say.

"I just wanted you to know that Dr. Howland was here to check on Liam, and he said he was doing great," Linda explained. "He didn't feel there was any need to move him back to the hospital as long as Rosalie continues to change and check the bandage."

Jessa huffed softly. And Cooper knew why. It meant she'd have to stay at the ranch. Of course, she could just hire another nurse and leave, and Cooper figured Jessa was already working on that.

He was working on making her stay.

Until the DNA results came back, Cooper wanted Liam under the McKinnon roof. And after he had the results... Well, he'd deal with that when and if the time came.

"Thanks, Mom," Jessa said. "Give Liam a kiss for me."

Jessa put her phone away and continued to look out the window. Cooper did his own share of looking, too. First to make sure they weren't being followed by anyone but Colt, who was driving behind them in his truck.

But Cooper also looked at Jessa.

No matter how many times he told his eyes to stay off her, they didn't listen. Partly because of the worry and fear still on her face. Partly because he shared the same concern about Liam's safety as she did.

However, it was her jeans and snug red top that were giving him the most trouble.

There was nothing particularly special about the items of clothing, except they looked damn good on her. Hugging her curves. Making him well aware that beneath her A.D.A. facade, there was a red-blooded woman.

One who stirred his own blood.

And that couldn't happen.

Hell.

He wasn't in any position to start a relationship, especially with a woman who thought he was lower than grit on a horse's hoof. And besides, he had to focus on getting things straight with this adoption and the attack. It wasn't as if he didn't have enough to keep him busy.

"You keep looking at me," she grumbled.

Yeah, he did. "It's nothing personal," Cooper said, and then silently cursed. Obviously, her jeans had also rendered him stupid.

Because a man gawking at a woman was indeed personal.

"I meant it doesn't mean anything," he corrected. "It's just you look, well, different. Sort of naked without one of your suits."

What he should have done was just shut the heck up instead of babbling like an idiot.

Her eyebrow slid up. "Naked?"

He groaned. Best to go another round of trying to clear this up. "Normal. Like you fit in around here."

She looked at him as if he'd sprouted an extra nose or something. Obviously, he'd missed the mark.

"If I fit in, I won't get the respect I need," she said, her voice crisp. The clothes might be different, but that ice-queen voice was the same. "I'd be just one of the good ol' boys."

"No one would ever suspect you of being a boy," he grumbled.

However, it was interesting that Jessa thought she had to keep her outsider status to do her job. He might not like the accusations she'd made against him, but he'd never wanted her to feel that she had to build up walls to stay professional.

She stared at him, whispered something he didn't catch and looked away. "Whatever this feeling is between us, it can't mean anything."

That sounded pretty good, but then she gave him one last glance. Or rather she gave that glance to his jeans.

Oh, man.

One-sided personal was bad enough, but two-sided could get them in a mess of trouble. Thankfully, he got a reprieve from putting his foot in his mouth because the GPS announced they had arrived at their destination.

The modest redbrick house was in a subdivision in an equally modest part of town. Definitely not the home of a lucrative baby broker. Of course, it could be a front, so as not to draw attention, and that meant they needed to take precautions. If Peggy had been the one to hire those two men, then she might have even more men and guns inside.

Cooper waited until Colt was parked and out of his truck before he motioned for Jessa to exit.

"Yes, I know," Jessa said without his prompting. "I stay behind you, and I don't take any chances."

But she would take chances. To protect Liam, she'd do anything, and that was why he had to watch her as carefully as he watched Peggy. If he'd thought for one minute that Jessa wouldn't have followed him for this visit, he would have just demanded that she stay at the ranch.

They walked to the porch, with Jessa between them, and Cooper rang the bell. There was a camera mounted just above the door and it didn't take long before the woman's voice poured through the little intercom just beneath the camera.

"May I help you?" she asked.

Both Colt and he flashed their badges. "I'm Sheriff

Cooper McKinnon. This is Deputy Colt McKinnon and A.D.A. Jessa Wells. We need to talk to you."

The door instantly opened, so fast that Cooper nearly reached for his gun, but the woman he came face-to-face with wasn't armed. She was a tall, attractive blonde in her mid- to late thirties, and there was little chance she could be carrying concealed in the gauzy white summer dress she was wearing. It fit her like a glove.

The woman's attention snapped right to Jessa. "Jessa Wells?" Peggy asked, her breath already revved up. "Did something else happen to the little boy you adopted?"

Well, at least Peggy wasn't going to claim that she knew nothing about the reason for their visit, and she certainly wasn't acting like a woman with anything to hide.

Of course, she could just be a really good liar.

Jessa nodded in response to Peggy's question. "Someone tried to kidnap him yesterday."

"Oh, God." And Peggy just kept repeating it while she motioned for them to come inside.

They went in, Cooper's gaze firing all around to make sure they weren't about to be ambushed. At first he thought he heard someone talking, but he realized it was music. Peggy apparently liked country music and white furniture. In fact, the whole place was pretty sterile looking. Nothing, however, to indicate she was making big bucks with illegal adoptions.

"Sit down, please," Peggy said. "Could I get you a drink or something?" Again, her focus was on Jessa.

"No, thank you. We're just here to find out about the man who attempted to take my son." Jessa glanced at Cooper, silently asking how much she should say. He didn't want all the details spilled about the DNA test, not yet anyway, so he took things from there.

"Two men wearing masks showed up at the hospital,"

Cooper explained, and he looked for any sign of guilt or recognition in her eyes. "One was killed. The other is Vernon Graham. He was injured, but he was able to talk today." He paused, kept watching Peggy's face. "And he claims you hired him to kidnap Liam."

Well, he got a reaction, but it wasn't one of guilt. Peggy's breath burst out, and she got to her feet. She pressed her hands against the sides of her head. "This can't be happening. It just can't be."

Cooper stood, positioning himself in front of Jessa just in case Peggy panicked and tried to run. But she didn't appear to be on the verge of doing anything but breaking down into tears.

And yeah, they came.

The tears started to streak down her cheeks. They were sort of convincing for an innocent woman, except guilty people cried crocodile tears all the time.

"You know Vernon Graham?" Cooper asked.

"No, of course not." She leaned forward, catching Jessa's hand. "I really just want to help people. Women like you. I have a large circle of friends, and when I hear of someone who's chosen to given up her baby, then I look for the right family for the child."

"You're a baby broker," Cooper concluded. "You get paid to do what you do."

Peggy's mouth tightened a little. "Yes, I get paid. Not as much as you'd think, and I'm not a broker. I think of myself more as a matchmaker. I find the perfect fit for babies."

"Admirable," he mumbled, and he hoped he didn't sound too sarcastic. It was hard to give the woman an inch of leeway when she'd been named a felony suspect. Of course, she'd been named that by yet another felon. "So why did Graham say you'd hired him to kidnap Liam?"

She instantly shook her head, her blond curls swinging around her face. "I don't know. But something suspicious is going on. I'm almost certain that someone's been following me, and then three days ago, I got a visit from a P.I."

Jessa and he exchanged glances. The timing was certainly suspect because that was the day of Jessa's car accident. Also the day that Cooper had requested a DNA test on Liam. He'd made waves to get the court order for that test, and in doing so, he could have stirred up some trouble from someone who didn't want trouble stirred.

Cooper snagged Peggy's gaze so he could watch her reaction to his question. "What makes you think someone's following you?"

"Just a feeling I keep getting. Like I'm being watched."

Cooper didn't discount it. Gut feelings had saved him more than a time or two, but he didn't like the gut feeling he was getting about Peggy, either.

"What P.I.?" Jessa asked the woman.

More head shaking from Peggy. "I can't remember his name. He only spoke to me for a minute or two. Said he was representing a client who was considering adoption. All he wanted to know was how I handled my paperwork for the adoptions. I told him there was no paperwork, that it was all done by word of mouth. I've been doing this for years, but that's the first time I've had a visit from a P.I."

"And he didn't say anything specifically about Liam?" Jessa pressed.

"No. He didn't ask about any of the babies that I've helped place, and there have been dozens of them." Peggy paused. "Do you think this man was working for the kidnappers?"

"Possibly," Cooper answered. "And that's why we need his name."

"I have his card somewhere around here." She stood and went to a rolltop desk in the corner. When she lifted the top, Cooper saw the stacks of papers and books. Definitely not as sterile and pristine as the rest of the house. Peggy began to dig through the heaps.

He hoped there wasn't a gun hidden in that mess.

Just in case there was, Cooper moved to the edge of his seat so he could watch Peggy better. "Where'd you get Liam?"

"I didn't *get* him. That's not how it works. I simply put Hector Dixon in touch with this friend of a friend who had the baby. The baby wasn't even her own child. If I remember correctly, she said someone in her family, a teenager, had given birth and couldn't keep the baby."

"I need that friend of a friend's name," Cooper insisted. "Or have you forgotten it, too?"

For just a moment she got a deer-caught-in-headlights look, but then she nodded. Swallowed hard. "What if the person who hired these kidnappers sends someone to come after me?" Peggy asked.

"Why would he?" Cooper pressed, though if the woman was an innocent pawn in all of this, he knew a good reason why. Peggy could be a dangerous loose end for someone trying to cover up an illegal adoption.

"I can arrange for you to have some protection," Cooper offered.

Peggy nodded. Stared at him for a moment and continued to dig through the papers. She finally extracted what appeared to be a bill with something jotted on it.

"It's not the P.I.'s card, but it is the name of the friend of a friend who contacted me about Liam." Peggy scanned through the notes. "Her name was Carol Sealey."

Jessa shook her head, no doubt because the name meant nothing to her. But it sure as hell meant something to Cooper. Colt, too. He opened his mouth to say something, but Cooper gave him a stay-quiet look.

Hell.

This had just taken a really bad turn.

"I have another desk in my bedroom," Peggy said. "I'll look for the P.I.'s card there."

Cooper didn't tell her to stop, and he didn't go after her. Heck, he wasn't even sure he could move. He just sat there and waited for the woman to scurry out of the room.

"Who's Carol Sealey?" Jessa whispered.

"She works as a personal assistant for Donovan Bradley," Cooper managed to say.

Judging from the way her eyes widened and the hard breath she sucked in, Jessa not only knew who he was. She also knew of Donovan's connection to him.

Of course she did.

There was still a lot of gossip about Donovan and him, and Jessa would have uncovered it when she was investigating him for those unfounded obstruction-of-justice charges.

"Donovan hates Cooper," Colt offered.

"He was once engaged to your late wife," Jessa added. "And then he was involved with Jewell's younger sister. Not in a good way, either. I've heard there was possibly some physical abuse."

Yeah, she knew the whole story, all right. What she didn't know was that in addition to the pain Donovan had inflicted on his aunt, the man had also tried to cause Molly and him as much trouble as possible. Nothing criminal, just the constant flow of malicious rumors and attempts to destroy Molly's reputation and the day care and preschool that she'd worked so hard to get started.

Jessa made a soft gasp, no doubt coming to the conclusion that Cooper and Colt had already reached. If Donovan's lackey, Carol Sealey, had some part in the adoption, then it was likely Donovan had, too.

And that would mean Donovan could have stolen Liam.

But how?

Molly had been swept away in the flood. She'd drowned. Cooper had seen her body, and there'd been no signs of foul play. Nothing to indicate that the baby could have survived, either.

But he could have.

No gasp this time. Jessa huffed, got to her feet. "Don't jump to conclusions."

Too late. Cooper had already made the jump. "I need the results of that DNA test." And he took out his phone.

"Please, no," Jessa whispered.

Cooper looked up at her, bracing himself for her to try to stop him from making the call. But her words seemed to be a prayer. No doubt praying that Liam's DNA didn't match his. But now that Donovan's employee was the one who'd arranged for Liam's adoption, it was the only thing that made sense.

Unless Peggy was lying.

Since Jessa had heard the stories about Donovan, Molly and him, it wasn't much of a stretch that Peggy could have heard them, too.

Cursing, Cooper jumped off the sofa, and drawing his gun, he hurried down the hall where he'd last seen Peggy. There were three rooms off the hall. Two doors were open. The other closed. That was where Cooper headed.

"Peggy?" he called out.

No answer.

Gun first, Cooper stepped into the doorway, his gaze

slashing from one side to the other. Movement caught his eye, and he took aim. However, it was only the wind stirring the white curtains in the window that was wide-open.

Peggy was gone.

Chapter Seven

Jessa's mind was running wild, and it was hard to tamp down the bad thoughts when there were so many of them. She hadn't wanted any of the danger to be connected to the adoption, but with every turn, they kept coming back to it. And now someone who could have given them answers was missing.

Where the heck was Peggy?

Jessa couldn't hear the phone conversation that Cooper was having with Tucker, but judging from his body language, the search for Peggy wasn't going well. He was pacing the sunroom that stretched across the back of the McKinnon house. He was barking out orders, too, but so far none of the orders or the search had turned up anything. It was as if the woman had vanished.

"It's amazing how fast babies heal," Rosalie said as she changed Liam's bandage. She finished up, gave him a kiss on the cheek and stood from the wicker chair where she'd been seated.

Jessa thanked her, something she'd been doing a lot lately. She thanked her mother, too, and glanced at Liam to make sure he was okay. He was. He was totally engrossed in the book Linda was reading to him.

"I can watch Liam," Rosalie offered, "if you and your mom want to take a nap. You both look exhausted."

Jessa didn't doubt what Rosalie was saying, but a nap was out of the question for her. No way would she be able to let her body and mind rest with so much up in the air.

"I can't lose him," Jessa mumbled. She hadn't meant to blurt that out, but she was doing it a lot lately.

Rosalie nodded, and she gave Jessa's arm a pat. It was more than just sympathy coming from the woman. From what Jessa had heard, Rosalie's newborn daughter had been kidnapped, never to be seen again. Rosalie knew what it was like to lose a child. Cooper did, too.

And it was something Jessa never wanted to experience.

"I've been investigating missing children," Rosalie said. "I've made plenty of contacts. I could ask around and see if anyone knows something about the circumstances surrounding Liam's adoption."

"There's nothing to find," Jessa insisted. *I hope.* "But if you hear anything that'll lead us to the kidnapper, that would help."

Rosalie nodded, assured her that she would do just that and walked away.

Cooper finished his call and looked on the verge of cursing a blue streak before his attention landed on Liam. That softened his expression a bit.

"No sign of Peggy, and no one's been able to reach Donovan Bradley," he explained, shaking his head. "Carol Sealey no longer works for Donovan. His new assistant said she has no idea where Carol is and that Donovan hasn't been in his office all morning."

Too bad because with both Peggy and Carol now missing, Donovan might be the only one left who knew what the heck was going on. "What about Hector? Does he have any idea where Peggy would go and why she'd run?"

"I think it's pretty obvious why she ran," Cooper

grumbled. "She's got something to hide." And with another glance at Liam, he believed that *something* was an illegal adoption.

That gave her another jolt of panic and fear.

"I can take Liam upstairs for his nap," her mom offered. Jessa hadn't told her mother about Cooper's suspicions, but she obviously saw the tension between them. Anyone could have, including Liam, and even though her son was young, it wasn't something she wanted him to sense. Especially since he was still recovering from surgery.

Jessa didn't stop her mother from leaving with Liam. She wanted a chance to talk to Cooper alone so she could beg him to, well, she wasn't sure what yet, but she had to do something. It felt as if he was trying to snatch Liam away from her.

"Hector's on the way over here," Cooper added before she could say anything. "He wants to talk to you."

Mercy, that didn't sound good. She prayed he wasn't coming to confess he'd done something illegal to secure Liam's adoption.

"I don't trust Hector," Cooper went on. "So while he's here, I don't want Liam or you alone with him. If he's trying to cover up his part in the adoption, he might consider you both loose ends."

Hearing that spelled out turned her blood to ice, and she forced herself to remember another side of this. "I plan to go through all my recent cases to see if there's someone who could be out for revenge. That might be all this is. Someone who wants to get back at me because I put him or her behind bars."

Cooper nodded, made a sound of mild agreement, but his attention wasn't on her. It was on the two people who came out of the guesthouse about twenty yards away.

Cooper's sister Rayanne and his stepbrother, Seth.

Like the other times Jessa had gotten a glimpse of Seth, he was dressed in a black suit. Very much FBI, and Jessa would have asked for his help if she thought she could trust him.

She couldn't.

Even though Seth and Cooper were at odds, it didn't mean the agent would be willing to help the A.D.A. who had put his adopted mother behind bars.

Rayanne and Seth appeared to be involved in a heavy discussion, but that stopped when they got within earshot of Cooper and her. Cooper's sister threw open the door to the sunroom, stepped in and aimed a glare at Cooper. The glare held when her attention settled on Jessa.

She didn't actually come inside. Rayanne stood in the doorway and ignored the steamy heat that was pouring in around her. "Are you plotting how to keep my mother in jail?" Rayanne snarled.

Jessa wasn't feeling her strongest, but that put some steel in her spine. She nodded. "Because the evidence points to Jewell's guilt."

Rayanne's eyes took on some steel, too, and she got right in Jessa's face. Even though she was Rosalie's twin, there was little resemblance between the two women. Rayanne's eyes were harder, and it didn't help that she looked ready to start a brawl.

One that she could win.

Jessa had heard rumors that Rayanne's boyfriend had dumped her and then been killed. On the very day that she'd learned her mother was about to be arrested for murder. This wasn't exactly a good time in Rayanne's life.

Just like the rest of them.

Cooper stepped between his sister and her. "Jessa's

an invited guest in this house," he told Rayanne. "You'll treat her as such."

"Invited," she grumbled. "And I wasn't. If that was meant to insult me, big brother, it won't work." Her index finger landed against Cooper's chest. "I'm staying to make sure you don't team up with your invited house-guest here to put the screws to an innocent woman."

"Rayanne," Seth warned. "Pull your claws back. This is a fight we'll win in court, not here on the ranch. That's the reason I've been telling you to move into the guest-house, so you won't be under their roof."

Now it was Seth's turn to glare, but his went to Coo-per. "Tell me what's going on with the attempt to kidnap the A.D.A.'s son. Is it connected to our mother?"

"Our mother?" Cooper repeated, clearly riled by that. Maybe because his mother had abandoned him. Maybe because Jewell had adopted Seth.

Maybe both.

There were a lot of reasons for Cooper to be upset, and Jessa could share some of those reasons with him.

"I can't find a connection between this and Jewell," Cooper finally said. "And I don't want you looking for one, either. You'll stay out of my way," he growled.

Seth met him eye to eye. "And you'll stay out of mine."

With that, Seth turned like a sleek jungle cat finished with his prey and walked back toward the guesthouse.

"I know I've already brought this up," Jessa said after Rayanne left, "and you've dismissed it, but what if all of this really is connected to Jewell? Not just the kidnapping attempt but my car accident and Peggy's disappearance."

This time Cooper didn't jump to dismiss it or defend his brothers and father. Nor himself. He just shook his head before his gaze came to hers.

"Someone could be trying to manipulate the investigation. Yeah, I've considered it," he added when she blinked. "Someone could be trying to use Liam to get one of us to tamper with evidence."

And that in turn led back to his mother.

Or maybe to someone who wanted the case against her dropped.

There weren't many people in that camp—Rayanne, Rosalie, Seth and Jewell herself. The only one she could rule out was Rosalie. Yes, it was clear she loved her mother as much as Cooper hated the woman, but Rosalie didn't seem like the sort to cut legal corners, especially when she had her own battle going on—the search for her missing baby.

But maybe someone else had a hand in this.

It wasn't much of a stretch for her to believe someone was trying to tamper with the murder charges against Jewell. After all, someone had stolen or misplaced evidence. Until now, Jessa had figured Cooper or his brothers might have done that, but she had a better understanding of the family dynamics now. The rumors of the rift between mother and sons weren't just rumors. She doubted any of the McKinnon men would lift a finger to help Jewell.

"It's almost as if we're on the same side when it comes to Jewell," she mumbled.

That sent a shot of fire through his eyes. "We might be if you'd quit accusing me of obstruction of justice. I don't care what happens to her. I only care how it affects my father and brothers. But I wouldn't destroy evidence to keep the mud off us from Jewell's arrest."

No. He wouldn't. She knew that *now*. But knowing it and knowing Cooper better didn't make her situation easier.

"I'm scared," she admitted. And Jessa could tell from

the look he gave her that he knew she wasn't just talking about the kidnapping attempt.

Cooper nodded, mumbled some of that profanity he'd held back earlier and reached out. Took her by the arm. And pulled her to him.

Almost immediately she felt him stiffen, and he no doubt would have snapped away from her if Jessa hadn't caught him. Why, she didn't know.

Okay, she did.

It was because that brief moment in his arms had felt darn good. Reassuring. And safe. She hadn't felt safe in days, but it was a mistake to look for that safety in Cooper's arms. And the sound that rumbled in his throat let her know that he agreed.

But he didn't move.

Neither did she.

Jessa just stood there with one of his arms hooked around her. Their gazes met. Held. And she felt that tug again. The one deep in her belly that she didn't want to feel.

"This is *not* going to happen between us," she reminded him, and herself.

The corner of his mouth hitched, and he pulled her even closer to him. Against him. And kissed the top of her head. It was chaste and comforting. Or at least that was what he'd likely intended it to be. But the fire she felt was anything but comforting.

What the heck was wrong with her?

Jessa stepped back. "I have a bad history with men," she said. Then she frowned when Cooper didn't even react to that. It was because he knew about her history, especially the parts she had wanted to keep shut away.

Knew about the nightmare of a relationship that had put her in the emergency room four years ago.

He knew that she'd allowed herself to become a punching bag for a man who'd professed to love her and who had once given her the same tug she was feeling now.

Almost.

This tug for Cooper seemed stronger. Different.

That didn't make it right, and it was no doubt just a response to the danger. In fact, that was all it could be. Even if they semiagreed about Jewell, the trial would still cause trouble between his family and her.

No near smile this time. A muscle flickered in his jaw. "I did read what your ex did to you."

No surprise, but it put a lump in her throat, and the memories of the pain and shame flickered through her.

"I'm sorry," Cooper added.

There it was again. The sympathy fueled the tug. Or maybe Cooper alone was doing that. It was a reminder, a bad one, that it'd been way too long since she'd really been kissed. And Cooper certainly looked as if he knew how to do that.

She felt herself leaning closer to him, and it took her a moment to realize that was because Cooper still had hold of her arm, and he was pulling her back toward him. He was mumbling more profanity, too, as if this was the last thing on earth he wanted to do.

And probably was.

Still, that didn't stop him from touching his lips to hers. Just a quick touch. That went through her like an inferno. She actually lost her breath for a moment.

Her mind, too.

Because she didn't put up a fight to stop what couldn't happen between them. In fact, Jessa was reasonably sure she would have returned the kiss. A real one. Long, slow and deep. If Cooper's phone hadn't buzzed.

He shook his head. Cursed again. And yanked the phone from his pocket.

Jessa stepped back. Way back. And this time she told that tug to take a hike. Kissing Cooper wasn't just stupid. It was dangerous.

"Your adoption attorney's here," Cooper relayed to her once he'd finished the call.

She certainly hadn't forgotten about Hector's visit, but Jessa hadn't quite braced herself for it. Because this conversation could be dangerous, too, if he ended up admitting that the adoption was illegal.

That gave her the attitude adjustment she needed.

Jessa followed Cooper through the kitchen and to the living room at the front of the house. Hector was standing in the center of the room, and she only needed a glimpse to see the nerves. His tie was askew. Suit coat, too. There were dark circles under his eyes, and his five o'clock shadow was well past the fashionable stage.

"I don't know what you've started," Hector said, his narrowed eyes pinned to her, "but I want it to stop now."

Jessa shook her head. "What are you talking about?"

Hector used the back of his hand to wipe some sweat from his forehead. "Someone broke into my office. They stole my computer and ransacked my files."

Her heart slammed against her chest. "Please tell me you have security cameras."

"No," he mumbled and dropped down onto the sofa. "And no one saw them coming or going. They took your file."

That didn't help her already unsteady breath.

"Anyone else's?" Cooper quickly asked.

"Not that I can tell. Just Jessa's."

Oh, mercy. And that led them right back to an illegal adoption. Or maybe someone who wanted to make it look that way. But Jessa couldn't think of any reason someone would want to do that.

Jessa walked closer, stared down at the man she'd once praised for locating a precious baby for her to adopt. No praise now. She just needed answers. "Do you have any idea where Peggy is?"

"No." Another quick answer. "But she's probably facing the same kind of harassment I am. Now I have an FBI agent calling and demanding to see me."

Cooper and she exchanged glances, but judging from the way Cooper's forehead bunched up, this was the first he was hearing about it, too.

"The agent called a few hours ago, insisted on seeing me and made an appointment for three o'clock. He didn't come out and say it, but it sounds as if I'm under some kind of investigation." His gaze snapped to Cooper now. "What the hell did you say or do to get me into this mess?"

"I didn't say or do anything. I want the name of the agent," Cooper insisted without pausing.

"Gordon Riker. Why? You don't trust him?"

"No, I don't. Don't trust you, either. But in the case of the agent, he could be a fake. If you're not the one trying to cover up an illegal adoption, then maybe this person is."

That brought Hector to his feet. "I'm not covering up anything, and I won't have my livelihood destroyed with questions and accusations from the two of you."

"I'll ask all the questions I want to get to the truth." Cooper went to Jessa's side, and the look he shot Hector was a lot more intimidating than one she could have managed. Added to the fact that Cooper towered over Hector.

"Was anything about this adoption illegal?" Cooper demanded.

"No." Hector made another swipe at the beads of sweat

popping out all over his face. "And from now on, you'll communicate with me only through my attorney." He extracted a card from his pocket and dropped it on the coffee table.

Hector started to leave but then stopped and looked at Jessa. "I don't deserve this."

"Neither does Liam." Her voice cracked, and Jessa hoped she didn't lose it before she could get her point across. "My baby's in danger, and I need to find out why."

Even if it would crush her heart, she had to know. She couldn't go on like this, with a threat hanging over his head.

Hector closed his eyes a moment. "I don't know why, but I swear to you, it had nothing to do with me."

Now he walked out, and while his parting line had sounded reassuring, it wasn't. Hector had earned plenty of money from Liam's adoption, and he'd handled several others that same month. The cash alone was motive enough to cut corners.

"Have you asked for a check of Hector's financial records?" Jessa asked.

"Yeah." Cooper went to the front window and watched Hector get back in his sleek silver sports car. "Not just him, either. I've asked for checks on everyone involved in this."

"Including me?" Jessa mumbled.

He glanced back at her. "You, too. I would apologize, but you'd do the same in my position."

Jessa couldn't deny that. She would. But considering that almost kiss they'd just shared, it seemed uncomfortable. Like sleeping with the enemy. Too bad she was deeply attracted to this enemy. Also too bad that this particular enemy could end up crushing her heart worse than it'd ever been crushed.

His phone buzzed, and while Cooper continued to watch Hector drive away, he answered it without glancing at the screen. However, he quickly did a double take.

"Donovan?" Cooper spat out like profanity. "I've been looking... What?"

That got her moving closer to Cooper so she could hear what had put that stunned look on his face. "Let me talk to her," Cooper said a moment later.

Her?

Jessa moved even closer, but she only caught a word here and there. It wasn't a woman's voice she heard but rather a man's. A scared one, from the sound of it. The moments crawled by, and the man continued to chatter.

"Too risky," Cooper finally said.

She missed the man's answer, but whatever it was, it turned every muscle in Cooper's body to iron. Then he cursed. "I'll be there in thirty minutes. Don't make me regret this, or you're a dead man."

"What's wrong?" Jessa asked the moment he put his phone away.

"Donovan said Peggy's at his ranch, and she's holding him at gunpoint. And if we don't go out there now, Peggy says she'll kill him."

Chapter Eight

Cooper stopped at the foot of the circular driveway that led to Donovan's house. The place sprawled across the top of a hill, and even though he'd never been inside it, he figured there were at least thirty rooms. Too many places for Peggy to be holding Donovan at gunpoint.

If that was really what was going on.

As far as Cooper was concerned, both Donovan and Peggy were suspects in this mess of an investigation, and he couldn't rule out that they had partnered up to lure Jessa and him to Donovan's ranch.

Or maybe this was a ploy to separate him from Liam and Jessa.

No matter which way he went, it could be a huge risk, but since he was the sheriff and a man in need of answers, it was a risk he had to take. Still, he'd taken precautions and left Tucker and a dozen armed ranch hands to guard Liam.

Jessa was a different story.

She'd refused to stay, insisting that she come with him as Peggy had demanded. Jessa had even played her A.D.A. card and claimed she needed to question both Donovan and Peggy. Since their argument had eaten up precious time, Cooper had decided to take the most hard-headed woman in the state with him. That didn't mean he had any intention of letting her get close to what could turn out to be a hostage situation.

"Wait here," Cooper growled.

"I could maybe help," Jessa argued.

"Yeah, by doing as I say and staying put." Cooper looked at his deputy Reed, who'd just pulled up behind them and gotten out of his vehicle. "And you stay with her. If she tries to come in before I give the all clear, arrest her."

Oh, she didn't like that. Jessa hurled little eyeball daggers at him, but Cooper just hurled them right back. Jessa had taken enough chances just by coming here.

He waited until Colt had parked his truck, and the two started for the house. Not a direct route where they'd be in the line of fire. Cooper used some hedges for cover. However, he and Colt had only made it a few steps when his phone buzzed again. Donovan's name was on the screen, but it was Peggy's voice he heard when he answered and put the call on speaker.

"Bring Jessa Wells in with you," Peggy demanded. "I want you both to hear the truth from this lying—"

"Jessa's staying put," Cooper interrupted. "Once you've surrendered your gun and I'm sure it's safe, I'll let her in."

"Stop arguing with this nutcase!" Donovan yelled. "Get in here and do your job."

Cooper's jaw clenched. "My job doesn't mean putting a civilian in danger. Jessa stays put. Now, where are you two?"

"The foyer," Peggy answered. "The door's unlocked. And don't try anything stupid because I'm watching you on a security camera."

So that was how she'd known that Jessa wasn't making her way to the house. It also meant that ducking behind the hedges wouldn't do any good. Of course, if Peggy wanted him dead, she would have already fired.

Cooper looked up the steps to the porch, where there was a trio of front doors with panels of beveled glass. The light caught the bevels just right, making it hard for him to see more than shadows on the other side. He didn't know which one was Peggy.

"Where's the staff? Is anyone hurt?" Cooper asked.

"No one's hurt." Peggy again. "Not yet, anyway. I searched the place, and I only found two maids. I made them get on the floor. If their boss moves, I start shooting."

Hell. So not just one hostage, but three.

"She had me call my ranch hands," Donovan volunteered. "She had me give the same warning to them as she did to the maids. Personally, I'm hoping one of them or you will put a bullet in her."

Cooper heard a sound. A hoarse sob, and it took him a second to realize it was Peggy crying. "You have to believe me. I didn't steal any babies."

"I'm listening." Cooper forced his voice to stay calm.

Hard to do though with the whirlwind of emotions whipping through him. Because this showdown could lead to info about Liam. It could also get him shot. Jessa, too. And that was why he had to defuse things before they got any worse.

"Peggy, if you'll put down your gun and come outside, I'll listen to everything you want to tell me," Cooper assured her.

"What she wants to tell you is a pack of lies!" Donovan shouted. "I didn't steal a kid." Cooper didn't think it was his imagination that the man sounded a lot more riled than afraid.

"Like I said, I'll listen to her," Cooper went on. "And

if she convinces me that you've done something wrong, then I'll arrest you."

"I'll kill you before I let you arrest me," Donovan fired back.

Cooper huffed. That was their old rivalry rearing its ugly head, and he didn't have time for it now. If Donovan needed arresting, it *would* happen.

"Peggy, put down your gun and release your hostage," Cooper repeated. "If you're as innocent as you say, then you'll have a chance to prove it. And I'll help you."

Silence. For a long time. "Give your phone to Jessa," Peggy finally said. "I need to tell her something."

Cooper looked back at Jessa, who was already hurrying closer. Reed managed to get a hand on her shoulder, but that didn't stop her from shouting out to Peggy.

"I'm here," Jessa assured her. "And I'm listening."

Peggy made another of those hoarse sobs. "I have files that'll prove where I got the babies. I brought them with me."

"And I'll read them," Jessa promised, walking even closer to the phone. "Just please put down your gun so that no one gets hurt."

More silence, but Cooper hoped Peggy was at least considering surrendering. The woman didn't say a word, but several moments later, the front door eased open.

Cooper took aim in case Peggy came out shooting, but it wasn't Peggy. With his hands raised in the air, Donovan stepped out onto the porch. He looked pretty darn calm and collected for a hostage. There wasn't a strand of his dark blond hair out of place. Ditto for his expensive-looking dark blue business suit. But there was one thing off.

His hands were tied.

"The dingbat still has a gun trained on me, and she's

accusing Carol and me of being involved with illegal adoptions," Donovan said though clenched teeth. His steely gaze met Cooper's, and the man had the gall to smirk. "A good sheriff could have prevented this," he added.

"Living a clean life could have prevented it, too. Or maybe just a good security system."

"She came in with the trash." Donovan's smirk softened a bit, replaced by a scowl aimed back in Peggy's direction. "I had the gate open so the trashmen could come in, and she drove in right behind their truck. I didn't see her until it was too late."

Clearly, Donovan wasn't pleased about Peggy getting the drop on him, but he was aiming just as much displeasure at Cooper.

"Peggy?" Cooper called out. "Your turn now. Come to the door so I can see you."

Cooper held his breath and hoped like the devil that the woman would cooperate. Then he could question both Donovan and her and get a look at the files that she said she had.

But she didn't answer. She certainly didn't do anything to surrender her gun.

"Peggy?" Cooper called out again.

And her name had hardly left his mouth when he heard a sound he didn't want to hear.

A shot blasted through the air.

JESSA'S STOMACH WENT to her knees.

She didn't have time to react to the shot before Cooper came running toward her, yelling for her to get down.

Everything seemed to happen at once. Peggy gave a bloodcurdling scream. Cooper dragged Jessa to the ground behind some massive landscape boulders. Donovan jumped off the side of the porch and into some shrubs. And Cooper and his deputies all took aim at the house.

God, why had Peggy fired the shot?

The woman had already gotten everyone's attention by taking Donovan hostage. She hadn't needed to do anything else so drastic.

"Peggy!" Cooper shouted. "Put down your gun and come out with your hands up."

She didn't answer, but Donovan did. The man started cursing, calling Peggy all kinds of names. Jessa couldn't blame him. Peggy had broken into his home and held him at gunpoint, but then maybe she'd done that because Donovan deserved having a gun pointed at him. Still, Jessa kept going back to the same question: How would Donovan have gotten Liam in the first place?

He ran a very successful cattle-broker business and was filthy rich. There was no need for him to get involved with adoptions.

Unless Liam's adoption was somehow personal for him.

Considering his history with Cooper, it could very well be that, but it still didn't make sense.

Another shot rang out; this time the bullet struck the cement just yards from them. Cooper moved her, pushing her behind the truck, and looked around. Not at the front of the house.

But at the roof.

"The shot came from up there," Cooper mumbled.

Because her heartbeat was crashing in her ears, it took Jessa a moment to realize something wasn't right about that, either. How could Peggy have made it from the foyer to the roof so quickly?

And then she got her answer when she caught a

glimpse of the man dressed in black. He was armed with a rifle, and he leaned out of one of the dormer windows.

Definitely not Peggy.

That meant she'd brought along some help.

But then, why had she screamed?

Another shot came at them. Then another. The deputies scrambled behind Colt's truck, using it for cover. Cooper pushed Jessa even lower to the ground, but he didn't follow suit. He levered himself up and fired.

The shot was deafening, and the tinny echoes clanged in Jessa's head. Still, it was worth it if Cooper stopped this monster.

But he didn't.

The shooter fired several more shots, each of them ricocheting off Cooper's truck and nearby boulders. She prayed none of the shots hit anyone.

After what seemed an eternity, the shots stopped. Jessa sucked in her breath, waited. Prayed some more, too. But the shooter didn't pull the trigger again.

"Stay put," Cooper warned her, and he motioned for Reed to move behind the truck with her.

The moment his deputy was in place, Cooper and Colt began to inch their way to the house. They kept cover behind the shrubs, but Jessa knew that wouldn't give them much protection from bullets.

"You stay down, too," Cooper said, and she figured he was talking to Donovan.

The man obviously didn't listen.

"I know you're not deaf," Cooper growled, "so that makes you stupid. Stay down!"

"It's my house," Donovan argued. "Besides, I want to get my hands around that witch's neck."

Jessa heard a thudding sound, and she peered around Reed's shoulder to see Donovan tumbling onto the porch.

Judging from Cooper's body language, he'd been the one to put him there. He turned his gun on Donovan when the man started to get up.

Donovan stayed put.

But he gave Cooper a glare that would make Hades freeze over.

There were stone inserts between the glass doors, and Cooper used one of them for cover. "Peggy?" he tried again.

Still no answer.

He said something to Colt that she didn't catch, and a split second later, the two pivoted into the partially open doorway. They looked inside.

And both cursed.

"She's gone," Cooper relayed to Reed.

That brought Donovan to his feet. He'd managed to get his hands untied, and he flung the rope aside and barreled into the foyer. Cooper stopped him from going any farther.

"Get Jessa inside," Cooper told Reed. "In case the shooter is headed your way."

That put her heart right back in her throat, and both Colt and Cooper became backup for Reed as he hurried her inside. Cooper immediately positioned her so that her back was to the wall and he was in front of her. Protecting her again.

Jessa looked around the massive foyer and the equally massive rooms that flanked it.

No sign of Peggy.

Just two terrified-looking women in maids' uniforms. They were on the white-carpeted floor in the living room.

"She ran toward the back," one of them said.

Cooper tipped his head for Colt and Reed to go in that

direction. "Find her. The shooter, too. They're probably escaping together."

"She's not going anywhere," Donovan snapped, and he would have followed Reed and Colt if Cooper hadn't grabbed a handful of Donovan's jacket.

"Start talking," Cooper ordered.

Donovan threw off his grip and looked on the verge of throwing a punch. His nostrils flared. Eyes narrowed. But then he stepped back and shot Cooper another of those smirks that made Jessa want to slug him. That was no doubt the reason he'd used it—because she could tell it infuriated Cooper, too.

"Start talking?" Donovan coolly repeated. He adjusted his jacket and brushed off some bits of the shrubs as if he had all the time in the world. "Why should I respond to that woman's lies? Peggy's clearly mentally unbalanced. You sure she's not a relative of yours?" he asked, looking at Cooper. "Insanity seems to run in your family. Killers, too."

If Cooper had any reaction to that, he didn't show it. "Why would Peggy say you were the one who gave her the baby that Jessa adopted?"

Donovan lifted his shoulder. "Mentally unbalanced people say a lot of things that aren't true. I can't believe you'd listen to a word she said."

"She said she had proof," Cooper reminded him.

"Where?" He lifted his hands, palms up. Then he leaned in. "You shouldn't believe everything crazy people say."

"I didn't say I believed her. I just want a straight answer. Did you give Peggy a baby that was meant to be adopted?"

They got into a staring contest that crawled on and on. Donovan was the first to break eye contact, and he laughed. "Me with a baby? Really? Do I look like the baby-handling type? I'm not, and if Molly were alive, she'd vouch for me on that."

Because Jessa had her hand on Cooper's back, she felt his muscles go stiff. "What the hell does that mean?" Cooper snapped.

"You want me to spell it out? Well, here it is. Molly and I were lovers—"

"And she broke off things with you and eventually married me," Cooper interrupted. "Old water, old bridge. Why bring her up now?"

"Simple. I was just making a reference. Molly knew I wasn't the daddy type, and that's why she eventually left me and went to you. Because she knew you'd give her a kid."

Cooper gave him a flat look. "I think you glossed over a few things, like Molly realizing you're a jerk and ending a toxic relationship."

Donovan lifted his shoulder, adjusted his suit again. "Obviously, she told you a different version of the truth. If I gave up Molly over my no-kid rule, then why the heck would I want to get into the baby business?"

"I don't know," Cooper fired back. "Why don't you tell me?"

"There's nothing to tell. Even if I'd wanted to be part of the *wonderful world* of adoption, why would I go looking for some kid to give to a whack job like Peggy? If I wanted to make money selling black-market babies, I sure as hell wouldn't use her for a middleman."

He sounded convincing, but Jessa didn't trust him. She certainly hadn't liked the way he'd thrown his relationship with Molly in Cooper's face.

"You need to come with me to the sheriff's office,"

Cooper said, sounding all business now. But Jessa could still feel his knotted muscles.

"I don't have time to play cop with you." Donovan smirked again.

Cooper didn't back down. "You'll make time. Several felonies were committed here, and that means paperwork."

Donovan stared at him, again looking as if he might challenge Cooper's authority. And he might have done just that. If they hadn't heard the footsteps.

Colt and Reed hurried back in, both shaking their heads. "No sign of Peggy or the shooter," Colt relayed.

"Great, just great," Donovan snarled. "You let them get away."

Cooper didn't even spare him a glance. He kept his attention on his brother. "What is that?"

Jessa had to go on her tiptoes to see over his shoulder, and she spotted what appeared to be a piece of paper in Colt's left hand.

Colt unfolded it and held up a flash drive. "I found it in the kitchen on the counter by the back door. Peggy left it." He looked down at the writing on the paper, then shook his head. "The note's addressed to you, Jessa."

Cooper reached out and took the note from his brother. Jessa quickly moved to his side so she could see what was written there.

Ms. Wells, the answers about the adoption are somewhere in these files. Read them and you'll learn the truth about your son.

Chapter Nine

Cooper's eyes were burning, but he forced himself to keep reading the computer files that Peggy had left on the flash drive. Jessa was doing the same on another laptop that she'd positioned on the other side of his desk in his home office.

"Anything?" he asked when she made a soft sound. But he quickly realized it was a sound of frustration.

"Nothing." She checked the time, glanced at the baby monitor that she'd brought downstairs and mumbled something about Liam waking up from his nap soon. Jessa would want to check on him. Cooper would, too.

"Did you find anything?" she asked.

He had to shake his head. Nothing in the thirtysomething files he'd already gone through, but they had twice that to go. It wasn't as straightforward as Cooper had thought it would be, because Peggy's adoption notes read more like a disorganized personal diary of her feelings over the placements that she'd helped arrange.

But she hadn't used names.

And sometimes she'd handled several adoptions at the same time and had merged those notes with ramblings of why she preferred one set of prospective parents over another.

That meant wading through page after page and trying to figure out which of the babies was Liam.

Read them and you'll learn the truth about your son, Peggy had said in her note. Cooper only hoped she was telling the truth about that.

His phone buzzed, and Cooper answered it right away when he saw Colt's name on the screen. He also put it on speaker because Jessa looked as ready for news, any news, as he was.

"Please tell me you found Peggy." Part of him wanted to be out looking for her himself, but that wouldn't be wise, since it would leave Jessa and Liam without protection. Besides, someone had to go through Peggy's files, and the people with the highest stakes in that potential info were Jessa and him.

"No sign of her, but I followed some footprints I found at the back of Donovan's house, and they led to a heavily treed area. I'm pretty sure the footprints were hers and that's where she'd left a vehicle, because there were tire tracks."

Yeah. And it was reminder for Cooper that he'd screwed this up big time. He should have moved one of his deputies to the rear of the house to prevent Peggy and the gunman from escaping. But he truly hadn't believed it was an actual hostage situation. In fact, he'd thought Donovon and Peggy might have been in on this ruse together.

"There's more," Colt said. "I found a second set of footprints and tire tracks on the east side of the property. Judging from the size of the footprints, they probably belong to the shooter."

Jessa's gaze met his, and he saw the question there in

her eyes. Why hadn't Peggy and her hired gun driven to Donovan's together?

And that brought him back to the first shot that'd been fired.

"Peggy had screamed," Cooper said, thinking aloud. "And it didn't sound fake, either. It sounded like the reaction of a woman who'd been surprised. Terrified, even. So why would she have reacted like that if she'd known all along what was going to happen?"

"Maybe her hired goon jumped the gun and wasn't supposed to shoot?" Jessa suggested.

It was a good theory, but Cooper had another possibility that only created more questions than answers. "Or maybe the hired gun wasn't working for her. Maybe he was working for Donovan."

"Or he could have been working with our hospitalized gunman, Vernon Graham," Jessa added. "Think about it—Graham is the one who implicated Peggy, and she in turn said Donovan was guilty. All this finger-pointing muddies the waters and might be leading us in the wrong direction."

"The direction of illegal adoptions," Cooper finished for her. "But if it's not about the adoptions, then it takes us back to Jewell or some other case that could cause someone to go off the deep end like this."

Colt made a sound of agreement. "I found something else at the second scene," Colt went on. "A scuff mark on one of the trees near the tracks. Looks like the vehicle ran into it while the driver was making an escape. I got some black paint chips. Already sent those to the lab. We might get lucky identifying the type of vehicle."

Yes, and maybe that would in turn lead them to the driver.

"Tucker's putting out feelers in case the driver brings the vehicle in for repairs," Colt added. "I'll go back to the hospital and have another chat with Graham. When I'm finished with him, I'll see how Reed is faring with Donovan."

Cooper doubted Donovan would say anything of importance, and the man darn sure wouldn't incriminate himself. In fact, Cooper knew from Reed's earlier call that Donovan had lawyered up before he'd even stepped foot in the sheriff's office.

"When you talk to Donovan, ask him how a gunman could have gotten on his roof without him knowing about it," Cooper said. "His place has to have state-of-the-art security, and I find it hard to believe that Donovan or his staff didn't hear or see anyone suspicious."

"Will do," Colt assured him.

"What about the FBI agent that Hector Dixon said had contacted him? Gordon Riker. Any luck talking to him?"

With everything else going on, Jessa had forgotten all about the man. Thankfully, Cooper hadn't.

"He doesn't exist," Colt said. "Well, he doesn't exist by that name, anyway. So either Hector made him up or else someone called him using an alias. Someone who maybe wanted to feel him out and find out how much he knows."

Yes, and maybe silence him if he knew too much. Of course, Hector had likely heard what'd happened with Peggy at Donovan's house, so hopefully the man was being more vigilant. If he was innocent, that was.

"You making any progress with Peggy's files?" Colt asked.

"None," Jessa and he said in unison.

"But I think we should do a deeper background check on Peggy," Jessa continued. Then she paused. "Because

I'm not sure we're dealing with someone who's mentally stable."

She looked at Cooper as if he might disagree, but he couldn't. Maybe Peggy just had a bad case of attention deficient when it came to her notes, but she certainly rambled a lot. And so far there was nothing of importance. However, it did make Cooper wonder how Peggy had gotten started in this whole baby-brokering operation. She didn't seem to have a lot of business sense, or any other sense, for that matter.

"I'll ask Tucker to do another background check," Colt said. "Unless you want me to involve the FBI in this."

The image of Seth and his mirrored shades popped into Cooper's head. "No. We'll keep this between us for now."

Cooper ended the call and went back to the notes. But he didn't get far. He heard sounds coming over the baby monitor. Not a cry exactly, but Liam seemed to be fussing. A glance at the screen and Cooper saw the little boy moving around in the crib. It got Jessa to her feet, and with Cooper right behind her, she hurried out of his office.

"Sometimes, when he first wakes up, he picks at the bandage," Jessa said from over her shoulder.

That was a good reason for her to hurry, especially since her mother had told them she'd be in the kitchen with Rosalie and the cook. But Cooper thought Jessa's urgency had just as much to do with this latest attack. She was terrified for Liam's safety.

Jessa practically ran once she reached the top of the stairs, but she stopped in the doorway. That sent a jolt of concern through him, but when Cooper reached the door, Jessa put her index finger to her lip.

"He went back to sleep," she whispered.

She didn't move, and neither did Cooper. They stood there and watched. Well, until Jessa looked up at him. And frowned. Probably because the emotion was written all over his face every time he looked at the little boy. Jessa wasn't the only one who was worried for Liam's safety.

And his future.

"I don't want this," she said, moving from the door. She leaned her back against the wall opposite the guest room where Liam was sleeping.

No need for her to qualify what *this* was. If she had her way, she'd shut Cooper out of Liam's life. Cooper understood that, but he wasn't going anywhere.

"I should leave," she added a moment later. "I should hire some bodyguards to protect us in a safe, hidden location."

He could see the panic starting to bubble up inside her. Cooper wasn't about to dismiss that, either. But he also couldn't let her do anything stupid.

Cooper took her hand when she reached in her pocket for her phone. "You're both safe here."

She huffed when her gaze dropped to the grip he had on her, and jerked away from him. But she didn't reach for her phone again and she didn't tell him to keep the heck away from her son.

"I just need this to be over," she said, her voice breaking on the last word. "If we knew who was behind the attacks, then we'd know how to stop them."

"Yeah," Cooper settled for saying. And because she looked as if she needed it in the worst way, he hooked his arm around her neck and pulled her into a hug.

Now she resisted. She put her palms on his chest as if to push him away. That didn't happen, either. A small sob sounded in her throat, and she dropped her head to his shoulder.

"It's not right for me to be here like this," Jessa mumbled.

He couldn't argue with that. It wasn't right even if it felt like it was. Because when Cooper caught the jerk responsible for the attacks and put him behind bars, there would still be unsettled issues with Jessa. His mother's murder trial, for one. These ever-growing feelings he had for Liam, for another.

And finally, the attraction between Jessa and him.

He seriously doubted it was just going to vanish when the danger ended. It certainly wasn't going anywhere now.

"Let's just get it over with," he said.

Her gaze snapped to his, and before she could ask if he'd lost his bloomin' mind—which was a strong possibility—Cooper put his mouth on hers. He caught the slight sound of surprise she made. Caught her scent and taste, too. All in all, it was enough to prove he was stupid to play with this kind of fire.

Did that stop him?

Nope.

He just kept on kissing her. Kept on reining her in, closer and closer, until Jessa was plastered against him.

Cooper deepened the kiss. Waited for her to stop him. And waited some more. During that wait, he didn't let up, and when he had Jessa gasping for air, he dropped some kisses on her neck.

And got a darn good response.

Well, it was a good one if his intentions were for this to continue. She made a sound. A silky little hitch in her voice that came from deep within her throat. But that wasn't all. She slid her arms around his neck and pulled him down so she could do some kiss deepening of her own.

Oh, man. They'd both lost it.

Not good. Cooper had figured the attraction would get the best of them, but he'd hoped that the craziness would be limited to one at a time. So the other could do something to stop it.

Neither of them was stopping anything.

Somewhere way in the back of his mind, Cooper reminded himself that they were in the hall. Where they could easily be seen. He wanted to keep kissing Jessa. Hell, he wanted to haul her off to bed. Not only was that a really bad idea, but the timing also sucked.

Obviously coming to her senses, too, she stopped kissing him at the same time he stopped kissing her and they backed away from each other.

She opened her mouth. Closed it. Opened it again and then shook her head. "Why?"

Since that could encompass a lot of different areas, Cooper just shrugged. And waited. Jessa would no doubt lecture him on why kissing was totally inappropriate and a judicial conflict of interest.

But she didn't.

She swallowed hard. "You read what happened in my last relationship, and you know I'm not ready for this."

He nodded and rubbed his thumb over the back of his left ring finger, where he used to wear his wedding band. It wasn't there now. Not physically. It was in the nightstand drawer next to his bed. But there were times when he still felt plenty married.

Not now, of course.

But other times.

Funny though—those times seemed farther and farther apart since Jessa had stormed into his life.

"We should make a pact or something," she said. "To make sure this doesn't happen again."

Cooper lifted his eyebrow. He was about to remind her that no pact would have prevented what just happened when his phone buzzed. Maybe this time it'd be Colt with news that they'd found Peggy or that Donovan had confessed to a felony or two.

But it wasn't Colt.

It was Dr. Howland.

"Cooper," the doc said the moment Cooper answered. But then he paused. "There was a break-in at the lab where I sent Liam's and your DNA. There's security footage, so you might be able to find out who did it, but the bottom line is the samples were destroyed. Someone set fire to them."

Hell. He didn't want to go through asking Jessa for another sample, but that was minor compared to the big picture. The person who'd destroyed the samples had likely done so in order to cover something up. And that brought Cooper right back to Peggy, Hector and Donovan.

Jessa, too.

She probably hadn't heard exactly what Dr. Howland had just said, but she could no doubt see the change in Cooper's body language. She knew something was wrong.

"We'll need to repeat the DNA test," Cooper said to the doc.

Jessa made a soft, helpless sound and touched her fingers to her suddenly quivering lips.

"No need to repeat it," Dr. Howland insisted. "I sent out two sets of samples. The first was the one that was destroyed. I used fake names on the second set and sent them to a different lab. Considering everything that was going on with Jessa and that car accident, I thought it was for the best."

Everything inside Cooper went still.

"And?" Cooper asked the doctor, though he wasn't sure how he was able to speak now that his throat had clamped shut.

Dr. Howland cleared his throat. "I just got back the DNA results...."

Chapter Ten

Jessa watched as Cooper staggered back a step. His breath was gusting now, and he squeezed his eyes shut.

"You're positive?" Cooper asked the caller, his voice hoarse and raw.

She'd seen Dr. Howland's name on the phone screen and had thought he was calling to check on Liam. No such luck. There was only one thing that could have caused Cooper to react like that.

The DNA test was back.

Jessa waited, her own breath racing. Cooper finally hit the end-call button, but it took a moment for his gaze to come to hers.

And she knew in her heart what the doctor had just told him.

That Liam's DNA was a match to his.

"No!" Jessa frantically shook her head and kept repeating it because she didn't know what else to say.

She turned to bolt away from him so she could take Liam...and do what, exactly, she wasn't sure. However, everything inside her was screaming for her to run, and that was exactly what she would have done if Cooper hadn't caught her arm.

"You can't go," Cooper insisted.

The emotions slammed into her all at once. The fear.

Denial. The sickening dread. "You're lying. The doctor's lying. Liam can't be yours. Because he's mine!"

She tried to bolt again, and this time Cooper took her by the shoulders and put her against the wall. He got right in her face.

"Think this through," he said, not easily. Like hers, his words sounded strangled. "Doc Howland did the test, not me, and he has no motive for lying about the results."

"He's your friend!"

"And he's honest. He wouldn't even do the test without a court order."

That tore at her heart like jabs from a razor-sharp knife. Jessa didn't want logic. She wanted the results to prove that Cooper's suspicions had been wrong. Because if they were right…oh, God.

Then he would have a claim to Liam.

The sob made its way up her throat, and Jessa batted away Cooper's hands when he tried to hold her in place.

"Just stop a minute," Cooper said.

Her gaze snapped to his, and that was when Jessa saw something that she didn't want to see. The emotions rifling through him, too. His were a different kind, though. While he was coming to terms with learning his son was alive, she was faced with the nightmare of losing Liam.

"You can't take him from me," she argued. But she was arguing with herself.

Cooper's grip melted off her, and, forcing out several deep breaths, he leaned against the wall. Probably because his legs looked ready to buckle. He had his attention fastened to Liam, who was thankfully still asleep.

He shook his head. "I'd given up. But I shouldn't have. I kept feeling something." He rapped his fist against his heart. "Something kept telling me he was alive. I couldn't allow myself to believe it."

Each word crushed her. "I've been his mother since he was three months old," she said in a whisper.

"I know." He drew in a long breath and walked to the doorway, no doubt so he could get a better look at Liam.

Sweet heaven.

Cooper no doubt saw himself in Liam's face.

Jessa didn't want to see it. Just as she hadn't wanted to question why Liam had Cooper's rare blood type. She hadn't wanted to question anything.

She'd only wanted her son.

"He's awake," Cooper said a split second before she heard Liam stirring in the crib.

Both Cooper and she moved toward him, but Jessa made it to him first and scooped him up in her arms. She held him to her as if her life depended on it. Because that was exactly how she felt.

"How could this have happened?" Cooper mumbled.

Jessa had to shake her head again. "I got references for the adoption attorney. I followed the rules. I didn't do anything wrong."

"I didn't do anything wrong, either." Cooper reached out, skimmed his finger down Liam's cheek. Liam smiled, breaking her heart even more. "But someone did."

"Maybe not." Her heart was pounding, and she was still breathing too fast. So fast she might hyperventilate. Jessa tried to tamp down her emotions so she could think of a way out of this.

She couldn't lose Liam. That wasn't an option.

But the tears and the doubts came, anyway. And she cursed them. Silently cursed, too, the footsteps she heard in the hall. She didn't want to see anyone right now, including Cooper, though she figured he wasn't going away.

Tucker stepped into the doorway, his attention going

straight to his brother. "You okay?" His gaze swept from Cooper to Liam to her.

"I had a DNA test run on Liam," Cooper said. "It's a match to mine."

She had no idea how much he'd told his brother, but apparently not much, since Tucker seemed genuinely surprised. He gasped and caught the doorjamb. "But how? Molly and Cameron washed away in the flood."

"Only Molly." A moment later, Cooper repeated it.

"Well, that explains the phone call I just got from Colt," Tucker went on. "He said he's reviewing some security feed for a break-in at Merritt Labs. He's already got the footage, thanks to Doc Howland."

Cooper nodded. "Someone destroyed the samples of Liam's and my DNA at that particular lab." He paused. Touched Liam's cheek again. "Whoever destroyed those samples is no doubt trying to cover up their part in the illegal adoption."

Oh, God. And it was maybe the reason the kidnappers had tried to take Liam from the hospital.

"Help Colt go through the footage," Cooper told his brother. "Find out who did this." He turned his head, his eyes meeting Tucker's. "We might be looking for a killer."

Tucker nodded as if he'd already figured that out, but Jessa had to shake her head. "You think this person murdered Molly?"

"He or she got their hands on Liam somehow." Cooper's jaw tightened. "No way would Molly have just let someone take him from her."

He hadn't said that easily, and despite the emotional pain crushing her chest, Jessa could practically feel Cooper's pain, too.

"The autopsy proved that drowning was the cause of her death," Tucker reminded him. He came closer and put his hand on his brother's arm. "And there were no signs of foul play."

"Maybe because the foul play was the drowning itself. Someone could have kidnapped Liam...Cameron," Cooper corrected, "and then restrained Molly somehow and moved the car to the bridge so it'd be swept away with her inside."

Jessa couldn't argue with that. Though she wanted to. She wanted to dismiss all of this, but she couldn't.

She looked at her son. Really looked at him. At his eyes. His hair. The shape of his face. Liam seemed puzzled by the intense scrutiny he was getting from all three of them. Well, for a few moments, anyway.

"Horsey," Liam said, and he motioned toward the plastic horse in the toy box. The last thing Jessa wanted to do was let go of him, but when Liam continued to twist and squirm, she set him on the floor and he made a beeline for the toy chest.

It hit her then. The toys and the crib had almost certainly belonged to Cameron. When she'd first arrived at the ranch, she hadn't even questioned why these things would be there.

"I can't stay here," Jessa blurted out.

The brothers exchanged a quick glance, and Tucker headed for the door. "I'll see if Colt's making progress with the security footage from the lab."

Cooper didn't say a word to her until Tucker had left. "We need a truce. Right now our focus has to be keeping Liam safe, agreed?"

Jessa didn't have to think about that. She nodded. "But you can't take him from me," she repeated, positioning herself between Liam and him.

It didn't work. Cooper just moved around her and sat on the floor next to Liam. Her son obviously enjoyed having a new playmate, because he smiled and handed Cooper a toy from the box.

"A truce," Cooper repeated. "You won't try to take him from this house, and I won't do anything to take him from you."

Not now, anyway.

Cooper hadn't actually said those words, but she could hear them in his voice.

"Say that you'll agree to a truce," Cooper added. Even though it was an order—she had no doubts about that— he smiled back at Liam.

It was the last thing she wanted to say, but the only thing she could do. If she tried to leave with Liam, Cooper would stop her. Legally, Liam was still hers, but Cooper could change that by filing a motion for custody.

Which he would no doubt do once Liam was safe.

"Truce," Jessa finally managed to say, just as Cooper's phone rang.

Cooper continued to play with Liam while he took out his phone. Jessa saw Colt's name on the screen, and even though Cooper took the call on speaker, she sank down next to him so she could hear better. And so she could better monitor this playing session. Yes, she was being petty again, but it was the only control she had over this nightmare of a situation.

"I've got good news and bad," Colt started. "The bad is that whoever broke into Merritt Lab also disabled the camera. Not sure how, but it looks like some kind of electromagnetic device."

Cooper looked ready to curse. He didn't. Probably because of Liam. "You said there's good news?"

"Yeah. There's no footage of the person in the lab, but I got a picture of him or her stepping from the vehicle.

It's just the one shot because the camera was disabled immediately afterward."

"Please tell me you got the license plate numbers," Cooper said.

"No, it was obscured with something, but I have a good description of the vehicle. A late-model black Jeep Cherokee with some damage to the front right fender. That's a match to the paint chips that I found near Donovan's place."

So the person who fired those shots had likely broken into the lab.

"We're running the names of all owners of that particular vehicle model," Colt went on. "We might get lucky."

"What about the interview with Donovan?" Cooper asked. "You get anything?"

"Nothing. His lawyer advised him to stay quiet, and that's what he's done. I'm about to cut him loose."

"Not yet," Cooper argued. "I'll come in and talk to him."

Colt hesitated. "You're sure? Because it seems to me you got other things on your mind right now."

"I need to help. I need to end this so that Liam's no longer in danger."

Jessa wanted that, too. Desperately wanted it. But with the kidnapper caught and behind bars, it would leave Cooper free to pursue custody of Liam.

"All right," Colt finally said. "I'll email you all the updates and files so you can read them before you come in."

Cooper thanked him, ended the call and went back to playing with Liam. When Liam made a neighing sound with the toy horse, Cooper mimicked it, causing Liam to laugh.

"He's always been fascinated by horses," Jessa mumbled.

"Once he's all healed, we'll have to get him out to the pasture to see some real ones." Cooper looked up at her, maybe waiting for her to say that wouldn't happen, that she would be long gone by then.

"Remember that truce," she mumbled.

"I am. I'm remembering that kiss, too."

Jessa flinched. "What does that have to do with anything?"

Cooper gave her a flat look. "Everything, and you know it. If it weren't for this attraction between us, I would have already made a call to start custody proceedings."

Yes, she did know that. And it terrified her even more. Because what would happen when this attraction ended? She wasn't sure what troubled her most—that it would end…

Or that it wouldn't.

Jessa had no idea what she would do then—feeling this heat with the man who could destroy her.

Cooper's phone buzzed again, but this time she didn't recognize the name she saw on the screen. Arlene Litton.

"She's our horse trainer," Cooper explained, and he answered the call on speaker.

"Coop, we might have some trouble brewing," Arlene said. "I was out checking on some calves and spotted a car parked just on the other side of the east back fence. It's nestled in some trees, nearly out of sight. The engine's still warm and there's some fresh footprints leading from it and into the pasture. I wrote down the license plate number and called it in to Reed. He said he'd run it."

Jessa had no idea if this sort of thing happened often, but she was betting it didn't.

"What kind of car?" Cooper asked the woman.

"A black Jeep Cherokee."

Oh, mercy. That put her heart right in her throat, and she seriously doubted it was a coincidence that the vehicle matched the description of the one on the security footage from the lab.

Cooper got to his feet. "Look at the front fender," he instructed Arlene. "See anything?"

"Yeah." She must have picked up on the concern in Cooper's voice because it was now in hers. "It's bashed in real good, like he ran into something. What you want me to do about this, Coop?"

"Lock down the ranch and get some hands out to follow those tracks. I'll be right out to help. And, Arlene, be careful. This guy could be a killer, and we have to find him before he tries to come after Liam."

Chapter Eleven

Before Cooper even made it to the hall, Jessa caught up with him. "You're not really going out there, are you?"

Cooper nodded. "This guy isn't giving up, and he needs to be stopped." But he appreciated her concern. Not for himself, but for Liam. "I'll have Tucker stay here with you. Some of the other ranch hands, too. They'll surround the house and will have orders to shoot anyone who tries to get in."

Jessa opened her mouth as if ready to argue with that, but finally shook her head. "Just be careful."

Her concern took him back a bit, and he cursed that blasted kiss that had changed everything between them.

"You and Liam stay away from the windows," Cooper added, and he hurried out.

He didn't waste any time—he called Tucker and filled him in so his brother could start getting the ranch hands in place. Thankfully, Tucker was already inside. And Rayanne. Cooper didn't like the idea of relying on his surly sister for anything, but she was a deputy sheriff, and if it came down to it, she'd hopefully stop a killer from getting into the house.

Cooper hurried downstairs to his office and armed the security system, using the keypad by the front door. He'd be heading out soon, but before he did that he needed to check the cameras they had positioned throughout the property. He might get lucky and spot this guy.

Nothing was on the first camera in the part of the pasture where Arlene had spotted the Jeep. The camera angle was wrong for him to see the vehicle itself, but he had no doubt that it was there.

How far had the driver managed to get, and where the hell was he?

He saw some ranch hands on the second camera. They were hurrying toward the house. Good. As soon as they were in place, he'd be free to leave.

His father was on the third camera. Roy was also heading for the house, and he was armed with a rifle. Arlene, too. Even Seth was outside the guest cottage, and he was talking to one of the ranch hands, no doubt to find out what was going on.

But there was no sign of the man who'd driven that Jeep.

Cooper remembered the other attack at Donovan's. The guy had fired shots from the top floor and the roof there. He quickly panned the camera around as much as he could, and saw something that caused his stomach to clench.

There, on the roof of one of the barns, was a guy dressed in clothes that would have blended in with the other ranch hands—jeans, boots and a cowboy hat. The guy had a scope rifle next to him, but he didn't aim it at the house. Instead, the man aimed some kind of handheld device.

Cooper couldn't be positive, but judging from the way he was moving and adjusting it, the device was some kind of thermal-imaging equipment. If he was right, the idiot could use it to pinpoint not just how many people were inside the house but their exact locations. If he was looking for Jessa and Liam, he would have no trouble spotting them.

That got Cooper moving. He barreled up the stairs, taking them two at a time.

"Jessa?" he called out before he even reached the landing. He also fired off a text to Tucker so his brother would know the shooter's location. "Get Liam out of the room now!"

He figured that would scare her to death. It did. Jessa had no color in her face and was shaking from head to toe. But she had Liam sheltered in her arms when she came running out of the room toward him.

"Where's the gunman?" Jessa asked, her words running together.

"Too close. Come with me."

"My mother…"

"We'll let her know to hide, too."

Thankfully, Liam didn't seem to be aware of the immediate danger. He still had the toy horse and was wearing a cowboy hat that was many sizes too big for him. Later, Cooper would kick himself for allowing another attack like this to happen, but for now he just focused on getting them to safety.

The door to Rayanne's room flew open, and she came out, her gun aimed and ready. "What's going on?"

"There's a gunman on the roof of the barn nearest the house." He tipped his head in that direction. "Can you keep watch up here and make sure he doesn't come through the windows?"

She glanced at Liam. "He's after the boy?"

Cooper nodded and wanted to curse that he had to explain anything. If this were one of his brothers, there would have been no questions asked. "Yeah, he's after Liam," Cooper said.

Rayanne nodded. "If he comes through a window, how you want me to handle it?"

"Shoot to kill."

That she didn't question, but she did take out her phone. "I'm calling Rosalie to tell her to take cover."

"My mom, too," Jessa added. "They're in the kitchen together."

Rayanne just gave him a get-going gesture with her hand, made her phone call, and Cooper got Jessa moving again. When they reached the stairs, he spotted Tucker in the foyer, already standing guard by the front door.

"We're getting the hands out of the line of fire," Tucker relayed. "Away from the barn. If anyone tries to get in, the alarm will sound."

That was good, but the kidnapper didn't have to get inside to do some damage. He could start shooting through the walls.

"I'm taking Liam and Jessa to my office," Cooper said as they headed that way. It was on the opposite side of the house from the barn and the shooter. "Wait with them."

He'd been right about his brother not questioning anything. Well, not with words, anyway. He saw the hesitation in Tucker's eyes. Maybe because Tucker knew Cooper would hate to leave Liam. But he had no choice. It wasn't just his job to stop this shooter—it was what he needed to do to protect Liam.

With Tucker right behind them, Cooper led Jessa to his office. Liam immediately spotted the framed photos and some books. "Wanna see," he said, and he wriggled to get down.

Jessa held on to him and went to the computer monitor, where Cooper still had the feed from the camera on the screen.

And Cooper's heart dropped again.

Jessa pointed to the screen. "Is that the barn roof where you saw the gunman?"

Yeah, and he was no longer there.

Cooper bit back the profanity that he was thinking and called Arlene. "This guy's on the move. He's wearing jeans, a dark blue shirt and a tan hat."

"I'll find him," Arlene promised, but he knew that was a promise she couldn't keep. He could be anywhere.

Cooper searched through all the cameras again. "I think he's got an infrared or thermal-imaging device. He'd aimed something at the house."

Jessa's eyes widened when she looked at Liam. "He'll know it's Liam because of his size."

"Yeah," Cooper settled for saying. He snared Tucker's gaze. "Go to the closet where Dad keeps his hunting equipment. There should be one of those silver Mylar blankets." It wasn't a perfect solution, but it would stop the majority of the body's heat loss, making it harder for the shooter to spot Jessa and Liam.

Tucker hurried off to get the blanket, and while Cooper kept watch on the computer screens, he maneuvered Jessa and Liam to the floor and beneath his desk.

"It's a game," Cooper said to Liam, hoping that he didn't sound as worried as he felt.

There were no toys in his office, but Cooper took off his badge and handed it to Liam. "Tank you," Liam babbled, and he smiled from ear to ear.

Jessa certainly wasn't smiling, probably because she knew the desk wouldn't stop bullets.

Cooper took the laptop to the floor with him so he could position himself in front of Jessa and Liam and watch the screen at the same time.

There was a lot of activity. Ranch hands were running around and getting into position, but there were still a lot of areas not covered. His dad was trying to do something about that. Seth, too. But it was a big ranch with plenty of barns, stables and outbuildings that a gunman could use—especially if the guy had been able to pinpoint their position.

"Here," Tucker said, hurrying back into the room.

He shook open the foil blanket and they put it around Jessa and Liam. Of course, that wouldn't stop the shooter from using infrared to key in on Tucker and him, so Cooper took the laptop with him and they headed for the door.

"Make sure no one gets to them," he said to Tucker.

However, Cooper hadn't made it even a step when he heard a sound he darn sure didn't want to hear.

The security system.

It was just a pulsing beat. A warning that something or someone had triggered the alarm.

The gunman was in the house.

That sent Cooper right back to the security screen, and even though there weren't interior cameras, he could see a blinking light to indicate the point of entry. A window in the family room just off the kitchen.

Much too close.

Especially too close to Rosalie and Jessa's mom.

It didn't matter that the guy wasn't after them. This idiot might shoot them on sight to get to Liam. Hopefully, the women would both stay hidden, as Rayanne had told them to do.

He disarmed the security system to stop it before it went from a beep to a full blare. A noise like that would no doubt scare Liam and prevent Cooper from hearing the gunman's movement in the house.

"Rayanne," Cooper called out. "We've got an intruder."

She didn't answer. Maybe because she couldn't hear

him or had chosen not to hear. Or maybe she just didn't want to give her position away to a killer. Either way, Cooper couldn't count on her for help.

"Wait in here with Liam and Jessa," he said to Tucker, and Cooper ignored Jessa's whispered demands for him to stay put.

He peered out into the hall and didn't see anyone so he stepped out. Cooper motioned for Tucker to shut the door and lock it. His brother did, and Cooper went looking for the intruder.

There was no direct access to the family room from the left hall, so Cooper went to the right. Toward the front of the house and the stairs. If the Mylar blanket could fool the infrared device, then the guy might go to the guest rooms to look for Liam. At least that was where Cooper hoped he would go so he wouldn't be anywhere near Liam.

Cooper kept his gun ready, and he made a quick look around the corner and into the foyer.

No one.

However, he heard the footsteps. Slow and cautious on the stairs. Cooper pivoted in that direction, taking aim.

But it was only Rayanne.

She, too, had her gun ready. She didn't say a word, just lifted her eyebrow, but Cooper understood what she was asking.

Where was the intruder?

He tipped his head toward the other side of the stairs and in the direction where the security light had indicated the break-in.

Rayanne didn't make a sound, but some of the color drained from her face. Probably because she knew her sister was in that general area. It was too risky to call Rosalie and try to warn her—the gunman might be able to hear a phone ringing. Same with a text. If it made any kind of sound, it could be fatal for not just Rosalie but Linda, too, and whoever the heck else was in the kitchen.

Rayanne nodded, waited until Cooper started moving that way and followed along behind him. They inched their way toward the kitchen. No sound of footsteps, which could mean the guy was just lying in wait. If he was hell-bent on kidnapping Liam, then he might want to eliminate any obstacles first.

Cooper stopped when he reached the kitchen and looked around. Still no one. Not even Rosalie and Linda.

Where the heck were they?

He heard some movement in the sunroom, and both Rayanne and he took aim there.

"It's me," someone called out. Arlene. Cooper was about to tell her to get down, but she continued before he could say a word. "I think he's getting away." Arlene stepped into the doorway. "I heard him moving around in a couple of the rooms. Didn't want to shoot in case some of the hands were in there."

"Where'd the intruder go?" Cooper demanded, and he hurried to the family room where Arlene pointed.

"Stay here," Cooper told Arlene. "Rayanne, find your sister and Linda."

No one was in the family room, and he opened the door that led to the side yard. No sign of a runner. But he stepped outside, listening for any sound that would give away this idiot's position.

Nothing.

Cooper didn't want him in the house or even near it, but he sure as hell didn't want him getting away, either. He went to the side of the sunroom and looked around the corner.

And he cursed.

The kidnapper wasn't there, but he'd ditched his rifle and the thermal-imaging equipment, and he'd no doubt done that so he could escape fast. That didn't mean the guy wasn't armed, though. He probably had a handgun or two on him.

"Head there!" Cooper shouted out to several of the ranch hands. He pointed toward the pasture nearest the window.

Of course, the intruder had had precious seconds to use another way to escape. Or this could all be a ruse. The guy could be hiding, waiting for Cooper to go in pursuit, and then the bozo could use that opportunity to get back in the house.

"Any sign of him?" Arlene asked. She was in the doorway of the sunroom, her gaze firing all around, but she also had her phone sandwiched against her shoulder.

"Nothing. Where's Rosalie and Linda?"

"They're fine. They hid in the pantry."

Good. He hadn't wanted the intruder to take them as hostages. Or worse—harm them in some way.

"Who's on the phone?" Cooper asked Arlene while he kept watch.

She held up her hand in a wait-a-second gesture. "Yeah, I'll tell him." Arlene put away her phone and met Cooper's gaze for a split second. "That was Reed. He ran the license plate I called in. And he got a hit. The Jeep's registered to one of your suspects. Hector Dixon."

Chapter Twelve

Jessa prayed she wasn't making another mistake.

She'd already made so many by not keeping Liam safe, and she might be adding to that lack of safety. Ironic. Since she'd brought him to the Sweetwater Springs sheriff's office, a place where she shouldn't have to worry about repeat kidnapping attempts.

But then, she'd have to worry about that no matter where she was.

That was the reason she'd brought Liam with her when Cooper had said he was going to his office to question the suspects. She wanted a chance to confront Hector and demand that he explain why an armed intruder had used Hector's vehicle to drive to the ranch.

The front door of the office opened, and Jessa snapped in that direction, her body bracing itself for another attack. But it was only Tucker.

"Just checking on things," Tucker said. "Thought you might like an extra hand." And he slid his hand over the gun in his holster.

Jessa was glad for the extra protection, even if it was Cooper's family.

"Don't worry," Cooper said to her. "Hector will be here soon."

Yes. Colt had called and insisted that he come in. Hector would be questioned, along with Donovan, who'd also been ordered back in for another round. There'd been no sign of Peggy, or they would have had all their suspects under the same roof.

That only made her stomach churn more.

Because Liam would be under that roof right along with them. Her mother and Rosalie had Liam in Cooper's office at the back of the building, and Jessa didn't think a hired gun would be stupid enough to come to the sheriff's office. But then, she'd thought the ranch was safe, too.

Cooper had already told her that she would be able to observe the interviews from the two-way mirror off the interview room. Jessa was past the observation stage. She wanted to question both of them, but Cooper hadn't budged on it. With reason. If either man said something that could lead to their arrest, Cooper didn't want that compromised by her being part of the interview.

Or maybe he was just worried she'd fly off the handle.

Jessa couldn't deny that it was a strong possibility.

Cooper got a paper cup of water from the cooler and handed it to her. "You could wait in my office with Liam," he reminded her—again.

"I want to see Hector when he walks through that door," she reminded him right back.

A heavy sigh left his mouth. "You've had a lot hit you today—"

"So have you." And he knew exactly what she meant. More than the attack, more than the hunt for the person responsible. They were both dealing with the results of the DNA test.

"I'll want the paternity test repeated, of course," she said, but her voice broke. The emotion flooded through her. She hadn't cried since the attack. Hadn't come close to falling apart. But Jessa felt as if that might happen now.

Cooper took hold of her arm as if he expected her to crumple into a heap. Probably because she looked on the verge of it. He led her out of the main squad room, past his office and to the break room.

"I'll have the test repeated," he assured her. "Do you really think I'd lie to you about something like that?"

No. But that was what tore at her even more. He wouldn't lie, and that meant somehow she had to deal with a truth she wasn't sure she could face.

"I can't lose Liam." She'd been saying that a lot lately. Not just to Cooper but to herself. "And I'm not sure I can put this on the back burner while we try to catch this kidnapper."

Another sigh, and Cooper pulled her into his arms. She didn't want this. Okay, she did. But she didn't want to want it. She didn't want to want *him*.

"You can go ahead and cry if you think it'll help," he offered.

Just the offer was enough to make her want to choke back tears. She wasn't a crier by nature, and she'd been doing too much of it lately. Jessa stepped back from him. Not easily, though. Part of her wanted to stay in Cooper's arms and let him help her through this, but she knew that Cooper, and her reaction to him, was a huge part of the problem.

"We need to get answers from our suspects," she reminded him. Reminded herself, too. "Because everything points to someone trying to cover up an illegal adoption."

"Yeah," he said. "There are some open cases on missing babies. Our situation might be connected to those."

Jessa thought about that a moment and didn't like any of the conclusions she reached. Judging from the way Cooper's forehead bunched up, neither did he. It was especially troubling that his wife could have been murdered so that someone—a monster—could take Liam.

There was a knock at the door just a split second before it opened. It was Colt. Even though Jessa was no longer in Cooper's arms, she stepped back farther to put more distance between them. That only made Colt give his brother a suspicious glance. She figured Colt wasn't stupid, and he could see the attraction between Cooper and her.

"I got the financials and background checks on Hector and Peggy," Colt said, handing Cooper a half-inch-thick file. "There's plenty to read in them, but some highlights—there are some suspicious deposits in Peggy's account. By suspicious, I mean two or three times a month, she makes cash deposits of anywhere from five to ten grand."

"Money she's getting from being a baby broker," Cooper supplied. "Do the deposits line up with the dates of the adoptions?"

"Hard to tell. Those records she left Jessa are a mess, and we're still trying to untangle them." He paused. "Our FBI *stepbrother* offered to help."

Cooper pulled back his shoulders. For a second, anyway. "Let him help. If he thinks he can make sense of it, let him try."

"He's not doing this for us," Colt reminded him. "But because he wants to help Rosalie find her missing daughter."

Cooper nodded. "I don't care why he's doing it. We just need to get to the truth." He thumbed through the file, and she saw something highlighted that had caught Cooper's attention.

"Two days ago Hector made a payment to Vernon

Graham," Jessa said, moving closer so she could get a better look.

"Well, Hector didn't make the payment directly," Colt explained. "It came out of his business expenses. His assistant actually signed the check."

The amount was only a hundred dollars. Not exactly enough for a hired gun. Still, it was a direct connection between Hector and Graham.

Or was it?

Her attention landed on another highlight on the next page. A payment that Peggy had made to Graham for the same amount—a hundred dollars, and the check had been made out on the same day as Hector's payment.

Cooper shook his head. "This is starting to look like a setup."

"I agree," Colt said, "But it could be a reverse psychology. If all our suspects look guilty, then we don't know which one to arrest."

"Yeah." Cooper looked up from the papers. "Make that call to Seth and ask for his help."

Colt hesitantly nodded and turned, no doubt ready to make what Cooper would see as an unholy alliance with their stepbrother. However, he stopped when the front door opened.

"I'll call Seth in a few minutes. Right now, it's showtime," Colt said. "Hector Dixon's here."

Even though Cooper tried to stay ahead of her, Jessa didn't let him. She hurried past Colt and practically ran to the reception area. And Hector was indeed there.

His gaze narrowed immediately when he saw her. "This is your doing—again. I'm fed up with you and the sheriff accusing me of wrongdoing."

"Someone tried to kidnap Liam again," Jessa settled for saying, though she wanted to say plenty more to him.

Actually, she wanted to make him tell her the truth, and it sickened her a little that she was ready to use force to do that.

Her news softened Hector's glare, but she couldn't be sure if his reaction was because he genuinely felt sorry for her or because he was faking it to take suspicion off himself.

"This way," Cooper insisted, tipping his head to one of the interview rooms. He picked up a laptop, some files, and led Hector inside. Once there, Cooper met his brother's gaze, and Tucker took Jessa into the observation room so she could watch.

"I know about the DNA test," Tucker said the moment his brother was out of earshot. "I talked to Doc Howland about it to make sure there was no chance it was wrong. He's positive that Liam is indeed Cooper's son."

Oh, God. If the doctor had talked to Tucker about it, that meant soon it could be all over town. Everyone would know, and all those people would be telling Cooper how happy they were for him. His family would no doubt be pressing for him to claim Liam and kick her out of the picture.

"The doc was worried about Cooper," Tucker went on. "About you, too. And he wanted me to make sure you were both okay."

"We're not okay," Jessa said under her breath.

Tucker just stared at her. No sympathy. No assurance that all would be well.

He looked a lot like Cooper. Same gray eyes. Same dark hair. But Jessa knew Tucker had a reputation for being a ladies' man. And a reputation for bending the law. He would do anything it took to make sure she didn't stand in the way of Cooper getting his son back.

"Cooper nearly died when he lost them," Tucker continued. He didn't look at her now. Instead, he fastened his gaze to his brother on the other side of the glass. "He won't go through another ordeal like that."

But Jessa certainly would, and it broke her heart to think of just how quickly she could lose the child she'd raised. It made her want to snatch up Liam and run. Anywhere. Anyplace where Cooper couldn't claim him. However, she could be running straight into the arms of a kidnapper.

Or worse.

It'd occurred to her that the person trying to cover up the kidnapping might be willing to do anything to make sure Liam couldn't be linked back to him.

Anything.

Tucker cursed, caught her arm and put her in the only chair in the room. "Are you about to faint?" he snarled.

She must have looked pretty bad for him to think that, and Tucker seemed as uncomfortable playing nursemaid to her as she was to be on the receiving end of it.

"Just breathe," he grumbled.

She couldn't do that well, either. But she did watch Cooper, and she prayed he'd get a break in the case to end the danger.

Then she could think of running with Liam.

Cooper took a piece of paper from the file Colt had given him and he slid it Hector's way. "That's the registration for your Jeep Cherokee. A man used it to drive to my family's ranch. He broke in, and I believe he tried to kidnap Liam."

Hector started shaking his head before Cooper even finished. "I keep that vehicle out at my hunting cabin. Anyone could have borrowed it to set me up for this."

He hadn't hesitated on the answer. Maybe because he'd been expecting the question. Still, it seemed risky for Hector's hired gun to use a vehicle registered to him. But again, Hector could have done that, hoping it would smack of a setup.

Cooper looked through the rest of the papers. "I don't see a hunting cabin listed in your assets, but there's one in your sister's name."

"It belongs to both of us, but her name is on the deed. We don't use the place very often. That's why I wouldn't have noticed the Jeep was missing."

"I'll send the Rangers out to the cabin." Cooper glanced back in Tucker's direction, and his brother made the call to get that started. "If the Jeep is there, they'll process it for any evidence." Cooper went to the next page. "Do you know Vernon Graham?"

"I know of him. He's one of the men who tried to kidnap Liam. Last I heard, he was in the hospital."

"You never had any dealings with him?"

"None," Hector insisted.

Which meant he'd just lied.

Cooper slid another piece of paper Hector's way. "Then why did you pay Vernon Graham a hundred dollars?"

Hector looked at the transaction as if seeing it for the first time. "I didn't pay him. But my assistant often gives contributions to various charities in my name."

It was either a very convenient answer or Hector had messed up and left a paper trail connecting him to a man he'd hired to kidnap a little boy.

Hector opened his mouth to say something else, but his phone rang. "I'll turn it off," he mumbled, but then seemed to freeze when he looked at the screen. "I think the caller might be Peggy."

That got Cooper's attention. He took the phone from Hector and answered it on speaker.

"Hector?" the caller immediately said. "Where are you?"

It was Peggy, all right, and Tucker hurried from the room, no doubt so he could try to trace the call. Jessa didn't stay put, either. She went to the interview room and threw open the door. Hector spared her a glance. A nasty one. Before he turned his attention back to Peggy.

"I'm at the sheriff's office *again,*" Hector answered.

"Don't hang up," Cooper warned the woman. "Tell me where you are."

Peggy didn't jump to answer, and Jessa prayed she'd stay on the line until Colt and Tucker had a chance to pinpoint her location. "I'm someplace safe, I hope. I know you don't believe me, but someone's trying to kill me."

"I might believe you if you turned yourself in. You held a man and two women at gunpoint. You need to answer for that."

"And I will. When you have this would-be killer behind bars so he can't get to me." She paused. "But I might have been wrong about Donovan. He might not be behind the illegal adoptions."

"You seemed pretty sure he was guilty when you were holding him hostage," Cooper reminded her.

"Yes, but I think Hector could have misled me so he could cover up his own guilt."

"Right," Hector snarled. "Point at me now, will you? Well, I'm not the one who did something wrong. Hell, Peggy..." He stopped, obviously struggling to keep a leash on his temper. "Quit slinging mud at me so we can get to the bottom of this. Someone tried to kidnap Jessa's boy again."

Peggy made a sound. Hard to interpret what it meant, though. "I didn't know."

"Well, you do now," Cooper snapped. He grabbed one of the papers from the file. "Now tell me about these deposits made to your bank account." He started reading off the sums and the dates.

"I told you. People pay me to find the perfect match for the babies."

"But I wasn't perfect," Jessa said. "I was single."

"The *perfect match* for someone who can afford it," Peggy corrected in a very loud voice. "You paid for your son, and it's payments like yours that keep the adoption wheels turning. If I had to work elsewhere in a day job, I wouldn't have time to find babies in need of adoption."

Then people would have to go through normal channels. Channels that Jessa hadn't taken because it would have been years, if ever, before she'd gotten a child. It sickened her though to think that cutting corners had brought them to this point. Not just her, but countless others.

"Did you steal Liam?" Cooper came right out and asked.

"No." Peggy didn't raise her voice. She merely sighed and then hung up.

Cooper hit Redial and stuck his head out into the hall. "Did you get her location?"

"Sorry," Tucker said a moment later. "It's a burner."

Cooper and Jessa both groaned, and he added some profanity when the woman didn't answer. A burner was a prepaid cell that couldn't be traced. However, that did cause Jessa to snap in Hector's direction.

"How did you know it was Peggy who was calling?" Jessa demanded.

He lifted his shoulder. "Peggy's called me before,

and it's appeared on the screen as unknown name, unknown number."

"It's how she called me," someone said. Jessa hadn't heard him come up the hall, but it was Donovan. And he wasn't alone. There were two men wearing suits standing behind him. His lawyers, no doubt.

"You're going in there," Cooper ordered Donovan, and he pointed to the interview room across the hall.

Donovan walked closer, that oily smile on his mouth. She figured that smile got to Cooper, because it sure as heck got to her. There was nothing about this situation that warranted a smile.

"Cooper," Donovan said, his tone as condescending as that smile. "I know you'd love to see me suffer. But this vendetta against me has got to stop. In fact, my lawyers are here to tell you that there'll be no more questions… unless you file charges against me."

Jessa knew Cooper couldn't do that. Not yet, anyway. The only evidence they had against Donovan was Peggy's accusations, and considering Peggy's situation, those weren't nearly enough to bring charges against the man.

"Now, if you don't mind," Donovan said, casually checking the time on his pricey watch, "I'll just be going. I have a business to run."

Donovan turned as if ready to leave, but he stopped and looked at Hector, who was still in the interview room. "Don't I know you from somewhere?"

Hector shook his head. Maybe too quickly.

"Funny," Donovan remarked. "I could have sworn I've seen you around Sweetwater Springs."

With that, Donovan smiled again and strolled away. Jessa sure didn't smile, and neither did Cooper. They just stared at Hector, waiting to see if Donovan had hit a nerve or was just blowing smoke.

"I was here in town after the flood," Hector finally said.

He didn't have to clarify what flood. Jessa knew from Cooper's suddenly blanched expression that Hector was talking about the one that had swept away his wife.

"A former client lives here," Hector went on, "and she had some flood damage. Not Donovan, but a rancher just outside of town. Norma Cullen."

Jessa knew the name, had seen it on records for an old embezzlement case, but she'd never met the woman.

"Norma asked me to come out and take a look at the damage," Hector went on. "I don't normally handle that sort of thing, but I made an exception because she was an old high school friend."

"That's all there was to the visit?" Cooper said, and it sounded like some kind of accusation.

"That's all," Hector snapped. "I don't know how Donovan found out about me being in town, and the only reason he brought it up was to implicate me in all of this."

"You're already implicated," Cooper reminded him. He opened a file on the laptop. A file with photos of a white car and another of Molly. "Did you see my wife, that car, the baby, anything?"

Hector studied the photos and shook his head to each of the questions. "Donovan's just muddying the waters. And now, if you'll excuse me—and even if you don't—I think I'll take a page from Donovan's book and leave. When and if you have more than just speculation, contact me."

"Oh, I will. Maybe as soon as the crime scene folks find something in that Jeep that will lead right back to you."

Hector stopped, stiffened. "If you find anything, it's because someone planted it." He walked out. Or rather, stormed out, slamming the door behind him.

Cooper stood there, staring after the man's hasty exit. But he didn't stand there alone for long. Colt went to one side of him. Tucker, the other. A united front. A family. Even with the shadow hanging over them from Jewell's trial, they were still very much a family.

One that would make sure Cooper got his son back.

Jessa got that urge again. To grab Liam and run. But then Cooper looked over his shoulder at her.

"I'm sorry," he said, his voice far more soothing than it should have been. He walked closer to her. "I wanted to get more out of them."

And he surprised her—surprised his brothers, too— by brushing a kiss on her mouth. It was quick. Barely a kiss. But she felt it all the way to her toes. Colt and Tucker no doubt felt something entirely different.

Confusion.

They probably thought Cooper had lost his mind.

"Come on," Cooper said to her, ignoring his brothers' stares. "We'll get Liam back to the ranch." He put his hand on the small of her back, easing her in that direction.

But he stopped.

Jessa followed his gaze to the glass front door and the woman who stepped inside. Rosalie.

"We need to talk," Rosalie said, not to her brothers but to Jessa.

She didn't like the sound of gloom and doom in Rosalie's voice. There'd already been way too much bad news. Jessa couldn't handle more.

"You remember I told you I'd been investigating missing babies? Like my own daughter," Rosalie explained.

Not trusting her voice, Jessa just nodded.

"Well, I found out something," Cooper's sister continued. "About Liam."

Chapter Thirteen

Cooper just stood there, staring at his sister. He tried to tamp down his hopes. But it was hard to do that when Rosalie might have exactly what he needed to put an end to the danger.

And reclaim his son.

Of course, he couldn't do that without hurting Jessa. Maybe Liam, too. After all, Jessa was the only parent Liam remembered having. Still, that didn't mean Cooper would just hand him over to her and bow out of Liam's life.

However, that left him with one Texas-size question: What was he going to do?

"What did you find out?" Jessa asked Rosalie.

Jessa was definitely wearing her heart on her sleeve. Her voice was mostly breath. She was pale and shaky. And she, too, looked as if she were trying to tamp down something—a panic attack, maybe.

Rosalie took a moment to gather her breath. "I've been working with criminal informants and just about anyone else who could give me information about my missing daughter."

Cooper almost gave her a stern scolding for that. It was dangerous, and she should leave that sort of thing to the cops. Still, he knew what Rosalie was going through, and he would have bargained with the devil himself to get his son back. Rosalie no doubt felt the same way about her own child.

"One of the informants told me about a woman who found a baby," Rosalie continued. "The timing and circumstances are right for it to have been Liam."

"But you're not sure," Jessa jumped to say.

There was sympathy in Rosalie's eyes, and she volleyed glances between Jessa and Cooper as if asking if she should continue. Cooper just nodded.

Rosalie took another deep breath. "The woman refuses to talk to me, and the informant wouldn't give me her name even when I offered him money."

"If you think he's telling the truth, I'll offer him enough money so he'll talk," Cooper assured her. "What's his name?"

"Calvin Brinton. He lives in San Antonio. And he has a record a mile long, mainly for petty stuff, but he did some time for forgery about a decade ago."

Cooper looked at Colt. "I'm on it," Colt assured him, and he hurried back to one of the offices, no doubt to make a call to locate everything he could about this criminal informant.

"Brinton said a woman who was a friend of friend had found a baby boy nearly two years ago after the flood," Rosalie continued. "According to this woman, the baby was floating in his car seat, and she rescued him."

God, it was hard to hear this. His son could have been out there on that raging creek. A dozen bad things could have happened to him. If this woman was telling the truth about rescuing him, then she had also saved his life.

Jessa started shaking her head. "Why didn't the woman report it?"

Cooper had the same damn question. He'd died a thousand times after Molly's death and his son's disappearance. And yeah, he was thankful for the rescue, but not thankful that his baby had been kept from him.

"This is where the story gets a little sticky," Rosalie went on. "The woman says she'd heard of someone who would pay big bucks for a healthy newborn, so she made some calls and arranged to meet with this person."

That immediately got his attention. "Peggy Dawes?"

"No. I'm sorry." She turned to Jessa. "She said the woman was *you.*"

"Then she's lying," Jessa insisted. "She's lying," she repeated to Cooper.

He ignored her for the time being. "What else did the woman tell your criminal informant?"

Rosalie didn't look especially eager to continue, but she nodded eventually. "She said that Jessa wanted the adoption to look aboveboard, so she gave the woman the name of a baby broker who was in turn supposed to contact an adoption attorney."

"I didn't," Jessa protested. She caught Cooper's arms, pulling him around to face her. "I wouldn't do anything like that."

"I know. But we could still get some truthful information from this woman if we can find her. My guess is that she's covering for the real kidnapper and purposely gave that false info about you to the criminal informant."

Jessa stayed quiet a moment, obviously giving that some thought, and he saw the muscles in her arms and shoulders relax a bit when she realized he wasn't accusing her of anything.

"We need to start by locating the criminal informant and pressuring him to give us her name," Cooper said, and he met Rosalie's gaze. "Thank you for bringing this to me."

Rosalie nodded, but she didn't get a chance to say anything because Tucker spoke first.

"Who else knows about this Calvin Brinton and what he told you?" he asked Rosalie. Unlike Cooper, Tucker's question sounded more like an interrogation.

Rosalie lifted her shoulder. "I'm not sure. I've talked to a lot of people, and Brinton's someone I use often when I'm following a lead."

Cooper and Tucker exchanged glances, and Cooper knew what had triggered his brother's question.

Hell.

"This could put both Brinton and you in danger," Cooper told his sister. "The woman, too. Until we get this situation under control, it's best if you take some precautions. Don't go anywhere unless one of us or your sister is with you."

Cooper had expected that to frighten Rosalie, but it didn't. She only gave a resolute nod. He wanted to add that she should back off from her investigation for a while, but a mere request from him wouldn't stop a parent in search of her missing child. Heck, once the danger was over for Liam and Jessa, Cooper would jump to help Rosalie himself.

Tucker mumbled plenty of profanity. Maybe because he didn't like being joined at the hip with a sister they no longer considered a sister. At least that had been the case when Rosalie had first shown up at the ranch with Jewell's entourage. However, Rosalie had more than pulled her own weight by helping to take care of Liam. And now she'd given them a lead.

Maybe.

If it wasn't already too late.

One glance at Tucker and Cooper realized his brother was thinking the same thing.

Tucker took out his phone. "I'll find out if there are any missing persons reports or dead bodies that might match this woman who found the baby."

"But you don't know anything about her," Rosalie interrupted.

"She must live near the creek," Cooper explained while Tucker proceeded with the call. "And she's probably not elderly if she walked down to the creek so soon after the flood. Also, since she was willing to commit a crime by selling the baby, then she possibly has a criminal record."

Of course, it still could turn out to be a needle in a haystack, but it was a start.

Jessa went closer to him. "I know I sound like Hector, Peggy and Donovan, but I didn't do anything wrong."

"I know." And Cooper would have given her more reassurance than that if Colt hadn't finished his call.

"It's not good," Colt told them right off the bat. "I just spoke to a friend in San Antonio P.D., and Calvin Brinton was found dead just a few hours ago. Murdered, execution-style."

Rosalie's hand flew to her mouth, but Cooper could still see her lips trembling. Jessa wasn't faring much better. Maybe because she was thinking this would implicate her in a murder, but in Cooper's book, it didn't.

"It's not your fault," Cooper immediately said to Rosalie. "I wouldn't be surprised if the person behind these attacks paid Brinton to contact you just so he could implicate Jessa."

Jessa nodded, but she lost more of the color on her cheeks. "He wants us divided. He wants me to take Liam and run. That way I'll be an easier target."

Cooper nodded, too. "I figure this guy will do anything to eliminate any chance that Liam could be linked back to him."

There'd already been a lot of effort made to cover up that link. The kidnapping attempts. The break-in at the lab to destroy the DNA sample. Now Brinton's murder.

Colt finished another call and joined them. "I've put out feelers. Whoever this woman is, we'll find her. Hopefully alive," he added in a mumble.

"Come on," Cooper said to Jessa. "We should get Liam back to the ranch. Rosalie, too."

"Wait. What are you gonna do?" Tucker asked with his hands on his hips and his gaze firmly planted on Cooper.

He didn't think Tucker was talking about the danger now. "I'll have to sort it out with Jessa," Cooper settled for saying.

That caused Tucker to huff. "For Pete's sake, Liam's your son, and you've already lost too much time with him."

Colt made a sound of agreement. "All you have to do is show any judge those DNA results, and that'll start the process to revoke the adoption."

Cooper couldn't deny what his brothers were saying. Neither could Jessa. If he pushed, he could have custody of Liam by the end of the month. No matter which way he went with this, it would mean a drastic change in all their lives.

"Well?" Tucker prompted. "Please tell me you aren't just gonna let her take him."

"No." Cooper's gaze came to hers. "I'm going to do what's best for Liam. I'm having Jessa and him move to the ranch and live with me."

Chapter Fourteen

Jessa paced outside Cooper's office while she waited for him to finish the family meeting with his father and brothers. There wasn't much else she could do—especially since Cooper hadn't invited her to join in on the discussion.

Liam had been bathed, fed and was down for the night. Her mother had said good-night, too. The ranch house was quiet, well guarded, and Jessa should be trying to settle herself so she could get some rest.

Fat chance of that, though.

She wasn't resting until she had a chance to confront Cooper about his idiotic insistence that she move to the ranch. He certainly hadn't made it sound like an invitation. More like one of his orders. And yes, their relationship had gotten a little friendlier.

All right, a *lot* friendlier.

However, that didn't mean it was a good idea for them to be under the same roof for an extended period of time. It would only make things harder for her to distance herself from him. And distance him from Liam.

As if she could.

No, Cooper wouldn't just let Liam go, but she had to find a way to minimize the damage and guard her heart in the process.

The sound of voices snagged her attention again. Jessa could hear parts of the conversation from the four Mc-Kinnon men. Some parts were easier to hear than others because the meeting involved some raised voices. Apparently, she wasn't the only one who thought the moving-in order was a bad idea. Tucker was especially against it.

No surprise there.

Like Cooper, Tucker had been especially critical of her pressing for Jewell's arrest. And like Cooper, his criticism hadn't been because he wanted to defend Jewell but because he saw the investigation as a threat to the rest of his family. Especially his father.

However, his father didn't agree with Tucker on the matter of Cooper's order. Roy was all for the idea of Liam and her moving to the ranch. Permanently.

She heard a phone ring. A moment later, the door flew open and Tucker stormed out. Not before giving her a glare that could have withered every blade of grass in Texas. Jessa fared somewhat better from Roy. He whispered an apology—for what, he didn't say—and walked away.

Colt was on the phone and didn't even make eye contact with her when he came out. Still, she was pretty certain they blamed her for this. They probably thought she'd managed to talk Cooper into this stupid moving-in-with-them idea.

She didn't wait for an invitation from Cooper. Jessa went inside the office and immediately spotted the baby monitor on his desk. It was on, and she could see her son sleeping peacefully in the crib. She was pleased about that but not pleased that Cooper was already acting like a parent.

Jessa mentally groaned. Of course he would think that he had a right to act that way. And he did. But she hated that there was nothing she could do to stop him from chipping away at her claim on the child she'd raised.

There was more proof of that on the desk.

The DNA results that proved Liam was Cooper's son. Not some handwritten note, but the actual lab report. She'd used reports just like that to prove a case in court.

Cooper would no doubt use it for the same reason.

"Doc Howland sent it over," Cooper explained. "He's keeping it under wraps for now. And since he didn't want anything on file, that's the only copy."

Cooper's eyes met hers. For an instant she saw the bone-weary fatigue there. However, he must have seen the fight in hers, because he frowned and mumbled some profanity under his breath.

"Why ask me to move in with you?" she demanded, and didn't wait for his answer. "Did you think it was the fastest way to get custody of Liam?"

"No. I thought it was what I should do for Liam. And for you." Cooper scrubbed his hand over his face, walked closer.

That threw her for a moment. Jessa had braced herself for the kind of stubborn, riled attitude she'd gotten from Tucker. But Cooper just seemed as exhausted as she was.

"I love Liam," Cooper went on. "And it wouldn't do anyone any good to push you out of his life. It sure wouldn't be in his best interest."

"It wouldn't do anyone any good except for you," Jessa corrected.

"Yeah. I'd have my boy to myself, but it'd come at a high cost." He paused, glanced at the photo of his wife on his desk next to the baby monitor. "Liam doesn't remember Molly, but he sure as heck knows you. It wouldn't be fair to cut you out of his life."

Jessa hadn't braced herself for a lot of things, including fairness. It softened her anger a lot more than she wanted it to.

"But moving in here at the ranch?" she questioned. "You can't think that's a good idea."

He lifted his shoulder. "We could make it work."

"Really? For one thing, your family wouldn't like that." Then she pointed to Molly's photo. "And you're still in love with your late wife."

Cooper didn't deny either accusation, but he did take the photo, and after a long look, he eased it into his desk drawer and shut it.

Jessa sighed. "I didn't say that to make you put the photo away. I'd hoped it would make you see that we're not suited for living with each other."

His eyebrow lifted. "Really?" he repeated.

She felt the heat rise on her cheeks. And elsewhere. With just one word Cooper could remind her of that mistake of a kissing session. Except it hadn't felt like a mistake at the time.

Sadly, it still didn't.

And that was why it was indeed a mistake.

"We're attracted to each other," he pointed out.

"Attraction's not enough," she insisted. Though there were times, like now, when it certainly felt as if it could help them overcome a lot of things.

"We're both committed to Liam," he said, coming toward her. Cooper stopped just inches from her. The weariness vanished from his eyes, and he pointed his finger at her. "And if you repeat that part about attraction not being enough, I'll remind you otherwise."

Jessa swallowed hard. She was all too familiar with Cooper's reminders. The kisses. The smoldering looks. Her body being in a continuous state of arousal just by being around him.

"Being committed to Liam and this attraction aren't enough," she reminded him.

"It's a start," he reminded her right back.

Okay. She was clearly losing this argument, and it was one she couldn't afford to lose.

Could she?

Would it really be that bad if she gave in to his order?

For just a moment Jessa allowed herself to think about living with Cooper. Not just for the immediate future until the danger had passed. But, well, forever. It would have some advantages. Like no messy custody dispute over Liam.

And maybe even sharing a bed with Cooper.

She couldn't stop that from creeping into her mind. However, she still shook her head. She didn't say a word, but her answer to the ridiculous living arrangements must have been all over her face, because Cooper hooked his arm around to snap her to him.

And he kissed her.

Jessa put her hands against his chest to push him away. At least some small part of her wanted to do that, but the other parts won out, and she found herself falling deeper into his arms.

All in all, not a bad place to be.

With her body pressed against his, and his mouth moving over hers as if he knew exactly how to set her on fire.

Jessa tried to hang on, tried to voice some kind of reminder that this wasn't going to help their situation. It would only muddy already muddy waters. But did she say that?

No.

She just stayed put in his arms and returned the kiss. Boy, did she. Jessa was the one who deepened it, and she was the one who tugged Cooper closer and closer until they were plastered against each other.

Until she was burning for him.

Soon, very soon, all thoughts of Cooper's order for her to move to the ranch slipped from her mind. Common sense did, too. She wanted to blame it all on the fact that it'd been so long since she'd been kissed like this. So long since she'd been held and wanted. But this wasn't about time.

This was all Cooper's doing. And she was terrified that even if this continued, it wouldn't leave her satisfied for long, that she would only end up wanting him more.

Cooper reached behind him and locked the door. She realized then what he had in mind. To take this much further than a scalding-hot kissing session.

That still didn't stop her.

Since this was going to be a massive mistake, Jessa figured she might as well enjoy it.

And pay the price for it later.

COOPER DIDN'T QUESTION what he was doing. He just went with it. He pushed aside the investigation, the looming custody fight. Even his insistence that Jessa move in with him.

And he just let himself get lost in her.

It wasn't hard to do. She tasted like Christmas and all the other good things rolled into one. Felt that way, too. With her breasts against his chest. Cooper did something to make the pressure even better—and worse—by catching the back of her leg and lifting it so that her sex met his.

Damn good.

And once he got his eyes uncrossed he did something about ridding her of some of the blasted clothes between them.

Jessa was doing some clothes removal of her own. Not easily. She stayed with the kissing until she was out of breath and gasping. She broke away only long enough to pull some air into her lungs and then continued unbuttoning his shirt. She finally managed to get it off him.

Her touch was instant. Her fingers against his bare skin created some instant heat inside him. Not that he needed more. He was already crazy enough, but it sped things up for Cooper, and he rid Jessa of her top. Then her bra. She was small, firm. Perfect.

Tasted perfect, too, he discovered when he lowered his head and kissed her there.

Jessa reacted. Man, did she. She made a little sound of pleasure and pulled him closer for even more. That sent him fumbling to get them to the sofa. He darn sure didn't want to wait to take her upstairs. Everything inside him was yelling for him to take her *now*.

But something else yelled through his brain.

"I don't have a condom," he let her know. Not easily. He damn sure didn't want this to end.

With her breath still gusting and her fingers on his zipper, Jessa froze. Met his gaze. She seemed to have a split-second debate with herself and yanked him back to her for another kiss.

"I'm on the pill," she said through the frantic flurry of kisses she showered on his face.

That was the best news he'd heard in a long time. Cooper knew he should still back off, but he would have had a better chance of telling his heart to stop beating. This was going to happen even if it didn't make sense.

Jessa obviously felt the same way.

She went after his zipper again. He went after hers.

They weren't exactly graceful when they landed on the sofa. That gracefulness went down another significant notch when she worked her hand into his boxers and took hold of him.

Oh, man. He was in big trouble here.

Her touch made everything seem more urgent, and Cooper rid her of her jeans. Panties, too. And even though he was burning, he still took the time to look at her.

And taste her.

Yeah, she was perfect everywhere.

Jessa made more of those sounds of pleasure. Slow, silky moans that purred from her throat. But there was nothing slow about her touch. She was frantic when she pushed off his boots and jeans, and by the time she made it to his boxers, she was well past the frantic stage.

Cooper was right there with her.

As soon as he was free of his boxers, he caught her and sank deep and hard into her. The pleasure shot through him, robbing him of his breath. He wanted to savor this, too, as he'd done with the sight of her. But Jessa lifted her hips, and savoring was a lost cause.

Cooper moved inside her and Jessa moved with him, keeping up the already desperate pace. That pace would end all of this too soon, but there was nothing he could do to make their bodies slow down. That fierce need pushed them hard to complete this and find mind-numbing release.

Too bad that release wouldn't last long. But Cooper refused to deal with that now. He only dealt with Jessa, and the frenzied rhythm of the strokes inside her.

"Finish this," she whispered. "Finish *me.*"

That was the plan. Cooper pushed into her, felt her body give way to the maddening strokes. He felt her *finish*. But she didn't go alone. Nope. Jessa hooked her arm around his back and pulled him down for a kiss.

That was the last straw for him.

Cooper buried his face against her neck and let Jessa finish him off.

Yeah, he'd been right about the mind-numbing part. Right about a lot of other things, too.

Now all that was left was dealing with the aftermath of the mistake he'd just made.

Chapter Fifteen

Jessa felt the instant change in Cooper. The muscles in his back tightened, and while he couldn't exactly roll off her without landing on the floor, he did move to his side.

He didn't say a word. Didn't need to. She could also feel the fierce debate going on inside him.

Because she was having the same debate with herself.

For days they'd been skirting around this heated attraction, and her body welcomed the satisfaction. The release. But she figured it would come at a high price, and she didn't want Cooper—or herself—making assumptions that this meant anything. Anything other than great sex, that was.

It'd been so long since she'd been with a man. And never like this. Why the heck had he been just as good as he looked?

Jessa mentally sighed. It would have been so much easier if she just felt indifferent toward Cooper. Or if she'd just left him alone. After all, this was the man who could destroy her life, and here she'd landed in bed with him.

Well, on the sofa, anyway.

"This doesn't mean I'll move in with you," she let him know.

He lifted one eyelid, and it looked as if he tried to

glare at her. Hard to do that, though, while butt naked and squished on a sofa together. "Didn't figure it did."

Her feelings were all over the place, and while his words were right, they didn't make her feel so right. Because if he hadn't used sex to sway her into moving in with him, then that meant this attraction had just gotten the better of both of them. It also meant the attraction would only get worse.

Until it burned itself out.

Then what?

They'd be at odds under the same roof. Maybe Cooper couldn't see the problem with that now, but he would certainly see it later. And being at odds with her might prompt him to get her off the ranch.

Without Liam, of course.

There was no way Cooper would let her leave with Liam now that he knew the little boy was his son.

"Don't know if you know this, but your nostrils flare when you're getting upset," he drawled. "So other than the obvious, what's upsetting you?"

She wanted to bring up the argument that she'd just mentally had with herself, but one look at him and Jessa knew he was well aware of what she'd been thinking.

"Just the obvious," she settled for saying.

Cooper made a sound of agreement and glanced at the baby monitor, prompting her to do the same. Thankfully, Liam was sleeping just as he should be. And it was a reminder she should be upstairs with him.

Jessa moved, forcing herself to get up, and she wished the room was suddenly pitch-black so that Cooper couldn't see her naked. He seemed to have no such concerns. He stood right in front of her.

Mercy.

The man had a great body.

Perfect. All those toned muscles earned from hard work on the ranch. The rugged face. It didn't help that she still had the taste of him on her lips.

And just like that, she felt herself go all warm again. A warmth that Jessa tried to push away so she could gather up her clothes and get dressed.

"How bad are you regretting this?" he asked just as he zipped up his jeans.

"Not bad enough." Especially considering that she was still fantasizing about getting him back on the sofa with her at the same time that she was worrying about his claim on Liam.

Cooper chuckled. Leaned over and kissed her. Not a postsex kind of peck, either. It was a full kiss that reminded her that one round of sex wasn't going to rid her of this sudden need she had for Cooper.

"How bad are you regretting this?" she asked, throwing the question back at him.

He pushed her hair from her face. Dropped another kiss on her forehead. Then met her eye to eye. Jessa was instantly sorry that she'd opened herself up for this conversation, because the last thing she wanted to hear was Cooper say he would do whatever it took to get custody of Liam.

Even though that was exactly what he would do.

And she would fight him equally hard.

"Let's table that for now," he said just as his phone buzzed.

Jessa thought maybe she'd like to table that particular discussion for a lifetime and have things go on as they had been.

Well, minus the danger, of course.

And when she saw Colt's name on Cooper's phone

screen, it was a stark reminder of not just the investigation but the danger that had set all this in motion.

"I found something," Colt said the moment Cooper answered the call and put it on speaker. "I'm pretty sure I found the woman who talked to Rosalie's criminal informant. Sonya Eakins."

Cooper shook his head. "I don't know her." And he looked back at Jessa, who had to shake her head, too. She quickly started dressing in case they had to go to the sheriff's office to question this woman.

"She lived in a little place just a quarter of a mile from the creek," Colt added.

Jessa didn't miss Colt's use of the past tense. "Sonya Eakins is dead?"

"Yeah," Colt verified. "SAPD found her body this morning. Killed execution-style."

Sweet heaven. This just kept getting worse.

Cooper cursed. "You're sure she's the right woman?" he asked his brother.

"Pretty sure. Everything you said about her fits. About six months before the flood, she rented the house within walking distance of the creek. She was young, early thirties, and had a long rap sheet for embezzlement and theft."

And to think Liam could have been in this woman's hands. At least Sonya hadn't hurt him, probably because she'd seen him as goods to sell.

"I got access to Sonya's bank accounts," Colt continued, "and there was a five-thousand-dollar deposit made less than a week after the flood."

Well, it wasn't absolute proof, but coupled with everything else, it was enough to convince Jessa that this woman had sold Liam. That sent her heart racing.

Because each piece of this maddening puzzle pointed at only one thing—that Liam was indeed Cooper's.

"What about our other suspects—did any of them have cash withdrawals around that time matching the deposit amount that was in Sonya's account?" Cooper asked.

"I checked. Didn't find anything, though."

Probably because the buyer had made sure it couldn't be linked back to him or her, and that would have been easy enough to do for someone rich, like Donovan, or for Hector, who had a thriving law practice. For that matter, Peggy, too, could have had that amount of cash on hand so there'd be no record of it. Now the person—Peggy, Hector or Donovan—whom Sonya had entangled in this black-market-baby deal had likely murdered her or had hired someone to do the job.

Cooper stayed quiet a moment. "I'll call you back," he said to his brother. He hit the end-call button and eased back around to face her. "The person who killed her likely murdered the criminal informant, too," Cooper mumbled. "A person who has murdered twice isn't likely to stop."

Jessa wished she could disagree, but she couldn't. "And now he or she has taken aim at Liam and us."

The *us* part she could handle. But she seriously doubted this monster wanted to kill Cooper and her and then leave her son alone. No, they wanted to sell him again or at least make sure no one could connect Liam to the illegal adoption.

"We need to do something," she whispered.

"Yeah." That was all Cooper said for several long moments. "I have a plan. You're not going to like it much, but I think this is our best shot at keeping all of us alive."

Jessa pulled in her breath, not sure she even wanted

to hear this, but knowing there was no guaranteed certainty in any plan they came up with.

"Whoever's behind this wants Liam," Cooper continued. "And we can make this person think that they can have him."

"What?" Jessa couldn't say it fast enough. "We're not giving them Liam." She'd die first before she let that happen.

"No, we're not. But I want this SOB to *think* that, and here's how we'll do it." Now it was Cooper's turn to take a deep breath. "We can pretend that Liam's had some kind of complication from his surgery and that we're taking him back to the hospital—"

Jessa was shaking her head before Cooper even finished. "I don't want Liam out there, especially at night where we wouldn't even be able to see our attackers before it was too late."

"Liam's not going anywhere," Cooper corrected. "But I am. I'll get out the word that Liam's running a fever and that I'm taking him to the E.R. Then I could make it look as if he's in the truck with me."

It didn't take Jessa long to figure out where Cooper was headed with this, and she didn't like this plan at all. "And then you'll set yourself up as bait so the kidnapper will come after you."

He darn sure didn't deny it.

"It's too dangerous," she said on a huff. "As you pointed out, this person has already murdered at least two people, and I'm sure he or she would love to add you to the list. Good grief, Cooper, this isn't a smart plan at all."

"It wouldn't be, if I didn't take precautions. Which I will. I can take one of my brothers with me, and he could stay low on the seat and out of sight."

"While you wait to be ambushed." Jessa threw her

hands in the air. "What if this person just starts shooting? What chance will you have then?"

Cooper caught her shoulders. "I have a better chance of stopping this idiot than he or she does of stopping me. That's because I'm fighting for Liam. For me this isn't about greed or covering a crime. I'll do whatever it takes to keep my son safe."

Jessa felt the same way. Whatever it took. "But this plan could backfire."

"Possibly," he admitted. "That's why I'd make sure the house is well guarded. I could move all the ranch hands near the house. They'd be armed. Plus, we'd set the security system, of course."

"And if the kidnapper is having the house watched, then he'll know that something's up."

"True," he answered so fast that it sounded as if he'd already considered that. "But I could keep the ranch hands out of sight."

Maybe. But Jessa thought of another problem with this so-called plan, and it was a huge flaw. "If I'm not with you in the truck," she said, "the kidnapper will suspect it's a trap."

Cooper stared at her a moment and then started to curse. "No way in hell will I let you go out there."

She huffed. "But you'd let yourself do this."

"Because I'm a cop. It's my job to take risks."

"This isn't a risk. It could be suicide."

"Yeah, if it's not done right. And the way to make sure it's right is to be ready. Tucker and I can be armed to the hilt, and if the kidnapper tries to force us off the road or something, we'd be right there, returning fire."

Jessa threw off his grip from her shoulders and reversed their position so that she had hold of him. She had to make him see that this wouldn't work.

Well, not without her, anyway.

"If I'm not in that truck, the kidnappers will likely just head here to the ranch. Without you around, they'll see that as their chance to find out if Liam's really here. And even if they don't manage to take him, there'll be shots fired. Do you really want Liam in the middle of a gunfight?"

"No." He backed away from her, cursed and then repeated it. "But it's only a matter of time before they try to come after him again."

"Agreed." Though it sickened her to think of her baby being in danger again. "And that's why I have to be in the truck with you. The kidnapper has to believe this is some kind of frantic rush to the hospital. That's the only thing that'll prevent him from coming here."

She could tell he wanted to argue with her, but he didn't. Instead, he paced. Cursed. And blew out another of those long breaths. Jessa knew him well enough to hear the argument going on inside his head.

An argument he was losing.

"I can't ask you to put yourself in that kind of danger," he finally said.

"You don't have to ask. Like you, I'd do anything for Liam." This definitely qualified as *anything*. "So how would we get out the word that we're on the way to the hospital?"

Still, he didn't jump to answer. Probably because he was still trying to think of another way around this. There wasn't one, and his profanity let her know he was well aware of that, too.

"How do we do it?" she pressed.

Cooper rubbed his hand over his face. "I can make a call to Doc Howland and make sure he lets everyone know we're bringing Liam into the E.R. I figure the kidnapper has someone watching the hospital."

Jessa figured the same thing. Watching the hospital, her house, the ranch and any other place that Cooper and she might go. That led Jessa to her next question.

"What if our plan causes a shoot-out at the hospital?" She cringed at the possibility of all those innocent people being caught in the cross fire.

"The idea is to find this nut job before a shoot-out can occur." But then he lifted his shoulder. "The best way to do that is to lure him and his goons away from the hospital and to the road where we can stop him."

"How? Unless you think Dr. Howland's phone line is somehow insecure."

"It's possible his line's been tapped, but we can't count on it to get the word to the kidnapper. I can use the squad radio to give Reed the false info," Cooper went on. "Then we can wait about fifteen minutes to make it look as if we're getting Liam ready to leave, and we can pretend to put him in the truck."

The squad radio was a good idea, because it wasn't secure. People tapped into them all the time. Considering how badly the kidnapper wanted them, he or she would almost certainly be listening to any communication coming in or out of the sheriff's office.

However, there was another potential problem.

"How will you get Colt to the hospital without making it look suspicious?" she asked.

"I can have him follow along behind us. It wouldn't be unusual for an uncle to go with his sick nephew to the hospital. Plus, I seriously doubt an extra lawman in tow will prevent this lunatic from coming after us." He groaned. "And that means you have to get down and stay down if anything goes wrong."

"I will, but I want to be armed, too."

That tightened his jaw muscles, because it was a reminder that this would almost certainly end in gunfire. Best-case scenario would be for them to see the kidnapper's vehicle and disable it by shooting out the tires, and then Cooper and Colt could arrest the culprit.

Worst-case scenario was for the kidnapper and his or her hired guns to be so well hidden on the road that an attack could start before Cooper, Colt or she even knew what was happening.

Judging from his suddenly stark expression, Cooper no doubt wanted to call the whole thing off, but like her, he knew the bottom line here. There'd been two kidnapping attempts in two days. She could add her car accident to that as well, since that had likely been the first attempt.

And there would be others.

Soon.

"We're already on borrowed time," Jessa reminded him.

Cooper stayed quiet a moment, then nodded. "Come on. Let's get this started."

Chapter Sixteen

Cooper hoped he wasn't making yet another mistake tonight. Not that he was certain that sleeping with Jessa had been a mistake.

The verdict was still out on that.

But while the experience had been pretty amazing, it'd stalled him from thinking solely about how to end the danger for Liam and them. Maybe he could redeem himself with this plan.

If it worked, that was.

For that to happen, Cooper had to make sure a lot of things were in place. He'd already called Dr. Howland and Reed to get the word out that he would be bringing Liam into the E.R. He'd told the doc and Reed to be generous with spreading the news, and by now it was probably all over town that Liam had had a medical setback. That was one of the good things about living in a small town. It didn't take long for people to hear news, both good and bad.

Step two involved the ranch hands. That had been a little trickier, since Cooper hadn't wanted to make it obvious that they were standing guard. The hands were instead keeping watch from their nearby bunkhouse but would be ready to respond if anyone tried to sneak onto the property to test if the hospital trip was some kind of ruse.

Of course, it was impossible to watch the entire ranch, so Cooper only hoped the hands would be looking in the right places at the right time if something went wrong.

Step three was for his father, Tucker, Rosalie and Rayanne to all be in position inside the house, armed and with the security system activated so they would know if someone tried to break in. Hopefully they wouldn't be needed, and while Cooper was hoping, he added a prayer that Liam would sleep through all of this. Maybe his son would even wake up in the morning without the shadow of this kidnapper looming over them.

Step four was finished, too, and it involved Colt. His brother already had weapons in his truck, but he had armed himself with more, along with putting on body armor beneath his shirt. Cooper didn't figure the kidnappers would just start shooting—if they genuinely thought Liam was in the truck—but he didn't want to take any additional risks with his kid brother.

Or with Jessa.

But she was a different matter entirely.

Yeah, he'd also had her put on body armor that she had concealed with a bulky sweater, and Cooper had given her a gun, but he wasn't even sure she could shoot well enough to defend herself. And the body armor sure wouldn't stop a shot to the head. That meant she had to stay out of the way and as safe as possible once this attack by the kidnapper started.

The final step was to get more security for the drive from the ranch to the hospital.

Easier said than done.

It'd been hard to assemble people he could trust on such short notice, but Cooper had finally called in two sheriffs from nearby towns. They wouldn't come to the ranch but rather join up with them separately on the drive to the hospital. Cooper had made it clear he didn't want them to look like lawmen and not to make it obvious that they were doing security detail. The idea was for the kidnapper to feel bold and safe enough to come after them. Jessa included.

A thought that sickened him.

After all, this kidnapper had already killed, and he or she wouldn't hesitate to do it again.

"Don't second-guess this," Jessa warned him, as if she knew exactly what he was thinking. Maybe she did. Cooper figured his expression said it all: this could be dangerous as hell.

"As long as they think Liam's in the truck, they won't shoot," she added.

Yeah, as long as the ruse worked. If it didn't, well, Cooper hoped he had enough backup security in place to stop Jessa and the others from getting hurt.

Colt's phone beeped, and he glanced down at the text that he'd just received. "It's from Reed," he relayed. "He got some deputies from Appaloosa Pass to guard the hospital, and they're getting into position now. Reed needs to know if you want them visible."

"Yes." Cooper didn't have to think about that. The last place he wanted a showdown was a hospital filled with people, and the deputies might deter that from happening.

Cooper waited until Colt had answered the text before he continued, "If we get all the way to the hospital and still haven't spotted the kidnapper, then we'll need to turn around and come back."

And come up with a different plan.

Cooper wasn't sure what that would be yet, but he didn't want these morons coming anywhere near Liam.

"You ready, then?" Colt asked.

His brother was geared up and standing by the back door. The only visible weapon he had was his sidearm, which wouldn't draw suspicion since he was a deputy, but if the kidnapper got a close look at Colt's face, then he would no doubt see the concern that was mirrored on Cooper's.

And Jessa's.

Cooper gave her one last chance. "You can stay here," he reminded her again. "And I can come up with a plausible lie to explain why you aren't coming to the hospital with us."

That earned him a huff, and she took the bundled doll from Rosalie. "No one would believe that I wouldn't be in that truck with my son. Besides, the plan's already been set into motion," Jessa insisted. "Rosalie found this doll in Rayanne's and her old room, and with the blankets around it, it'll look about the right size for Liam."

Yeah, the plan was indeed in motion, but that didn't mean Cooper had complete faith that he could keep Jessa safe. He hated that she had to be in danger, but they were both on the same page here, and that meant putting Liam and his safety first.

Cooper considered going upstairs to give Liam a kiss, but that felt too much like a goodbye. And he was determined to keep Jessa and himself alive so they could... Well, he wasn't sure what their future held, but he wanted time and the chance to figure it out without all this danger hanging over them.

Colt, Jessa and he hurried out the back and didn't waste any time getting in their respective vehicles. Jessa went through the pretense of putting the doll into a car seat. Cooper didn't miss the long look she gave the house in the side mirror as he drove away.

"Where are the sheriffs who agreed to help us?" she asked, also glancing at Colt, who was in his truck directly behind them.

Cooper hated the tremble in her voice. And her resolute expression when she took the gun he'd given her from her pocket. She was scared and determined to end this. A bad mix, and he prayed that she didn't have to take any more risks tonight.

"The first sheriff is about two miles up in a black truck. He'll pull out behind Colt and follow us into town. The second won't join us for another five miles." Still, he'd be close enough to respond if something went wrong. "He'll be in a silver-gray SUV, which should make it easy to see."

"Good." She nodded, repeated it and kept a white-knuckle grip on her gun.

Cooper took the turn from the ranch onto the farm road that led into town. Part of him was relieved that the gunmen hadn't been ready to ambush them so close to the ranch. He didn't want gunfire anywhere near Liam and the others.

But then the waiting began.

Each second crawled by while he fired glances all around them. There were plenty of old ranch trails and farm roads where the kidnapper could lie in wait, ready to attack. He thought of Jessa's car *accident* and how fast the driver had managed to come at her. In broad daylight, no less. That was why he had to keep watch and make sure that didn't happen again. The darkness could hide a killer, and running Jessa and him off the road would make them easier targets.

"Maybe the kidnapper didn't get the word about us taking Liam to the hospital," Jessa mumbled.

Maybe. But they still had a good ten miles to go before

they reached town, and they hadn't reached the most isolated part of the road yet. At the halfway point there were no farms or ranches in sight. No one to witness an attack.

Or so the kidnapper might think.

Cooper breathed a little easier when he saw the first sheriff ease onto the road behind Colt. He now had two lawmen as backup, but they still had a long way to go. It felt even longer with each mile just crawling by. Every shadow looked like a waiting killer.

His phone buzzed, the sound shooting through the truck. Through him, too. And he went on instant alert. Jessa did as well, because she sucked in her breath loud enough for him to hear. When he took it from his pocket, she darted across the seat to see the name on the screen.

Rosalie.

Hell, he hoped nothing had gone wrong with Liam. Cooper hit the answer button fast.

"I'm so sorry," Rosalie immediately said. "God, Cooper, I didn't see him before it was too late."

JESSA'S HEART SLAMMED against her chest, and she grabbed the phone away from Cooper. She prayed this was some kind of bad joke, but she knew Rosalie wouldn't joke about something like this.

"What's wrong, Rosalie? What happened?" Jessa demanded.

But Rosalie was no longer on the line.

That sent a jolt of terror and adrenaline through her. Through Cooper, too, because he hit his brakes and, with the tires squealing and smoking, made a U-turn to take them back in the direction of the ranch.

Jessa pressed the redial button, but Rosalie didn't answer. She tried again and got the same results.

Oh, God.

What was going on?

Jessa didn't like any of the possibilities that came to mind, especially since Rosalie had said she would stay with Liam while they were gone.

I didn't see him before it was too late.

Him.

That had to be the kidnapper or one of his or her henchmen. But that didn't make sense. Cooper and she had taken plenty of security precautions to make sure no one got near Liam. So maybe Rosalie was mistaken. Or maybe Jessa had misheard her. She held on to that hope and prayed that her little boy and Rosalie were all right.

The phone buzzed again. Still no Rosalie. This time it was Colt. Both he and the sheriff had made the same U-turns and were following behind Cooper's truck, but Colt no doubt wanted to know what was going on. Jessa answered it, and because she didn't trust her voice, she held it out so that Cooper could respond.

"There's a problem at the ranch," he told Colt. "Rosalie might have been taken hostage. Maybe Liam, too."

Those words had not come easily, and they nearly sent Jessa into another panic. But she forced herself to stay calm. Well, as calm as she could manage, but they couldn't get back to the ranch fast enough.

"Call the others," Cooper added to Colt. "Find out what the hell's going on."

Cooper snatched the phone from her, ended the call with his brother and tried to contact Rosalie again.

Still no answer.

Cooper was already going way too fast, but that caused him to speed up, and he called Tucker next. Thankfully, he answered, but Tucker's hesitation put Jessa's heart right in her throat.

"I'm not sure how it happened," Tucker finally said.

"But someone got into the house…and into the room with Liam."

There was no holding back that panic now. Jessa's breath vanished, and her heart started slamming against her ribs. This was her worst nightmare come true.

"Where's Liam?" she practically shouted.

"We're not sure, but we're looking for him."

That didn't make sense. None of this did. "How did this person get in the house?"

"I don't know yet. We didn't hear anything. Didn't see anyone. There were no indications that we had an intruder. Even the security system didn't go off." Another hesitation from Tucker. "The kidnapper hit Rosalie with a stun gun, and he took Liam and your mother."

It's a good thing she wasn't standing, or her legs would have buckled. This monster had her son and her mother. A monster who'd already murdered at least two other people.

For several moments Jessa had no choice but to give in to the terror. To allow it to paralyze her. But then the image of her son popped into her head, and she knew this fear wouldn't help. She had to think. To do something. Anything. To get Liam and her mother back.

"Did they leave the ranch?" she asked Tucker. "If they did, please tell me you're in pursuit."

But Tucker didn't get a chance to answer. Another call came through on Cooper's phone. No name or number.

Just *unknown caller* on the screen.

Jessa knew what that meant. Knew that it wouldn't be good, and she tried to brace herself. Hard to do, though, with her baby and mother missing.

"The kidnapper's calling us," Cooper told his brother, and he switched over to the new call.

Nothing.

For several snail-crawling moments. That didn't help her tamp down the panic, either.

"Cooper," the caller finally said. He or she was using some kind of voice scrambler so Jessa couldn't tell who it was. It could be any of their suspects.

Or none of them.

"You'd better not hurt my son," Cooper said through clenched teeth. Jessa shouted out the same.

"Well, that all depends on you two. Both Liam and his grandmother will stay safe if you do as you're told."

"What do you want?" Jessa asked.

"The DNA test results. I know that Cooper has the original, and it's the only copy. I also know it's somewhere at the ranch."

It was. She'd seen it on Cooper's desk in his office.

"Bring it to the old hay barn on the back-east corner of the ranch, and I'll exchange it for Liam and Linda. You've got fifteen minutes. And if you're late or if you bring anyone else with you, the deal's off. You'll never see either of them again."

The kidnapper hadn't shouted the threat, but it certainly shouted through Jessa's mind. She had to do something to stop this now.

"Let me speak to my mother," she insisted. "I need to know they're okay."

But she was talking to the air because the kidnapper had already hung up.

"Hit Redial," Cooper told her, and he took the final turn back to the ranch.

He was going so fast that the truck skidded. For several heart-stopping moments, Jessa thought they might crash, but he managed to keep the truck on the road and sped toward the house.

Even though her hands were shaking almost uncontrollably, Jessa managed to hit Redial. The terror sky-rocketed with each unanswered ring.

Finally, she heard the voice.

"Unless you're calling to say you already have the DNA results, we have nothing to discuss," the kidnapper said.

"But we do. Let me speak to my mother. If you don't prove she's alive, you won't get that report."

It was an empty threat, but maybe the kidnapper wouldn't hear that in her voice. Even if he didn't let her talk to her mother, Cooper and she would still take the report to the barn. They'd still try to negotiate with the devil to get Liam and her mother back.

"Put my mom on the phone now," Jessa insisted, sounding a lot stronger than she felt.

It seemed to take an eternity, but she finally heard some movement. Then a voice.

"Jessa?" her mother said.

There was a split second of relief knowing her mother was still alive. Followed by the terrifying realization that the kidnapper hadn't lied. He actually had them. He had her son and her mother.

"Is Liam okay?" Jessa immediately asked.

"Yes, he fell back asleep. He doesn't know what's going on."

Jessa was beyond thankful for that and had to figure out how to get to this monster before he harmed her family. "Who kidnapped you?"

But this time there was no answer. Jessa only heard a shuffling sound and knew her mother had been moved away from the phone.

"Time's ticking away," the kidnapper said, coming back on the line.

"Who are you?" Cooper demanded.

"You'd better hope you don't have to find out. Best if I keep my identity out of this, because not knowing who I am will ensure all of you stay alive."

Jessa desperately wanted to believe that. She wanted to hang on to the hope this could all be resolved in the next few minutes and she could once again hold Liam in her arms. However, she kept going back to the reminder that they were dealing with not just a kidnapper.

But a killer.

"Get me that DNA report," the kidnapper added. "And remember the part about you coming alone—just Cooper and you. I'm using a thermal detector so I'll know if you try to bring somebody with you."

Sweet heaven. That meant Colt wouldn't be able to follow them to help. No one could.

"We'll get you the report," Jessa said, "but there's no reason to hold Liam and my mother. You're obviously already on the ranch, and you can come after us then if we don't hand over the report."

She knew she was grasping at straws, but she had to try something. Anything.

The kidnapper laughed and made a tsk-tsk sound. "I'd rather not face down a bunch of cowboy lawmen tonight. No, you and Cooper will come alone. If I see anyone else with you, your mother dies and Liam disappears forever."

Like before, the line went dead.

It took Jessa a moment just to get control of her voice so she could speak to Cooper. "What are we going to do? How do we get them back?" Because she refused to consider the alternative.

"For starters, I give this snake the DNA results," Cooper said. "Then I figure out a way to make him pay for this."

He brought the truck to a quick stop in front of the

house. Tucker and his father were already on the porch, but Cooper barreled right past them. No doubt headed toward his office.

"He needs the DNA report," Jessa explained. They obviously knew what she was talking about because no one questioned her.

Rosalie stepped out of the house, and despite Tucker trying to hold her back, she hurried to Jessa. "I'm so sorry," Rosalie repeated.

Jessa nodded, and because she looked as if she needed it, she gave Rosalie's arm a pat. "Are you okay? Did the kidnapper hurt you?" she asked, eyeing the bruise on Rosalie's head.

"I'm fine." A hoarse sob left her mouth. "I'm so sorry," she repeated. "When I went to check on your mother and Liam, the kidnapper was already there in the dark room."

"Who was it?" Jessa demanded.

Rosalie shook her head and wiped away tears from her already red cheeks. Her eyes were red, too. "I don't know. The person was wearing a ski mask and used a stun gun on me. By the time I was able to get downstairs, the kidnapper already had them out of the house."

Her voice was shaking so hard it was difficult to understand her. This was no doubt bringing back horrible memories of the time her daughter was stolen.

"How did they get in?" she asked, and when Rosalie only shook her head again, Jessa looked up at Tucker.

"It looks as if someone tampered with the security system. Probably the person who broke in earlier."

Oh, God. Jessa hadn't thought that was anything more than just another failed attempt to take Liam. But the intruder had done exactly what he'd come to do.

To prepare the way for a real kidnapping.

It made her wonder what else he'd done and what he'd

managed to get into place so he could get that DNA report and take Liam for good.

"So this person could have been in the house for hours," Jessa mumbled. "He could have heard everything we said about the fake trip to the hospital."

Tucker nodded, and she saw his jaw muscles at war with each other. "I'll go with you to the barn. I can hide in the truck—"

"No," Cooper said hurrying back to the truck. He had the DNA report in his hand. "He's got infrared, and he'll know if we're not alone. Plus, he'll probably have someone search the truck before we can get near him."

Tucker cursed. "You can't go out there. This is a trap and you know it."

Cooper only nodded. "Once I'm in the barn, I'll try to keep the kidnapper distracted. Use the Mylar blankets to make your way there, but put something dark over the silver so it won't be easy to see. Go on foot. The heat from another vehicle or horse could be detected."

He didn't wait for Tucker's answer. Probably because he knew his brother would do exactly as he'd said. Cooper threw the truck into gear, and the moment that Jessa was inside he hit the accelerator.

"This *is* a trap," he said, repeating Tucker's warning to them. He stayed on the dirt road that coiled around the various outbuildings on the ranch. "And this SOB will want us both dead. Probably your mother, too."

Jessa swallowed hard. She didn't want to die. Didn't want Cooper or her mother to die, either. "Liam has to come first," she insisted.

"Yeah." The emotion was there, clogging his voice. Cooper reached over and gave her hand a gentle squeeze. "No matter what happens, we get Liam out of there."

Ahead, on the horizon, Jessa saw the barn.

Chapter Seventeen

Cooper didn't have time to stop and think if this was a mistake or not. He was dead certain that it was. But he was also certain he didn't have any other choice.

Thanks to a full moon, he had a decent view of the barn. It was a good mile from the house and at the back part of the ranch. These days, the only time it got used was during hay-baling season, but since it was summer and the cattle still had fresh grass to graze on, the barn would practically be empty.

Well, except for a kidnapper, Jessa's mom and Liam.

There might be plenty of gunmen inside, too.

Cooper didn't see any sign of them. In fact, there was no sign of anyone. There didn't appear to be a light inside either, and there were no vehicles parked nearby. Of course, the property-line fence was only about fifty yards away, so it was possible the kidnapper had parked there and walked to the ranch.

The fact that no one had noticed him or her meant that the kidnapper had blended in—again. It also didn't rule out Peggy, since she could have disguised herself as one of the ranch hands.

Beside him, Jessa leaned closer to the windshield, her gaze combing the barn and surroundings. Her breath was still way too fast, and she had the same bleached-out look on her face as the day of Liam's surgery.

Yeah, she was terrified.

So was he, but along with that fear for his son, Cooper also had a massive amount of rage that he hoped he had a chance to aim at the idiot who'd set all of this in motion. Liam was in danger, again, and someone was going to pay and pay hard for that.

"See anything?" Jessa asked, and she moved her hand to the door handle. She was no doubt planning to bolt the moment he stopped.

That wasn't going to happen.

"You're to stay in the truck," he insisted. "And no, that's not negotiable, so don't argue."

She looked at him as if he'd lost his mind. "But it is *negotiable*. The kidnapper said we both have to come. If we don't, he said he'll kill my mother and Liam will disappear forever."

Cooper remembered the threat verbatim, and it would give him nightmares for years to come. However, he had to be a little sensible here and try to minimize the risks for Jessa. Even if she didn't want them minimized.

"He didn't say we both had to go in there and give him the DNA report," Cooper clarified, "only that we had to come."

At least that wasn't part of the demand that'd been spelled out. Cooper intended to use that loophole to try to buy some time for Tucker and the others to make their way to the barn. He figured they'd need at least twenty minutes, since they were traveling on foot and would have to cut through the pastures and then some wooded areas.

"We have to get Liam and my mom out," Jessa mumbled, her voice all breath and nerves, and she just kept repeating it.

Inside, he was doing the same thing.

Cooper came to a stop in front of the barn. He kept his headlights on bright and aimed them right at the closed double wood doors. Anyone peering out from the cracks might be blinded enough that they wouldn't be able to see his brother and the others. Plus, the lights gave Cooper enough illumination to see anything or anyone coming from the sides of the barns.

"Remember, you stay put," he warned Jessa. He started to open his door, but she grabbed his arm.

She opened her mouth but didn't say anything. Not right away. "Please be careful," she finally whispered.

Cooper nodded, and because he thought they both could use it, he leaned over and brushed a kiss on her mouth. He kept it brief and tried not to notice the tears shimmering in Jessa's eyes. Those tears only ripped at his heart, and right now he had to focus on Liam and Linda.

He reached for the door again, but reaching was as far as he got. His phone rang, and he saw the now-familiar unknown caller on the screen.

The kidnapper obviously wanted to chat.

"You barely made it on time," the kidnapper snarled. "Hope you weren't talking to your kin about planning some kind of attack. FYI, that wouldn't be a smart thing to do."

Maybe not smart, but Cooper figured it was the only way he would get his son safely out of there. Yeah, it would put his brothers at risk, but if their situations were reversed, he would do the same for them.

"I've got the DNA report," Cooper said, putting the call on speaker. "And I'm bringing it to you now. Once you have it, you'll turn over the hostages to me."

The kidnapper laughed, and even though the voice was still scrambled, that laugh managed to sound intimidating. Of course, anything at this point was unnerving since this sick dirt wad had Liam.

"Now that we've got your little fantasy scenario out of the way, here's how it's really going to work," the kidnapper said. "You and Jessa will get out of the truck and walk toward the barn. Put your weapons—*all of them*—on the ground."

"Sounds like your fantasy isn't workable with mine," Cooper snarled. "What guarantees do I have that you just won't gun us down when we get out?"

"None. But that's a chance you'll have to take. In fact, I'm betting you'll do whatever I say for a chance to get your son back."

It was the truth. Cooper knew it. So did the kidnapper. But Cooper wasn't about to say the words out loud. Jessa was already close to the breaking point, and there was no need to spell out that this could go wrong. Fast.

"Now get out of the truck," the kidnapper continued. "And if you broke the rules and brought someone with you, I'll know."

Cooper heard the whirring sound, and he spotted the camera on the eaves of the barn. It certainly wasn't something his family had installed, so the kidnapper had likely brought it with him. The camera turned slowly, no doubt so the kidnapper could see the truck bed and what was inside.

"Good. You listened to that come-alone part," the kidnapper said several moments later.

"We've done everything you asked," Cooper reminded him. "Now let them go."

"All in due time. Maybe I'll give you a gold star for following the rules. Now, don't forget the really big rule about putting the guns on the ground," the kidnapper added.

Cooper had every intention of doing that. Well, one of

his weapons, anyway. He had another in the back waist of his jeans, and he hoped he'd be able to get to it in time if he needed it.

And he figured he would need it.

Jessa was another matter. Even though there were some other weapons in the glove compartment, Jessa only had one gun. One that he wasn't even sure she could use, and in her case, being armed might turn out to be a detriment. If the kidnapper just planned to shoot them on sight, then Jessa wouldn't get a chance to draw, anyway. And if she tried to keep the gun on her and the kidnapper saw it, then Jessa could be shot just for breaking a *rule*. They could be damned if they did or damned if they didn't.

Cooper held his hand over the phone so the kidnapper wouldn't be able to hear what he was about to say to her. "When we get out, toss your gun toward the barn and then stay behind the truck door."

It wasn't ideal protection, but along with the body armor, it might be enough. Might.

"You'll stay behind the truck door, too," Jessa insisted.

Maybe. But Cooper doubted this SOB would allow that. It was going to be hard enough just to get that concession for Jessa.

He took his hand from the phone. "We're getting out of the truck now," Cooper informed the kidnapper.

With the DNA report tucked under Cooper's arm, he and Jessa opened their doors together and both stepped out. Almost at the same time, they tossed their guns in front of the barn.

And they waited.

"Move out so I can see you," the kidnapper said.

Cooper huffed. "Give me proof that my son and Mrs.

Wells are all right. And if they aren't, don't expect to get out of this alive. Because I will kill you."

Another laugh. It made Cooper wish he could tear through the barn wall and beat this idiot senseless. He still might get a chance to do that before this was over.

"Proof of life," the kidnapper continued after the laughter had died down. "Still think you're the one calling the shots here?"

Cooper's phone dinged, and he looked down at the screen. It was a text from Tucker.

Found a gunman near the house. He's been neutralized. Am on the way.

Cooper didn't want to risk texting back because he didn't want to take his attention off the kidnapper, but it was good news. One down and heaven knew how many to go.

"You don't get the report, or us, if we don't have proof that Liam's alive," Cooper argued with the kidnapper. "Or maybe you should consult your henchmen to make sure you have plenty of help keeping me under control."

Silence.

Cooper wasn't sure the kidnapper would actually hear the veiled threat, but the silence could mean the person was trying to get in touch with the gunman. The one Tucker had already neutralized.

"What's the matter?" Cooper asked. "Is your hired gun not answering?"

More silence. He didn't want the kidnapper to get desperate and start shooting, but he also wanted the idiot to understand he was on his own here.

Well, maybe.

Maybe there was only one other gunman, but if there

were more, Cooper hoped his brothers would find them. He wanted to focus just on the jerk in the barn and not worry about being ambushed.

"I want some proof of life," Cooper reminded him.

"Okay," the scrambled voice finally said. Maybe it was his imagination, but the kidnapper didn't seem nearly as confident as when they'd first arrived. "You'll get that proof. And since I don't want to stand around here and nitpick, you and Jessa step away from the truck at the same moment that the barn door opens. My advice? Don't shoot, because it won't be me standing there."

Cooper heard some movement, and it didn't take long before he heard the creaking sound of the hinges. The barn door eased open.

"Don't go out there," Cooper whispered to Jessa.

Maybe, just maybe, he could keep her hidden away enough to find out what they were up against. He still didn't know how much backup the kidnapper had in there with him.

Thankfully, Jessa did as he told her. She stayed hidden behind the door, but Cooper moved as fast as he could. He still had his phone in his left hand, but he wanted to have his shooting hand clear in case he had to fire.

"Jessa?" someone called out.

It was Linda, and a moment later the woman appeared in the doorway. She had Liam bundled in a blanket in her arms.

"Mom," Jessa said, but thankfully she stayed put.

The truck headlights blazed on Linda like a spotlight, and while she didn't appear to be injured, she was pasty white and shaking. She had clearly been through an ordeal since she'd been in the barn with a killer for the past half hour.

Cooper couldn't see Liam; the blanket completely covered him. Nor could he see the kidnapper. The person remained in the shadows near the door, but Cooper could see enough of the outline that he knew where to aim if he got the chance to take out this moron.

"Tell Linda to move now," the kidnapper said to Cooper from over the phone, and Cooper relayed that to her.

Linda gave a shaky nod, and she walked out of the barn. Not far, though. Just a few steps away from the front of the barn and directly in Cooper's path. Whoever this jerk was, he or she knew what to do by keeping Linda in the line of fire. No way would Cooper risk taking a shot when Linda or his son could be hurt.

"Now, Jessa, it's your turn," the kidnapper said, his voice taunting through the phone. "You want to see your baby boy, don't you? Well, have a look and you'll see that he's as right as rain."

Still trembling, Linda shook her head just a little. Just enough for Cooper's stomach to twist into a knot.

And that was when he saw the glint of metal from the kidnapper's gun. Aimed not at him.

But right at Jessa.

"DON'T GO OUT THERE," Cooper warned her again.

Even though he'd only whispered it, Jessa heard Cooper's warning loud and clear, but the last thing she wanted to do was stay put.

She had to get to her son.

"If you go out there, he'll kill you," Cooper told her when she started away from the truck.

That wouldn't have stopped her, but the sound of the kidnapper's voice did.

"Your son and mother aren't in any real danger, *yet,*" the kidnapper said through the phone scrambler.

"Yet," she repeated.

The threat was clear—the danger would be worse if she didn't cooperate. It chilled her. Angered her. And sent a dozen other emotions through her.

Part of her wished she could hurt this person the way he was hurting her while another part of her only wanted to shout for her mother to start running so that Liam and she could maybe get out of there.

"Well?" the kidnapper prompted. "I've kept my part of the bargain, and you two need to keep yours by coming out from behind that truck."

Jessa glanced at Cooper, and she knew from his expression that they were on the same wavelength here. The kidnapper would almost certainly gun them down when they stepped out.

And Liam and her mother would be caught in the middle.

She had no idea what they could do to defuse this, but Jessa gasped when Cooper stepped out.

Right into the line of fire.

Jessa nearly went after him, but Cooper shot her a stay-put glare, and he made his way toward the barn doors.

"Where should I put this DNA report?" Cooper asked.

She saw the gun in the back waist of his jeans, and Cooper kept his right hand by his side so he could hopefully get to it in time.

"Bring it to me," the kidnapper insisted. "Jessa and you together."

"Why do you need Jessa for this? Don't you want to see the report first?" Cooper asked. "To make sure it's the real deal."

"It is. You wouldn't be stupid enough to bring me a fake."

Cooper lifted his shoulder. "I might if I didn't trust

you. Or if I thought you didn't have any backup gunmen with you."

What the heck was Cooper doing? He shouldn't be antagonizing this person. Or did he have some other plan up his sleeve that she didn't know about?

Cooper cautiously walked to the doors and positioned himself between her mother and the kidnapper. Cooper turned his head a little and whispered something to her mother. Something that Jessa didn't catch.

"Here," Cooper said, holding out the report.

"Come closer," the kidnapper snapped.

And Cooper did. Jessa held her breath, praying and waiting. Her mother appeared to be praying, too, and she had her attention fixed not on Jessa, but on something over Jessa's shoulder.

"Now," she heard Cooper say.

Her mother ducked down, and with Liam still cradled in her arms, she scrambled to the side of the barn. Cooper quickly followed them. Out of the line of fire.

Maybe.

But Jessa was terrified the kidnapper would just start shooting and that the bullets would go through the wooden-plank siding on the barn.

The kidnapper didn't shoot, but he let out a string of profanity. Definitely male, but his voice was still partly muffled. He no longer sounded like the cocky person who'd first spoken to him. He was quickly coming unhinged, and that could be bad news for them. Of course, not much about this was good news, except that maybe her mother and Liam were now in a better position to get away.

"What's the matter?" Cooper called out. "Where's your backup?"

There was only one reason that Cooper would keep

bringing that up—someone had managed to find the kidnapper's henchman and had stopped him. That explained the message Cooper had gotten right before her mother had stepped out of the barn.

"You think I don't have someone else out there who can help me handle this?" the kidnapper said. But he didn't sound confident about that, either.

The kidnapper was no longer using the scrambler, but she thought maybe he had a cloth or something over his mouth. No doubt still trying to protect his identity.

While keeping her head low, Jessa looked around, hoping to see if she could spot any of henchmen or Cooper's family, but the only thing she saw was the darkness.

"Time's up," the kidnapper barked. "If Jessa and you don't come out now, this is over."

"You haven't even looked at the report yet," Cooper said immediately. "Why have me bring it all the way out here if you're not even going to look at it?"

"Oh, I think you know why you're here. I could have broken into the house and stolen that report at any time."

That chilled her to the bone. Because she knew it was true. "You were watching the place," she said, and even though she was scared, there was plenty of anger in her voice.

"Watching through cameras. You people really should have given the house a good once-over after the break-in. My assistant managed to put a few bugs and cameras in place."

The chill turned to a sickening feeling. This monster had spied on them.

"I think your mom might be surprised to know that you're sleeping with the sheriff," the kidnapper went on. "Do you think that'll maybe convince him to let you keep Liam? I think not," he said before she could speak.

In fact, she didn't get a chance to do anything.

"Time's up," the kidnapper repeated.

And the person stumbled out of the barn.

Chapter Eighteen

Cooper saw Peggy the moment she came out, and he also saw the gun she had gripped in her hand. He shoved his phone in his pocket and nearly fired, but something caused him to hesitate.

It was the dazed look on Peggy's face.

Something was wrong.

However, Cooper didn't get a chance to figure out exactly what before the shot zinged through the air.

"Get down!" Cooper shouted to Jessa, and he prayed she would do just that.

He pushed Linda farther back and leaned out, ready to return fire.

But there wasn't another shot.

Peggy stood there, still dazed, her gun pointed at the ground. She certainly hadn't been the one to fire. Cooper could see that even though she was indeed holding a gun, her hands were tied with clear plastic cuffs. Maybe the kidnapper had figured Cooper would shoot her first and ask questions later.

If he had, Peggy would have been dead, and he might have killed an innocent woman.

Jessa was still crouching behind the truck door, but she glanced at Cooper, her expression asking if he knew what was going on. He only shook his head and motioned for her to get down. As long as they stayed out of range, the kidnapper wouldn't be able to get to them. Not all at once, anyway. And if he started shooting at Jessa, Cooper was in a position to return fire.

At least he would be if Peggy got out of his way.

"I didn't do anything wrong," Peggy said, her words slurred. It sounded as if she'd been drugged. "Please help me—"

Another shot blasted through the air. Again, not from Peggy's gun. Cooper could see that her trigger finger hadn't moved.

But Peggy certainly did.

The woman made a raspy sound that came deep from within her throat, and the gun slipped from her hand and to the ground. A second later, Peggy crumpled in a heap next to it.

It was only then that Cooper saw the dark stain spreading across her shirt. *Blood.* She'd been shot in the back. If she wasn't already dead, she soon would be. He had to get an ambulance out here, but even that was too risky.

"Told you time was up," the kidnapper taunted. He was still inside the barn.

"You didn't have to kill her!" Jessa shouted.

"Yeah, actually, I did." His voice was shaky now. Maybe because killing a woman had gotten to him or maybe he was coming to realize that his plan was falling apart. "She could have maybe linked me back to Liam."

Maybe.

And if he would kill on a *maybe,* then he'd damn sure kill Jessa and him if he got the chance. Not just Jessa and him, either, but anyone who might connect him to the crimes, including Linda and even Liam, since Liam's own DNA proved that he'd been stolen and put up for adoption.

"I want you to run," Cooper whispered to Linda. "Stay on this side of the barn, away from that camera. Keep Liam close to you and stay low."

Linda gave a shaky nod, and the moment she took off running, Cooper leaned out from the corner of the barn and hoped the sound of his movements would cover any noise that Linda was making during her escape.

"So are you Hector or Donovan?" Cooper asked. He figured any distraction would help right now. Help Linda get to cover and give his brothers time to arrive.

"Come in here and you can see for yourself," the kidnapper growled.

Cooper watched as Linda ducked behind a tree. It wasn't ideal cover, but it got her away from the barn, and the tree might be able to stop any bullets fired in that direction.

His phone dinged again, and Cooper ducked back around the side of the barn so the kidnapper wouldn't notice what he was doing. He saw the text that he'd been waiting for.

Second gunman caught, Tucker wrote. I can see your truck lights from where I'm standing, and there are no other gunmen around.

Get Linda and Liam out of here, Cooper texted back. He would have loved to include Jessa in that rescue, but it was too risky.

Liam had to be rescued first.

Plus, Jessa was still too close to the shooter. If Tucker tried to get to her, Jessa and he would just be gunned down like Peggy.

"I want you to give me that DNA report now!" the kidnapper yelled.

Yeah, the guy was definitely losing it, probably because he knew both of his hired guns were out of commission. Were there more? Maybe. But if so, Cooper hoped this idiot called his backup to the barn so it would give Tucker a safer path to escape with Linda and Liam.

Without warning, a shot rang out and blasted into his truck.

Cooper's heart went to the ground, and he quickly looked to make sure Jessa hadn't been hit. He saw her scramble back into the truck and across the seat. Good. He hoped she'd stay there.

But she didn't.

When the kidnapper fired again, Jessa stuck her hand out from the open door. Cooper saw the gun she held. One that she'd no doubt taken from the glove compartment.

Jessa pulled the trigger. The bullet slammed into the barn door, and she didn't stop there. She fired another shot. Then another.

"Big mistake!" the kidnapper yelled, and he called her a name mixed with some raw profanity. He made a sound of outrage, the kind of sound a crazy man would make, and the shots started coming.

Nonstop.

The bullets began to pelt the truck, ripping through the glass, one of the headlights and the metal, and Cooper knew it was only a matter of time before one of the shots hit Jessa.

Hell. That couldn't happen. It couldn't end like this.

She didn't give up and sure as heck didn't get down on the seat. Jessa returned fire until she ran out of ammunition, and judging from what Cooper could see of her, she then began to rifle through the glove compartment for more.

"Stay down!" Cooper yelled to her, and he started running. Toward the back of the barn.

His best bet was to sneak up on this guy and take him out. Maybe he'd be alone, but if not, Cooper would have to deal with that, too.

With only one headlight left on his truck, it was hard to see, but Cooper made it to the back of the barn. The doors were shut, of course. Fate wasn't going to make this easy. But he peeked through the cracks in the wood.

Just as the shots stopped.

Cooper heard the movement then.

Footsteps.

Not near the back of the barn. But the front. He saw the doors there fly open. And Cooper knew he'd just made a huge mistake coming back here.

Cooper started running toward his truck. Toward Jessa. But the fear slammed right into him when he spotted her. Not inside the bullet-riddled truck where he'd last spotted her. But outside, several yards away from it.

The kidnapper was behind her and had her at gunpoint.

"I'M SORRY," JESSA SAID, the fear obvious in her voice and in every part of her body. Not fear for herself, but for Cooper, her mother and her son. She hadn't wanted it to come down to this, because the kidnapper could use her to draw out Cooper.

Cooper gave her a glance and took cover beside the barn. He leaned out, his gaze connecting with hers. It was hard to see his expression, but she knew he was feeling the same thing that she was.

"Please tell me that Liam is safe," she managed to say.

"He's safe," Cooper assured her, without taking his attention or aim off the man behind her.

She still hadn't seen her captor's face because he'd been wearing a ski mask when he'd first come at her and dragged her from the truck. However, the mask had come off in the struggle when Jessa had managed to get out of the truck and run.

She hadn't gotten far before he'd caught up with her.

"Liam's safe *for now*," the man snarled. He had something over his mouth, a bandanna, and it was muffling his voice. "It won't stay that way if I have anything to do with it."

She wasn't immune to that threat. Every word hit her like a fist, and she hated that this monster had any say in what would happen to her son.

"You don't need to disguise your voice any longer," Cooper challenged him. "And you don't need to hide behind Jessa. Let her go, and we'll deal with this—just you and me."

The man didn't say anything else, but he was moving. Not in the direction of the barn but rather back to the truck. God, was he planning on trying to use it to escape with her? A hostage could get him off the ranch. Of course, he'd try to kill Cooper and his brothers first.

"Donovan," Cooper spat out like profanity. He was staring right at the man and could no doubt see Donovan's face.

Jessa's stomach clenched even more. If the kidnapper had been Hector, she thought she could have reasoned with him. Maybe by offering him money. But Donovan hated Cooper, and that made this attack personal. Donovan wouldn't stop because of anything she might say.

"Let her go," Cooper repeated.

"Not likely." Donovan shoved the bandanna from his mouth. "She's my ticket out of here. My ticket to freedom."

Jessa tried to elbow him in the stomach, but he curved his arm around her neck and yanked her back. He put so much pressure on her windpipe that she thought she might lose consciousness. Not good. Because she had to be able to fight if she got the chance.

"Why the hell did you take my son?" Cooper asked. The pain was in his voice. His face. Every part of his body. He was no doubt reliving the horrible memories of losing his wife and believing his son had been lost, too.

"This isn't a good time for conversation." Donovan eased up the pressure on her neck. Probably because he didn't want to have to carry an unconscious woman. Besides, she was only of use to him if her body shielded his.

From the corner of her eye, she saw Donovan glance all around them. Yes, she was his human shield, but that wouldn't prevent one of Cooper's brothers from attacking him from behind. Jessa prayed that would happen before Donovan got a chance to kill Cooper.

And Donovan would do that.

She needed to do something to give Cooper and herself a fighting chance, so she dug in her heels when Donovan continued to drag her back toward the truck.

"I want to know," Cooper tossed out there, "what was going through your head two years ago when you found out Liam was alive."

"*You* were going through my head!" Donovan practically shouted. "You and Molly, and the way you treated me. You deserved to lose them both. The flood took Molly, and I got your son."

Cooper's expression didn't change, but she figured the words had to hit him like fists, too. "How did Sonya Eakins know to bring Liam to you?"

"Why does it matter?"

"It matters." Cooper paused and took a deep breath. "It hurts to hear it, but I want to know."

"*It hurts?*" Donovan snarled, his tone taunting again.

"Well, then, I wish I had a million details to give you. And to crush you. Sonya worked for me, briefly and off the books. She knew how much I hated you, so after she found the kid, she came to me."

"How did she know Liam was mine?"

"She saw Molly's car, recognized it." Jessa couldn't be sure, but she thought Donovan might be smiling. It nearly made her gag. "Go ahead and ask if Sonya could have saved Molly."

"Could she have saved her?" Cooper's voice sounded as strangled as Jessa felt.

Donovan laughed, obviously enjoying this little torture session. "No. She got there too late for that. She only found the kid. She thought I'd want to use the baby to get you to cough up lots and lots of money. But I figured that'd be too easy, and I didn't want you to have any part of Molly."

Yes, definitely like fists. It crushed her, too, because she'd been part of this monster's plan and hadn't even known it. Jessa didn't regret adopting Liam, but she hated the pain this had caused Cooper.

"Now come on out," Donovan demanded, "and take your punishment like a man."

"Cooper didn't do anything to be punished," Jessa reminded him. It only caused Donovan to jam the gun harder against her head.

For a second, anyway.

Then he turned the gun. Took aim at Cooper.

And fired.

The sound blasted through her and would have brought her to her knees if Donovan hadn't kept a firm grip on her. It took her a few moments to realize the bullet had torn through a chunk of the barn, but it hadn't hit Cooper. Thank God he was all right.

For now.

Donovan kept looking around them, kept maneuvering her to the truck. She figured he couldn't just kill her because he'd lose his protection, so Jessa kept struggling despite the choke hold he put on her.

"You planted evidence to make Peggy and Hector look guilty," Cooper said, glancing around the corner again.

Donovan fired another shot.

Mercy, this had to stop, but the more she fought, the more Donovan fought, too. If he got her into that truck and off the ranch, he would no doubt use her to bargain with Cooper. Maybe to keep Cooper silent or to get him to obstruct justice or something.

Either way, Donovan would kill her when he was finished with her.

"Taking me won't get you Liam," Jessa reminded him. "Cooper won't trade him for me. Nor would I want him to."

"I don't need Cooper to choose between his son and you," Donovan insisted. "Though since he's your lover, that would be a nice way to give the knife another twist."

The man was sick, along with being a sadistic killer. Cooper probably hadn't known just how much Donovan hated him, but he certainly knew it now.

"What about the DNA report?" Cooper shouted. When he glanced around the corner again, Donovan fired another shot at him. Each bullet ate away more of the barn and more of Cooper's cover. "You wanted it badly enough to demand that I bring it to you."

"That was then and this is now. I don't care if you have proof that Liam's yours. Don't care what happens to him or you. Time for me to regroup, but trust me, this isn't over. I'll be back to finish this."

She'd doubted some of the other things that Donovan

had said, but Jessa didn't doubt that last part. If he managed to escape, he would indeed kill her and then come back. For Cooper and Liam. For anyone who'd gotten in his way. And next time, Cooper might not be able to keep Liam out of this monster's path.

Donovan gave her a fierce jerk and climbed onto the truck seat, dragging Jessa right along with him. Despite all the glass littering the seat, he got behind the wheel and kept her positioned between Cooper and himself.

He fired another shot at Cooper, enough to get him to duck back behind cover. Then Donovan started the engine.

Oh, God. He was getting away.

Jessa looked around for anything she might be able to use as a weapon. Her fingers closed around a large piece of glass from the windshield, and she brought it up to jab it in his eye.

She didn't get far.

As if he'd known all along what she planned, Donovan knocked the glass away, and in the same motion he drove his elbow into her chin. He hit her so hard that Jessa not only lost her breath, she saw stars. She had to fight hard to stop herself from losing consciousness.

Donovan loosened the grip he had on her slightly, and he didn't waste even a second before he slammed his foot on the accelerator.

And he drove the truck right at Cooper.

Chapter Nineteen

Cooper didn't have time to think. He could only react. He dived to his right, barely in time. The truck's fender bumped into him, but he managed to stay on his feet.

He got just a glimpse of Jessa then. At the stark terror on her face. Donovan still had his left arm hooked around her neck, and even though he was holding his gun in his right, he somehow managed to get off another shot.

Cooper had lost count of how many shots Donovan had fired, but he prayed the man ran out of ammunition soon. While he was praying, he added that Tucker had managed to rescue Liam and Linda. There'd been no other texts from his brother, and he hoped nothing had gone wrong.

With Donovan, anything was possible.

Cooper had always known the man hated him, but he'd had no idea just how much until tonight. Donovan wanted to make him suffer in the worst way possible and then kill him. Jessa, too. And it didn't seem to matter that others would know of his guilt. Donovan was just hell-bent on getting even for what he considered an old, unforgivable wrong—Molly no longer loving him.

"Watch out!" Jessa shouted to Cooper when Donovan turned the steering wheel, aiming the truck right at Cooper again.

Cooper didn't want to run toward the tree where he'd last seen Linda and Liam. They could still be there or nearby, and it was too big a risk to take. There was no other nearby cover, so Cooper went behind the barn instead.

Donovan followed right along behind him. So close that Cooper could feel the heat from the engine on his back and legs. He couldn't risk shooting at the SOB because he could accidentally hit Jessa. She was already in too much danger without him adding more. However, Cooper did aim for one of the tires. He missed.

Cooper made it around the barn, hoping it would take Donovan several seconds at least to maneuver the vehicle. It didn't. Despite being hindered by a struggling Jessa and a weapon clutched in his hand, Donovan just kept coming.

And he fired another shot.

This was one didn't hit the barn, and it put Cooper's heart right in his throat. Liam was out there somewhere, and that bullet could have come close to him.

Or worse.

Cooper got back to the front of the barn, and he ducked around Peggy's lifeless body and inside the still-open doors. Maybe when Donovan reached him, Cooper could somehow get Jessa out.

However, Donovan didn't slow down enough.

Nor did he turn away from the barn.

He swerved around Peggy, and the truck bashed through the doors and came right at Cooper. He had no choice but to run again and try to get back outside. If he stayed inside, Donovan could hit one of the thick posts while trying to get him, and since Jessa wasn't wearing a seat belt, she could be thrown through what was left of the windshield.

Jessa screamed, and Cooper glanced over his shoulder to see her sink her teeth into Donovan's arm. The man cursed and let go of the steering wheel so he could bash the gun against her head.

Cooper could have sworn that he saw red.

Cooper darted to the side, hoping he could still try to pull Jessa from the truck. But Donovan regained control. Not just of the steering wheel but also his weapon.

He fired at Cooper.

And this time Cooper wasn't so lucky at dodging bullets. The pain sliced through his arm.

Hell. He'd been hit.

He couldn't take the time to figure out how badly he was injured, because the truck was coming right for him again. Worse, Jessa was dazed or something. Her eyes were half-closed, and she looked ready to faint. Donovan had obviously hurt her when he'd hit her.

And that made him a dead man.

Cooper couldn't stop the shout that roared from his throat, and he turned, not to get away from the truck. But rather to face it head-on. He took aim, praying he had a clear shot so he could stop Donovan for good.

Donovan came right at him as if he was playing a game of chicken. Cooper cursed because he still didn't have a clean shot.

"Be seeing you," Donovan said, smiling.

He gave the steering wheel a sharp turn to the right and plowed through the back door. The splintered wood burst out like daggers, some of them slicing across Cooper's face, but they didn't stop him. He barreled out the gaping hole and hurried outside.

Donovan was getting away.

Cooper hadn't thought that knot in his stomach could get any tighter, but he'd obviously been wrong. Donovan was taking Jessa God knew where, and there was no telling what the man would do to her to get back at Cooper.

Again, he couldn't shoot because he had no idea where Liam and the others were. But Cooper started running. He had to get to the truck before Donovan managed to get off the ranch. He took out his phone, and without slowing down, he hit the button to call Tucker.

"Don't let Donovan get away," Cooper insisted, and he shoved his phone back in his pocket in case he had to fire.

His heart was already racing, but it started to pound against his chest. It only got worse when he heard Jessa scream again. Cooper could only see shadowy movements in the cab of the truck, but it looked as if Jessa was in another fight with Donovan.

And then Cooper heard the shot.

This bullet hadn't come at him; he was pretty sure it'd stayed in the cab of the truck.

Hell.

Had Donovan shot Jessa?

That only made Cooper run faster, even though he knew he'd have a hard time catching up with the now-speeding truck. That didn't stop him. No way. Somehow he had to get to Jessa and make sure she was all right.

Ahead of him, he saw the bloodred flash of the brake lights, and it took Cooper a moment to figure out why Donovan had done that. But there were several horses in the pasture, and Donovan had nearly run right into them. If he had, it would have not only injured or killed the horses, it would have disabled the truck. That was probably the only reason he hadn't crashed into them.

That delay gave Cooper some much-needed seconds so he could close the distance between him and the truck. Even over the engine, he heard Donovan curse. Saw more of the struggle going on in the cab.

Thank God.

It meant Jessa was alive, but she wouldn't stay that way for long.

Cooper was still running when he saw the truck door fly open, and he caught just a glimpse of Jessa trying to get out before Donovan hit her with the gun again. He dragged her back inside with him, slammed the door.

"Jessa!" Cooper yelled, just so she'd know that he was close. He wanted her to keep fighting. Wanted her to stay alive so he could get to her.

Donovan must have realized it, too, because he floored the accelerator. Maybe it was because of the struggle going on inside the truck.

Or maybe Donovan suddenly had a death wish.

Either way, Cooper could only watch as the truck slammed right into a tree.

JESSA WAS SO caught up in her fight to get away from Donovan that she didn't see the tree in time to brace herself for the impact.

Not that she could have done much.

She wasn't wearing a seat belt. However, she was squeezed against the driver's-side door and Donovan, and he was the one who went through the windshield first. Jessa wasn't far behind. She smashed into him.

The pain slammed through her, so hard and fast that it blurred her vision and knocked the breath out of her. She did a quick assessment and didn't think she was hurt too badly. But Cooper could be a different story. She'd seen the shot that Donovan had fired at him in the barn.

And she'd seen the blood.

He was hurt. Maybe it was a serious injury, and she had to get to him to see if he needed help.

Jessa forced herself to get moving. Not easy to do.

Both Donovan and she were on what was left of the hood of the truck, and they were wedged against the tree. Worse, Donovan had somehow managed to hang on to his gun. She reached for it, but that was as far as she got.

Donovan's eyes flew open, snaring her in his gaze.

God, no.

He should be dead or at least unconscious, but here he was ready to attack her all over again. And try one more time to kill Cooper. He latched on to her wrist, digging his fingernails into her skin.

And he fired.

The shot blasted past her, but she knew it could have hit someone. Maybe Cooper. Heaven forbid, maybe Liam. It crushed her heart to think of her baby being hurt, and all because of this monster and his hatred.

"Jessa?" she heard Cooper call out, and she spotted him running toward her. He was alive, thank God, but even in the milky moonlight, she could see the blood on his shirt.

"Donovan's still armed," she warned Cooper. He was close, but not close enough to stop Donovan from getting off another shot. She had to be the one to stop him, or this time he might succeed in killing Cooper or her.

Jessa rammed her elbow against the man's jaw, and while it wasn't enough to loosen the gun, it did cause him to let go of her. She didn't have much wiggle room, but she used her hands and feet to get some leverage, pushing herself away from the truck, the tree and him.

She made it the rest of the way through the broken windshield and was finally able to roll off the hood.

She didn't land on her feet. She was too woozy for that and instead fell to her knees, but Jessa got up as quickly as she could.

However, it wasn't fast enough.

Donovan slid off right behind her.

Just like before, he put the gun to her head, and he ducked down behind her. Unlike before, Cooper didn't have the cover of the barn to protect him. He was out in the open, running toward her.

"Get down!" Jessa shouted.

She braced herself for Donovan to fire again. But he didn't. Maybe because he was running low on ammunition. He'd already fired a lot of shots.

"Let her go," Cooper ordered. He stopped about ten yards away from them and took aim. Not that he could shoot. She was in the way again, and Donovan did his best to keep hidden behind her.

"You're not going to win this time," Donovan spat out, the venom heavy in his voice.

Cooper shook his head. "Your beef's with me, not Jessa. Let her go."

"Right, so you can just gun me down," Donovan snarled back. "By my calculations, I have just one bullet left. I've got extra ammo in my pocket, but by the time I got to it, it'd be too late."

"Yeah, it would," Cooper assured him, and he inched closer. He bracketed his right wrist with his left hand. "And that's why you need to put down your gun and surrender. It's over, Donovan."

That wasn't the right thing to say. She felt the muscles in Donovan's body turn to iron again, and his breath rushed out like fire.

"It's never over!" Donovan shouted. "I could live as long as I knew you were grieving every single day. But you're not grieving now, are you? You're sleeping with Jessa, knowing it'll help you breeze through getting custody of your son."

Cooper took another step, held his aim. "Not that it's any of your business, but that's not why I slept with her."

Donovan laughed. "Please," he said, stretching that out a few syllables. "You haven't looked at another woman since Molly. You've been moping around town, all dark and tortured. Just the way I wanted you to feel."

Cooper didn't argue with that. "You made sure I felt that way by kidnapping my son and keeping him from me."

"Yes, I did." Donovan sounded pleased, but Jessa heard another sound. He was shifting the gun, no doubt so he could aim it at Cooper. He'd said he only had one bullet, but one was enough.

"Ironic, though, that you'd figure out a way to get your son back," Donovan snarled, "and replace Molly at the same time."

Despite the pain from the wreck and Donovan's blows with the gun, that riled her to the core. "I'll never replace Molly," she fired back.

In fact, she couldn't be sure that Cooper hadn't slept with her just because of Liam. He wouldn't have done it intentionally.

No, he was too honorable for that.

But Cooper could have been drawn to her simply because he was so thankful to have found his little boy. It would be easier on her heart if it'd been the same for her, if her feelings for Cooper had been because of Liam.

But they weren't.

Jessa could see that now. She knew that she cared deeply for Cooper, despite the fact that if they survived this, he might take Liam from her.

"Time's up," Donovan repeated. "No more happy times for you." And he raised the gun to fire at Cooper.

Just as Jessa dropped to the ground.

The men fired their guns at the same time, and the combined blasts created a thundering boom that seemed to echo through the darkness. Jessa was terrified to look in case Donovan had hit his intended target. Terrified also that Cooper hadn't hit his.

She lifted her head, but she didn't even get a glimpse of Cooper before Donovan slumped against her, knocking her face-first to the ground.

"Jessa?" Cooper called out.

She was still fighting to get Donovan off her when Cooper made it to her and pulled away the dead weight so she could scramble back and stand. Jessa saw him then. Donovan's lifeless eyes fixed in a blank stare.

Unlike Cooper's.

There was plenty of life and concern in his eyes, and he slipped his arm around her and pulled her to him. He brushed what had to be a kiss of relief on her forehead before his gaze fired all around.

Mercy. He was looking for Liam and her mother. They definitely weren't by the tree any longer, but she couldn't see them anywhere in the pasture.

"Where's Liam?" she managed to ask.

But Cooper just shook his head. "Come on. We have to find him."

Chapter Twenty

Cooper ignored the throbbing in his arm and scooped Jessa up so he could get her away from Donovan and find Liam. Jessa had already seen too much blood tonight, and there was no need for her to see more.

"Tucker?" he called out.

No answer, so he managed to take out his phone and handed it to Jessa. "Call my brother."

They'd been through hell and back, but there was no worse hell than not knowing if their son was all right.

He mentally repeated that: *their son.*

And while it packed an emotional wallop, Cooper decided to table it for now. The only thing that mattered was getting to Liam and then making sure that everyone was okay.

That included Jessa.

She was bleeding on her hands and face. Hopefully just minor nicks and cuts, but he wouldn't know for sure until the doctor had checked her out.

"He's not answering," Jessa said. She was shaking all over, maybe even going into shock.

Cooper could hear the rings on the other end of the line, and he held his breath until he finally heard something he wanted to hear. Tucker's voice.

But not on the phone.

"Over here," Tucker called out to them. Cooper spotted his brother holding a flashlight, halfway between them and the house.

"Where's Liam?" Cooper and Jessa asked at the same time.

"He's here with me," Linda answered. "We're both okay."

The relief nearly brought him to his knees, but Cooper kept running and Jessa slipped out of his arms so they could go even faster together.

As they got closer, Cooper could see Tucker and Colt. And the man kneeling on the ground. One of Donovan's hired guns, no doubt. He'd been cuffed, and Colt was holding him at gunpoint.

Linda stepped from Colt's truck with Liam in her arms. His little boy was still sacked out, thank God. He hadn't seen any of this horrible mess.

"We got both gunmen," Colt volunteered. "One didn't make it." He tipped his head toward the barn nearest the house. "The ME's on the way to get the body."

"Bodies," Cooper corrected. "Donovan's dead, too."

Other than some sounds of relief, no one had much of a reaction to that. Good. Cooper didn't want to give Donovan anything, especially not a lifetime of anger over what he'd done. Donovan had already claimed enough by keeping Liam from him all this time, and he'd given them enough nightmares. Especially Jessa.

"Peggy's dead, as well," Cooper explained. "I'm pretty sure Donovan kidnapped her and brought her here. Her hands are cuffed, and she appeared to have been drugged."

And with Peggy, that meant Donovan had murdered at least three people. All to get back at him and cover his tracks.

"You're hurt," Tucker said, glancing Cooper's arm.

It was just a flesh wound. He'd deal with that later, too, but for now he and Jessa hurried to Liam. They both reached for him at the same time, but Jessa froze and drew back her hands.

Oh, man.

He didn't want her to feel that she didn't have a right to hold the child she'd loved and raised. Cooper eased Liam from Linda's arms, kissed his cheek and held him for a few precious seconds before he passed him to Jessa so she could do the same.

She did.

But then she burst into tears.

"It's okay," he tried to assure her, and he lowered his head, intending to give her a reassuring peck on the forehead. Too many nicks there, so he just went for her mouth.

And Cooper really kissed her. Long, slow and deep.

Jessa didn't stop him, either. She just melted into the kiss as if they were the only people on the ranch. It went on for so long that Tucker cleared his throat, reminding him that they weren't alone.

"Why don't you go ahead and take Jessa, Liam and Linda back to the house?" Colt suggested. "Tucker and I can tie up loose ends here. I've already called the doc and he's on the way. Looks like he'll need to do some stitching up."

Yes, there were cuts on Jessa's face and arms, each one of them an angry reminder of how bad things had gotten. And how much worse they could have been.

Cooper thanked both his brothers, not just for handling the loose ends but for everything they'd done tonight. And not done. They hadn't made a fuss about him kissing Jessa.

Cooper got Jessa, Liam and Linda into Colt's truck and started the short drive to the house. It was so quiet, you could almost hear a pin drop, and that was when Liam woke up. His eyes popped open and he sat up, looking first at Jessa.

"Mama," he said, smiling. He snuggled into her arms as if he might go back to sleep. Then he spotted the cuts on her head and frowned. "Got bad boo-boos." And he lifted his shirt to show her the bandage from his surgery.

"Mama's fine," she whispered, her voice surprisingly calm. "Grandma and Daddy are, too."

Liam's gaze went from Linda to Cooper. He stayed quiet a moment, as if trying to figure out why Jessa had called him the *D* word, and he gave Cooper a hard once-over.

"Daddy's got boo-boos," he said.

Good thing Cooper hadn't been standing, or his legs might have buckled. It was the first time his son had called him Daddy, and it wouldn't be the last. *Daddy* was something he'd never tire of hearing.

Cooper stopped the truck directly in front of the house and got them inside. Away from the chaos that was about to happen with the arrival of the medical examiner and his crew.

However, there was a crew of a different kind inside.

Roy, Rosalie and Arlene were all in the foyer waiting. Rayanne was at the top of the stairs, and she glanced at each of them and must have decided the danger was over and that a family moment was to follow. She turned, heading back toward her room.

"Thank God you're all right," his father said, and Arlene and Rosalie echoed the same.

Rosalie gave Liam a quick checkup, but then shook

her head when she examined Jessa and Cooper. "You both need to see the doctor."

"We will." But not right now. Now he wanted to deal with the aftermath.

Maybe the future, too.

"I need a long soak in the tub," Linda said, making her way up the stairs. "Maybe a shot of Jack Daniel's."

"I'll bring some up to you," Arlene offered. "Could use a drink or two myself." She made a face when she looked at Cooper's arm. "If that's the worst of it, then I guess we made out all right."

Yeah, they had. Partly because of luck and partly because of help from Jessa and his family. Together, they'd kept Liam safe and all but Peggy alive. Excluding her, everyone who counted was in one piece.

"Want me to take Liam?" Rosalie offered.

Jessa and Cooper jumped to say no. Cooper figured it would be a while before they let him out of their sight. Rosalie smiled and excused herself.

His father and Arlene gave Cooper knowing looks. Which was strange. Since he wasn't sure how the next few minutes would play out. Cooper only knew these would be some of the most important minutes of his life.

With Liam still in Jessa's arms, they went upstairs to the guest room. When Liam saw his crib, he motioned to get in it, but Cooper soon realized it was just to play with the toy horse on top of the covers. Cooper made a mental note to get him more toy horses.

A real one, too.

While he was at it, he went through the rest of his mental notes, which started with Jessa. Except she spoke before he could.

"I'll move in with you," she said.

Okay. That was a good start, but Cooper wanted a heck of a lot more. "You told Liam I was his daddy."

She nodded, swallowed hard. "Because you are. He needs you, Cooper." Another nod, and her gaze cautiously came to his. "I need you."

The corner of his mouth lifted. That definitely qualified as more. Cooper eased his arm around her, brought her to him and kissed her. It didn't go on nearly as long as he wanted. Of course, a lifetime might not be long enough. But Jessa broke the kiss and looked up at him.

"We still have things to work out," she said. "With your mother's trial, for instance."

Yeah, that. "I don't see a way around it. You'll have to excuse yourself as prosecuting attorney or else someone could claim a conflict of interest." He eased her back to him. "And just in case you're wondering, there will be a conflict."

He kissed her to show her just how much of one there'd be. Like the kiss in the pasture, it went on a little too long, and Liam started to laugh.

"Mama and Daddy kiss-kiss." And he got in on it by leaning out from his crib and motioning for them to kiss him.

They did.

The moment was perfect, but it didn't last. Jessa got that pained look on her face again. "What I said back there is true. I know I'll never be able to replace Molly."

Well, Jessa was certainly hitting the high points, things that definitely needed a clearing of the air.

"I don't want you to replace her. Molly will always be here." He tapped his heart. "And here." Cooper ran his hand over Liam's hair. "You're your own woman. And you're Liam's mom."

"Daddy," Liam proudly announced.

"Yeah, I am." And Cooper hoped to be a lot more when it came to Jessa and his son.

The tears came, watering Jessa's eyes. Maybe because she had expected him to tell her what he'd figured out after nearly losing both of them to a madman.

"I'm in love with you," he said.

He wasn't a man who said the words easily, but they came easily tonight. Clarity had a way of doing that, of boiling everything down so that Cooper could see what was most important.

And what was most important was in this room with him.

"I'm in love with you, too," Jessa said, but then she shook her head, almost as if in disgust. "But love doesn't make it easier. Your family—"

He kissed her to cut that off. And because he just wanted to feel her mouth on his. "My family will accept you just fine. Now, let's go back to that other part that you rushed right over. The part about you loving me."

She nodded. "I do love you."

"I wove you," Liam piped in, causing them to laugh. Liam obviously enjoyed their reaction, because he started repeating it.

Cooper gave his son a kiss on the cheek. "I'm going to ask your mama to marry me." There was no way Liam could have known what that meant, but he smiled, anyway. "Should she say yes?"

Liam bobbed his head. "Yesss."

With that seal of approval, Cooper turned back to Jessa, waiting for her to answer. But he didn't have to wait at all. She landed right in his arms.

"Yes," she said. "Yes, yes, a thousand times, yes."

That was the exact answer Cooper had wanted to hear.

He kissed her, hard and long. Then he gathered up Liam and kissed her again.

Finally, Cooper had everything that he wanted right in his arms.

* * * * *